CITY OF SHATTERED LIGHT

CLAIRE WINN

flux®

Mendota Heights, Minnesota

First Edition
First Printing, 2021

Book design by Jake Slavik
Cover design by Jake Slavik
Cover illustration by Sanjay Charlton

Flux, an imprint of North Star Editions, Inc.

Library of Congress Cataloging-in-Publication Data (pending)
978-1-63583-071-2

Flux
North Star Editions, Inc.
2297 Waters Drive
Mendota Heights, MN 55120
www.fluxnow.com

Printed in Canada

To Drew, who believed in me even when I didn't.

Part I:
THE MONSTER IN THE WIRES

chapter 1

DEADEYE

Riven Hawthorne could never turn down a challenge. As she climbed the rusted ladder, the city whispered of violence—she tasted it in the slow, sinuous *thud-thud* of a muffled bass rhythm, in the blare of distant sirens, in the satisfying *snick* as she loaded her revolvers' cylinders. Scavengers chattered in the hideout across the street, unaware Riven's crew was about to rob them blind.

Her feet hit the balcony, and an eager tremor buzzed through her. This was a chance to prove herself. Rumors about her would ignite like sparks on the oil-stained streets.

"I don't trust this, Riv." Ty peeked over the balcony's edge. Despite the sweltering heat, the hood of his black-and-yellow vest shadowed his boyish face.

Riven pulled Ty up by his wrist. "Good. I'd be worried your head had come unscrewed otherwise." Of course it was risky. The matriarchs tested smugglers by throwing them into vipers' nests.

"I'm serious." Ty caught his breath against the broken railing. His blue eyes reflected the sunset haze of holoscreen billboards and neon lights. "They're scouting. Aggressively. As if they're already looking for us."

"No way they've seen us yet." Riven thumbed her revolvers on instinct, her trigger fingers itchy. She couldn't back out now, with a chance to pull her crew off the underworld's dirty bottom rung.

She needed *one* job to go right—one night she could rest easy, not worrying whether they could pay rent for their ramshackle hideout. And once she'd made a name for herself in Requiem's neon-soaked streets, none of the crime syndicates would dare threaten her crew.

Samir was last to reach the top. He grunted as he pulled himself up, weighed down with a tailored armor vest and the rifle slung across his back.

Here, in the shadows between the buildings, not even the merciless sun could see them. Her crew was ready to move.

Riven flipped the scan-glass over her eyes, watching for their target. Any second now, it would be in range. "Think of it as a game of capture the flag, Ty. We rush in, grab it, and run like hell." If only it'd be that easy. Her vision zoomed in on the scavenger hideout a few floors below, where two scouts patrolled the balcony. Captions scrolled by on her scan-glass, describing the chatter within—*no, honestly, I heard he had cybernetic nads installed after that accident in the GravSphere arena*—confirming most of the scavs were probably drunk.

"I've never played a game of capture the flag where you get shot if the other team nabs you," Ty whispered. He hit the release on the tether line, unfurling the wicked concrete-piercing barbs. When strung between this balcony and the top floor of the scav hideout, the cable might be enough to hold their weight, one at a time. And a hell of a ride, to boot.

Samir's vivid yellow eyes flicked over the alleyway. "Nobody's getting shot if we play our cards right. Security's only tight because they're paranoid." His pupils were vertical like a cat's, from the dark-vision mods in his eyes—but with over thirty hours of scorching daylight left on this moon, he wouldn't need them. "I'd be, too, if I were sitting on a bounty that big."

"Then we're doing them a favor. Giving them one less thing to worry about," Riven said. The scav hideout was crawling with security-mechs. A nasty, deadly annoyance. There was *one* thing in there worth protecting—the rest was probably trash scrounged from the desert outside the city's atmo-dome.

Then Riven glimpsed what she'd been waiting for. A scout drone flew through the alleyway. "Incoming." A thrill built in her chest. Her wristlet's cracked screen flickered on as Galateo booted up. "Start a remote hack, Galateo."

"Bypassing security feed," her AI companion chirped in his pompous offworld accent. "Alarm triggering soon—"

Riven crouched beneath the balcony railing. Ty bit his lip and ducked next to her as the drone whizzed toward them. Its eye-beam scanned the overfilled trash bins in the alley below.

Galateo clicked, beginning the hack.

"Please tell me you at least have an exit strategy," Ty said.

Riven shot him a grin she hoped was reassuring. "Bet you twenty denar Samir and I can wreck their mechs before the idiots know what hit them." She gave *Verdugo,* her right-hand revolver, a spin on her index finger. Protecting Ty was her responsibility. Even if the job went south.

"My lady," Galateo said from Riven's wristlet, "your current account balance is only fourteen denar."

She made a face at her wristlet's camera lens. "Hush. I'll have it when we finish this job."

That earned a small smile from Ty. "If I'm not patching you up instead." He crossed his arms over his slender frame, peering through the railing bars. "Look, I know getting on Matriarch Sokolov's good side means a lot to you. But . . . be careful, Riv. Please."

I can't lose you too was left unspoken.

Riven nodded. She wouldn't lose him either—the day Ty's brother had died, she'd made a promise. And she certainly didn't intend to break it today.

"Connection formed," Galateo said. "Triggering alarm in six seconds . . ."

"Heads up," Samir said.

Riven tore her gaze away from Ty and steadied her breaths, heart rate revving, waiting for the cue. Her old-tech revolvers waited in their holsters—her executioner and her wildcard. *Blackjack* carried her stun-rounds and disruptors, and *Verdugo* would come out to play if things got messy.

The matriarchs' Code listed nasty punishments for murder between syndicates. Since rumors whispered these scavengers had ties to the Boneshiver syndicate matriarch, Riven wasn't allowed to break their skulls. But their mechs were a different story.

The security-drone's eye lit red. "Time to go!" Samir said as alarms blared across the street.

Galateo picked up voices in the hideout, echoing in her earpiece. "*Dammit!*" one of the scouts yelled.

"Breach. Lower level!" barked a scavenger with a trio of green mech-eyes on his forehead. "All of you, get down there!"

As planned, the scavs rushed toward the elevators, except two who lingered on the balcony. Their backs were turned. The path to their vault was wide open.

Idiots.

Riven peered down *Blackjack*'s iron sights and fired across the alley. Two stun-rounds, two clean shots. The scavengers crumpled to the concrete, convulsing.

Ty latched the tether to the balcony and fired it. It anchored itself to the concrete on the other side, forming a crude zip line. Samir grabbed a carabiner, jumped, and slid across.

Her turn. Riven grabbed the second carabiner and leapt off the edge.

Her stomach plunged as the cable dipped under her weight. Then, it bounced until her glide evened out. Sparks flew from the carabiner, and she stole a glance at her boots as they dangled over the ridges of broken Etri crystal lining the street. Hot wind rushed across her face.

She hit the scavs' balcony running.

She vaulted over the tattered couches, skidding into a crouch behind the bar. By her knees, shards of glass caught the kitschy palm tree neon lights.

Beside her, Samir was already in place. "So. I hear you have twenty denar on us destroying these mechs?"

She smirked. "Unless you're planning on slowing me down."

Spidery mechs crawled the walls, a patchwork variety of stolen tech. In five seconds, they'd send out more scan-beams—and bullets would follow.

Four.

In a single breath, Riven was ready. *Time to come out and play.*

Her revolvers slid out of their holsters. This was her favorite part—the pulse, the rhythm, the firecrackers at her fingertips.

Three.

She spun *Verdugo* and *Blackjack* until their barrels were trained on the mechs. Their pull-back hammers clicked into place. The guns were unhackable old tech—no wires, no circuit boards. Guided by *her* hands, not some AI.

Deadly calm came over her. All the gun training she'd done since Emmett's death had built to this.

Two.

Somewhere beyond the pulsing adrenaline was Samir shouting to *Quit showing off, Riv!*

Her fingers twitched.

Crack. Crack.

One by one, her bullets exploded through the metal shells. The mechs burst into showers of sparks and shattered metal. Steel spider legs fell from ceilings. Her silver-blonde braid whipped over her shoulder as she ducked beneath a salvo of bullets from a turret.

Between the rhythm of recoil and the snaps of gunpowder, she felt alive. She let the rhythm suck her under, losing herself in the merciless pull of the triggers.

"Get down!"

At Samir's warning, she dipped into a shoulder roll. She

spun backward as a wolf-shaped mech lunged at her face—and one of Samir's disruptor rounds tore through its head.

Samir reloaded his rifle as the mech crashed to the floor with a sparking hole through its skull. "You got cocky, as usual."

"That's why I keep you around."

"To keep your ego from suffocating us all?" Samir mimed a gagging motion and then grinned. He'd kept her ego in check ever since he'd been her senior-year mentor at a military academy on Earth. And, well, he was good backup in a gunfight.

"Please. My ego isn't half as bad as your nagging." Now no red lights winked in the dark. It was clear. Riven stood up, reloading *Blackjack*. "What'd I tell you, Ty? They barely even saw us."

Ty didn't answer. She glanced around the room—at the slouching couches, the static on the holoscreens. Where *was* he? Ty was good at staying hidden, but he usually kept close. Maybe he'd gone ahead.

"Ty?" Beyond the blaring alarms, the speakers hummed an irritatingly upbeat pop song. Riven tasted raw, acrid gunpowder at the back of her throat, and something darker with it. Why had he left her side?

"Ty, where are you? We need to move," Samir said into his wristlet comm. He was right. Any second now, the scavs would realize they'd been duped.

Finally, Ty's voice came through, punching Riven with fleeting relief. "Guys. Come up the stairs. There's something you should see."

Riven rushed to the stairwell, cramming bullets into

Verdugo's chambers. As soon as the door slid open, she found Ty crouched over a corpse.

A deep slice through the dead scavenger's bulletproof vest revealed cybernetic ribs. Blood darkened the ratty carpet, dribbling down the steps.

Samir swore, lifting his rifle.

"This definitely wasn't one of your bullets." Ty leaned in to inspect the wounds.

A warning shrieked in the back of Riven's mind, louder and angrier than the hideout alarms.

Someone else is here.

She tried not to imagine what failure would bring—the rumors of what Matriarch Sokolov did to accomplices who disappointed her. Smugglers thrown like bait into the mech-fighting pits; thieves broken down for parts, both metal and flesh.

It wasn't happening to her crew. This trespasser wasn't getting away.

"Stay close, Ty. Change of plans."

"Maybe we should turn back." Ty's eyes were wide, and for a second, they were his older brother's eyes—fearful, pained, pleading to Riven even though she couldn't save him.

She shook away the memory. "We can't. We're seeing this job through." They were in too deep. Whoever was here, she'd teach them nobody interfered with one of Riven Hawthorne's jobs. "I'm going to greet our intruder. Samir, check the vault."

"On it." He headed up the steps past Ty.

Ty pulled out his switchblades. "I'm with you, Riv."

She frowned. Though Ty was too squeamish to touch a gun, he still tried to protect her. "Just stay behind me."

The corridor split—Samir headed toward the vault, and Riven scouted the other hallway. A few telltale spots of blood on the carpet meant someone had fled. Maybe they'd been chased. Riven ignored the gnawing in her gut.

Within seconds, Samir's voice came over the comm. "Vault's empty. Seems our visitor got here first."

She swore. Someone had taken advantage of their distraction. "We need to cut them off."

"I'll be there in a second."

As they climbed to the upper floor, muffled shouts resounded from behind a battered door with light straining beneath it. Riven put a finger to her lips, and Ty followed. She kicked the door open, raised her guns, and saw their culprit.

Compared to the boarded windows of the scav hideout, the sunlight of the rooftop was blinding. The scents of exhaust and ozone and greasy smoke hit her with an oncoming breeze.

And at the edge of the roof, a small girl crouched over a fresh corpse.

"Oh. Was wondering how long it'd take you to show." The girl—no, a woman, probably a few years older than Riven—popped a pink gum bubble between her lips.

Her brown curls were swept into buns, her fingernails coated in chipped pink enamel. A stark contrast to her armor vest and the bloody cybernetic blade running along her forearm. An expensive body-mod—the blade was anchored to her bone somewhere, her flesh parted in surgical steel.

The woman pulled the blade from the dead person's neck,

and they seized one last time. "Thanks for the distraction. Thought I'd have to kill a few more of these." She kicked the corpse with a pink-and-black sneaker. "This little piggy tried to make a break with my cargo."

Everything about her made Riven's hackles rise. Riven clicked back *Verdugo*'s hammer with her thumb. "I don't know who the hell you are," Riven said, "but you'll have a bullet in your skull unless you hand over those fossils." This woman had killed here, violating the matriarchs' Code—meaning Riven didn't need to hold back.

"Here's what's going to happen in ten seconds." The woman flicked blood off her forearm with a skin-crawling grin. "My ship shows up, I leave, you screw off forever, and we all live happily ever after."

"Not going to happen." Riven scanned the woman from head to toe. She had their cargo, but where was it? "We know you cleaned out the vault."

Footsteps approached behind her. "With her reputation," Samir said, "I don't think *happily ever after* is an option." He emerged beside Riven, his rifle drawn. Even in body armor, he composed himself like a gentleman. "Pleasure to meet you, Morphett Slade."

The woman—Morphett—cocked her head. "Seems *you're* not as stupid as you are pretty."

Riven tightened her grip on the revolver. *Morphett Slade.* She'd heard the name and the rumors with it. A bounty hunter who'd taken down an entire Federation platoon to settle a grudge, whose cybernetics alone might be worth half of Requiem. Riven had expected her to be . . . taller, maybe.

"Last chance, Tiny." Riven's finger slid onto the trigger. "You have two guns on you now."

With a low roar, a boomerang-shaped ship rose at the edge of the roof. *NEPHILIM* was scrawled in black letters on the hull, and the sunlight was bright enough on its chrome-and-onyx paint to silhouette Morphett. The humming thrusters knocked empty bottles across the concrete roof and blew Ty's hood off, whipping his rust-blond hair.

Morphett held her hands up, and the cybernetic blade folded and retracted into a seam in her forearm. "Fine," she snarled. "It's yours."

Morphett crouched over the corpse and tugged a small canister off its belt. Riven frowned. The cargo—the fossilized Etri bones—should be in a slender black case, but this seemed too small.

It was hard to see against the gleam of Morphett's ship, but Riven recognized that shape.

"Grenade!" Samir called.

Before Riven could shoot it, Samir's steel-vise hands gripped her shoulders, and he crushed her to the concrete. The ground shook, and everything went impossibly bright. All she saw was the inside of Samir's elbow and a blinding blast of white.

Her elbows stung, shredded by the concrete. Her ears throbbed, ready to explode. And her hand was empty. Where was *Verdugo*?

Smears of blue-black dissolved as the world came back into focus. Her pulse roared through her ears. Her shoulder was pressed against a sheet of dented steel—a shipping crate. Samir had pulled her to cover.

And Morphett was getting away.

Samir pushed himself to his knees, heaving. Riven's ears rang dully. "She found a flash-bang," Samir yelled, but his voice sounded so distant.

With a pang of nausea, she remembered Ty. But he was nearby, rubbing his eyes and panting. Riven groped along the concrete, grabbing *Verdugo* in shaking fingers.

Morphett's docking hatch was already closing.

"Dammit!" Riven pushed herself to her knees, the ground swaying beneath her.

Morphett had already disappeared on board. But as the hatch slid closed, Riven caught a glimpse of their cargo—a long black capsule strapped to the inner wall of the ship.

Riven didn't care about the money—not now—but Morphett was taking her cargo. *Her* job.

Her future with the syndicate, going up in smoke. Her reputation ruined.

She aimed *Verdugo*.

"Riven," Samir warned. "Scale it back."

She ignored him. If she wasn't getting the cargo, Morphett wasn't either. Nobody got away with swindling her. There it was—the uncontrollable flare, the angry rush of wounded pride.

That alone was reason enough to pull the trigger.

Despite the blue-black staining her vision, Riven peered down her iron sights. Her finger on the trigger twitched.

She never missed.

The canister exploded, shards of crystallized bone raining

onto the floor of Morphett's ship. A perfect shot. The last thing she heard was Morphett's shrill cussing as the doors clenched shut.

Riven fired another shot to dent the *Nephilim*'s pretty hull.

The ship was already in motion, cutting above the skyways. Morphett could try to salvage the cargo—but it was worthless now. Good. She'd regret crossing them.

"Well, damn," Samir said, voicing what all three of them were probably thinking.

"Hawthorne," a deep voice crackled in her earpiece, grating against the ringing in her ears. "Matriarch Sokolov's dropship will arrive in twenty seconds. Have you secured the cargo?"

She couldn't answer. The numbness of defeat was settling over her. It was gone. All her aspirations, shattered like the Etri fossils.

"Hawthorne?" the voice insisted. "Answer me."

She turned off her comm and glanced at Samir and Ty. Ty pulled his hood back up, looking bewildered, and Samir gripped the balcony railing, white-knuckled. They'd lost. The three of them stood silently as alarms blared and speeders honked in distant skyways. Requiem's towering spires and glitching holoscreens walled them in. No easy way down from here.

Either the scavs would find them, or Matriarch Sokolov's bruisers would. Sokolov would be furious. All the nasty rumors about her whispered from the edges of Riven's mind.

"Riv," Ty said. "We are in *such* deep shit."

chapter 2
THE FLIGHT
AND THE FALL

When Asa stepped into the show hall, her nerves were already fraying.

Flashing camera-drones and reporters formed a gauntlet to the stage. Sentry-mechs stood like ancient suits of armor along the massive crystal bridge, their cold lenses glaring down at her. Here, it wasn't only her father's surveillance systems watching her every step—news outlets across the planet were too.

It was time for the biggest test of her life.

They won't be forgiving just because of your parentage, her father had said. *And neither will I.*

Asa strode into the chaos, armed with only her false smile and the red ball-gown skirts swishing across her legs. Beneath the arches of smoky-white stone, onlookers' shouts and reporters' questions crashed like waves. She tuned out their voices, steadying her breaths and her nerves until there was nothing but her measured footsteps and the stage ahead.

Under those spotlights, the world would see *her* work. Her father would have no choice but to respect her, to name her heir to the largest tech firm on Cortellion. And someday, she'd finally be free of his lengthy shadow.

"Damn. They're like vultures." Her sister Kaya fell into step beside her. "All eyes on you. You ready?"

"As I'll ever be. They're hoping I'll freeze up and make Dad take over." No doubt the rumor mill would love to grate her to a pulp.

"Well, they're going to be disappointed." Kaya grinned. "You're going to channel all that whip-crack expertise from whenever you explain your tech to *me*. Right?"

"Easy for you to say." Kaya never froze up. As they stepped onto the bridge—Asa's red skirts trailing on the polished crystal, Kaya swaggering in her chunky leather boots—Kaya radiated confidence. Her starfield-black hair was pulled into a messy ponytail, her lime-green cocktail dress bright in the camera flashes.

Unlike Asa, Kaya didn't have the pressure of becoming heir. Their father hadn't molded her from birth for this.

The self-doubt whispered at the back of Asa's mind. She swallowed with a dry throat. Someday, once she'd made a name for herself, he wouldn't be able to control her.

A spherical camera-drone slipped in to block her path. She flinched as its flash erupted in her face.

"Miss Asanna!" came a voice through its speaker. Through the blue-black afterimage in her vision, she saw the lens swivel, scanning her up and down. "How do you respond to rumors that your father's new tech caused permanent neural damage in previous test subjects?"

"I've heard no such rumors," Asa said awkwardly. Her father's tests were rigorous, but never dangerous. His worst critics constantly spread conspiracy theories. Better to ignore them.

And it had *better* not be unsafe, with Kaya doing mind-link tests.

When Asa tried to dodge the drone, it glided back into her face.

"Why the deflection?" the reporter's voice said. "We're livestreaming on VNet, and over seventy thousand viewers need to know."

"Excuse me, I'm going to be late," Asa said, her smile hardening.

The drone bumped her on the collarbone, stopping her dead in her tracks. "Are you admitting complacency? Has your father forced you to—"

Asa was tempted to grab the drone and hurl it into the crowd, when the drone's light went out and the speaker cut.

"Didn't you hear her?" Kaya's voice was icy. "She's not interested in talking to you." She snapped her fingers at the camera lens. Immediately, the drone seized up and fell to the floor, sparking.

Asa bit her lip as a new wave of questions rippled through the crowd. So much for subtlety. "We were supposed to save that for the stage," she muttered to Kaya. She was grateful her sister looked out for her, but Dad might count this against her.

"Is this the new Winterdark tech?" someone shouted.

Kaya stepped over the dead drone. "It's a preview." She flashed her impish grin at the cameras and tapped the metal node embedded behind her ear—her brain-tech link. Her voice lowered as she caught up to Asa. "And now they know what happens when they harass my sister. That guy's lucky I just powered his drone off, instead of flying it straight up his—"

A cheer went up from the crowds as the stage lights dimmed and the house-sized holoscreens lit up with the company's white-and-gold logo. It was beginning. Fitting for her father to make his dramatic entrance here—on a stage carved into an ancient Etri palace, the remains of a civilization lost to time.

Asa picked up her pace, slipping behind the seated audience until she reached the stage's side ramp.

". . . and please welcome our keynote presenter, Luca Almeida," a voice boomed over the loudspeakers.

Asa stood with Kaya, waiting for their cue. She inhaled a lungful of overcooled air and tried to exhale her jitters.

Her father emerged at center stage, spotlighted in his crisp white suit. The most powerful tech mogul in the star-system. The screens zoomed in on his handsome face, frozen in medically modded youth. His true age was a mystery even to Asa, but with his laser-straight teeth and perfect carbon-black hair, he could've passed for her older brother.

The applause rolled like thunder. Here, her father was a king.

"We take pride in pushing the boundaries of the human mind and its interactions with technology." As Luca addressed the adoring crowd, he wore a genuine smile—one that was never for Asa. A wolf-mech followed him onstage, part of the company's flashy military tech.

"He sure knows how to make an entrance," Kaya muttered.

"Tonight," Luca continued, "I invite you all to witness Almeida Industries' new breakthroughs—new ways to control our technology as an extension of ourselves. To begin . . . I'm ecstatic to show you a preview of the company's next generation. No wires, high precision. This part of Project Winterdark was developed by my daughter, Asanna Almeida, who has *insisted* on showing us her work."

Asa's nerves sizzled as she and Kaya ascended the ramp. The spotlights and afternoon sunlight were as bright and scrutinizing as a microscope lens. She glimpsed herself on the holoscreens—her hair tousled perfectly, the rose-pearl necklace draped over her collarbones, her dress blossoming into fiber-optic fabric that shifted between red and gold. She almost didn't recognize herself, after only seeing her haggard reflection in her brushed-steel tool cabinet for the past few days.

Asa steadied her breaths, shaking away the sleepless night in her garage perfecting every circuit. The transition from Grease Monkey Asa to Debonair Heiress Asa was always weird. But since she'd turned seventeen last week, she'd be in the spotlight more often now. If today went well.

The applause quieted in anticipation. Debonair Asa had to come out, *fast*. She stole a glance at her father.

Go on, his steel-hard eyes demanded. *Impress me.*

Asa bowed as another scalding spotlight came down on her. "I'm honored to debut on the world stage today," she recited as the microphone hidden behind her ear made her voice boom through the crowd. She froze under the weight of every stare in the room. Could she live up to the stars in their eyes? "And to be part of Project Winterdark, and Almeida Industries."

Across the stage, she caught Kaya's stealthy smile. This morning, when Asa had been up bleary-eyed until dawn, Kaya had brought her caffeinated mango soda and a croissant. *I know you can do this*, she'd said. *You've worked your ass off.*

Even though Kaya was her opposite, the night to her day, she believed in Asa. That one glance was enough.

Asa straightened her back. Her father hadn't introduced her sister, but it was Kaya's first time onstage, and she deserved a piece of the spotlight. "My sister, Kaya Almeida, has worked tirelessly to test this technology. So, together, we'd like to show you a bit of what it can do."

Though Kaya preferred art to tech, she'd been a lab rat since they were kids, and she kept the details secret. Their father had chosen Kaya's path, like he'd picked Asa's—but promised Kaya permission to attend art school if she worked hard in the lab. For Asa, success had to be its own reward.

Asa reached into the storage container at center stage and clicked the switch on her phoenix-mech. Gasps rippled through the crowd as she lifted the bird into the stage lights. The carbon-weave feathers Kaya had painted glowed like living fire.

Asa smiled as the bird shuddered to life, perching on her forearm. She'd spent weeks syncing its intricate circuits to the Winterdark software in Kaya's brain-jack. Finally, the world was witnessing something Asa had built herself.

The phoenix ruffled its wings as Kaya made her connection. On Asa's wristlet screen, the link lit green. So far, so good.

Then, with only a thought, Kaya called the bird toward her. The phoenix's wings unfurled as music stirred, vibrant strings and sullen drums, and flames danced across the holoscreens. As Kaya lifted her arm, the bird banked a perfect pirouette around her wrist, following her movements with precision only a creature sharing her mind could. She ran along the ramp and it glided with her, then swooped over her shoulder blades as she lunged.

Cameras flashed, and excited cheers erupted from the crowd.

"*Incredible!*"

"*. . . never been done this well wirelessly. Are you seeing this?*"

The applause grew louder as the bird flew over the crowd. For a moment, Asa's smile was real. The precision aerodynamics in those wings were working perfectly.

Then she noticed Kaya wincing with the sharper movements, and her stomach flipped. *Oh, god.* Kaya was rubbing her temple—was this one of her headaches? It'd been weeks since her last one.

The bird flew higher, and higher still. Asa squinted into the sunbeams. This wasn't what they'd rehearsed. Kaya was supposed to fly it back to the front of the stage for their finale.

But the phoenix soared toward the layer of reinforced glass holding the heavy chandeliers in place. It rose until it was only a silhouette against the snowcapped mountains and the distant sky.

Clink. The bird's razor-beak slammed into the transparent layer.

No. What was Kaya doing? Asa straightened her back, mimicking her father's confident posture. The presentation was bound to have some hiccups. What mattered was that the bird was flying, and her presentation could continue. "The military and aerospace applications for this technology—"

Thunk. The bird slammed into the glass, harder. Its purple eyes had turned orange. That was new.

She shot a glance at Kaya, and her heart dropped. Kaya was clutching her head, grimacing. This wasn't just another headache—she was in real pain. On Asa's wristlet, the connection had turned red. Kaya had cut it. She wasn't in control anymore.

But if Kaya wasn't, who was?

Thunk. One of the phoenix's wings was bent, and it flew lopsided. A crack was growing across the glass shield at the impact point. The hanging chandeliers shuddered, creaking precariously above the seated audience.

Asa squinted into the stage lights, hitting the emergency diagnostics on her wristlet. The bird was running a program she hadn't authorized. She hit the fail-safe—the switch that would bring the bird back to her on autopilot. But the bird kept slamming into the ceiling.

Worried murmurs erupted through the crowd.

"Kaya?" Asa whispered into her earpiece on a private channel. "What's happening?" Was someone trying to sabotage her presentation? She tried to force a shutdown.

The phoenix didn't stop. It had a mind of its own.

Thunk. Crack. Asa was so focused on her wristlet that she almost missed the growing shriek of microphone feedback. The music cut out, and when she looked up, the stage holoscreens had gone dark.

"Asanna." Her father's voice rasped in her earpiece. She saw him across the stage, scratching his ear to conceal speaking into his microphone. He still smiled, as if nothing was wrong, but the urgency in his voice said otherwise. "Reconnect her."

Cameras flashed. Nervous murmurs rippled through the audience. A few people headed for the aisles, watching the ceiling.

Asa glanced at her sister. "But Kay . . . she's hurting. What's going on?"

Kaya was hunched over, hand clapped over her mouth. Her cool exterior had evaporated. If Asa reconnected her, what would happen? "I hear whispers," Kaya said into the comm channel. "My head . . ."

"Ignore it," Luca snapped. "Hurry. Before they notice that thing is here."

"What thing?" Asa said. "A virus?"

"Not the time, Asa. She can handle it. I won't ask again. *Reconnect her.*"

Asa's finger hovered above the button. The bird flapped harder, flew faster. The glass panel shuddered as the bird slammed between the chandeliers. The brilliant gems jostled, swaying, as the crack grew to a rift across the clouds. If she didn't act soon, the crowd would clamor for the exits. She'd never seen a glitch this bad.

Whoever was in control was *trying* to bring the ceiling down.

But Kaya was hurting. Her chest heaved as she swayed, on the verge of collapse.

Her father glared at her across the stage. He'd given her a command. Maybe this was part of his test. If she disobeyed, he'd never treat her as more than a child. She'd be nothing more than a broken-off piece of him.

And with the ceiling cracking—people might be in real danger. Her father only cared about the public fallout, but there was more at stake.

Kaya could forgive her later.

Asa bit her lip and restarted the connection on her wristlet. Kaya gasped, shooting her a worried look. Asa forced a smile. *Please, Kay. Just another minute.*

Her sister's face was unreadable as she staggered back to her feet. The bird shuddered, its eyes turning purple again. The holoscreen static went dark, and the microphone feedback silenced.

The bird's dented wings flapped, lifting it back into the sunbeams. When it reached the apex of the stage, Asa hit the switch, and small jets of flame trailed from its wings. A flurry of golden feathers ejected, catching the high sunbeams like falling embers.

Asa clicked her microphone back on. "Progress is . . . never easy," she improvised, salvaging an explanation for the disaster, "but our work can shatter even unseen barriers to progress."

It was nonsense, but the crowd seemed to buy it as avant-garde. Hesitant applause rose for her and her father.

Luca strode back into the spotlight. "Well done, Asanna," his voice washed over the crowd. "As you can see, her brilliance makes her a worthy successor, and I'm proud to have her as the heir to Almeida Industries, and to Project Winterdark."

The heir. She'd done it. Her father's pride was so rare and hard-earned it ached. But Kaya . . .

Kaya took a staggering bow as her spotlight went dark. Blood was trickling from her ear.

Asa found Kaya vomiting in their backstage dressing room.

"Oh god. I'm so sorry." Asa held back her sister's thick layers of hair as Kaya retched over the trash bin. "I shouldn't have—"

"Not your fault," Kaya said bitterly between heaves. The

blood on her ear was drying, and guilt gnawed at Asa. Why had she allowed this to happen onstage?

"I didn't know what was happening." A flimsy excuse. She could fix tech, but she was helpless to fix her own sister.

"I think she'll be fine," came a deep voice from behind her. Josiah, her father's chief scientist, had stayed nearby since escorting Kaya offstage. Now, he stood at the private dressing room's minibar, silhouetted by a glass wall overlooking the spires of Himmeltor. The towers of Cortellion's capital city glinted like knives, catching the light of dusk.

Josiah cracked open a hissing can of soda and stirred pain meds into it. Asa felt better having him here. He'd worked for her father as long as she could remember, though she rarely saw him outside the lab.

"Should we call a medic?" Asa said.

Josiah brought a cloth napkin and the drink to Kaya. "The med-scan says it isn't serious. And Kaya is tough." Carefully, he dabbed at the drying blood on Kaya's ear. Concern deepened the lines on his face. Unlike her father, Josiah didn't use antiaging mods, and his sallow cheeks and graying blond beard looked worse by the day. "The two of you composed yourselves excellently today. That could have been much worse."

"*Could've been worse* isn't exactly a high bar," Asa said bitterly.

A smile quirked Josiah's thin lips. "How's this, then? Your phoenix was phenomenal. And it seems congratulations are in order. Welcome to Project Winterdark, heir official."

Kaya stared pensively into the trash bin. Then she sat up and chugged the med-soda.

Though it was all Asa had wanted this morning, the welcome

was hollow. "You saw what happened onstage, right? That weird malfunction wasn't from my tech."

Josiah's near-colorless eyes flickered. "No, Asa. It wasn't you. We hadn't thought that thing could leave the lab."

A strange chill crept over Asa. "What *is* it? A virus? An AI?"

He looked uneasy. "It's complicated."

Asa sat up straighter. "I'm heir now. I have a right to know."

"I suppose that's true. Winterdark has its costs." Josiah let out a slow breath, folding the bloodied napkin, then shook his head. "Asa, there are still some things you should leave to your father and me. You needn't worry about them."

Asa huffed. Yet another person treating her like a child. She'd heard enough of her father's *you wouldn't understand* and *my rules are here to protect you.* "Answer this, then: did Dad know this jack could hurt Kaya?"

Part of her didn't want to know the answer. She'd seen her father work mechanists to the bone and lay them off before the final product was released. Always a strategist, treating people like pawns. But his own daughter?

"I think he miscalculated. Luca told me he'd fixed things, but you've surely seen how his tenacity gets the better of him. He was reckless in allowing tech from the lab onstage today."

And maybe Asa had been reckless for reconnecting Kaya. But whatever had gone wrong onstage wasn't an accident.

"We need to take better care of Kaya," Asa said. "From now on, her safety is priority."

"Of course, Asa. I trust you'll make the right decisions in

guiding the company." Josiah stood up, brushing his rumpled suit straight. "Now. Kaya, if you're feeling better—"

"I'm fine." The fire was returning to her voice. She glanced at Asa, and something in her eyes said *we need to talk.* "Thanks for your help. Asa can handle it from here."

Josiah gave a brisk bow. "If either of you need help . . . you know where to find me." With that, he left.

"Just when I thought today couldn't get better," Kaya said as soon as the door clicked shut. "That cryptic *Winterdark has its costs* crap? Dad's up to something, and Josiah knows it." Kaya sank onto one of the marshmallowy couches. That impish light had returned to her eyes, but something bleak was boiling to the surface. She'd never seemed resentful of the experiments before.

"I'm sorry about making you go through with that." Asa sat down, her red-and-gold skirts pooling around her. "Dad said you could handle it. Has this ever happened before?"

Kaya avoided Asa's eyes, tilting her face toward the marble arches and the holographic rose petals falling, bright as bloodstains. Even here, Asa felt they were being watched. Opposing mirrors reflected the sisters to infinity, creating a crowd of other Asas and Kayas to spy on them.

"Dad pushes me," Kaya finally said. "He insists it's fine, that I just need to concentrate harder. And for the past few years, it's been okay. But lately . . ." Kaya shuddered. "Last week, my head hurt so badly I thought I was dying."

A sympathetic headache throbbed behind Asa's eyes. Winterdark went far deeper than cutting-edge tech that augmented minds and linked them to machines. What had she inherited today?

"Can't you quit the project? Dad will understand."

Kaya scoffed. "Are you joking? He wouldn't let me go. None of the other test subjects have gotten the results I have." Kaya rubbed the metal node in her neck. "And besides. I still have Lakespire to think about."

Right. Her dream art school. Kaya had two more years before he'd agreed to consider sending her. "Don't worry about that. I'll make sure you get whatever you need for art school. One benefit of being heir, right?"

Kaya's smile was brief, a twitch. "And if quitting means he kicks me out of the house? He's already worried I'll rub off on you. If I'm gone, you'll have nobody to sneak you out past curfew."

The thought of Kaya leaving left a black-hole pit in her insides. Kaya had always hated Luca's rules—he'd forbidden them from taking ships offworld or attending social events without an armed escort. But some breezy summer nights, Kaya had sent her encoded messages promising concerts, malls, a taste of normalcy—if Asa would help her rig the security systems. And she'd agreed.

Until the day they'd gotten caught. It was the last time Asa ever snuck out. They settled for adventuring in VR worlds now.

Asa wiped her sweaty palms on the dress. Her sister couldn't leave.

"Dad doesn't want to hurt you," Asa said. "Listen. I'm heir official now. And I'm going to find out what he's up to." Though they played their roles onstage, they were a family when the cameras stopped rolling. He wouldn't let Kaya truly get hurt.

At least, not if Asa could help it.

"I was hoping you'd say that." Kaya's eyes sparkled with mischief. "But I hope you're not planning to just *ask* for answers."

Asa frowned. "What's that supposed to mean?"

"I mean we can't trust them to tell us everything. But there's another way. Dad's putting you on all the projects. *All* the labs."

Asa froze. Her hand scan would probably unlock every door now. Even the areas she'd been forbidden to enter. "Do you know what kind of trouble we'd be in if we snuck in?" Heir or not, going behind Luca's back would be betrayal.

"Which is why we won't get caught." Kaya tapped her brain-jack. "You can open the doors, and I'll handle the security cameras."

"Kay. We can't." The last thing Asa needed was to be confined to her bedroom for weeks again. Or worse. He could always choose a new heir—or *design* one—even after all she'd done.

"Not even Josiah is going to tell you what's happening."

Asa wasn't sure. Josiah had been a friend since she was little—helping her with complicated engine builds her father hadn't approved. If he was keeping secrets, it was at her father's request.

"Dad has plans for me," Kaya said. "Winterdark is bigger than a brain-jack. And who knows how much more of this I'll have to deal with?"

Asa chewed one of her red-lacquered nails. If something happened to Kaya during the next stage of Winterdark, she'd never forgive herself. And after all Kaya had endured for her today, Asa owed her.

Sneaking in was one way to make things right. She had to know exactly what she'd become heir to.

"All right," Asa said. "Tomorrow night. I'll be your key."

chapter 3

DEEP SHIT

T rue to the name, one of Matriarch Sokolov's bruisers was
crushing Riven's wrists in his meaty hands.

"Ease up, big guy," Riven grumbled as the cyborg's fingers wrenched her arms tighter, dragging her further into the matriarch's throne room. Along the steel bridge, Sokolov's grunts pointed pulse-rifles at her crew. "I'm obviously not going anywhere."

"I'm not stupid." The bruiser's metal jaw clicked. "I know what happens when those hands of yours get anywhere near a gun." His breath was hot against her neck and stank of exhaust. He'd probably earned his body-mods in Sokolov's service. Riven had never bothered with mods, except the grafts in her scalp that streaked her silver-blonde braid with permanent magenta. Her prowess was *hers*, not artificial.

"I've got no reason to point anything at Sokolov." Riven had done everything right this time—the diversion, the stun-bullets, the plan. Morphett had just gotten there first.

If she got out of this alive, Riven would make her pay for it.

The bruisers stopped the three of them on a platform suspended above an armory, with power-armor awash in the glow of guttering flames. Unlike other syndicates, Staccato's matriarch didn't have a physical throne—she stayed on her feet, ready to throw a punch. Steel trusses spitting gouts of fire illuminated her dais. Sweat beaded on the back of Riven's neck, and it wasn't just from the heat.

"Ah. They arrive." Matriarch Sokolov's dark hair covered half of her weathered face. She crossed her arms, widening her muscular shoulders. Fitting. Of the five factions that ruled Requiem—beneath the Duchess herself—Staccato was the least subtle, known for its raw firepower.

With that reputation, Sokolov wouldn't let them off easily. Riven kept her chin up.

"Matriarch Sokolov." Samir gave a small bow. Ever the diplomat. "Our deepest apologies—"

"No groveling in my court," she snapped. "I should've known better than to entrust this job to a bunch of kids."

I'm eighteen, thank you very much, Riven thought, flicking her silver-blonde bangs out of her eyes, *and I'm better than most of your thugs.* Ty was a year younger than her, and the only one of them who'd qualify as a *kid.* But Sokolov would probably throw even a five-year-old into a pit of anteleons if they crossed her. No chance for mercy there.

"So far, we haven't been able to pry any footage from your Galateo-unit." Sokolov tossed the tiny spherical drone into the air and caught it. "What model is this?"

"I am unique," Galateo chirped. "A Galateo 91-E Personal Assistant modified for improved machine learning." Chatty, the way Emmett had programmed him—and with little pieces of Emmett left behind. It took all Riven's willpower to keep from lunging onto the platform and grabbing him from Sokolov.

"No matter." Sokolov chucked the drone over Riven's head. One of the bruisers ducked as he whirred to life and reattached to Riven's wristlet. "I think we know everything we need to. Which is that you took a job, and you failed."

Riven inhaled sharply. "Only because Morphett Slade—"

Sokolov swiped a hand through the air like a blade, cutting her off. "My operatives don't make excuses. You were assigned to retrieve one of the purest Etri fossils found in the mines lately. Do you have any idea what it was worth?"

"A lot more than the two thousand denar you offered us." The tech moguls on Cortellion would dish out a fortune for that stuff. The Etri bones helped them calibrate cybernetics tech. Despite being a dust-bowl moon with a single city, Requiem's long-dead alien remains were a commodity—both the faster-than-light ship fuel from their mineral deposits, and the fossilized bones they'd left behind.

"Ten times that. And my buyer is now *very* disappointed." Sokolov strode around them, her heavy footsteps making the platform shudder. Ty cringed, and Samir lifted his chin defiantly. Sokolov ignored them and locked eyes with Riven. "You owe me, Hawthorne. And I'm sure the cargo was worth more than those revolvers and that piece-of-scrap ship of yours combined."

Riven narrowed her eyes. *Boomslang* had originated in a junkyard, sure. But she'd never give up her venom-green ship, even if Sokolov demanded it. "Say we can't pay you twenty-k denar right now. What then?"

Sokolov gave a humorless grin. "You might have something else worth almost as much." She gestured to one of the bruisers, who slid a silver chest toward Riven. "Go ahead. Open it. See what happened to the last aspiring smuggler to disappoint me."

Riven hesitated, fighting back the nauseating buzz of pain at the back of her head. The pain she called *white noise*, since it had no name she knew. It always chose the worst times to hound her.

The chest was small, the size of a cockpit control screen, with temperature readouts on the sides. Bio-support. Something inside it was *alive.* And probably for sale.

This was an intimidation tactic, and it was working. Riven couldn't open it, couldn't bring herself to see what remained of the former smuggler.

"If that's what I think it is," Ty murmured, "we really shouldn't be opening it in a non-sterile environment."

Sokolov glared. "Shut the hell up."

"I get it." Riven stared at the latches on the case, her vision tunneling. With one slip, all the power she'd wanted to hold was crashing down on her. "You have organ pirates under your thumb."

She was pretty sure Matriarch Sokolov didn't want *her* organs—for over a year now, her nervous system had been rotting from inside. But it wouldn't stop Sokolov from trying. And Samir and Ty . . .

Her guns were still hot in their holsters. If the bruisers tried to touch her crew, she was going out shooting, no matter how many rifles were trained on her.

"Yes," Sokolov said. Riven flinched as she snatched the scan-glass off Riven's temple, inspecting the tiny metal frame. Dammit. She'd paid good money for that thing. "So unless you can get me twenty-k by Dawnday—in full—you'd better hope your organs are worth that much."

Dawnday. They had time, but not much. Requiem's sun would set soon, and they'd have a few standard Earth-days before it rose again. Still, twenty-k was more than they'd earned in the past few months combined.

Samir shot Riven a look. *Don't do anything stupid,* it said.

Riven's restless trigger fingers calmed. "We'll do it. I promise."

"Good." Sokolov brushed aside her rough-cut curtain of hair. "Because you don't get any more chances."

***

"Dammit." Riven kicked an empty can across the concrete. Broken glass in the street was crushed so fine it glittered in the evening sun.

She could feel the matriarch's spies monitoring them from every lens in the city streets. Nowhere in Requiem would be safe until they coughed up twenty thousand denar.

"We could have resolved that much more gracefully. I don't suppose either of you have a plan?" Samir wiped sweat from his perfect hairline and stubble beard. Somehow it was even hotter in the streets than the throne room. Requiem's atmo-dome baked the city like the cockpit of a ship left too long in the sun.

"We bask in the sunlight, and never take it for granted again." Ty let out a small, delirious laugh, leaning against a rusted *NO LOITERING* sign on the brick wall. "Oh my god. I thought we were dead."

The sunlight wouldn't last forever. It was thirty-three hours to dusk, and another one hundred fifty-four until the sun rose again. The city seemed to be holding its breath for nightfall, when neon would bleed into the streets and the bass would come alive. Riven wouldn't complain about the fading heat, but their deadline was coming, and small jobs wouldn't cut it.

"We might be dead, come Dawnday," Samir muttered. "I doubt the cash will just fall out of the sky."

Fall out of the sky. Riven tilted her head back. Above the spines of Etri crystal shearing the skyline, a massive crescent of marbled blue streaked across the horizon—Cortellion, the planet Requiem orbited. Wealthier than Earth, and home to bastards who had everything, who could drop twenty-k on a batch of stupid alien bones. If anything there went missing, it'd be worth something.

Morphett Slade probably chased those bounties. Big ones, from people with deep pockets. A plan sparked in Riven's head.

"I know where we can get twenty-k." Speeders whizzed across the skyways above, a barrier between her and the heavens. "And *then* some."

Samir slid his metal-plated knuckles into his pockets. "I'm sticking to my rule—no drug smuggling. The last thing we need is to be on some glitch kingpin's hit list."

"Please not anteleons either." Ty shuddered. "Or anything with teeth."

"No." Riven grinned. They were out of cash, but not out of ideas. It was time to be a little more drastic. "We're going to rob Morphett Slade."

chapter 4

THE WINTERDARK VAULT

Breaking and entering was probably a bad idea.

Asa zipped her polycarbon jacket against the chill. It was an hour to midnight—an hour past curfew—and the moon, Requiem, bathed the water-gardens in dusty blue light, giving an eerie cast to the tiered fountains and rock waterfall.

Beyond the breeze rustling through the palm fronds, she heard the whir of stalking security-mechs. She tried not to think about their grasping stun-claws, or the face waiting at the other end of the security cameras.

Her father would be furious.

"Here it is," Kaya said. Ahead, through the cluster of ather-blossom trees, a door marked the laboratory's back entrance.

"You sure about this? I don't even know what we're looking for." Heir or not, Dad wouldn't appreciate spying.

"I know exactly where we're going. All you have to do is scan us in, Miss Heir." Kaya gave a dramatic flourish, gesturing to the scan-pad. When Asa hesitated, her smile faded. "Please, Asa. This is important."

Asa tucked her hands into the pockets of her well-worn jacket. The breeze whispered behind her, through the gardens where they'd played as children. Their world had transformed over the past decade, and now they both sat atop a dangerous pedestal.

"Fine. But you still owe me an AbyssQuest mission in the holodeck later." Asa pressed her hand to the scan-pad. A beam of light slid down the screen, and the door's dead bolt gave a *click.*

"Thanks." Kaya slipped past her.

Asa slowed her breaths as she stepped inside the world that would someday be her birthright. The familiar lab corridors felt menacing in the dark. A dim strip of green light wreathed the ceilings, replacing the bright clinical fluorescents. Above, every camera lens and powered-down control screen seemed to be watching. Some were.

"Security cameras," Asa said.

"Now they see us . . ." Kaya pulled a cord from her pocket and plugged it into her brain-jack. She connected herself to the security terminal and closed her eyes. Sparks fell from the control panel as Kaya let out a sharp gasp. Her mind was inside, gliding through the patterns and locks of the security systems.

Not for the first time, Asa felt a pang of envy. What was it like to feel the pulse in the circuits, to speak to them through your mind instead of your fingertips? Kaya created art when she wasn't stuck in laboratory tests, and the murals she painted of circuitspace—the maze of data and intricate locks—were nothing short of breathtaking.

And fortunately, Kaya was good at finding her way through. The tiny lights on the security cameras winked out. "And now they don't." Kaya unplugged herself. "Security systems should be out for a while."

The new silence was a shroud. Asa tiptoed past the tall robotic sentries, their heads hanging dormant. She kept her distance, still wary of those arms reaching for her.

Kaya clicked on a flashlight and beckoned her to a narrow door that looked like a janitor's closet. Inside, a cramped staircase plunged downward, with tiny lights illuminating the edges of the winding steps. Hidden in plain sight.

The farther they went, the stronger the fear pricked along Asa's spine. Something was hidden close by, something her father didn't want her to find. She followed Kaya's flashlight down the steps, letting the door creak shut behind her. The dark swallowed them like a tide before Asa opened the next door, revealing a corridor that smelled like sterilizer. The hall ended in a massive door.

A door she'd never seen.

"This is it," Kaya said. "The Winterdark Corridor."

The door was brushed steel, with a circular vault lock. Biohazard stickers marked its edges, and three dead security cameras stared overhead. Crisscrossing the surface of the metal, nearly invisible, was a lattice of sensor lasers.

"What is this?" Asa breathed. Some deep instinct whispered, *Turn back.*

"It's where he's keeping the next phase of Winterdark. My fate, I guess." Kaya inhaled sharply, pointing to a set of control panels on the wall. "You should be able to access some of the data here."

Apprehension burned at the back of Asa's neck. This felt like betrayal. There had to be a good reason her father was keeping this a secret—but what if it involved hurting Kaya?

She swallowed the lump in her throat and scanned her palm on the data terminal. Winterdark's austere logo filled the screen. She scrolled through the experimental records and groaned. "This is thirty years' worth of data. It'll take *hours* to go through."

Kaya stepped forward, her brown eyes barely a gleam in the dim light. "Hmm. My project is more recent, but try these keywords . . ."

That narrowed the list down. Sweat prickled at Asa's fingers as they ghosted across the keypad, entering Kaya's search terms.

She found a file on Kaya. *Subject Prime*, it read.

"Holy hell." Kaya leaned closer to the screen. "They created this entire phase of the experiment . . . based on me. Tens of millions of denar . . ." She shuddered. "I really am just a commodity to Dad."

Hadn't they tested on *anyone* else? Asa dug deeper into the files and noticed something. "Wait." Another main subject file. "It looks like you weren't the first."

When she opened the file, a picture of Kaya stared back at her.

Except the woman wasn't Kaya. She looked just like her—the same sharp cheeks and bowed lips and long, wavy black hair—but the name at the top of the file read *Sofi Almeida*.

"What the hell?" Kaya whispered.

Dread turned her insides cold. "Have you heard that name before?" With her face and her last name, the woman had to be a relative. Asa scrolled down—this "Sofi" was the first subject for Project Winterdark. "The next phase . . ." She could barely speak the words. "Dad's been working with living Etri samples, in an effort to . . . reprogram the human mind."

"Like hell he's going to reprogram anything." Kaya slammed her shaking palm against the wall. "I should have known the tests wouldn't be parlor tricks forever. This is bad. He's messing with people's brains here. *My* brain."

Asa steadied her breaths. It was impossible. Tinkering with human minds was risky, but no way he had an Etri. "Calm down, Kay. I'm sure it's just a prototype." The Etri had been extinct even before humans reached the Alpha Centauri star-system to settle Requiem and Cortellion. All that remained of Etri civilization were crystalline ruins and fossilized bones.

But what if it *wasn't* just a prototype? If her father had found a way to use those fossils, to build something living . . . Luca Almeida prided himself on doing the impossible.

"I don't care! If he wants to take my mind and . . . " Kaya clenched her eyes shut. "I need to know what happened to this Sofi girl."

With trembling fingers, Asa finished scrolling. The most recent report was a lab test.

Inconclusive, read the final line.

"It doesn't say what happened to her," Asa said. It was hard to focus on the screen with her heart pounding in her ears. What had her father done?

"The log ends in 2168. Twenty years ago. Two years before I was born." Kaya shuddered. "I'm sure my file won't say what happened to me either."

The knot in Asa's stomach twisted tighter. "I swear, Kay. I won't let him touch you—"

The fluorescent lights flickered as the breathy roar of the ventilation system rose.

"No." Kaya's eyes were hollow. "Listen, Asa. I've been thinking about this for a while, but this is the final stroke. Whatever happened to this Sofi girl, I'm going to be next. If Dad's invested all this into me . . . what if he never intends to let me go?" She chewed her lip. "I need to run. Somewhere he'd never find me."

"*Run away?*" It hit Asa like a kick to the gut. Running away from their father never ended well. "Remember what happened last time we snuck out?"

They'd been caught after looping the security cameras and heading to a music festival downtown. It only took an hour for one of their father's bounty hunters to find them.

What followed was two weeks of being locked in their rooms, with lectures playing on their vidscreens. Terrible news reports of what happened to *girls like them* who weren't lucky enough to have wealthy fathers to retrieve them. Horrific photos. Missing persons reports. Mug shots.

What happened if someone else had found them first? The images still haunted her.

"Dad's controlling, but we're safer here," Asa said. "And even if you run, he'll—"

"He won't find me on Requiem."

Requiem. Even worse. "That city would eat you alive! There's a reason Dad's security won't even set foot there." The moon's mining colony was the most dangerous place in Alpha Centauri. The city had once been a tourist trap and art project, but now crime syndicates and firepower replaced the law, and death whispered in the shadows behind its neon lights. Reckless kids from Cortellion bragged about visiting its nightclubs, but Asa was pretty sure they were lying.

Kaya, however, was dead serious.

"Exactly. I'm more afraid of whatever's behind that door than Requiem. I'll get by."

"And what about school? Home? Everything?" *What about me?* she thought, selfishly.

"I'm not smart like you. Our futures aren't the same." Kaya tapped the screen, pulling the image of Sofi Almeida back up. "Even if it's dangerous, I can't let Dad mess with my head for the rest of my life. And I won't end up like her." She put a hand on Asa's shoulder. "I don't think you're safe here either. You should come with me."

"Kaya . . ." Asa closed her eyes. She'd never imagined a future without Kaya.

But Luca had given them the world. Without the estate's marble ballrooms, the magazine interviews, the future he'd carved out for her, Asa would be nothing. She was born for a life here, a life of aspirations and discovery—not a life on Requiem. The uncertainties of her father's shadow were safer than whatever lay outside it.

"If I do nothing else as heir," Asa said, "I *swear* I will convince Dad to take you off the project. Do you understand?" She'd talk to him on equal terms. There had to be another way. "If I can't fix this, I'll go with you. That's a promise."

"You can do what you want, Asa." Kaya pulled away from the terminal and faced the massive vaulted door. "And I'll wait for a bit longer. But I'm not going to let him drag me behind that door and—"

Her voice was swallowed by a breathy shriek.

Asa spun backward, sure they'd been caught. But the noise seemed to come from everywhere—growing in pitch and volume, like an approaching maglev train. Something almost human mingled with a mechanical scream, like no motor Asa had ever heard.

The sound was coming from behind the door.

"Shit," Kaya hissed. "It's here."

One by one, the green laser-diode panels gave way to darkness. Then, they flickered back on—orange this time.

"That virus," Asa whispered. The one that had possessed the phoenix.

"We need to go. Now." Kaya grabbed her wrist.

But as they turned, the stairwell door slammed shut. Not its usual automated slide, but a loud *bang* that rattled Asa's teeth.

"Dust and bones," Asa breathed, but the noise drowned out her voice. She pressed her palm to the scanner, but the orange keypad wouldn't activate. She slammed her hand—no response.

"Need to do this the hard way." Kaya pulled the cord out of her pocket.

Asa's heart pounded. "Don't, Kay. You'll get hurt again—"

"And you want to wait here and get caught?" Kaya sounded scared—*really* scared. "Dad cannot know we're here."

Kaya plugged her brain into the panel and chewed her lip in concentration. Sweat glittered on her brow in the aux lights. She gasped in pain as the door gave a crude whine.

Asa grabbed her shoulders to steady her, and the door sputtered open. Asa's thoughts were a blur as she pulled Kaya, stumbling, back into the stairwell.

Something really didn't want them here.

Kaya was shaking, on the verge of collapse. As they ran, a dark, wet line trickled from her ear.

Blood.

What is happening to her?

Asa braced Kaya as they burst through the exit. She gasped as the verdant scent of the water-gardens hit her. She'd never been so glad to taste fresh air. "Kay, are you okay? We can still make it back before—"

A blinding spotlight hit her square in the face.

"Face-scans confirmed," the mech droned, its footsteps clicking. "Asanna Almeida and Kaya Almeida." Asa held her forearm over her eyes, squinting into the spotlight beam. The mech was as slender as a human skeleton, with a face like a hatchetfish. "It is nine minutes to midnight. You are not authorized to be outside the manor." The drone's stun-claw crackled.

Kaya held up her hands. "No resistance here. We'll go back—"

"Violation of curfew. And unauthorized laboratory access. Consequences will be decided—"

"Dad, if you're listening—this was my idea, not Kaya's!" Whatever happened next, Asa needed to take the fall.

"Asa. Don't," Kaya whispered. The blood on her ear was bright as rose petals.

"Do you hear me?" Asa said to the mech, louder. "None of this is her fault."

A few moments of silence. Static.

Then, a familiar voice came through a speaker on the mech's ribs.

"Asanna." Her father's voice was smooth but simmering. "Come to my office. Now."

———————————————

As soon as the office door opened, Asa had the lie ready on her tongue.

My fault. Not hers.

"Asanna." Her father's voice echoed as he turned his high-backed chair toward her. "Come here."

She walked softly, her footsteps barely audible. Luca Almeida's private office looked like a hollowed-out moon—sterile white walls curving into a sphere, crater-like indentations where holoscreens flickered, dormant. One wall cut away to glass, and the darkness beyond glittered with a thousand lights—the glow of distant cities, fairy lights in the gardens below, the stars themselves. As if he'd bought himself a piece of the night sky and mounted it on the wall.

"I don't have all night," he said.

Though her father spoke a dozen languages when interstellar media outlets surrounded him—Portuguese, Mandarin, French—he only spoke English at home, and he expected Asa to do the same. The most commonly spoken language across human civilization, one he'd insisted she excel at for business without using audio translators.

She clenched her fists and approached, the image of Sofi's face still burned into her brain. *Maintain your composure. Never crack. This is your last chance to make things right.*

Luca didn't look angry—but then again, she never could read his face. His dressing robe was as regal as any suit, as if waking up to midnight security alarms were part of his job. Thanks to subtle body-mods and a concoction of serums, he might be immune to sleep anyway.

Beneath the scan-glass over his eyes, his gaze skimmed her. "What have I said about slouching?"

She instinctively straightened. *Confidence doesn't slouch,* he always said. But right now, her confidence was a lie, like everything else in this room.

"I expected better from my heir." His restless fingers drummed on the chair. "I want a thorough explanation. This contempt for my rules is disgraceful."

Disgraceful, she wanted to say, *like everything you've been hiding.* She wondered how old her father had been during Sofi's tests. And how old he'd been when Asa was conceived *novus vitro*–in an artificial womb.

But all she could mumble was "Sorry," as she stared at her boots.

"Did your sister talk you into this?"

"No." Asa knit the lie together. "It was my idea. I was anxious to see the new prototypes. I asked Kaya to help me get in with her brain-jack." She forced a shy smile.

He saw right through it. "Kaya knows better. She's a bad influence on you."

"It's not her fault. I was curious." She remembered the noise in the lab, the shriek like a vengeful ghost. "After that glitch crashed my presentation."

"And you chose to investigate the Winterdark Corridor?" His features darkened. "You need to stay far away from there.

We have it under control, but you put yourself in danger tonight."

Under control. As if he knew where the malfunction had come from.

"You're grounded. I'm changing the passcodes to your garage and your speeder. Your free time will be spent on company duties."

Asa nodded halfheartedly. It was better than being taken off Winterdark or denounced as heir.

"You are not to leave your room for the next week, Asa. And you are forbidden from contacting your sister. You two need space to sort out your priorities, and I need her focused. She has an important project next week."

Next week. So soon.

Asa's chest tightened. "Listen, Dad. I'll do whatever you want. I'll put in twice as much lab time. But . . . I have a request. As your heir, and as a project engineer for Winterdark."

Luca laced his fingers together. "This isn't a good time to push me, Asa."

Maybe not, but she had to say something. It'd devour her otherwise. "I want Kaya taken off the project."

His face never changed. "That is a ridiculous request."

She swallowed hard. No backing down now. "The brainjack is hurting her. I'm worried about her safety."

"Her safety?" He rose from his seat. "Are you worried I've made a mistake, Asanna?" Anger flickered beneath his placid features.

She'd hit a sore spot—one that probably involved Sofi. "At least give her a *choice* about the next project phase," Asa pleaded, shrinking. If he didn't listen to his business partner, maybe he'd listen to his daughter. "If you need to, use someone else. That's all I ask."

Her father let out a shuddering breath, exhaling the hostility. When he spoke next, his voice was calm. "Asanna." She tried not to flinch as he set a hand on her shoulder. "Everyone in this family makes sacrifices. You do, I do, Kaya does."

He tapped his wristlet, and the holoscreens along the walls displayed old pictures and vidclips of people—and some she recognized. But none of them were Sofi.

He strode to an image of her great-grandmother, her velvet-black hair whipping in front of a mountain landscape. "Your great-grandmother sacrificed the entire life she'd known on Earth to be one of the first colonists here."

Mara Almeida herself. She'd helped sponsor Cortellion's terraforming, decades after she founded Almeida Industries.

"But under my parents' leadership, the company nearly went under." The vidclip showed her grandparents—her grandfather laughing as he kissed her grandmother's cheek, while they hiked through some Earth rainforest. "They were idealists. They didn't understand what it meant to set aside other aspirations for the company they'd inherited. They were squandering their fortune on environmental conservation efforts for Earth. The one who saved this company from the brink of ruin was *me*. Because of *my* sacrifices."

Asa stared at the picture. They looked so happy. She'd searched social networks and snooped into old files to hear their voices, see their faces—photos and vidclips of massive family gatherings on Earth, dozens of relatives and cousins she'd never met. But Luca had forbidden Asa from contacting any of them, and her grandparents had died when she was eight.

Was it possible to miss someone she'd never met?

Her father clicked off the screen. "I raised you with the expectation that the next generation wouldn't make their mistakes." He lifted her chin. "That someone brilliant would carry on our legacy."

My grandma wouldn't have hurt her child, Asa thought, gritting her teeth to keep the words in. But if she'd inherit everything their family had worked for, what choice did she have?

"Kaya knows her role here. Her results have far surpassed the other subjects'. She is extraordinary. As are you," Luca said as the pictures scrolled. "I'm proud of you, Asa."

She looked up at her father, his features softening. Her face was an echo of his—his gentle chin, his fierce brown eyes.

"Do you understand now? Why Kaya's contributions are necessary?"

Her jaw clenched. She and Kaya owed him everything, but he didn't own them. He couldn't dictate their entire lives.

Except he absolutely can, part of her whispered. *He can do whatever he wants.*

Making him angry was the last thing she needed. Helping Kaya meant lying low, at least for now. "I understand."

"Good. Though this doesn't mean you aren't grounded." He kissed her on the forehead. "I want you to recognize how much freedom I *do* give you. And I hope you'll use that freedom productively. Onstage . . . you were composed. Dignified. Everything I'd dreamed of."

Asa returned his smile with a hollow one. "Thank you." Normally the praise would've made her heart soar. But what was his approval worth, if she was still powerless?

She'd failed to help Kaya. Which meant she had a terrible promise to keep.

As the security-mech escorted her to her room, her mind rushed through solutions like dead ends in a maze. There was no way out of this. Either way, she might lose Kaya.

She messaged Kaya on their secret text channel. *Dad is a no-go. But please, just give me more time.*

But even as the bolt in her bedroom door slithered shut behind her, Kaya hadn't responded.

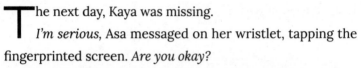

chapter 5
THE HEIR

The next day, Kaya was missing.

I'm serious, Asa messaged on her wristlet, tapping the fingerprinted screen. *Are you okay?*

She paced her room, her bare feet padding on the seafoam-and-gold carpet. Lightning flashed outside, sending stripes of light flickering through the tall windows. It was nearing noon, and she hadn't heard from Kaya since last night. Her messages weren't even showing as read. Asa had checked AbyssQuest in the holodeck, and her sister's username hadn't logged in for four days.

Asa gave three light raps on the wall between their rooms, then pressed her ear to it. No footsteps inside, only the faint hum of the security system.

Was Kaya avoiding her? Or had she already left?

AbyssQuest mission, Asa messaged, more frantic. *We need to replay the one with Shadowlord Drom and Aidan Thornslinger. You owe me, remember?*

AbyssQuest. The game they'd created in virtual reality together—a secret world where they could explore fantastical worlds outside the estate, especially when grounded. Asa had programmed the gameplay, and Kaya had poured her artist's soul into the landscapes and characters. Their shared creation.

Thunder rumbled, so hard the door rattled on its hinges.

Today was the city's weekly storm, and the pink-tinted mineral rain pounded the countryside. Not a great day to run away.

Asa stared at her wristlet screen until afterimages shifted when she blinked. A minute ticked by on its clock, but still no messages. Dammit. Where *was* she?

I need to know you're okay, Asa messaged. *Please respond.* Kaya had promised to wait. She couldn't have left for Requiem already.

Unless something had happened, and she'd needed to disappear. Asa shook the thought away.

The wind picked up, shrieking through the balustrade on the terrace outside and sending raindrops pattering against the windows.

Then: *Ping.* A message.

Her nerves plunged. Her fingers shook as she clicked on the screen.

It wasn't from Kaya. It was from her father.

Asanna. Meet me in the lab. I have a task for you.

Fear crept through her like snow-chill at the demand. What if her father knew exactly where Kaya was?

Don't think about it, she told herself. *She's fine. You'll find her.*

At her father's behest, the bolts on her bedroom door clicked open. She slipped into the hallway and tested the gold knob of Kaya's bedroom. It didn't budge. Locked.

Numb, she clicked on her service drone, and it floated beside her, forming a rain-repelling dome. She headed for the lab, slogging through the rain-soaked groves of the water-gardens more on instinct than conscious thought, her vision tunneling so she barely felt the humidity.

She couldn't let herself think about what he might want. It was hard enough to keep her mind from tumbling down horrific paths.

Just wait, she thought. *Wait and see. Don't think. Don't worry. Yet.*

When she reached the lab door, it still opened at her touch. Compared to the clouded skies, the lights inside were blinding, and a deadly quiet had settled over the corridors.

In the laboratory lobby, her father waited for her in a high-collared suit fitted with pearl cuff links. More suited to meeting an interstellar ambassador than for lab work.

"You wanted to see me?" Asa's voice cracked weirdly.

"Asanna." His hands were clasped behind his back. "I need your help."

She couldn't speak, but nodded. She followed him through the tiny door—the not-closet Kaya had shown her—and down the winding staircase. Once again, she faced the vaulted door.

This time, no mechanical screams emanated; everything was eerily quiet. Her father pressed his hand to the scan-pad, and the massive wheel at the door's center twisted and clicked. The lattice of tiny lasers went dark, and the door slid aside.

"I have an assignment for you. Your most important project as my heir."

He seemed so calm—too calm—as he showed her the Winterdark vault. All the secrets he'd kept. All the lies he'd told. Her instinct screamed *don't look, turn back*, but she forced herself forward.

Ahead, the room was dim. A heart monitor chirped a steady rhythm, and she glimpsed the glow of a life-support pod.

Someone was inside. Her heart dropped.

Oh please no oh no–

"She will not speak to me." Her father's broad back obscured her view of the machine. "But perhaps she will speak to *you*."

"She?" Asa whispered, finding her voice. "What did you–"

She sidestepped her father. Lying in the life-support pod was Asa's worst fear.

There, with her dark hair frayed, monitor nodes stuck to her skin, and her face blank as if asleep, was Kaya.

Asa choked down the shriek building in her chest. "What did you do to her?"

She was too late.

"Relax, Asa. She's fine." A razor-sharp smile split her father's perfect mouth–genuine excitement, different from the one he'd worn onstage. It made Asa's blood curdle. "The transfer was successful."

Whatever *transfer* meant, Asa knew it was horrible. Thick cables connected Kaya's pod to a set of control panels, with a cylindrical capsule latched into the center. Inside the biocapsule was a squishy blue-gray organ, pulsing–and definitely not human. An Etri brain.

Inside the life-support pod, Kaya's chest rose and fell, but her skin was gray, the flesh beneath her eyes sallow.

It looked like a coffin.

What had he done? His own daughter, hooked up like an experimental frog for dissection, a piece of equipment. Asa's heart threatened to rise into her throat and choke her.

"Human brains never took the reprogramming well." Her father strode to the biocapsule holding the pulsing organ. "But now we have a living Etri organ. It took us twenty years to develop. And we—"

Shut up, she wanted to scream. *Stop talking about your experiments and think about your daughter.* "What. Did. You. Do. To. Her?" Asa's teeth would break if she clenched them any harder.

"Kaya is my first successful mind upload." He ran his fingers over the plexicarbon cylinder of the biocapsule. "Human brains cannot interface with computer data, but Etri brains can—and their neural structure can be wiped and rewritten like software. Which is why I've rewritten this with her mind." He tapped the biocapsule.

"She can communicate through the machine," Luca continued, "but she refuses to speak with me. Even after all I've given her . . ." He sighed. "Minds are much easier to work with when they're willing. But the best thing I ever gave her was a sister. I hope she'll respond to you." He fixed his dark eyes on Asa. A demand. "Talk to her, Asanna. Command her to wake up."

Command her. Like a computer program. A subservient thing. Inside the machine, Kaya was cold, alone, probably terrified.

She should've listened. She should've taken her sister's hand and boarded that ship with her at the first opportunity. She should've stood up to Luca, *demanded* he take her off the project, threatened to leave. Sabotaged his experiments herself. *Anything.*

But she'd failed.

"Put her back together," Asa said through a rising sob. "Use someone else!"

"Do you not realize what a breakthrough this is? We can erase negative traits, upload new skills—"

"I do *not* care about your breakthrough. She's not a machine." The world lurched and swayed. Asa caught herself against a control panel. All of this was her fault. She'd kept her suspicions buried, too willing to convince herself Luca had better intentions.

The bright control readouts silhouetted her father in a haze of green. "I know she planned to betray me. She will be far less defiant when I've finished with her."

Bile threatened to heave up her throat. This was about control. Not his studies. "Don't you dare change her."

Luca turned away, sighing. "I know this might be difficult to accept. If you need time to process this, I understand."

"I don't need—" Her legs trembled. Dad wouldn't do this. He couldn't.

"Asa, dear." He smoothed a stiff hand over her hair. "You're young yet. One day you'll understand better."

She tried to lift her hand, to swat him away, but her whole body was rigid. *Don't talk down to me*, she wanted to say. *You're a monster.* She opened her mouth to yell at him, but the world was out of focus, as if she were underwater. The words died on her tongue.

And, as soon as it occurred to her that she might need to sit down, everything slipped into darkness.

Asa awoke on her bed's rumpled lace duvet, covered in a cold sweat, her limbs impossibly weak.

For a while, she couldn't move. It was only her and the agony and the sheets clenched in her fists, the tears soaking her pillow. She'd failed. Her future was collapsing around her, and it had taken the only person she'd cared about. The only person who saw Asa as a friend, and not a business opportunity. Time stretched, each second an eternity of raw solitude.

I can't stop him.

I should have intervened.

What could I do? He took Sofi, he took Kaya, he was always going to take Kaya . . .

I have to help Kaya before he erases her.

And if he uses me too? Replaces my brain?

The emptiness made it hard to breathe. Her sister's mischievous grin wouldn't appear outside her window to steal her away for adventures in disguise. The vibrant horizon of AbyssQuest would remain unfinished, and the second VR headset would collect dust. And nobody would giggle with her at the dirty romance novels they'd downloaded while sipping mango sodas.

Reprogramming. He'd change her. The Kaya she knew would be gone forever.

Your fault, that awful voice nagged. *You self-centered coward.*

But the life-support pod had been active. There had to be something she could do.

Asa steadied her breaths. If she'd learned one thing as Luca Almeida's daughter, it was that you hadn't lost until you'd given up. He was always a step ahead—he'd known Kaya had planned to escape. But he would've never guessed Asa had wanted to go with her.

Maybe he still didn't know.

She stumbled out of bed, wiping her tears on her bare arm.

No more crying until you've done everything you can. The skies had cleared, and Requiem's glassy-blue moonlight sheared through the starfield. Only a few hours had passed since she'd blacked out.

A shrill *ping* made her jump. Her wristlet, again.

For a moment, she wanted to unhook the braided rose-gold strap and hurl the thing across the room. But it was Josiah, not her father.

Asa. I heard what happened, the message read. *I can't abide by what your father has done. I feel it's only right I leave the company.*

Josiah. How much of this had he known about?

You picked a heck of a time to gain a conscience, Asa responded.

It seemed like forever before the next message came. Then: *I'm trying to save her, Asa. I have a plan to put her back together. Before he can change her.*

Asa's heart leapt. She dialed him on voice, on the secret channel she used to call Kaya without their father tapping in.

"How?" she demanded as soon as she heard static on the other line. "You really think you can fix her?"

"I can't talk much here," Josiah said. "I'm already en route to Earth. My former research team can help her. But there's a problem, and I need your help."

"Anything." She'd cling to this opportunity if it killed her.

"Your father was keeping her body in the cryo-lab. As soon as I found out what he'd done . . . I had to help. I managed to get her out a few hours ago, but I miscalculated. Her mind is still in that biocapsule. I couldn't retrieve it from the vault. But you can."

She frowned. He'd acted so *fast.* "You already have her?"

"This was the least I could do for her. I owe it to the two of you. I should have done something earlier."

How long had he known? "Did you try to save Sofi Almeida?"

The question must've caught him off guard, because he went quiet. Only garbled voices in the background. Then: "That was before I joined the company. But the way your father speaks of her . . . I can't let that happen to Kaya."

"There's still time," Asa whispered, more to herself than Josiah.

"Yes. But I can't save her unless you bring that biocapsule. I know it's a lot to ask."

It was *everything* to ask. Asa ran her fingers across a painting Kaya had made for her—the ridges of acrylic forming a crumbling castle in a fantasy landscape.

I don't think you're safe here either, Kaya had said. *You should come with me.*

Asa knew her choice. "I'll do it."

That night, Asa stole through the gardens one last time, ready to betray her father.

"I'm almost there," she murmured into her wristlet as she slipped into the atherblossom grove.

"Keep going." Josiah's voice was rough and rasping in her earpiece. "You won't have much time once you open the vault."

The thought of confronting her father still made her sick with fear. But even if she couldn't stand up to his face, she could steal from behind his back.

She swallowed the lump in her throat as she passed

everything she might never see again—her garage and the cherry-red speeder she'd built herself for her seventeenth birthday, the swimming pool where holographic dolphins flipped and squealed on warm summer nights. Her school, the tech-shows, her future.

This is my choice, she told herself. *No matter what it costs.*

The straps of her grease-stained backpack dug into her shoulders with every step. She'd stuffed it with everything she could fit—some self-defense tech, her tools, the vintage fantasy comic books Kaya had bought for her birthday—while leaving room for the capsule she'd steal.

She commanded the lab doors open with the touch of her palm. As she entered the sterile darkness, Asa activated her fade-suit. It cloaked her, blurring her limbs into rippling water to scramble camera detection. Even if her lab entry was authorized, cameras wouldn't show her.

Inside the Winterdark vault, the horror washed over her again at the sight of the capsule.

The final piece of Kaya pulsed in the suspension fluid. Small bubbles glowed sickly green under the dim aux lights. Asa took a steadying breath, wiping her sweaty palms on the fade-suit.

I will not be afraid. I owe her more than that.

Beneath the capsule's cold plexicarbon surface, the organ throbbed in time with Asa's frantic heartbeat.

If she stole this, there would be no coming home. But home wasn't home without her best friend, the only person who knew the dreams she kept secret from their father.

I can do this. I have to.

Asa punched the stolen passcode into the machine. With

a soft hiss, the steel arms holding the capsule unlatched like the maw of a spider. Asa stuffed the capsule into her backpack.

Her first betrayal. So quick. So simple.

"Asa," Josiah said. "My ship's about to depart. She's safe in the cargo hold."

"Her body, at least." Asa tried not to think about her sister in pieces, or how Josiah had gotten her out. No doubt he'd taken advantage of her father's trust, like Asa was.

"I'll contact you soon." Josiah had been in a dangerous position since stealing from her father, so he couldn't wait. The hard part was up to her—alone. "Remember: get to the port quickly, and find a cheap transit that isn't taking face-scans. Send me your coordinates when you arrive within Earth's gravitational field, and I'll pick you up. I promise we'll put her back together."

When he put it that way, it sounded easy. "And what about Federation customs paperwork? School enrollment? What happens once I'm settled on Earth?"

A pause. "Don't worry about that yet. Just focus on getting here."

Asa bit her lip as the Winterdark vault grated closed behind her. Within minutes, she'd become a fugitive. She'd robbed the man who'd given her everything, and now she had to run.

She slammed her palm on the scanner for the final door. She had Kaya.

No turning back.

chapter 6

THE GIRL WHO FELL

The worst part of being a fugitive was the uncertainty.
With every bump and lurch of the rickety passenger transit, Asa braced for a boarding party to kick open the airlock and drag her back home.

Home. Through the dirty porthole, Cortellion's crystal-blue oceans and lush jungles shrank to a cloud-streaked marble in the distance—but even thousands of miles away, she wasn't safe from her father. And up here, there was nowhere to run.

Asa gasped as the ship shuddered, jerking her against the seat harness. She squeezed the backpack tighter between her boots, feeling the steady pulse of the Etri organ inside. All of Kaya—her memories, her mischief—was mute and vulnerable inside this plexicarbon pod, and Asa had spent most of the trip trying to hold herself together.

She wished she could apologize.

"Heads up," a voice lisped over the ship's speaker system, punctuated by a shriek of feedback. The ship's owner held a button on his cybernetic jaw as he swaggered down the row of seated passengers, electromagnetic boots clicking against the floor grates. "We're having engine trouble. Might make an emergency stopover soon."

Asa gripped the harness. Engine trouble. Just what she needed today. If only she could've stolen her dad's personal ship instead of this junker.

"One hell of a ride, huh?" murmured the pixie-like girl in the seat facing Asa. She tucked a caramel-brown curl into one of her hair buns. "You worried? You look like you've seen a ghost." The girl leaned forward, and Asa caught a whiff of bubble gum and cigarettes.

Asa met the girl's eyes, cautious. That seat had been empty when the ship left port. She must've boarded at the fuel station, when Asa had her nose buried deep in a fantasy novel on her wristlet.

"I'm fine," Asa said, though she was certainly *not* fine. "Just . . . haven't slept in a while."

She kept her gaze low, avoiding the other passengers' gazes—hollow-eyed glitch addicts; body-mod junkies with pointed carbon ears, hunched over holoscreen gamepads; a beefy mercenary with a flickering blue cybernetic eye. None paid her a second glance; without the makeup and ball gown, she didn't look like the girl on the cover of *Eon Magazine*'s "20 Future Leaders Under 20" issue two months ago.

Fine by her. Asa could play the part of a traveling mechanist.

The girl chuckled. "I've run away from home before too." She tapped a talon-sharp pink fingernail on the armrest, jingling the silver charms of her bracelet. Upon a closer look, she was probably half a decade older than Asa. Not really a *girl*, but tiny. "Sucks to travel alone at first, but you get used to it. And sometimes the emergency stopovers turn into the best stories."

Asa wasn't *that* obvious as a runaway, was she? "Why do you think—"

"Oh, come on." The woman's amber eyes flitted over Asa's dirty jacket, her rose-pearl earrings, the backpack at her feet. "Overstuffed backpack. Bloodshot, terrified eyes. You might as well stick a 'runaway' sign on your forehead. Need one of these?"

Asa prepared to turn down a cigarette, but instead, the woman offered a foil-wrapped stick of bubble gum. She hesitated—but bubble gum might ease the nervous metallic flavor on her tongue.

As she reached for the gum, the lights flickered, and the ship gave another lurch. Asa mouthed curse words she'd never dared use in front of her father. The ship had power issues. That could doom their landing.

The owner clacked down the aisle. "Strap in. There's a navigation issue, and we're having an emergency inspection. Our next stop will be Requiem, not Earth."

Angry muttering erupted among the other passengers. "A *navigation issue*?" said a mercenary with silver tattoos crisscrossing his cheeks. "Why the hell can't you control your own ship?"

"We're preparing for the landing." The ship's owner turned to a man in a char-marked mechanist jumpsuit, and his voice dropped to a whisper. Asa leaned over the armrest, trying to overhear. "It's rerouted itself, somehow," he murmured. "Never seen anything like it."

Navigation issue? Those were rare—unless there was a glitch, or something worse.

Beyond their voices was a low roar. It rose to a mechanical, pseudo-human shriek that tugged at the corner of her memory.

The same one she'd heard in the Winterdark vault.

Asa's throat went dry. It sounded like the security program with the orange lights, the one that slammed the doors shut. Had it *followed* her?

Unless she was so tired her mind was playing tricks on her.

Out the porthole, Requiem drew closer for the landing. The colorful sprawl of the city—covered in an atmo-dome in the middle of a hellish desert—sparkled like rivers of radio-active waste. The faster-than-light relay, which pulled ships between Alpha Centauri and Earth's solar system, was still a distant point of light.

The engine was grating horribly. At this rate, they'd either be stranded on Requiem and at the mercy of smugglers and bounty hunters, or the ship would make a nice crater on its surface. If that noise was truly the thing from the Winterdark vault, it was here for her.

Asa had to do something.

"Excuse me." So much for not drawing attention to herself. But there had to be a thousand girls roaming Alpha Centauri looking for mechanist work. "I need to see the engine."

The ship's owner snorted. "You? Why?"

She winced as the roar of the engines rose to a bone-splintering wail. Murmurs erupted among the passengers, who covered their ears or winced. Asa had worked on hundreds of engines, and no functioning engine made that noise, ever.

They had bigger problems than a detour. Namely, turning into a meteor of scrap metal.

"We can't land yet," she blurted. "I think there's a power issue, and if the nav-board is glitching . . . you need to shut it down while someone fixes the power. Otherwise, it could give out when we land. With no lift, we'll crumple like a soda can."

He chuckled, and his voice dropped to a murmur. "Look. You're cute and all, chickling, but you should leave this to the professionals."

Asa's cheeks warmed as indignation built in her gut. "What makes you think I'm not a professional?" Nobody ever talked to her like that. Nobody who knew her name, anyway.

His lips quirked into a smile above his metal jaw. She felt his gaze slide over her, straight through her baggy jacket and trousers. "Tell you what. If you really are a professional . . ." He hooked his thumbs under his belt. "You can inspect *my* engine."

That earned him a few snickers from the mercs behind him.

Revulsion crept up Asa's spine like an angry tarantula. But before she could retort, her gut flipped as the artificial gravity released.

Gasps echoed through the cabin as the ship plunged into darkness. Only the red emergency lights and moonlight pouring through the portholes remained.

"*Landing commencing in six minutes,*" a mechanical voice droned over the loudspeaker. "*Power failure imminent.*"

Asa grabbed the seat harness as the gravity kicked back on, its dizzying weight washing over her like a lull on a roller coaster. "You hear that? That's a bad combination of alerts!"

The man's bushy eyebrows scrunched. "Our mechanist already knows something's wrong."

She unbuckled her harness and stood. Today, she was done asking nicely for what she wanted. She and Kaya weren't going to die in a fiery landing because of one stubborn idiot. "Listen," she demanded, "I'll bet your dropout mechanist on this junkyard ship doesn't know a wrench from his own—"

"Junkyard ship?" His eyes narrowed. He grabbed the lapel of her jacket and shoved her against the emergency med cabinet. Asa winced as pain pounded through her skull. "I don't know who the hell you think you are, but I don't take orders from little girls."

Asa bit back her protest. If he knew she was Luca Almeida's daughter, he'd grovel and beg forgiveness. If he knew she'd finished two years at the Naat—Cortellion's best automation school—he'd let her see the engine without question.

But without her former identity, she was a homeless runaway.

The colossal man glared down his nose at her, silhouetted by the moonlight. "I ought to throw you in the cargo hold for a while. That'll shut you up."

"Don't touch me." Asa struggled against his grip, wishing she'd pulled the stolen stunner out of her backpack. "I'm telling you. None of your mechanists will know how to fix this!"

"You heard her, Steel-Jaw," said a smooth voice behind them. "Don't touch her."

"You want to go in there with her? You'd better—" His hands suddenly released. As he turned to the woman who'd spoken, the fury in his eyes turned to horror.

Behind him stood Bubble Gum, pink-taloned hands on her hips. "I'd better what, now?"

The woman was half his size, but he backed away like she was a snake. "*Morphett Slade?* Oh, god. I'm so sorry. I didn't know you'd boarded my ship. I swear—"

"Shame you don't take orders from little girls," Bubble Gum—*Morphett*—said, popping a cherry-pink bubble over her shiny lips. Something dark danced behind her eyes, and the smile splitting her face was deadly. "Because your engine's failing, and you've got a capable mechanist who says she can fix it. It's probably a good idea to let her see it, hmm?"

The man's eyes were wide as dinner plates. Asa panted, straightening her jacket where he'd grabbed her. Whatever he knew about Morphett—whatever he saw beneath her bright exterior—it wasn't good. But it was saving Asa.

"Y-yes. Of course. Go down there and tell Cyclops I sent you. And if there's anything you need—"

"I need you out of the way," Morphett said with lazy confidence.

He nodded quickly and wedged himself between empty seats, giving Morphett the entire aisle.

"That's better." Morphett leaned under the seat to grab Asa's backpack, then shoved it into her arms. Asa grunted as it hit her. The woman was stronger than her size suggested. "I hope you know what you're doing." Morphett waved her toward the hall.

Asa chased Morphett past leaking pipes and dirty portholes. "Wait. Why did you stand up for me?" The woman was smaller than Asa, but surprisingly quick.

"Because you're the only one who can fix this piece of scrap."

"And why do you think that?" The name *Morphett Slade* traced a familiar groove inside Asa's mind, as if she'd heard it before.

"Something about the way you talk. You're trained. And I'd rather not die at the hands of these idiots." She flashed a grin, weirdly chipper for how screwed they were. "So make us both look good when you save this ship."

She couldn't deny the appeal.

Asa was reaching for the engine-room door switch when the ground whipped upward. She gasped as the ship tilted violently, and her feet were knocked from under her. Instinctively, she pulled the backpack against her chest as she rolled over the floor grates, her hips and shoulders knocking against the metal.

"*Rear port thruster offline*," droned the voice over the speaker. "*Commence repairs before landing in five minutes.*"

No, no, no. Asa rolled into the wall, her back stinging from new bruises. Blood rushed to her head as the ship plummeted, like the dizzyingly fast elevators at her father's office. Requiem's gravity was pulling them in. With the ship tilted almost forty-five degrees, it'd crash and roll as it hit the ground—worse if another thruster gave out.

Asa pulled herself along the tilted floor, grabbing the steel grates for support. She hit the switch for the engine room, and the blue light blinked as the door slid aside.

Inside, sparks rained from the ceiling as a frantic mechanist clutched the control board in his cybernetic fingers. The screech of the engines rattled through her bones. A memory flashed of the laboratory lights turning orange, of the blood trickling from Kaya's ear.

Whatever had followed her, Kaya had counteracted it once, hadn't she? There had to be something Asa could do.

"Are you here to help?" A cybernetic third eye glowed through the hair on Cyclops's forehead. "Something's wrong. My eye's acting up. I keep seeing—" He gasped, running his skeletal fingers over the eye. The eye flickered orange, confirming Asa's worst fear. "I don't know what to do."

"She'll handle it," Morphett said. "Just stay out of the way."

Good that *someone* had faith in Asa. The colorful tangle of engine processes displayed on the holoscreens behind Cyclops were an absolute mess.

Asa took a deep breath and ducked into the engine crawlspace—a tight squeeze with her backpack on. Time to get her hands dirty.

Between the whirring timing belts and heaving pistons, the engine hummed a deadly purr around her. The ship shuddered, buffeted by the atmosphere. Not much time. She reached deeper within the engines, avoiding the hot breath of the vents and power cables.

The automated alert sounded over the loudspeaker: "*Impact approaching. Fasten harnesses. Emergency: power failure imminent.*"

Asa pulled up the diagnostic screens. She'd only seen a power failure this bad in test simulations.

The landing would be rough. Even if they survived, this ship would probably never fly again. She'd be well and truly stranded—on Requiem, of all places. In a city that swallowed people whole, a runaway heiress would be an expensive morsel.

She closed her eyes and lost herself in the crescendo of the whirring engine. This was her place—where the gears whispered a symphony and fell into place at her command. If only for another minute, she had to be Asanna Almeida, the girl who could do anything.

She had an idea. She grabbed an emergency comm on the wall, shouting for the captain to unlock the thrust controls. When the lock disengaged, she rerouted the power cables, dividing the electrical supply of the three active thrusters among all four. Had to be enough power for one last blast to break their fall. The landing wouldn't be smooth, but they might not die.

No matter how this ended, Asa wasn't going back home.

Asa slammed the cable box shut and stumbled toward a landing harness, bracing for whatever awaited below.

chapter 7

THE CITY OF
SHATTERED LIGHT

"*Twenty seconds to impact*," the automated voice chirped over the loudspeaker.

"Strap in!" Morphett shouted over the emergency alarms. "This is going to be rough!"

The ground rushed to meet them. Seconds left. Asa tightened the straps on her harness so she wouldn't hit the ceiling with the force of the plummeting ship. She imagined crashing the airship in AbyssQuest, the glaring *GAME OVER* screen she'd programmed with whiny, sympathetic music—except this was real.

"*Emergency: power failure imminent.*"

The descent slowed as the thrusters gave one last kick, just like she'd hoped. She clutched the dirty backpack as the ship leveled out, the thrusters humming weakly.

And then came the drop. The thrusters died with a harsh whine—all of them. A gut-turning fall, and they were crashing.

A tremor rattled the ship as the hull gave a sickening *crunch*. Asa squeezed her eyes shut. Metal grated as the ship slid across carbon and concrete. The landing gear had shredded—now the hull. If it crumpled further, they were doomed. The lights flickered out, for good this time.

After a hard lurch, the grating stopped. Everything was so quiet, Asa could hear the ringing in her ears. Nothing but darkness stretched ahead. Her head spun.

Am I dead?

The ship shuddered, punctuated by the groan of metal. A muffled sob resounded through the ceiling from the cabin above. Somewhere in the dark, Cyclops's eye clicked on.

"I'll be damned." Morphett's voice cut through the darkness before a flashlight beam skimmed across the floor, reflecting light onto her pixie face. "You did it."

"Oh my god," Asa whispered. The relieved, broken exhaustion she'd been putting off since stealing the capsule rushed over her. She unbuckled the harness and pressed her cheek to a warm control panel. "We're . . . we're alive."

Slowly, Asa unzipped her backpack and inspected the bio-capsule's silver-tinted surface. No cracks, and the vitals were stable. Thank the stars.

"That was one hell of a landing," Morphett said.

Asa let out a half-delirious cackle. Her knees stung with growing bruises, but nothing else hurt. She'd *saved* them. "That," she laughed, "is called *lithobraking!*"

She tapped her wristlet to send a message about saving the ship, but realized she couldn't tell anyone. One of the most impressive things she'd ever done, and nobody—not Kaya, not her few friends at the Naat—would know.

Morphett put a finger to her lips. "This ship's the least of our problems. We have to move."

"Move where?" Asa's head spun. Right. They were on Requiem, and far from safe.

As Asa's eyes adjusted, she could barely make out the engines. Judging by the tilt of the floor, they were crushed. She winced. As she'd expected, the ship was toast.

But if Asa and Morphett were safe in the lower level, the passengers in the cabin above definitely were. Their muffled footsteps and chatter drifted through the ceiling.

Beyond the creak of settling metal, she heard a deep, strange pulse. A rhythm.

"Come on." Morphett pulled Asa to her feet. Her legs were jelly. "We're trespassing in syndicate territory with a busted ship."

"Trespassing?" Asa's stomach lurched.

Morphett pulled her toward the emergency hatch. The doors were warped, and the access panel was dead. Morphett gave the doors a hard kick, mumbling under her breath.

In the dim flashlight glow, Asa caught a glint of steel at Morphett's fingertips. A tiny saw blade ejected from behind one of her pink fingernails, and she jimmied it into the bolt holding the doors together.

Cybernetic implants. Asa shivered. What else was Morphett hiding?

The blade folded back into Morphett's finger, and she gave the door another kick. "Eyes up." A shaft of reddish light flooded into the corridor. "You'll want to see this."

With the doors warped apart, that low, ominous pulse became louder. *Thump-thump*, pause. *Thump-thump*, pause. A bass. It buzzed through Asa's boots, like the city's beating heart.

She followed Morphett through the hatch, onto the

concrete rooftop where they'd landed, and Requiem knocked the breath out of her.

Among the sprawl of holoscreens and neon lights, it was hard to tell where the streets began and the night sky ended. Glass bridges and skyways crisscrossed between the glowing buildings, and bright advertisements scrolled across billboards, sending colors glinting off the carbon-fiber hulls of passenger speeders. The sun had set in a blaze of deep-violet streaks, and far above the bleeding inferno of city lights, stars flared across the sky. Beyond the roof they somehow hadn't crashed through, Requiem's electrified skyline was a mishmash of mock-Gothic spires, beaten-gold domes, and twisted glass monstrosities, blinking their colors into the haze.

And between the stars, a silver-blue crescent of planet-light arced over the city.

"Cortellion," Asa breathed. So far away now. Everything she'd ever known was on that patch of light.

Compared to home's water-gardens and verdant fields, Requiem was garish, fast, *cramped*. And so much brighter, with ancient, lacerated Etri crystals forming opalescent ridges between the buildings. Each crystal refracted the galaxy of city lights like a thousand prisms.

The city of shattered light. The place Kaya had wanted to start her life over. Despite the rumors, Asa couldn't deny it was beautiful.

Kaya, she thought, squeezing the backpack, *we're here*. Tears pricked her eyes as the guilt came flooding back. If she'd left when Kaya had asked . . . her sister would be here with her, whole. At least until this city got the better of them.

Morphett stared at the vibrant skyline and took a deep inhale of night air, as if the scents of exhaust and fried street food were sweeter than the cigarette between her teeth. As if she'd arrived home.

"Just in time for sunset. Night breaks like a fever in this city, huh?" Morphett's pixie smile grew as she touched the cigarette with a metal lighter node in her fingertip.

"It's . . . *alive*." An ad for data-chip tattoo services scrolled across a nearby tower. Distant music stirred through her, a steady rhythm beneath the whirring and honking of the speeders. Pretty as the city was, Kaya still needed her, and she had to find a way offworld before her dad caught up. She was about to call Josiah when a small drone scudded up to her and sent out a green scan-beam.

Asa held a hand in front of her eyes, blocking any face-scanners. But the drone seemed more interested in the ship. The scanner flitted over the hull, illuminating grapefruit-sized dents and dramatic scrapes where it'd crumpled against the concrete.

"What's that?"

"Scavengers are sizing up the damage. They'll be here any second to pick this ship apart. Us, too, if we linger. Come on."

"Pick *us* apart?" Asa didn't like the sound of that. She winced as gunshots resounded somewhere in the distance, and all the awful stories about Requiem whispered ferociously at the back of her mind.

Morphett beckoned her to a rickety fire-escape ladder, and Asa followed her down into a dimly lit alley. She wasn't letting Morphett leave her behind.

The alley was crowded with overfilled dumpsters and spine-backs burying their snouts into the plastic bags. Everything smelled of fry-grease, and despite the reek of rotting vegetables, Asa's mouth watered. It'd been a while since she'd eaten.

"Mechanist." Morphett's expression was stern under the alley lights. "We both need a ride to Earth, yeah?"

Asa nodded slowly. "I . . . yes. Do you have a way out?"

"I've got friends picking me up. We have room for one more, if you need it."

Dust and bones, yes. It was perfect. Asa had a few thousand denar she'd hastily pulled from her dad's account before leaving—an amount small enough to prevent him from getting an alert. "How much will it cost? I can pay."

"No worries. I owe you after you saved that ship."

Relief flooded Asa. "Oh. That would be *great.*"

"Good." Morphett tightened the pink laces on her sneakers. "We're going to pass through the Crush, so the rule is: *you stick by me.* No wandering. No slowing down. Try not to look anyone in the eye." Asa nodded, though her knees and wrists trembled, aftershocks from the crash. "And have one of these. It'll calm your nerves a bit."

Morphett held out the packet of foil-wrapped bubble gum, and Asa gladly accepted this time, cramming a stick in her mouth. It was sticky and warm from Morphett's pocket, the flavor a chemical imitation of strawberries imported from Earth. The sweetness trickled through her, calming her nerves.

And she needed every bit of calm as they entered the Crush. Beneath rusted, graffiti-smeared overpasses were streams of pedestrians with brightly colored hair and strips of light glowing beneath their skin. The scents of spicy noodles, candy vapors, and engine exhaust nearly knocked her over. Spiny succulents topped with alien floral blooms lined the streets. At the center, a twisting Etri crystal glowed faint purple over tattered awnings of tattoo stalls and the broken-glass storefronts of cybernetics dens. All contraband tech, no doubt.

Was this place really as awful as the rumors suggested? She certainly understood why her classmates had boasted about coming here. The pulsing bass rhythm rocked through Asa's bones, an undertow that threatened to drag her down and suffocate her. Requiem was overwhelming, but there was something seductive about it.

Come to think of it, everything felt fuzzy. Maybe she was in shock, her nerves fried from the landing and the rough night. She'd stopped shaking, but now she felt oddly numb. She worked the bubble gum across her teeth, sucking out more of the weird strawberry flavor.

Around her, terse murmurs rippled through the crowd.

"*Third one this week.*"

"*Poor bastard probably deserved it.*"

The crowd was gawking at something behind her. Asa followed the angle of their holo-goggles and tattered hoods upward to the skyway system, and instantly regretted it.

Tacked to a billboard at a skyway station was a corpse.

The lower jaw was missing, the face open in a silent scream. The empty chest cavity was pinned open, bloodless, the cut edges sealed off with melted steel.

Neon-orange paint was smeared into letters on the flickering screen behind it. *ORGANS ARE WORTH MORE THAN LIARS.*

Asa turned away, but the image had already wormed its way into the darker parts of her head. This city would eat her alive, and nobody would care.

The dizziness worsened, and she caught herself on a grimy sidewalk railing.

"I told you to stay close," said Morphett behind her. "Almost lost you."

"Who—" Asa cut herself off. She didn't want to know.

"Someone who snubbed the Code. The Fed troopers here are paid to look the other way, and the only law is the Duchess's. Golden rule being *don't piss off any of the matriarchs*."

A chill fingered up Asa's spine at the mention of the Duchess. Requiem's ruthless leader was a legend. Rising above the skyline was a golden spire with a pair of holographic wings spreading and folding behind it. The Duchess's Citadel. The queen among matriarchs.

"Of all of them, the Staccato matriarch is one of the nastiest," Morphett said. "We're in her territory."

Suddenly, Asa was glad she wasn't staying.

Asa closed her eyes as the nausea rose. Images flashed through her head—the strung-up corpse, but with Kaya's face, her brain destroyed. Asa's head spun so badly she couldn't tell whether she was still standing.

What's wrong with me? She had to be in shock. She needed to leave this moon before she collapsed. No telling what would happen if she fell unconscious here.

Morphett caught Asa as she stumbled up the steps to the docking bay. Trams trickled past in blurs of color. Asa's mind was a swamp of throbbing bass, glaring corpses. She was in no condition to navigate by herself.

She rested a cheek on Morphett's shoulder. Since she'd left home, Morphett was the only person who'd protected her. The only person she could trust right now.

Morphett had believed Asa's engine skill without question. She hadn't even asked Asa's name before offering to help her.

Wait. Asa braced herself, trying to catch her breath. Her head swam. Something was wrong, but she couldn't pinpoint what.

"You okay?" Morphett's scalpel-sharp eyes said she knew exactly what was wrong.

Then it clicked.

Asa spat out the gum, clumsily groping for her stunner. *The bubble gum. Dammit!*

But Morphett was faster—especially given Asa's current state. Morphett grabbed her neck, and a metal node on her palm erupted into searing pain. Asa gasped as the stun-blast lanced through her, locking up her legs and knocking her over. She writhed from the aftershocks, feeling like she'd been dropped into a deep fryer.

"You're working for my dad," Asa slurred.

"Well," Morphett purred, her pink-laced sneakers padding lightly at eye level. "Maybe you aren't so gullible after all."

chapter 8
BOOMSLANG

Stealing Morphett Slade's bounty was a gamble, but Riven was feeling lucky tonight.

The sun had crashed beneath the horizon, sending aftershocks of purple sunset through the glass wall of Eidolon Docking Bay. Below the control tower where her crew waited, the sprawl of lights hit the rainbow of Etri crystals and ship hulls.

It was a good night for payback and profit.

"Not long now." Riven rested her palms on her revolvers' varnished oak handles.

Ten minutes ago, Morphett's lackeys had landed her ship, *Nephilim.* Any second now, Morphett would arrive with her bounty—soon to be *Riven's* bounty. From Cortellion, if her informant was right. Easily worth twenty-k, maybe more. If this didn't cover their debt to Matriarch Sokolov, nothing would.

And Riven couldn't resist the chance to beat one of the underworld's dirtiest bounty hunters at her own game.

"Still no chance I can sit this one out?" Ty's ginger-blond hair was tangled where he'd been tugging it. "What if this bounty's a seven-foot-tall glitch kingpin? With metal-plated knuckles like Samir's? And before I can use the sedative, they deck me in the jaw—"

"All the drug kingpins I've met have been scrawny and

strung-out." Samir peered down the scope of his rifle, scanning the bay. "Besides, you have backup. You'll be fine."

"Bullets don't care who our bounty is." Riven drew *Blackjack*, gave it a lazy spin on her finger, and holstered it again. "I've got plenty of stun-rounds." That was *Blackjack*'s job tonight—non-lethal rounds for their bounty. On her right hip, *Verdugo*'s cylinders were loaded with live, lethal rounds for Morphett and whoever else got in their way.

"Hope this is worth it." Ty crouched next to the platform's ledge, blue eyes flicking frantically over the bay. He'd admitted to having nightmares about her and Samir getting hurt beyond what he could fix. Like Emmett had.

But leaving this debt unpaid would be more dangerous.

"Just imagine how it'll feel to get back at Morphett," Riven said. "And when the matriarchs catch wind of it—"

"*Dust and bones*, Riv," Samir said. "This isn't about payback. This is about keeping our guts. We're not risking ourselves for your reputation, so keep the cockiness in check."

Too late. "Morphett has it coming." And when everyone knew Riven's name, it'd be like living long after she died. Which, at this rate, would be within a few years.

Even now, the white noise was a phantom dizziness at the back of her head, threatening to send tremors through her trigger fingers. If the white noise didn't eat her, this city would.

"Incoming," Ty said.

Samir adjusted his rifle, and the carbon-fiber scales plating his knuckles shimmered. He was even better at throwing punches than lining up shots, but getting within ten feet of Morphett Slade was a bad idea.

Sure enough, Morphett was striding through the west entrance, her bounty in tow.

Ty inhaled sharply. "*She's* our bounty?"

Not the bounty Riven had expected either. Instead of a beefy, metal-modded arms dealer, Morphett was dragging a struggling, half-limp girl.

"Our bounty took the damned bubble gum," Riven muttered. Rumors told of Morphett drugging her bounties with candy, but Riven hadn't thought anyone would be dumb enough to fall for it. Clearly her new bounty wasn't some criminal mastermind. So who was she?

Riven clicked her wristlet, releasing the zip-drone. "Galateo, give me a better visual."

"Of course, my lady." His drone scudded across the docking bay, clicking inquisitively. Her wristlet holoscreen showed a zoomed-in image of the girl's face. Messy black hair, fitted red jacket, elegant button nose. Pretty, in a helpless princess sort of way. The girl was around Riven's age, but probably not her type.

Galateo's drone returned to Riven's wristlet. "I am unable to match her face to any open bounties in the database."

Samir swore. "It's a private job, then. Someone hired Morphett. Someone with money."

"Even better," Riven said.

"No. Much worse," Samir said. "If we steal this kid, we might not get paid. Or we might piss off someone powerful at the other end of this bounty."

Ty bit his lip. "She doesn't look like a criminal."

"And Morphett doesn't look like a sadistic, thieving

cybernetic bitch, but here we are." But Riven could tell Ty was thinking the same thing she was—the girl probably wasn't cut out for wherever Morphett was taking her.

"What if she's in trouble? Shouldn't we help her?" Ty said.

"Oh, *now* you want to intervene?" No doubt the girl got bonus sympathy for being cute. "Doesn't matter who nabs her. Someone's getting her bounty, and it had better be us."

They were prepared to grab her and run. *Boomslang* waited in the dock below, sleek and poison green with stark black bands, her stealth-class Marauder ship with an anterior gun. It looked like the head of its namesake, a poisonous snake about to strike.

Riven's pride and joy. Emmett's last gift to her.

"Your ship, your decision, I suppose," Samir muttered, though there was a twinge of bitterness in his voice. "Let's hope collecting this bounty doesn't land us in deeper trouble." He clicked the safety on his rifle. "If we're getting into position, it's time. Remember: steady, subtle. On my count—"

Screw subtlety. It didn't matter if Morphett saw her coming. Better she see Riven's face one last time before Riven turned her into red smears on the corrugated steel.

Before Samir finished his count, Riven was halfway down the ladder. She leapt the remaining distance, landing in a crouch in front of the docking bay's massive glass wall.

Morphett had swindled her once. Riven was a dead girl walking, but nobody crossed her without consequences.

Above her, Samir groaned. "Why do I bother?"

She drew her revolvers. *Verdugo* and *Blackjack* were her best friends. Sometimes, her only friends.

She peered down *Verdugo*'s iron sights at Morphett and fired.

"Let me go!"

Asa knocked an elbow into Morphett's ribs. They were hard as steel, and the impact buzzed painfully through her arm. With Asa's hands cuffed and fog stuffing her brains, she was out of escape options.

"You really thought stealing from him was a good idea?" Morphett pulled out Asa's stunner and slung the backpack straps over her own shoulders. The muzzle of the stunner jabbed Asa's spine, urging her forward. "Runaways don't usually survive a night in this city. A little princess wouldn't last ten minutes. I'm doing you a favor by taking you home."

It wasn't a favor. All that awaited her back home was imprisonment, or worse.

But maybe Morphett was right. Why had she thought she could survive away from home? She'd trusted the worst possible person, and now she was paying for it.

The colors of the city blurred through the glass wall. *Stay awake,* she demanded. *Stay awake!* Asa closed her eyes, trying to ignore Morphett and her failure and the noise . . .

The noise.

At first, she thought the sound was in her head—the sedative distorting her hearing. But it grew louder until it was clearly a high-pitched whine.

The thing from the Winterdark vault had followed her.

Morphett gasped as the doors snapped shut behind them. A ripple ran through the security station doors as they, too, locked and bolted. The tram on the skyway ground to a halt, and inside, confused passengers shouted for the attendant.

The overhead lights flickered orange. The program—virus? monster?—was trying to trap her.

What did it want? The capsule? She could've sworn she heard the alien organ pulsing like a beacon, a secret that didn't want to be kept. But maybe it was only her own heartbeat, slowing with the sedative.

"Keep moving." Morphett pulled Asa across the steel-grated walkway between the ships. "Whatever your daddy has in store for you, it's probably a hundred times better than whatever that thing does."

She doubted it could be worse than having her mind trapped in a machine for reprogramming. No, she couldn't go home. Asa reached for the pen-laser in her pocket—anything to cut the cuffs, to buy her a second of time—

An ear-splitting *crack* tore through the air, and Morphett halted as a dent appeared in the candy-striped hull of a ship, a good inch from her ear. One of her curls twitched.

She shoved Asa to the ground as her gaze whipped toward the glass wall. Only then did Asa realize the noise had been a gunshot.

A few docks over, a girl had landed in a crouch, silhouetted by the glass wall and the expanse of towering neon behind it. She slowly stood—her feet planted, long braid whipping behind her—until her body covered the spire of the Duchess's palace. The fluttering holographic wings seemed to extend from her shoulders.

"Hey." The girl stared at Morphett, her eyes ringed in gunpowder-black smears of eyeliner. She leveled a revolver at Morphett's head. "Hear you've picked up some cargo."

Morphett laughed, cracking a smile both lazy and predatory. She pulled a pistol from under her black vest. "Riven Hawthorne. Looking for a rematch?"

"Send the girl over," Riven said from behind her gun, the corner of her mouth twitching into a smirk. Her braid rested over her shoulder, silver-blonde and streaked with magenta that matched her fraying vest. "Or the next bullet will be through your eye."

No matter how disastrously beautiful Riven was, the last thing Asa needed was another kidnapper.

"Do you even know who she is?" Morphett said.

"I know she's worth something to you." Riven spun her left-hand revolver around her trigger finger until it snapped back into position. "Last warning."

Asa forced her limp body to stand. Riven didn't know who she was, so Asa might be able to negotiate, if Riven could steal her. With that spark of hope, a plan began to take shape.

She had to ditch Morphett.

"You have a death wish?" Morphett said.

Riven fired. *Pop, pop.*

The pinpoint shots flew straight at Morphett's eye sockets, but they stopped inches from her face. They flattened like nailheads and fell, ringing against the steel walkway.

A holo-shield. A barely visible lattice of blue hexagons

hovered in front of Morphett. Expensive tech. A metal node was embedded in the exposed skin at Morphett's hip—the shield-generator. More cybernetics. Escaping would be tough.

Riven swore, and her cocky grin evaporated.

"You like the shield?" Morphett said. "Was expecting you to test it at the scavenger hideout."

Through the growing fog in her head, Asa saw a gleam on the upper railing, a long metal barrel trained on Riven. It took Asa an extra second to realize what it was, but—

"Sniper!" Asa blurted.

Riven reacted immediately, diving out of the way. A salvo of bullets peppered the walkway at her heels. She ducked beneath the hull of a docked cargo freighter, the bullets pinging its gray-blue cladding.

Morphett gave Asa's handcuffs a hard yank and pulled her toward a wicked-looking Sidewinder ship with its cargo hatch open. By now, Asa's attempts at kicking and flailing were closer to twitches.

"Galateo," Riven shouted into her wristlet, hunkered behind the freighter. Another sniper bullet whizzed above Asa's head, pinging near Riven. "Position *Boomslang*'s main gun. Now!"

The reply came from a synthy voice with a proper Himmeltor accent. "There are no viable angles to shoot from where *Boomslang* is docked. Perhaps you should have considered this before rushing into combat."

Riven made an exasperated noise. "Perhaps *you* should go fall off a bridge."

"Duly noted, my lady," Galateo, which must've been an AI, said. "A shame I'm strapped to your wrist."

Morphett urged Asa up the scaffold steps to the roof of her black-and-silver ship, with *NEPHILIM* painted in uneven letters. The roof hatch gaped, revealing the ship's cargo hold. With Asa's hands bound and her body turning to gelatin, she was in no condition to descend the ladder. Her stomach sank. Morphett was going to push her.

"My dad won't pay you if I'm injured," Asa slurred.

"He'll pay me well enough." Morphett's hot breath smelled like smoke.

"Cover me," Riven called, her gun trained on Morphett. "Sniper's targeting me. And our cargo's in my line of fire."

"Would everyone please stop referring to me as 'cargo'?" Asa muttered, wondering whom Riven was talking to.

Her answer came seconds later as a bullet whizzed through the air.

Morphett looked up, cursing, as a sniper turret sparked and fell from the control tower at the bay's west edge, disappearing between the docking bridges. Her backup fire was down.

Riven had a crew.

"Nice of you to bring friends, Morphett," a deep voice called from the opposite control tower. Asa glimpsed someone atop the platform, someone built like a soldier.

Riven cackled, scrambling back onto the walkway. "Good shot, Samir." Asa couldn't hear what Samir said over the comm, but she heard Riven's response: "She's *beyond* drugged. See if Ty can fix her."

"Fix her. That's rich," Morphett mumbled. She held Asa's bound wrists at the edge of the cargo hatch. The drop was at least ten feet. "It'll be a long ride. Get comfortable."

Then she pushed her.

For a second, Asa was airborne—bound and limp and floating, hoping the sedative would make the fall hurt less.

She landed in the waiting arms of a gray-armored woman who dumped her to the ground. One of Morphett's hired lackeys, no doubt. Asa's head spun as the woman growled at her to *stay right there.*

Not that Asa had much choice. She needed a strategy before she faded completely.

I am not going home.

Shouts and gunshots resounded atop the ship, and the hull shook. Morphett dove out of view as sickly yellow smoke rose around the hatch, the bay lights shining through like dirty sunbeams.

In the chaos, a hooded figure descended the ladder, quick as a spider. For a heartrending second, Asa thought it was Morphett, but it was a boy, and he was too tall besides.

"Who the hell—" Morphett's lackey had barely noticed him when he produced an electric switchblade and rammed her in the back of the neck. She jolted and crumpled to the ground.

The boy leaned over the mercenary, pressing a tiny gray patch against her neck until she went limp. "That's it," he whispered. "Sleep now."

He powered off the switchblade and knelt next to Asa. She glimpsed kind eyes beneath his hood. "Hey, don't panic. I'm not with Morphett. You all right?"

Oh, nice of you to ask. I'm sure your payout's bigger if I'm not injured. "Peachy." This must be whom Riven had told to fix her. "Are you Ty?"

Ty nodded. "You took the bubble gum, huh?" He had strik-ing eyes and ginger-blond hair. His delicate features reminded her of Aidan Thornslinger, an elf rogue character Kaya had created for AbyssQuest.

And he was pretty. Asa managed to stop herself from telling him as much. "Yeah." She worked hard to speak through her slackening mouth. "Last time I'll ever take candy from strang-ers." A trail of drool leaked from her lips, and a small, distant part of her was mortified.

His fingers flitted over Asa's pulse points. "Nasty sedative. Guess she knew you'd be trouble, huh?" A smile flickered over his face, quickly replaced by concern. "Slow, even breaths, all right? Just focus, and try not to panic."

She imagined being onstage beneath the glaring lights, where she'd crushed her fear until it was only a whisper. Her breaths slowed.

"Riven has Morphett distracted, so we need to act fast. I don't think I can carry you up the ladder, so I need you to stay conscious."

"Aren't you . . . trying to kidnap me too?"

Guilt flashed over his face. "I won't let anything bad hap-pen to you. I promise."

Asa closed her eyes. Going with Ty was risky, but it was better than a certain trip back home. She'd rather be in smug-glers' hands than her father's.

"Get the pen-laser from my pocket and cut my handcuffs." She managed to roll onto her side, giving him access to the pocket of her baggy mechanist's pants. "It's powerful, so don't look . . ." Her breaths came ragged. ". . . straight into it. Careful where you aim. The switch is the safety . . . the button turns it on."

His blond brows furrowed. "You sure this thing is safe?"

"I'm great at QA testing." It was a more intense version of the pen-lasers most mechanists used for precision cuts. Asa's quality assurance had involved cutting watermelons while wearing safety goggles.

Well, she'd also made a fissure in the lab floor, but Ty didn't need to know that.

The tension on her wrists slackened as Ty sliced the handcuff chain. "Can you move?"

She tried to push herself up, but her entire body was asleep. She pushed harder, lurching onto her knees.

Ty mounted a needle.

She groaned. "What's that for?"

"Adrenaline. It'll keep you conscious a little longer. You ready?"

She supposed it was too late to back out now. All her objections were drowning as the sedative pulled her deeper.

A sharp pain pricked her neck. Then, adrenaline hit her like a tidal wave of color and fear and anxious energy.

Asa's breaths turned to gasps as she wriggled her arms. She clambered to her feet, grabbing the ladder rungs. *Move,* she commanded herself. *Your sister needs you.* Somehow, she had to get her backpack from Morphett.

Ty steadied her, and it took all her strength to climb.

Atop the *Nephilim*'s hull, Riven and Morphett were locked in a blur of kicks and punches. Riven knocked Morphett onto her back, clenching her throat with one hand and raising her revolver in the other. Morphett grabbed her wrist, and Riven gasped and dropped the revolver as a stun-shock rippled through her.

Eyes blazing, Morphett held out her fist as a long cybernetic blade whirred and unfolded from her forearm. Asa was morbidly transfixed by the tiny mechanisms, the flesh parting along a line of surgical steel.

"*Dammit!*" Riven rolled out of the way as Morphett slammed the blade's curved tip toward her face, piercing the ship's hull instead.

Ty tugged Asa's wrist and gestured to the stairs. "Come on."

But climbing the ladder had taken everything she had. "Just . . . give me . . ." Asa knelt, her head spinning. She needed another minute. Or a nap. Everything was fading into a comfortable haze.

Move! screamed a small, determined voice, but it was quieter than before.

She could barely see the fight. Riven's purple-streaked braid whipped behind her as she tumbled off the polished black hull, crashing to the docking ramp below.

Asa winced. *You have to win, Riven. You're all I have right now.*

Morphett's shield flickered and encased her entire body like mesh armor. It would take an obscene amount of energy to cover her like that. No way her shield could take much more after Riven's gunshots.

Morphett intended to finish this quickly.

With Riven down, Morphett turned to Ty. She held up her pistol, brushing away a curl falling out of her bun. She looked unhinged—her doll-like eyes bright, her predatory nonchalance falling away.

"Who do we have here?" Morphett cooed, circling Ty. "I think you're out of your depth here, buttercup. But I can see why Riven keeps you around."

Asa had a clear view of Morphett's back. Riven's dropped stunner was nearby. Asa had all the mobility and speed of a shockworm right now, but she had to take one last shot.

Ty backed away, pulling a slender hilt from his pocket and ejecting the electrified switchblade. But Morphett simply smacked him with her gun and sent him sprawling.

Morphett's holo-shield flickered. Though it was a cybernetic implant, Asa had worked on that shield model before—it had a "blind spot" caused by the projector. A weakness.

And there it was, near the base of Morphett's spine.

Ty clutched the red mark on his cheekbone. *Go*, he mouthed when he caught Asa's eye.

Morphett stood over him, lazily brandishing her pistol. The backpack, *Asa's* backpack, still clung to her shoulders. With those ridiculous pink-laced sneakers and her small stature, she looked like a kid on her way to school.

All Asa could think was, *That's mine, you tiny mech-rat.*

Asa summoned every ounce of strength left in her slackening muscles. Her hand fell onto Riven's stunner, and she tilted it just enough to aim at Morphett.

Asa pulled the trigger.

The stunner blast arced, a jolt of electricity that sizzled through the holo-shield's sweet spot. Morphett yelped and fell forward as her shield shimmered and disappeared.

In the brief silence, distant alarms blared. The bay lights glared orange, and the corrupted screech grew louder.

"Everyone drop your weapons! This bay is being evacuated!"

Footsteps slammed on the corrugated steel, muffled by the throb in Asa's head. Helmets like blue beetles gleamed beneath the alarm lights—Federation soldiers had arrived.

Morphett swore.

"The backpack," Asa slurred as her eyes fluttered shut, hoping Ty would hear her. "I need it. Don't let–"

It was the last she remembered before blacking out.

Part II:

THE CITY OF NIGHTMARES

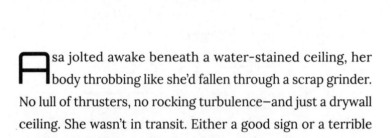

chapter 9

STRANDED

sa jolted awake beneath a water-stained ceiling, her body throbbing like she'd fallen through a scrap grinder. No lull of thrusters, no rocking turbulence—and just a drywall ceiling. She wasn't in transit. Either a good sign or a terrible one, depending on whose hands she was in.

Asa cursed the hammer-pulse in her head as she sat up, the ratty couch sagging beneath her. The walls were covered in wrinkled old posters of movies she'd never heard of—one had mustached men in Gold-Rush Earth attire, and another displayed an angry-looking man with half a cybernetic face. Mounted on the walls were old-tech guns with revolving cylinders and pull-back hammers. Like the ones Riven used, but probably even older.

Riven. Was this her place?

Better hers than Morphett's. Asa stumbled to the window and pulled aside the solar blinds. Glowing skyways arced across the dark horizon, crisscrossing over the maelstrom of crooked alleys, graffitied syndicate logos, and relentless holoscreens blinking into the electric haze.

Definitely Requiem.

If she'd helped Kaya run, maybe she wouldn't be in this

mess. She'd failed the one person who treated her like a sister and not a prodigy. Now, on Requiem, Asa was neither.

Floodlights bathed the streets in a harsh imitation of sunlight. The clock on her wristlet read 10:49—Requiem ran on Earth's twenty-four-hour cycle, not Cortellion's twenty-eight-hour cycle. It was morning by Earth standards, but still dark—Requiem's rotation was agonizingly slow. Night would last much longer, at least a few Cortellion days.

She was running out of time. The biocapsule could only sustain the organ for another week or so. Her only hope was that Riven hadn't figured out who she was. She had to take the biocapsule to Josiah, and—

Her backpack was gone.

"No, no, *no*." Asa pulled up the couch cushions.

The stained green carpet was cluttered with discarded clothes and empty microfilm pizza packets, but nothing big enough to hide the capsule. The last time she'd seen her backpack, Morphett had been wearing it. Bile rose in her throat.

Voices drifted through the closed door. An argument.

". . . can't just bend over backward for every pretty girl we meet." Riven's voice. The girl who'd kidnapped Asa. "Once we turn her in, she's out of our hands."

"And if Morphett comes after us?" This voice was probably Ty's.

"We'll deal with her. Damn if I wouldn't like to throw that gremlin out an airlock."

Asa's head pounded. If they had her backpack, it was pointless to run.

"Who *is* this girl, though? I mean, if Morphett's after her, she must be in deep—"

Asa pushed the door open. In a small, brick-walled kitchen with a sink full of dirty dishes stood Riven and Ty—her kohl-rimmed eyes dark and alert, his blue ones concerned.

"Where's my backpack?" Asa's legs faltered, and she caught herself against the table.

Ty put a hand on her shoulder, steadying her. "Whoa. You're awake early. That sedative Morphett hit you with was pretty powerful."

"Where is it?" Asa repeated.

Riven dangled the backpack strap from one finger, like bait on a hook. "Looking for this?"

"Oh, thank *god*." She reached for the backpack, but Riven jerked it away.

"You owe us an explanation. What makes you so valuable to *Morphett Slade*?" Riven unzipped the backpack, setting Asa's gadgets on the table. Asa winced as Riven set the EMPs down roughly—she probably didn't recognize them as grenades.

Riven produced the slender silver biocapsule. "And what the hell is this?"

Asa's mouth went dry. What could she tell them? Riven's crew knew she had a bounty. "I don't know what you're talking about. It was a mistake—"

"Morphett isn't stupid. And neither are we. She only gets her hands dirty for bounties that pay big. So I'll ask *one more time*. Who the hell are you?"

Ty turned over Asa's grenades, inspecting the white-

and-gold logo stamped into them. "Almeida Labs?" His eyes widened. "Where did you get this?"

Asa had to weave another lie, and quick. "I . . . used to know Luca Almeida. I stole the equipment—and the capsule—from him." Partially true. She could leave out the part about being his daughter.

At her father's name, a chill crept over the room. Riven and Ty shared a glance, and a deep, wounded anger flashed between them. The nape of Asa's neck tingled. She needed to tread carefully.

"Luca Almeida?" Riven raised an eyebrow. "How'd you manage to steal from that bastard?"

If you're going to lie, Asa, make yourself believe it, her father had once told her. He was an excellent liar, conning his way into business deals and convincing employees to sell their souls to the company. Much as it chafed her to imitate him, she didn't have much choice.

"Because I'm a mechanist in his laboratories," she said, spinning a story close to the truth. Her father wouldn't have leaked news of her disappearance—especially not when he already had Morphett after her. She only hoped Riven didn't pay attention to tech-industry news. "Was, rather. Before I defected."

"Defected? Now I'm liking this story." Riven set the biocapsule down, then sank into a chair and crossed her ankles over the table. "They say Almeida Labs are a steel trap guarded by mechs. Lots of shady shit happening in there. So what's in the capsule?" She tapped the tinted glass with a fingernail coated in chipped steel-gray polish.

Asa forced her voice steady. Clearly Riven knew something she didn't. "It's . . . the crux of the corporation's biggest project. The advanced human brain-computer interface. Project Winterdark."

Ty gasped. "Project Winterdark?"

Riven's voice was sharp as a razor. "The same Project Winterdark that wiped out an entire Earth settlement a year ago?"

Asa's blood ran cold. "I . . . I never heard about that." An entire Earth settlement? That couldn't be right. "What happened?"

Riven ignored the question. "Of course nobody on Cortellion heard about it. They probably scrubbed all those news reports."

A mechanical voice chimed in with, "This information is consistent with Earth media reports from last year, my lady."

Riven looked to her wristlet. "What'd you find, Galateo?"

A Galateo-unit personal AI was pricey, even by Cortellion standards. Asa didn't dare ask where Riven had gotten one.

"It seems the incident was, indeed, connected," Galateo said. "Project Winterdark was the test that lost control and wiped out the settlement at–"

"That's enough." In one fluid motion, Riven stood, pulled out a silver-purple revolver with *VERDUGO* carved into the side, and pressed the muzzle to the capsule. To Kaya. "So what you're saying is that this thing needs to be destroyed."

"No!" Asa blurted.

Ty held up his hands. "Riv, hear her out–"

"You'd better give me a damn good reason." Riven clicked the hammer.

"Because . . ." Asa stumbled over the words, anything to stop her, but all that came out was the truth. "Because that's my sister!"

Riven looked at her like she'd coughed up a slug. She slowly lowered the gun. "What?"

Asa's throat was impossibly dry. "Almeida uploaded her mind, as part of Project Winterdark. Her body . . ." She hesitated, but there was no point in hiding this part. She told them the rest of the story—about Josiah taking Kaya to Earth, the capsule containing her mind, their plan to put her back together.

Ty picked up the biocapsule, turning it carefully in his palms. When he flipped a switch, LEDs lit up inside the tinted glass, revealing the organ suspended in viscous fluid.

Riven squinted. The capsule cast a faint glow over her freckled cheeks. "What in hell?"

"It's an experimental organ." Asa eyed the pulsing blue-gray organ and the ropes of sinew tethering it. "And Project Winterdark can't proceed without it."

Ty's expression was unreadable. "Doesn't look like any organ I've ever seen."

"It's not human. It's Etri." Her father was fascinated with the Etri. One summer night, he'd pointed out stars in the sky and told her how the Etri had once ruled Alpha Centauri. *The Etri communicated in a way humans never can, Asa. Their brains seamlessly melded with each other, and the organisms they evolved alongside.*

The Etri had left behind only their ruins—and on Requiem, the salirium fuel mines that powered FTL travel. According to the Winterdark files, with two decades' worth of resources and connections to Requiem's mines, her father's scientists had somehow revived a living Etri. But only one.

"*Etri*?" Ty said. "How is that even *possible*?"

"Highest security in Almeida's entire facility. I had to pull a lot of strings to get it out." Less complicated—and more exciting—than hitting her palm on a scanner.

Ty put a hand to his forehead. "This keeps getting weirder and weirder. I think I need to sit down."

"I know it could be dangerous. But if you're willing to get me to Earth, I can pay." If they had reason to hate her father, maybe they'd help her.

Riven gave her a hard look. "How much have you got?"

She'd withdrawn eight thousand denar before leaving home—for emergencies. This certainly qualified. "I can pay seven thousand." Much more than the eighty-five she'd spent on that piece-of-scrap transit. But it should be enough to keep Riven's crew loyal, right? "If it's not enough, Josiah can pay you more once we get to Earth."

Riven snorted. "I'll be honest with you: if Almeida sends more hunters after your ass, this won't be worth seven-k denar. We need . . . twenty-five-k. Think your contact can pay that?"

Asa felt the blood drain from her cheeks. She was already asking so much of Josiah. But if he had the cash, he'd give it. At least, she'd tell Riven that. "Josiah can give you the rest. I promise."

Riven slid her fingers into the backpack's outer pockets, like a dealer searching for a hidden ace. "He'd better. As much as I'd like to find out how much Morphett was offered for you . . . I don't like Luca Almeida, and I especially don't like the nasty shit he's doing with Winterdark. Sounds like helping you means screwing over both him and Morphett."

"Almeida has done enough damage," Ty added.

Asa's chest coiled tighter. They'd help her, but if they learned the truth—the hours she'd spent hunched over lab tables, the tech-show she'd done for Winterdark . . . bounty aside, they would *hate* her.

But it wouldn't matter once they got to Earth. Only a few hours. She could bluff until then, and hope they didn't dig too deep.

"There's no Project Winterdark without that capsule," Asa said. "And I'm going to make sure he never touches it again." That, at least, was a promise.

"I'm in, then," Riven said. "We'll take that seven-k and get you the hell out of here. You're ours until your guy coughs up the rest. Fair deal?"

Asa swallowed hard, nodding. Still a hostage, but she at least had some negotiating power now. She pulled up her bank account, scanned her fingerprint on the wristlet screen, and initiated a transfer for seven thousand denar, wincing as the numbers dwindled.

"Give me your wristlet code so we can put you in our messaging system," Riven said. "And take an earpiece while we're at it."

"Did they restore the power to *Boomslang*'s bay yet?" Ty said as Asa entered her messaging code.

"Not yet," Galateo said from Riven's wristlet. "I still cannot form a connection with the ship."

The power. Asa vaguely remembered Federation soldiers

shouting about a lockdown. Her stomach churned. She'd forgotten the creature in the wires, following her, shrieking.

"Well, the lockdown can't last forever," Riven said. "If needed, we'll *convince* a dock worker to let us in."

Footsteps thumped behind the closed door. Then, a knock. "A little help?" said a muffled voice through the door.

Ty opened it.

A broad-shouldered man stumbled through, grasping plastic carry-out bags in his carbon-plated fists. Sweat beaded on his brow, but his dark hair was frozen in perfect waves.

"Or . . ." Riven glanced at the newcomer. "Maybe Samir's boyfriend can pull some strings for us."

"For the last time, Riv. Diego is *not* my boyfriend." Samir, Asa assumed, was the man she'd glimpsed in the control tower. He caught Asa's eye and flashed a grin, teeth white as the diamond studs in his ears. "Hey, our cargo's awake."

"Uh, hi," Asa said. Samir looked like the kind of guy who left a trail of broken hearts in his wake. All three of them did. Asa wondered if any of them had a history—but they seemed to get along, so probably not.

Behind Samir, a tiny dog scrambled into the kitchen, its nails clicking against the tile-patterned floor. Its tail wagged so hard its entire body wiggled. The dog nuzzled Samir's leg, shedding a mess of golden fur onto his black pants.

"The bar's serving chicktrill skewers today. Couldn't miss it." Samir grinned, unpacking the bags. "I figure if we can't pay Sokolov, we might as well splurge on something we can eat." The smell of fried meat, scallions, and buttery flatbread wafted from the cartons, and Asa's stomach ached in response. She hadn't eaten since before getting on the transit ship, at least half a day ago.

"Actually, we might have a way to pay Sokolov," Riven said.

Samir raised his eyebrows, his gaze flicking quizzically from Riven to Asa.

"Change of plans," Riven said. "We're getting her to Earth. I'll explain later."

"Uh. I'm Ty, by the way." Ty gave Asa a small, awkward wave. "Since nobody seems to have introduced you. That's Riven. This is Samir, and the dog is Zephyr." The little dog hopped onto Samir's lap, watching the food cartons expectantly. "What can we call you?"

She was *definitely* not related to Luca Almeida, the man Riven and Ty seemed to hate. "Tripp. Call me Tripp."

She'd earned the nickname in machine shop at the Naat after she'd gotten her boot stuck to an electromagnet and fallen face-first into a vat of coolant. It was all anyone in class talked about for days. And, unfortunately, the first name that sprang to mind.

"Tripp, huh." Ty cracked a lopsided smile. It made something flitter in her gut. "Good to have you on board."

As the others cracked open their carry-out containers, Asa found her table manners slipping—picking meat off the skewer with her bare hands. Eating was different when meals weren't guaranteed.

"If you're from Cortellion . . ." Ty said between bites of flatbread, "have you ever seen a bruttore?"

"Only in zoos." Asa noticed her elbows were on the table and quickly pulled them off. "Nobody wants them anywhere

near a human settlement." They'd been an apex predator before humans terraformed Cortellion.

"Did you guys know a bruttore's stomach coats its prey's
bones in an oily mucus, forcing it to vomit them up so they
don't enter its lower digestive tract?" Ty said cheerfully.

Samir groaned. "And why are you telling us this during
lunch?"

"I was reminded of it, by the way Riven's scarfing her food."

Riven reached over Ty and head-locked him, pulling his
forehead against the table. He didn't stop laughing. "I'll barf
all over you," she said. "Watch me."

The conversation should've mortified Asa, but instead her
chest ached with jealousy. Besides Kaya, she had few friends—
the other kids at the Naat didn't give her a second look until
they found out who her father was.

But no matter how charismatic these people seemed, it
was probably a façade. They were thieves, smugglers. Though,
come to think of it, wasn't Asa a thief by now too?

Galateo interrupted their teasing. "My lady, it might be of
interest for you to see the news. Check channel RQK."

"Turn it on, then," Riven said.

The holoscreen next to the table lit up, showing footage
from the docking bay. The bay lights sputtered, and panels in
the control tower exploded in small bursts of electrical fire.

"Damn. We make the news again?" Samir handed Zephyr
a nugget of meat.

"Shush!"

". . . *the accident at Eidolon Docking Bay stemmed from a*

virus that authorities have named Banshee, due to the bizarre screeching it emits. Sources are still unsure where the virus originated, or why, but the bay has been quarantined until further notice, with power cut–"

Riven practically spat out her mouthful.

Banshee. It had a name now. Though Asa wasn't sure it was a virus.

"Until further notice, all of Requiem's incoming and outgoing ship traffic has been halted without exception–"

"*All* traffic? Surely it isn't that bad?" Samir said.

". . . enforced by the Federation. This includes shipments, patrols, and passenger transport."

Riven flicked off the holoscreen. Nobody spoke. In the silence, Zephyr scarfed the rest of Samir's flatbread.

"Looks like roughing up a dock worker isn't going to cut it," Riven murmured.

"All of Requiem? Are they serious?" Ty said. "Does the Federation even have that kind of power?"

"There has to be some way off." Samir idly stroked the pup's head. "No way the Fed troopers can keep tabs on every port. The matriarchs would have them skinned alive if they tried. It's–"

He was cut off by a high-pitched beeping that set Asa's teeth on edge. Her first thought was *fire alarm*. A light above the kitchen door flashed with the noise.

"What is that?" Asa said through clenched teeth.

"Perimeter security," Riven said.

"Someone's prowling around in the tunnels." Samir coaxed

Zephyr into the room where Asa had woken up. "Guess we'd better take a look, Riv." He produced a slim rifle from the cabinet next to the door.

"Ty. Keep an eye on our cargo." The look Riven gave Asa was glacial. "But I'm sure Tripp knows what'll happen if she tries anything funny."

Asa *didn't* know what would happen, but she nodded vigorously. She slipped the biocapsule into her backpack and followed Ty into the back room.

"It was probably a spineback or a lost glitcher that tripped the alarm," Ty said, but there was a tremor in his voice.

With Banshee and Morphett after her, Asa didn't believe him.

chapter 10

BLACKJACK

Stranded on a strange moon in a strange apartment with a strange boy, Asa had forgotten what calm felt like.

She crouched between the sagging couch and the crooked solar blinds, resisting the urge to chew her nails bloody. Across from her, Ty leaned against a movie poster, the false sunlight from the street illuminating his tattered jeans and boyish face. A pair of stun-switchblades were sheathed at his belt.

"So. Corte, huh?" Ty's voice was soft and disarming. "Is it as gorgeous as they say?"

Cortellion. Home. Right now, she was on the bright spot of the moon that glinted above her home planet. The thought made the whole world seem to flip. "I glimpsed Almeida's estate once or twice. It's pretty, I guess." And she'd never see it again. The floating crystal chandeliers of the grand hall, the lazy brooks in the water-gardens, and the aura of inevitable success were nothing but memories. "Did you grow up here?"

"Nah. I'm an Earther. My brother and I grew up there with my dad, until he passed. Then Emmett met Riven, and we ended up here."

Her nerves began to settle as he spoke. He was obviously attempting to calm her, and it was working. "Your brother?"

Ty's lips pursed, like he couldn't summon the words. She'd

poked a sore spot—maybe he had secrets too. But Ty seemed out of place in this city, too kind for its violence and lies.

A fizz of static cut through the silence. A screen on the wall next to Ty blurred to twists of color, like radio waves.

Ty gave it a glance, then changed the subject. "I miss Earth's storms and beaches. Nothing but desert out there."

And no rain under Requiem's atmo-dome, since clouds couldn't condense under it. Asa wondered whether she'd miss the regulated weather on Cortellion, after enough time away.

He gave her a curious look. "What about you? Do you think you'll ever go back to Corte?"

"I can't. Almeida rules that place." Asa watched the screen. Why had it turned on? Its static was cutting through the quiet, erasing the calm she'd tried to settle into.

Then, she heard it.

Thump.

The noise had come from the kitchen. But the lights were out and the plasti-pots were still piled in the sink. Nobody was there.

"Riv," Ty whispered into his comm. "Was that you?"

"Was *what* me?" Riven's voice fizzed through the comm. "Is he there?"

Asa's stomach knotted. "Who?"

Riven swore under her breath. "Galateo's camlink showed him trying to get in. We haven't found the guy. Ever since the cams went dead, it—" Her voice dissolved into garbled noise.

Thump.

This time, Asa saw the kitchen door shake on its hinges.

This room had few places to hide—a closet, a couch, a desk. Her heart slipped into her throat.

Ty crouched, drawing his switchblade. "Samir? Riven?"

But there was nothing on the voice-channels but static.

Click.

The kitchen doorknob shuddered.

Click, click.

Asa looked for somewhere, *anywhere,* to hide.

"That isn't Riven." Ty gestured to the closet. "Let's go."

"Go where?" Through the kitchen was the only exit she'd seen. There was the window behind her, but—

Ty jammed the sliding closet door open. He pulled aside a panel in the closet to reveal a rickety spiral staircase. The scent of musty, stagnant air hit Asa.

He beckoned her into the darkness.

After he slid the panel shut, she followed him down the stairs to a tunnel system. Cracked white tiles covered the walls, streaked with grime, and two tarnished metal tracks lined the branching tunnel. An abandoned subway platform rose next to the staircase. "Is this a train system?"

"It's been empty for years. Don't worry about traffic. We need to find Riven and Samir."

Their footsteps sloshed in an inch of stagnant water—if it could even be called water. It looked like dirty motor oil. The scents of exhaust and mildew and other unsavory things greeted Asa, and she had to duck beneath hanging vines the color of dried blood. Above them, scarni chittered as they scampered through the vines, their bushy tails bobbing.

On a wall in faded yellow spray paint were curly letters: *LET IT ALL DEVOUR YOU.*

Not exactly reassuring.

Asa's breath hitched when Ty proffered a stunner, holding it by the barrel. "I saw Morphett take yours."

Asa slid the stunner into her jacket pocket, taking a deep breath. She hoped she wouldn't need it. When she looked up, Ty was still watching her.

"I, uh, meant to thank you earlier." He rubbed his shoulder absently. "You saved my ass back there in the docking bay. So . . . thanks. You're a lot tougher than you look."

Asa already knew she didn't look tough—she had next to no muscle and was still sometimes mistaken for a twelve-year-old—so it didn't mean much. "You're welcome." It came out high at the end, like a question.

"I guess I shouldn't be surprised." His sharp cheekbones were staining pink. "It must've taken guts to steal from Almeida. I mean—"

Static crackled over the comm.

Ty tore his gaze away, scouting the tunnel beneath the dirty glow of fluorescent lights. "Riv, Samir?" he said into his comm. "Come in."

The buzzing void in Asa's earpiece only intensified. Something was interfering. Something *close.*

"Do you think they would've gone that way?" Down the tracks was a broken crater, filled with more brackish water. A tunnel stretched beyond it.

Ty grimaced. "Better hope not. I'm drawing the line at

crotch-deep. That's a nest of venereal disease waiting to happen."

At a scuffing in the tunnel behind them, Asa immediately spun, raising her stunner. "There!"

Silhouetted by the dim lights, a figure stumbled along the tracks. Choked weeping echoed down the tunnel.

"Get down." Ty pulled her into a crouch behind a maintenance staircase.

The man ambled closer. His legs moved at different paces—one lurching forward, the other dragging reluctantly. He'd seen them.

Soon, Asa could make out his face—pitted cheeks, lank brown hair falling over his face. His pants were cut short on one side to reveal a cybernetic leg, with ropes of steel and silicon like muscles. He looked familiar.

On his forehead was a patch of gray steel, embedded with an eye glowing orange.

Orange.

Icy clarity washed over her. "Oh, no."

Cyclops. The mechanist from the ship. Infected.

"Don't come closer." Ty ejected one of his stun-blades. "We're armed."

Cyclops stumbled forward, pointing at Asa through the stair slats. "You. You're the one it wants."

"What are you talking about?" Asa's voice shook. She had a feeling she already knew.

"It feels like needles," Cyclops said, voice breaking. "And the visions—it won't let me sleep. Unless—" A ragged gasp. "I'm sorry."

He lunged toward Asa.

She fired her stunner as Ty rushed the man, slamming the blunt end of his stun-blade against Cyclops's shoulder. The man stumbled and fell, his eye flickering.

The orange glared brighter, and Cyclops pushed himself onto his knees. "It's telling me to take back what you stole. It hurts. *Dust and bones*, it hurts–" The fear in his eyes turned to rage.

Asa hit the trigger on the stunner again, but its charge was still building. Cyclops grabbed Ty's ankle and yanked him to the ground.

"Why did you bring it here?" Cyclops roared. He staggered to Asa, looming over her.

There was nowhere to run but the brackish water behind her. "I didn't mean to. It followed me!"

He ran his fingertips over his eye. "If you could see what it's telling me to do to you . . ."

Cyclops fell again, clutching his hip. Riven appeared behind him, a revolver smoking in her hand. She'd fired a stun-round.

Samir rounded the corner of the branching tunnel and grabbed the man from behind, jerking him into a chokehold. Cyclops gagged as Samir tightened his elbow across his windpipe. "You have five seconds to tell us what you're doing here."

"We told you two to stay put!" Riven glared at Ty and Asa.

Cyclops struggled against Samir's grip, veins on his neck bulging, his face turning red. "It's not my fault." He grabbed Samir's wrists. "I can't make it stop. It's showing me visions of a biocapsule. I . . . I'm sorry. Please–"

Asa bit her lip. "He's infected. It's Banshee." She'd brought this. And it was only getting worse.

The man's cybernetic leg flailed, making a faint screech.

"Did you think it'd free you once you hurt this girl?" Riven said.

"I don't know what to think anymore. But it's gotten worse." He gasped. "Please, just—"

Samir's carbon-plated knuckles clenched the man's throat.

Riven's gun locked onto Cyclops's cybernetic eye. "Stand back, Samir."

Samir let the man's arms go, cursing. "Riv, what are you—"

"No!" Ty sprinted toward her, hands up. "You can't just kill him."

"And why not?" Riven's glare was intense enough to melt steel. "He's as far gone as those soldiers at Sanctum's Edge, Ty. Like those Project Winterdark subjects. You want a repeat of that?"

Sanctum's Edge. The name was familiar, but Asa couldn't place it.

"But his mind is still his. He's not a mindless slaughter machine." Slowly, Ty put his hand on the barrel of Riven's gun and eased it down. "Please put it away."

She jerked the gun away and aimed it back at Cyclops. "I'm not taking any chances. Not this time."

Ty stepped back, stunned. With the flash of pain in Riven's eyes, Asa understood. Project Winterdark had cost them a friend. Her *father* had cost them a friend. A voice at the back of her mind whispered, *Your fault.*

Riven's hand was steady. "If you don't want me to shoot, you'd better convince me. Quickly."

Ty gave Asa an uneasy glance. "Why does it want that capsule?"

Asa shook her head. "Your guess is as good as mine." Either way, this man didn't need to die. "The virus has his cybernetics, Riven, but it doesn't control his mind." Not like whatever Riven had seen of Winterdark.

Riven lowered her gun. "Galateo. Are we safe from this virus?"

A few clicks. "I don't detect any hacking attempts on our networks, my lady. It's likely the virus can only transfer itself through wired systems."

So far, at least. Asa shivered. Something was very wrong here. No virus she'd ever heard of was smart enough to take over both ships and cybernetics, much less make demands. It seemed to be *thinking.*

Fresh tears rolled out of the man's flesh eye. "Help me get it out of my head. *Please.*"

"If your cybernetics are standard med-tech, I can power them down." Ty's voice became silken-soft, like the tone he'd used on Asa. "And a cybernetics den can debug you or get replacements. At least until someone finds a cure for this Banshee plague. We'll get you there."

"We will?" Riven snarled.

"I'll go too," Samir said. "Riven and Tripp, you can meet us at Diego's. We shouldn't leave Tripp or her cargo near this man."

"Who's Diego?" Asa wasn't ready to meet yet another underworld smuggler.

"Friend of ours," Samir said. "He knows everything that happens on Requiem. If a spineback dies in a sewer, he's heard about it. If anyone has a way off Requiem, he'll know who."

And would he know about a ship crash? A runaway heiress? Asa could be walking into a trap. But trying to flee would be worse. They'd know she was hiding something.

As Samir slung the man's arm over his broad shoulders, Ty gave Asa and Riven a long look. "Be safe."

She almost asked to stick with Ty. Being alone with Riven scared her. Riven's strong arms, her confident swagger, her lightning-quick triggers—she was capable, but lethal. As she followed Riven through the subway tunnels, she couldn't tell whether it was fascination or paranoia that kept her eyes glued to Riven's tapered waist, the intimidating shift of her shoulders, the silver-and-purple braid revealing soft freckles on the back of her neck. Asa shivered as her thoughts drifted, and she forced herself to focus.

Shouts and thumping bass emanated from the floor grates above them, and shadows from colored lights danced across the tunnel. Glowing rivulets floated within puddles of glitter and vomit and god knew what else.

Asa was in over her head. So, so deep. Trapped on this moon by something that wanted to destroy her.

How long before Riven decided she wasn't worth the risk?

She nearly jumped out of her skin as a buzz jolted through her arm, but it was only a message on her wristlet.

From Josiah. *I saw the news reports. Are you all right?*

She stole a glance at Riven, who was preoccupied sweeping her gun-barrel across the tunnel. Asa began tapping a message.

I'm alive, she responded. *Hired some smugglers who think they can get me out of the quarantine. Unless you can pick me up here?*

Minutes crawled by as she waited for the next message. Maybe the communication relay to Earth's solar system was slow. Or Josiah might be preoccupied.

Then, the response appeared. *Do they know about your bounty?*

"Tripp." Riven's black-smeared eyes locked onto Asa's. "Who're you talking to?"

"Um. It's Josiah." Asa angled her wristlet screen away from Riven.

They don't know the details, she replied. *But they hate my dad and want to help shut down Winterdark.*

Josiah's reply was quick. *Listen, Asa: Banshee is bad news. You're in danger, and so is Requiem. Only two people might be able to stop it: your father, and me. It's after the biocapsule.*

Why? Asa responded.

Because Banshee was part of Project Winterdark. It knows that organ is the key to shutting the project down—and that I can do it. But right now, not even your father can control Banshee.

So why didn't Banshee want Winterdark shut down? Something didn't add up. It wasn't her father's doing—he wouldn't sabotage his own experiments, and he had no reason to want Asa dead. Both the ship engine and Cyclops would've killed her.

I don't understand, she replied. *How are you going to defeat it?*

Just bring me the capsule. I'll save Kaya. I'll take care of everything.

Josiah was the only person she could trust, but he wasn't telling her everything. *What else do you need me to do?*

For now, he messaged, *lay low. Tell nobody who you are or what you have. If your friends get testy, make sure they know the only way to save their city is to get the capsule into my hands.*

Will you still be able to save Kaya? she typed. *Stopping Banshee won't hurt her?*

She'll be fine. I'll just need a tissue sample.

And he'd attached a picture. Within a green plexicarbon stasis pod was Kaya, blank as a corpse, her limbs peppered with tubes and monitors.

Kaya is safe here. But she can't wait forever.

Though Asa had a thousand other questions, she clicked off her wristlet, turning away so Riven couldn't see the tears welling behind her eyes.

Everyone on this planet was her enemy, and her secrets hung on a knife's edge. But she'd keep up the lies if it killed her. Whatever Requiem had in store for her, she had to survive.

Riven had expected to spend her Duskday in *Boomslang*'s cockpit, not in this dark-as-hell abandoned subway tunnel that smelled of piss and electric sweat. Night had only just fallen, with one hundred forty-three hours to go, and no way to leave on the ship she called home.

Maybe helping this girl had been a stupid decision. She

had half a mind to shoot that capsule and destroy Project Winterdark with it. But then Tripp's sister would die, just like Emmett. Another person she couldn't save from Almeida.

Screwing over Luca Almeida could *also* make her underworld-famous. She needed to make a name for herself, and soon. The white noise—worsening to pinpricks of pain in the musty air of the tunnels—was getting worse by the day.

When she'd said goodbye to Emmett a final time, he'd looked at her like her eyes held the universe, like her knobby fingers could shape the world. Soon, maybe, everyone else would believe in her.

And it started with ruling this hellhole city.

"Sorry," Tripp whispered. "I didn't expect to bring so many . . . complications." Though the air was muggy and hot, she wrapped her arms around herself and shuddered.

Something was off about Tripp. She was more than a helpless princess, and she certainly hadn't told Riven the whole story. And Riven wouldn't ignore it just because the girl had a pretty face and a weird, tantalizing spark beneath it.

"Whatever." The tunnel overflowed with silence. "Dumb name, *Banshee*. Sounds like an urban legend. Requiem already has the Overpass Ghost—you heard of it?"

Tripp shook her head uncomfortably.

"She's a spirit who sends flirtatious messages to nearby wristlets and lures their owners to an abandoned overpass. Only later does anyone find their corpses stuffed into the trash chute." It was a legend people whispered whenever shrieks echoed in the night—but there was a lot of shrieking on Requiem, no matter the time of day.

Tripp's elegant button nose scrunched, and she held herself tighter. It was kind of cute to watch her squirm, after she'd come from the planet where you never had to worry about the streets eating you alive.

Or so her story went.

"Riven . . . you weren't really going to shoot that man, were you?"

"Banshee was telling him to kill us. To hurt you. I would've shot, if it weren't for Ty." Damn Ty and that soft heart of his. Now Ty was off somewhere with that guy, and Riven couldn't protect him. Although Samir would take good care of Ty—like he'd done for Riven, when he'd been her mentor at Central Atlantic Academy—it wasn't the same.

Riven had made a promise to Emmett, that day at the lighthouse when bullets pelted the shoreline like raindrops. All she could do for Emmett now was keep his brother safe.

"Well, Ty was right," Tripp said. "You can't pull the trigger before you know all the details."

"Don't preach at me." She met Tripp's cautious gaze. "Surviving in this city means one second of hesitation can get you killed. So if pulling the trigger early means protecting Ty, I'll do it."

"What's the deal with you and Ty?" Tripp's eyes fell to the rusted tracks.

"What's it to you?" Tripp *had* been staring at him earlier. But getting involved with cargo was never a good idea. She'd be gone soon enough. "He's my brother. Not by blood, but . . . I made a promise. Smart kid, but he doesn't always think with his head. Someone has to look out for him."

"He seems capable."

"He is. But he won't touch a gun."

Riven's instincts sharpened as the tunnel grew darker. Broken wires dangled from the ceiling, and rust-colored paint peeled from the walls. The underground passage led to Nocturne, the district of wandering lips and jarring bass. Even the waste puddles were beginning to glow.

The abandoned underground fighting pits seemed to whisper as they passed. The first matriarchs had shut down the pits sixty years ago, after the mining-colony rebellion that ousted Federation control of Requiem. As the five lieutenants of the rebel leader Huifang—who became the first Duchess—the syndicates' first matriarchs shaped Requiem into what it was today: thriving, decadent, dangerous. Even decades of infighting, several assassinations, and a few underworld wars later, Requiem's traditions were passed down through the matriarchs' Code.

And Riven intended to make her mark as one of them.

Riven squared her shoulders and lengthened her stride. Though the pits were no longer used for prizefighting, they still teemed with thieves. If you looked like prey down here, there'd be no end of trouble.

"Hey," a voice called. Right on cue.

Verdugo was in Riven's hand, her finger parallel to the trigger guard, before she even saw the green-haired woman perched atop the crisscrossing ceiling beams. Sparks fell from the blinking fluorescent light, and Riven noticed a pistol in the woman's hand.

"Hey yourself." Riven aimed her gun in greeting.

"What do we have here?" From the abandoned electrical room, a man with steel studs covering his scalp emerged.

Wait. She recognized him. Diesel-Breath, the bruiser who'd dragged her into Sokolov's throne room.

He held an assault rifle, the stock braced against his shoulder. New-tech, with more firepower than Riven had on her. Whatever he wanted, it wasn't good.

"You come to apologize?" Riven said. "You damn near messed up my wrists."

The woman in the rafters giggled. "Not quite."

"You brought a friend." Diesel-Breath leered at them. "Both one hundred percent flesh? Wonder if your insides are just as pretty."

Damn. He'd come to collect. "Sokolov's given me until morning. That was the deal."

His laugh grated like breaking glass. "There's no way you're getting that bounty before Dawnday. Figure I'll get a cut if I make the harvest."

"We don't want trouble." Tripp held up her hands, her brown eyes wide as portholes.

"Organ pirates," Riven whispered. "*They* want trouble." Organs were hot commodities for high-paying Corte buyers—the planet's terraformed atmosphere and weird radiation created enough malformed guts for an organ shortage. And those people were too good for cybernetics.

Riven kept her gun trained on the man. She could make a gamble—hand over Tripp and hope the girl's bounty was worth something to Sokolov. But this jackass would probably steal all the credit, and she wasn't in the mood to negotiate. "You want to harvest? How do you feel about pulling a hollow point out of your chest?"

"You talk tough for someone with such a small gun." He crept forward, until the muzzles of their guns were close enough to touch. "How about you drop it before I shoot your friend in the neck?"

Riven wanted to tell him how *small* her .44 bullets would feel when they ripped through his guts, but she kept her mouth shut. She felt the warmth of Tripp at her back. For both of them, she had to stay calm.

"Avoid the lungs," the woman in the rafters said. "Lungs are selling for double right now."

Riven didn't flinch. *Couldn't* flinch. Tripp wouldn't be quick enough to draw her stunner. That left Riven, outnumbered.

But she'd never be outgunned.

"You really don't want my lungs. Trust me." Riven steeled herself, noting the way the man's finger hovered near his trigger. Two gunners, two options. It would only take one to kill her.

Diesel-Breath shuffled to one side, revealing the woman's pistol in the rafters behind him. He was moving out of his companion's line of sight, so she could take a shot at Riven.

Riven's heart pounded. In a moment, she'd be good as dead.

But Diesel-Breath made a mistake: his eyes flicked to Tripp. In that fraction of a heartbeat, Riven had her opening.

The shot wasn't perfect, but they weren't expecting it.

In one motion, Riven had clicked the hammer, angled *Verdugo* sideways, and fired at the woman in the rafters. A choked cry signaled she'd hit her target.

She barely heard the woman's pistol clattering to the ground as she drew *Blackjack* from her hip, using it to shove aside the man's assault rifle. Three shots from his rifle discharged wildly, deafeningly loud in the tunnel.

Riven smashed her knee into him. He staggered backward, dropping the gun.

He clutched his crotch as she shoved his head against the wall. Riven kicked his gun away, crouching next to him. She pressed *Verdugo* to his heart and aimed *Blackjack* at his forehead. "I talk tough, huh?"

Blood trickled over his neck from where his head had hit the wall. "You're nothing," he spat.

She should shoot him now. No hesitation. But the thought of Sokolov encouraging this nasty shit made her pause. Any matriarch who allowed this needed to be ousted.

Still. This was his choice. Not only had he insulted her guns, but he'd threatened her. Mercy wasn't an option.

"I'll give you a choice," Riven said. "*Verdugo*'s my executioner. All live rounds. *Blackjack* has a cylinder full of wildcards—you could get a stun-round, a plasma round . . . or a shrapnel-scattering disruptor." She swung out the cylinder and gave it a spin before clicking it back in. "*Blackjack* will sure as hell hurt, but it might not kill you."

At point-blank, the odds weren't in his favor.

"Those are some pretty guns, bitch. You wouldn't be so strong without them."

Riven felt a savage smile play at her lips. It was cute when muscle-heads thought bulky shoulders meant anything in a gunfight. "Having a gun doesn't make you strong, dumbass.

And humans didn't evolve for strength. We wouldn't last ten seconds against half the shit roaming the wilderness."

She pulled back *Blackjack*'s hammer with her thumb, producing a satisfying *click*. "You know how humans conquered two star-systems? Hmm?"

His only response was a whimper. Guess he didn't know.

"Because we are *clever* bastards," Riven continued. "We built spears, holo-shields, guns . . . and suddenly, all those nasty predators were nothing to us."

She pulled the trigger. *Blackjack* kicked in her hand.

Tripp let out a strangled cry as the back of the man's head exploded pulpy red over the grimy white tiles. Metal shrapnel from the bullet sparked in the mess.

"Of course it was a disruptor round," Riven muttered, standing up. "Expensive shit. You okay, Tripp?"

Tripp nodded, her eyes wide. Then she pointed to the rafters.

The green-haired pirate was still alive, clutching a gunshot wound in her shoulder. She pressed herself to the steel beam when she and Riven made eye contact, trying to hide from Riven's line of fire. Drops of blood pooled beneath the beam, painting the woman's fallen pistol.

Unarmed, and trapped up there. Riven could leave one alive.

"You there," Riven said. "Tell your friends if they mess with Riven Hawthorne or the rest of the Boomslang Faction, they won't have enough brain tissue left to sell afterward." In a single motion, she spun her Smith & Wesson revolvers by their trigger guards and slid them into their holsters.

The pain in her chest burned hotter with the adrenaline rush. Whether Requiem or the sickness got to her first, she'd be dead within a few years.

But with the right reputation, you could live forever.

". . . the hell is going on out here?" Voices, from the stairwells of the subway platform.

Diesel-Breath had friends. More of Sokolov's bruisers, maybe, with more guns. She had a feeling they'd hound her for the rest of the night. It was time to go.

She kept the swagger in her stride as she grabbed Tripp and pulled her around the corner. She could never let the fear show, never let anyone see her lose her composure.

No matter how badly she was falling apart.

"Tripp," Riven whispered, once they were out of sight, "this way. Now."

chapter 11
GNOSIS

It wasn't Riven's first time seeing brains splattered across a wall, but it seemed it was Tripp's.

The girl ran after Riven, her breathing ragged, mumbling, "*Oh god, oh god, oh GOD.*" Not a surprising response, if you'd never seen a bullet in action.

Only once they'd stopped at a tunnel intersection–where an abandoned train car sat derailed and rusted–did Tripp speak up. "Riven?"

Riven pointed *Verdugo* at the railcar, peering through a broken window. Indecipherable spray-paint curls covered the holoscreens where ads had once glimmered, and empty, dented glitch canisters lay on the seats. No signs of anyone inside though.

"What do you want?" Riven finally said.

"Why did you do that? I . . . I've never seen someone killed before."

Not this again. Riven rolled her eyes. "Well, congratulations. Now you've seen what happens when you run into people who want to steal your guts."

"You had them both disarmed." Tripp was panting hard, distraught. "You didn't have to–"

Riven's lip curled. "Would you like to have your guts packed into biocapsules and shipping containers right now? Don't be stupid. No way we would've passed without a fight. And the more people who know not to cross me, the better."

Tripp huffed. "I hate this place."

"Yeah? It probably hates you too. You might think you're too good for Requiem, but you'd better damn respect it. It'll devour you otherwise."

That shut Tripp up. Good. Riven waved her forward, past a waterfall of leaking ceiling pipes and burned-out neon lights from an old syndicate checkpoint. Fluorescent lights still shone overhead—Rio Oscuro's smugglers kept the lights on for cargo runs.

Eventually Tripp whispered, "We could've died back there." Tears brimmed in her startled eyes.

Riven had to look away before she started sympathizing with her cargo. If Tripp didn't toughen up now, she was hopeless.

"Just speeding up the inevitable," Riven muttered, watching for errant shadows. Clear, for now—the bullet through their companion's head might've discouraged the others from following.

Tripp wiped her eyes on her sleeve. "I won't get in the way anymore. I promise. Whatever you need, I'll help." Her whisper burned with resolve. Seemed her shell shock was wearing off. "I'm glad you were there. Really."

Riven couldn't help but smile. "Whatever I need, huh? You any good with a gun?"

Tripp shuffled nervously. "I'm an engineer. So mechs and circuits, I can deal with. No idea what it takes to be able to handle a gun like *that*."

"Used to practice for an hour a day." Riven gave *Verdugo* a spin. Her nervous habit. Either Tripp knew how to flip someone's switches, or she was genuinely impressed. Riven wouldn't complain.

Beyond the *hish* of falling water, she heard a faint scuffling. *Come on out,* she thought, keeping *Verdugo* up. "Being able to pull out my gun before the other guy has saved my ass quite a few times."

"And the spinning tricks?"

Riven grinned. "Make me more fun at parties."

"But you use old tech?"

"No electricity, no circuit board. Unhackable. When I fire, it's me aiming, and not some AI targeting system." She ran her thumb along *Verdugo*'s varnished-oak grip.

Truthfully, she'd watched an old Earth film from Phase I too many times when she was younger. One character had been dying of tuberculosis–but it never stopped him from spitting bullets into anyone who crossed his friends.

And ever since that day at Sanctum's Edge, Riven realized she needed to do the same.

"Could've fooled me," Tripp said. "Haven't ever seen you miss."

"That's because I don't." She pulled out *Blackjack,* giving it a twist in her left hand. This hand had been harder to master.

Tripp was looking her over. Riven couldn't tell whether it was respect, or sizing her up.

"Old tech's useful," Tripp said. "They'd be unscathed if I had to toss an EMP grenade."

Riven raised her eyebrows. She'd been so busy gawking at the biocapsule earlier, she hadn't examined Tripp's other gadgets. "Where'd you pick up EMP grenades?"

"I made them. But I haven't done much testing yet—don't know exactly how wide the knockout radius is. I'm saving them for an emergency." Tripp pursed her lips. "They'd shut down most tech, including our wristlets . . . and the biocapsule."

Riven frowned. Gadgets like that seemed outside an ordinary mechanist's pay grade. A piece was missing here, and Tripp couldn't hide it forever. Requiem had a way of cracking people open like eggs.

Even before they reached Gnosis, the nightclub's diabolical bass reverberated through the tunnel. The barred back door was flanked by two armed guards—the Boneshiver matriarch's sentries, wearing their standard red and silver. There was nothing uniform about them though—one wore a flanged helmet with mesh exo-armor, and the other a hooded wraparound robe that left most of his lithe body exposed. Javier.

"Shove off, this entrance isn't—" Javier squinted at Riven, then his face lit with surprise. "Riven Hawthorne. Been a while."

"Yeah. Need to get in." Javier still owed her, after she'd taken a job smuggling his rich aunt's pet bruttore to Earth. Despite an assload of sedatives and a pink shock harness, Truffles had made a wreck of *Boomslang*'s cargo hold.

Javier glanced at Tripp but didn't ask questions. "Better be on the lookout. Federation mechs have been on patrol all night. I think it has something to do with that Banshee nonsense."

Riven felt Tripp tense up beside her. "Will do. Thanks, Javier."

Javier lifted the crossbar on the door, and the flood of light and sound rushed through the opening. Riven braced herself.

"Chin up, shoulders back," she said to Tripp. "It's time to make an entrance."

───────

Asa watched Riven burst through the doors like she was arriving home, as if the brawling and reveling was all for her. The guns slung at Riven's hips accentuated her calculated, confident stride, and her magenta-streaked braid swayed behind her.

Something about Riven's roguish smirk and deadly confidence made it hard to tear her eyes away. Asa's cheeks warmed. She'd kissed girls before, in the storage room of machine-shop class when her professor wasn't looking, but it was stupid to think of Riven that way. To Riven, she was nothing but a payout.

Asa stumbled after Riven as the aggressive flashes of color blinded her. The bass pulsed so angrily it might've replaced her own heartbeat. She clutched her backpack straps tighter, following Riven through the jungle of sweating, gyrating bodies and wristlet screens blinking in the dark.

With Riven's every step, rings of colored light rippled from her feet, like stones dropped in a toxic pond. The animated floor reacted to the pressure of every footstep in the crowd.

"Where are we going?" Asa had to yell.

Riven grabbed her wrist and pulled her through the crowd.

The club was open to the night sky and the atmo-dome above the city. Crystalline arches with glaring lights crisscrossed between the glassy towers around them. Asa flinched whenever a light would flash orange.

Hell would break loose if Banshee ever got into a place like this. Maybe it was already on its way.

"Hey, Riven!" A man shouted over the thrumming bass, though he was close enough to touch. "Haven't seen you in a while."

"Here on business," she called without looking back. Riven seemed to know *everyone* in this part of town. "Can't talk."

He scuttled through the crowds, following them. His hair was pulled into a messy blue bun, and his smile revealed sharp metal caps on his teeth. "Who's your friend? She's cute." Asa shuddered. When Riven didn't respond, he turned to Asa. "You look like a glitch virgin. Ever done a Broken Saddle, chickling?"

Revulsion crept over her skin. Either he was talking about drugs, or something else entirely. "I'm not interested," Asa said firmly, hoping to absorb some of the confidence Riven radiated. No way this guy would hit on her if he knew she was an Almeida, and a thousand miles out of his league.

"There's a first time for everything." His grin widened, those teeth glinting under the strobes.

Asa winced, looking to Riven for support. Riven's gaze was leveled right at her. *Do it*, it said. *Tell him off.*

Asa took a deep breath, summoning her father's iron calm. So what if she didn't have a gun? She had Riven at her side, and that made her a little braver.

"Do I need to repeat myself? Or do you get a rise off badgering girls who don't know better than to avoid you?" With one last glance at his slack-jawed expression, she sauntered in the direction they'd been heading.

Riven chuckled and retook the lead as they sidled between mod junkies with feathered hair and silver beaks over their noses. "Not bad."

Damn, Asa needed to get out of this place. The image of red splatter on white tile was still etched into her head, and all she wanted was to be alone. Away from this neon-drenched city trying to sink its claws into her.

Riven dragged her up the steps to the bar, where excessively pretty androids of every gender served drinks. Asa had never been in a real nightclub, since she wasn't quite old enough for the ones on Corte. This was beyond any party she'd ever seen. Feverish, frantic, threatening. She was both invisible and prey at the same time.

Kaya would love this place. There *was* a certain freedom to being nobody. But Asa would've taken a mango soda over the dubious blue liquid in the glass tubes any day.

"Is Diego in his office?" Riven leaned over the bar counter.

The android's glassy, cartoonish eyes fluttered. Her metallic shell mirrored the bubbling drink tubes and reflected the flashing lights. "Diego?"

"I've got an overcoat in need of a wash."

It didn't make sense, so it might've been code. The wide-eyed innocence disappeared from the android's face, and a knowing smirk crossed her features. "He's not taking clients right now."

"I'll see about that. Give me the elevator code."

"Sorry, but due to the quarantine, elevator access to

Alcyone Tower is restricted to residents," the android recited in an irritatingly saccharine voice.

"Do you know the code?" Asa said. *Restricted* meant nothing to her. A plan was already forming, and she felt a thrill at the idea of showing off for Riven.

"I provide the information to residents and approved guests only."

Riven looked ready to pull a gun on the android. Asa grabbed her wrist, taking her aside. Drawing attention was the last thing they needed.

"What?" Riven hissed.

"I have a plan."

"How? Those elevators are guarded and equipped with scanners. We can't just sneak in."

Asa clicked on her tech-scanner, angling her wrist toward the android working the bar. Her wristlet screen displayed the internal wires, heat maps, processes—no flesh, all circuits.

Good. She felt less guilty about this idea.

"That robot has the code," Asa said. "It's programmed into her—um, *its*—head."

"And?"

Asa smirked. She was useless against organ pirates. But mechs? Maybe Riven needed her after all. "We can get it out."

A dark smile crossed Riven's face, mischievous and stunning. Instantly, the whole plan was worth it. "That might be my favorite thing you've ever said."

"All right," Riven said, once they'd settled into the private, curtained booth in Gnosis's upper deck. "You want to place the drink order, or should I?"

"I'm not old enough to order a drink." Asa's fingers wouldn't stop buzzing. If this plan fell apart, it was her fault.

Riven raised an eyebrow. "How old are you then?"

In Cortellion years, Asa was almost eight. Barely seventeen in standard Earth years—with twenty-eight-hour days and 688 days per year, Corte's years were much longer. But like every human settlement, they used Earth years. "Seventeen," Asa said.

"Hmm, I've got a year on you. Doesn't matter though—they don't ID here." Riven pulled up the touchpad on the round tabletop, tapping an order for a whiskey-cola.

"We're hacking one of those service androids, yes?" Galateo piped up. "Their coding is quite complex for bartending. I advise caution. They're impressively clever."

"Keep it in your pants, Galateo," Riven muttered.

"I assume you mean that figuratively, my lady."

Asa was restless as they waited for the order. This would be nothing compared to the tech she worked with at home, but this plan came at the risk of a pissed-off matriarch.

She peered between the curtains at the glass gravity tubes at the center of the club. Patrons clustered around the ring, walled between ropes glowing bright pink. The massive tubes were underlit with changing colors, rising into the sky.

Within the tubes, people tumbled. Wind-dancers like the ones at Cortellion carnivals, with suits like bat wings to control their motion within the harsh jets.

Silver glinted inside one tube, and Asa looked more closely.

No, not dancers. A man in a tight gravity suit was twisting into the jet, holding a weapon.

Gladiators.

Her stomach turned as a dark shape rose within the central glass tube. Shaggy and hunched on all fours, silhouetted by the glaring lights. A bruttore.

The wind jets activated, and the creature flailed, scrabbling at the glass, twisting and flipping as it tried to escape. Terrified.

Bruttore were deadly predators, but this was cruel.

The gladiator held his arms close to his body, diving into the wind until he was close enough to slash at the bruttore. A translucent blue holo-blade shot from his wrist, clipping the monster across its shoulder. A stream of dark blood flew up the tube.

And it reminded Asa of Requiem—a cage surrounded by bloodthirsty spectators. No escape. No mercy.

The crowd roared as the creature grabbed the gladiator in a massive fist and hurled him. He smacked against the glass wall, dazed—

Asa couldn't watch anymore. "Is this common? Killing animals for sport?"

"It's entertainment," was all Riven said. Asa wondered if she'd ever been in the ring. Riven seemed like she'd do anything to get by. Maybe that was the fate of anyone trapped in this city for too long.

The curtain pulled aside, and the android strode in with a drink tray, its eyes glowing and vacant.

Asa scooted along the bench until she was behind the

robot. As it greeted Riven and set the drink on the table, Asa clicked the safety off her pen-laser.

"Would you like to open a tab?" the android said.

Asa lunged, making a slice at the base of its neck.

It froze, hands on the tray. "Tampering detected. Enter maintenance code before alarm triggers in five—"

"Get the alarm!" Riven said.

"I know what I'm doing!" Asa yanked up the metal shell forming the back of the robot's head, pushing aside the shell-pink synthetic hair.

"Three . . . two . . ."

She used the pen-laser to sever the main relay circuit and popped a few panels aside until she'd exposed the motherboard.

"Hurry," Riven hissed.

"Shut up so I can think!" Asa chewed her tongue, plugging her wristlet into a port and overriding the encryption. She nabbed the list of access codes. For good measure, she wiped the robot's memory of the past three hours.

Even after she fitted the neck-plate back in place, a scar still marked the sleek metal. Asa wished she had better welding tools on her. "See that?" she said, heart pounding. "Like we were never here."

Riven grinned. "Gloat later. Let's move."

They pushed through the heavy curtains toward the elevators, leaving the android sprawled over the booth's benches as she rebooted, her pink hair a tangled mess.

Riven punched in the elevator code Asa had given her. As soon as the doors had closed behind them, Asa all but collapsed against the elevator railing.

"I can't believe we just did that." Nervous laughter burst from her. "We . . . we committed a crime." A crime against a stranger, not her father. Somehow, it was different.

Riven smirked. "You need to get out more."

As the elevator crept skyward, Asa caught her breath. Through the scrolling glass panes, she watched the dance floor of Gnosis, the bars, and the gravity tubes shrink into a field of colored lights.

"I mean, that was *perfect.* Alarms didn't trigger. Nobody noticed. You have to admit—that was cool."

Riven's glance slid from Asa's eyes down to her lips, and lower. "Okay, I'll admit it. You did a damn good job."

The compliment hit like a jolt to her chest. She had a feeling Riven didn't give them out often. And the way Riven was looking at her . . .

The adrenaline surge was intoxicating. "Maybe this place isn't so bad," Asa said. It was a delicious feeling of power to know she wasn't helpless here. With Riven's guns and her tech-jockeying, they could take down anything the matriarchs threw at them.

"Don't get comfortable. If this goes according to plan, we'll have you on a ship soon." Maybe—just maybe—that was a hint of regret in Riven's voice.

But she was right. Asa would be off Requiem in no time, and no matter how fast Riven made her heart beat, she wasn't sticking around. "You sure this Diego guy can get us out? Or that there are ships running at all?"

"There have to be ships running. No way the Duchess would take a Federation quarantine lying down. To cut all the salirium exports and water shipments . . . it'd be business suicide." Riven tapped into her comm channel. "Ty, Samir. I'm sending the elevator code. You're behind schedule—something happen?"

Silence. Five seconds. Ten.

"Uh, Riven," Ty's voice crackled through the comm. Breathy, strained. "We're on our way. But you're not going to like this."

Riven frowned. "On a scale of *'we stopped for pizza'* to *'we're stuck in the Duchess's chophouse,'* where are you?"

"Depends where you put *'run-in with Fed troopers'* on that scale." Samir's voice. "There was a bit of a kerfuffle in Ellyion, but we got out."

Fed troopers. That didn't sound good.

"Why were you in Ellyion?" Riven said. "Did you stop at the hideout?"

"Yeah. Personal reasons," Samir said, and a small *arf* interrupted him.

"Zephyr was stuck in the quarantine zone," Ty whispered, then shushed a high-pitched puppy whine in the background. "Couldn't leave him there."

Riven swore under her breath. "Our hideout is in the quarantine zone?"

"We'll be there in ten minutes," Samir said. "Sorry, Riv. You might want to look north."

Riven marched out of the elevator as soon as the doors to the fifteenth floor opened. Asa struggled to keep up as she ran to the end of the balcony, past battered apartment doors and hanging wires and drying bedsheets strewn over the shabby railings.

"Oh, hell," Riven growled.

When Asa reached the railing, the sight hit her like a gut punch. A chunk of Requiem had gone dark—a slice missing from the sprawling, light-polluted pie.

The quarantine zone was now massive. While the rest of the city glittered in an overexposed haze, the area they'd come from was a blackened, corrupted scar.

"They weren't kidding about the quarantine," Asa whispered. Suddenly matriarchs and organ pirates were the least of their problems. The quarantine was walling them in. Quickly.

Riven's jaw tightened. "Not just my ship. Now my goddamned hideout. We're going to shut this thing down."

"I'm with you. And so is Josiah. We can get off Requiem, and—"

"There had better be a Requiem to come back to. This city might be a hellhole, but it's *my* hellhole." Riven turned away from the balcony, beckoning Asa with a flick of her chin. "Come on. We've got a visit to pay. And we'd better not piss him off."

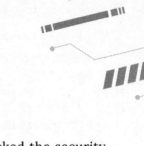

chapter 12
NIGHTFALL

As Riven rang the buzzer, Asa checked the security systems on her wristlet. Whatever lay beyond this door, she couldn't risk an underworld informant getting his grimy hands on her secrets.

Diego's office looked like every other apartment on the balcony of Alcyone Tower. But the windows were tinted, and the only exterior light was from flickering red neon letters proclaiming *LAUNDRY SERVICE*.

Definitely a façade. No doubt Riven's informant had other tricks too. Asa had to keep her guard up or she'd end up on an expensive one-way trip back to her dad.

As they waited for the door to open, the anger rolled off Riven like a quiet storm. She wouldn't look at Asa. Maybe she was considering throwing Asa into Banshee's corrupted zone and being done with her.

"Remember," Riven said, keeping her eyes on the security cam, "information is valuable. Let me do the talking."

Asa hadn't planned to talk. Riven could negotiate. And if Diego pried, she might have a few tricks of her own.

The intercom light flashed green, and the door slid open. Riven led her into a dim, sparse foyer. As Asa stepped through the door, a faint prickle, like static, washed over her. "Did you feel that?" she whispered.

"Feel what?"

"I think we were just . . . scanned." It wasn't an electro-magnet or interference—Asa's wristlet screen still clicked on. Dozens of hidden sensors and electric eyes probably watched her. What had Diego learned about her? And how much did Requiem's underworld networks already know about a runaway heiress?

If someone pushes you, her father had once said, *it's a test. Yield nothing. Threaten them with a smile.*

If this Diego had any brains in his skull, he'd know an Almeida girl could beat him at his own game. He wouldn't dare mess with her even if he learned her identity. Probably. Asa swallowed the lump in her throat and followed Riven.

The laundry service façade extended to the foyer. A holoscreen mounted on the peeling imitation-wood wallpaper displayed a muted episode of some noir film from Phase I, before humans had left Earth. Dust clung to clothing hanging from a rack, likely untouched for years. Most people walking through those doors must've known this wasn't a laundromat.

Riven strode to the deeply tinted window at the reception desk. "I'd like to place an order."

"Regrettably, the queue is too long," a heavily processed voice crackled through the reception desk speakers. "Please check back later."

"Tell Diego that Riven Hawthorne is here. I already sent a message. It's important."

"You do not have approved clearance."

Riven slammed her hands against the desk. "Diego!" she

called to the ceiling. "Your stupid robot friend is shutting us out."

No response, from either the robot or Diego himself—wherever he was.

Riven stepped to the wall and knocked so hard she almost punched a hole. Asa wanted to drag her out the door before things got messy.

Then, a voice—breathy and deep—trickled through the overhead speaker. "Get lost, Riven." A chill spiked through Asa. "I have a lot to deal with right now."

"Oh, really?" Riven said. "And if I have information about Banshee?"

A pause. "You're bluffing."

"You want to find out? I know what it's after."

A sigh over the intercom. Then, the wall Riven had been knocking on slid aside, revealing warm light and a plush sitting room.

"Inside," the voice commanded. "*Now.*"

Asa followed Riven in, glad to be out of the fluorescent lights that seemed to glare straight into her soul. This room was all bookshelves and scarlet carpets, and everything smelled faintly of sweet tobacco and cloves. A pleasant scent mingled with the spice—real books with musty pages and leather covers, like the ones she'd only seen in museums. Whoever owned this place had taste.

Diego sat in a high-backed chair, fiddling with a holopanel on his wristlet. A narrow meeting table stretched toward him, where he was barely visible in the glow of candlelight-colored laser-diode panels.

"Approach," he said.

"So demanding." Riven slumped into a chair.

"This had better be important. We can't spare many re-sources right now."

Asa took a seat next to Riven, and Diego's shadowed eyes sized her up across the table, peering through her makeshift disguise and straight into her. Like the surveillance androids lurking in every corner of her dad's estate.

"So. What are you after, Riven?" Diego said.

Diego caught Asa off guard. She'd expected someone older—maybe riddled with scars and gruesome mods, sitting on stockpiles of weapons. But Diego looked young enough to be sitting in one of her Naat classes. His sleeveless athletic shirt revealed a carbon-plated glove that extended from his fingers to his right elbow. If not for those deep, skewering eyes, Asa would've thought he was the wrong person.

Riven slung her feet onto the table, crossing her ankles. "Didn't you get my message?"

"I cut comms because of Banshee. The entire syndicate is on lockdown." Diego gave a strained smile. "And the last time I trusted your word, I had Fanged Invective assassins bursting through my ceiling."

"That was Samir's fault, not mine. And it was . . . resolved."

"With bloodshed."

"*Minimal* bloodshed."

No matter how hard Asa studied Diego, she couldn't burn his face into her memory. Somehow, he was both beautiful and plain. Tightly curled and close-cropped dark hair, a sharp jaw, and full eyelashes. He seemed clean-cut and collected, aside from the sunken circles under his eyes. As if he maintained a façade, close to cracking.

"And I wonder how much bloodshed we'll have to deal with this time," Diego said.

"Not a lot, if you can get us a ship." Riven crossed her arms. "We need a ride out of the quarantine. Can you pull some strings with Boneshiver?"

Diego narrowed his eyes. "Does this have something to do with your friend and the biocapsule in her backpack? You promised me information."

Asa's whole body stiffened. He knew about the biocapsule—probably from the scan. She glanced around the room, at the cameras undoubtedly waiting.

What she saw, instead, were spiders.

Hand-sized mechanical spiders with barbed, metallic legs clicking as they moved, and green eyes watching her in the dark. Surveillance tech. Asa fiddled with her wristlet under the table, starting a hack into the networks covering Diego's hideout. If she could slip into his systems—even a little—she might have some leverage if he used her identity against her.

Riven ignored his comment. "In exchange for you helping us out, we're going to save your city. Your matriarch, your syndicate, probably your job. Sound fair?"

"The answer is no, unless you give me the details. And if I knew the source of Banshee's ire . . ." Diego's eyes pierced Asa like needles. "You're aware I would be under a *hefty* obligation to report it to Matriarch Cerys?"

Asa looked at Riven for support. But Riven looked confident as ever, shooting Asa a wink. It kindled a spark in Asa's core.

"I think there's someone else you have a hefty obligation to." Riven leaned back in her chair, and it teetered on two legs. "And he's standing outside your door."

Diego's eyes widened as he clicked his wristlet. That placid veneer began to crack. "Samir's still with your crew?"

Riven grinned. "Yeah. He still hasn't gone crawling back to the Federation's straight and narrow. Surprised he's slipped under your radar, though. Wasn't he your favorite person to keep tabs on?"

Diego sighed. "Let him in."

The doors slid open, and Samir and Ty strode in. Ty held Zephyr, and the pup sniffed the air curiously, tail wagging. Asa was relieved to see Ty in one piece—and she had to admit, he looked damn cute holding a dog.

"Samir." Diego scrubbed a hand through his dark hair, his composure ironing out. "Didn't realize you were still in the smuggling business. I thought you would've headed home by now."

"I can't seem to tear myself away from this death trap of a city. And you and I have a debt to settle." Samir held an over-sized coin between two fingers, inset with red symbols that shone like embers. "Will you finally let me get rid of this?"

Asa frowned. A life debt? She'd heard of the coins being traded on Laurizon, a sprawling satellite orbiting Earth. Favors were money there—and a life debt seemed to be the biggest denomination of all. Was Samir really using one to help her?

"Half expected you'd have thrown that thing out an air-lock," Diego said.

"Nah. Even if I had, you wouldn't let me forget this *life*

debt nonsense." Samir set the coin on the table and flicked it. It skittered across the polished wood. "I'm sure Riven has told you we're in need of a hideout."

Diego turned the coin over. He gave Samir a look equal parts reverent and grudging. "Why now?"

"Oh, come on, Dee. Don't I get to choose what to do with it? You refused my last request."

Diego's eyes flashed. "Because your last request was a crude suggestion of where I could *shove* the favor."

Riven snorted. "All right. Can we agree this cancels out whatever other *obligations* you have to turn us in? Everything we're about to tell you stays between us. Not Boneshiver."

Something scathing in Diego's and Samir's gazes connected. They definitely had a history, but there was an undercurrent of suspicion. Of reluctant longing.

"That's my favor, Dee," Samir said. "You get us a place to stay and a ship out of here. Above all, you tell nobody. Sound fair?"

Diego slipped the coin into his pocket. "I will honor this. You have my word."

"Perfect." Riven chipped at her steel-gray nail polish. "Our friend Tripp here has a friend on Earth who might be able to fix Banshee. One of Almeida's scientists. We just need to get that capsule out of here."

Asa locked eyes with Diego. *That's right,* she thought, trying to send a silent warning through her gaze. *I'm a friend of theirs. And if you get too nosy, I'll sink your networks.*

Diego frowned. "Banshee doesn't act like any virus I've

ever seen. It seems strategically predatory in a way most algorithms aren't—"

"Like it's thinking," Ty said.

"Something like that," Diego continued. "Even Requiem's best hackers can't stop it. You really think you can shut it down?"

"It's the best option we have," Samir said. "Ty and I saw it creeping out of the quarantine zone. Even Federation tech is being hacked." He pursed his lips. "So first, I want you to verify Tripp's story."

Asa's blood turned to ice. Suddenly, all the eyes in the room were on her. "You don't trust me?"

"It's protocol. We're not risking my crew's necks until we confirm your story checks out." Riven's kohl-smeared eyes met Asa's. "Show him the biocapsule."

Asa gripped her backpack straps tighter. "It stays with me."

"He's not going to hurt anything," Samir said gently. "He just needs to pull up some data."

Diego returned her gaze, and it felt like a challenge. "She can come with me, if she wants. It doesn't have to leave her sight." He gestured to a doorway behind him. Waiting beyond the dark were blinking control panels.

If it was just her and Diego, she had a better chance at striking a deal. Asa let out a shuddering breath. She could do this. She had no other choice.

"All right. I'll tell you everything. Alone." Whether or not he knew her identity already was a gamble.

Riven gave her a hard look that said, *What are you playing at?*

"Protocol." Asa tried her hardest to smirk. "For my sister's privacy. And mine." If Riven didn't trust her, she wasn't going to return the favor.

"I suppose that's acceptable." Diego inclined his head. "Follow me."

Riven's glare followed Asa inside, so fierce Asa half expected it to melt the door as it slid closed.

"I'll tell you everything," Asa said. "But it doesn't leave this room."

Diego's eyes flicked over her, as if searching for weak points. Then he tapped a control panel to life. With his back turned, Asa parsed the lines of code and layers of security on her wristlet, still chipping away at his security systems. Even the tiniest piece of blackmail might be enough.

Her heart pounded. *What have I gotten myself into?* Going toe to toe with an underworld informant was a bad idea. Still, she had to show him who he was dealing with.

"I'll confess . . ." Diego swiped a holoscreen, and a familiar face appeared on it.

Asa's face.

Dolled up like a perfect heiress, on the cover of *Eon Magazine*.

"I've foreseen a lot of things happening in this city," Diego said. "But I never expected you, *Asanna Almeida*."

There it was.

Asa's boots froze to the floor at the mention of her name. Of course Diego knew. Still, she searched his face for any trace of uncertainty.

He fixed his eyes on her with perfect clarity, like she was a scarni caught in a snare. "I've known since the moment you stepped into my lobby."

The heiress-Asa on the magazine cover—with her wind-blown hair and pouty red lips—seemed to taunt her. Asa pushed for a final lie. "You don't seriously think that's me."

"Don't be so modest. You're a prodigy." He held up the spider she'd hacked, dangling it by one metallic leg.

Filthy curses threatened to spill from her lips. She had to pull her only ace. A bluff. "So we understand each other." She fought to keep the quaver out of her voice. "I'm sure you know, too, that my dad's security systems are far more advanced than your flimsy networks. I've already found a back door."

He chuckled, as if threats were as normal for him as the sirens blaring through the apartment walls. "I expected as much. You don't need to prove yourself to me, Miss Asanna. It really is a pleasure."

She stopped short of threatening to leak his files—the Boneshiver syndicate's data—all over Requiem's streets. She'd expected him to blackmail her. Not this. "What do you want from me?"

"I want to know why you're lying to them. I'm sure they know you have a bounty. So why the false name?"

She clasped her shaking hands together. She'd lied to protect herself when she'd woken up in a den of smugglers. Plus, her name was on Project Winterdark, and if Riven thought she'd helped with whatever happened at Sanctum's Edge−.

Maybe Riven would rather kill Asa than turn her in.

"I'd be a target," Asa said. "Riven hates my dad, and I'm just trying to survive."

"At least you're being honest now."

He was silent for a while, scrolling through web pages and reports with the Almeida logo stamped at the top of the page. Asa breathed deeply, her own sweat chilling her as she focused on the tangy smell of the oxygen converters in the vents. Was he considering whether to tell them? Had he found anything on Josiah?

Then Diego spoke again. "You're lucky your information checks out. A certain scientist by the name of Josiah Herron *has* left Almeida Industries recently. And Banshee's origin is traceable to a ship from Cortellion." His gloved hand maneuvered over the keys with soft clicking noises. "From what I can see, you're telling the truth."

"So you won't tell them my name?"

"For now, it's your secret to tell, not mine. But you realize the longer you wait, the deeper you'll be digging your own grave?"

She said nothing. Riven couldn't find out. Not ever.

"I'll still be monitoring you. Samir's crew is risking a lot to help you, and I owe him my life." He whirled toward her, his face suddenly fierce. Asa backed away until the light switches dug into her back. Diego pressed his hand to the wall next to her ear, his voice like honey laced with venom. "So if your identity starts to put him in danger . . . I'm going to test just how much of your threat is a bluff."

Without taking his eyes off her, he snatched a datapad off a table and sauntered out.

Numb and quaking, Asa followed him to a living area, where the others had settled onto the couches. She wondered what Diego's word was worth—for him, information was liquid gold poured between powerful hands. But if he was keeping his oath to Samir, maybe he'd protect her identity.

"Her info checks out," Diego announced.

The other three tore their attention away from the GravSphere battle on the holoscreen. Ty grinned at Asa, as if he'd trusted her all along. Guilt settled deeper into her gut.

"And this Josiah guy?" Riven said.

Diego tapped his wristlet, and a picture of Josiah appeared on the holoscreen. Just as Asa remembered him, with bruise-colored bags under his eyes and the unkempt beginnings of a graying beard.

"From what I've gathered," Diego said, "Luca Almeida and Josiah Herron are probably the only ones who can stop Banshee. And I doubt Almeida will be inclined to help."

"Well?" Riven said. "Can you get us that ship?"

"Already booked you a meeting with the captain of the Duchess's fleets." Diego's eyes were glued to his datapad.

"Unfortunately, it'll be hard to make a case if they discover you have what Banshee's after. Likely they'd confiscate it and hand it off to a Requiem hacker."

Confiscate it. Nobody in Requiem would know what to do with it. They'd pick it apart. "They'd destroy it," Asa said. "Josiah's the only one I trust to run tests while keeping my sister safe."

"Right," Diego said. "So, offer them your smuggling services. Convince them you can navigate contraband around Federation ships."

"The *Duchess*?" Riven blurted. "Shit, Sokolov is already threatening to steal our organs. Is the Duchess going to demand ritual sacrifice if we sneeze in her court?"

"This is your only shot. Unless you'd like to steal a ship from one of the matriarchs."

"That plan sounds more fun." Riven sank deeper into the embroidered couch.

Diego ignored her, furiously tapping his wristlet. "Your meeting's at the next Falsedawn. So rest up. There's couches and blankets in the spare room, if you need to sleep."

Another night in paradise, Asa thought. Falsedawn probably meant the next Earth-morning. It would take a few more sleeps before the sun rose here. She intended to be gone by then.

"I think we'll hang out here for a while." Riven kicked her purple polycarbon boots onto the floor, and Zephyr eagerly sniffed them. "If you don't mind."

Diego grumbled something about *new clients* and disappeared into one of the side rooms.

Asa felt impossibly tired, now that death and blackmail

weren't breathing down her neck. She peeked through the solar blinds at the dark patch looming beyond the glowing spires. Banshee was cutting a vicious path as it hunted her. Sirens blared in the distance, and when panic threatened to close her throat, she had to turn away from the window.

Riven and Samir sat together on the couch, flipping through holoscreen channels and laughing as they mocked the actors on a bad holiday soap opera. Ty crouched by Samir's ankle, dressing a recent wound and grumbling at him to *hold still*. Riven had been angry only minutes ago, but with her crew, some of her hardness melted away. They were broke and had lost their hideout, but they had each other.

Asa was alone. And her secret was a barbed-wire fence separating her from them.

"I'm going to bed," Asa announced to nobody in particular, heading to the spare room Diego had pointed out. "Still have a headache from that sedative."

"That's not a good sign." Ty unwrapped a fresh bandage. "Do you need me to look you over?"

"You've been *looking her over* enough already." Riven nudged him with her foot. "You're going to run out of gauze, with all that drool."

Ty's face was flushed, and his gaze lingered on Asa as she left, but her eyes were already blurring with tears and she couldn't make herself care. Only once she'd closed the door to the spare room did the fatigue crash over her like a wrecking ball. She collapsed onto the couch, and the momentary relief racked an ugly sob from deep in her chest.

She missed home—the privacy of her own bed, the scent

of cheese pastries wafting from the kitchens, the comfort of seeing her face on a magazine and knowing she had a future.

But that future had gone up in smoke. Her best friend was in pieces, a constant reminder her father could do whatever he wanted. Cortellion was no longer home.

Through her tears, she saw a fuzzy gold shape on the floor. Zephyr had followed her. He looked up, cocking his head inquisitively.

"Do you want to know my name?" Asa whispered. "You wouldn't care, would you?"

His collar jingled as he leapt onto the couch, nuzzling into her lap. She buried a hand in his soft fur.

She couldn't make friends here. Maybe never again, since she'd be keeping secrets for the rest of her life. And for the first time ever, her money was running out. Where would she work? What the hell was she *doing*?

This city would eat her, if Riven didn't get her first.

A burst of laughter erupted from the other side of the door, and the pang of jealousy came back. Asa curled onto her side, the capsule a steady pulse against her chest. There was only one person she wanted to talk to right now, and she might never hear her voice again.

She and Kaya had never been apart for more than a few days. Even when grounded, they'd sneak into AbyssQuest and meet virtually–

An impulse snapped some of the fog away. Was it possible?

Asa tapped her wristlet, finding she could still link remotely to her AbyssQuest server. She dug through Diego's closet, found a dusty old scan-glass, and slipped it over her eyes.

On the screen, AbyssQuest's horizon stretched and rendered before her—the feverish sunscapes and distant castles taking shape. The stormy oceans and quiet villages. The world given life by Kaya's art. A world that felt like home.

There was only one thing missing.

Asa plugged the biocapsule into her wristlet and held her breath.

"Kaya," she whispered to the petals on the false breeze. "Can you hear me?"

The sky flickered from sunset to night in an instant. Her breath caught. She wasn't alone.

"Come find me," Asa said. "I need to talk to you—"

Something was wrong. The stars in the sky shifted, pulled inward by a gasping void. The edge of the horizon disintegrated as blackened veins crept over the landscape, like something out of a nightmare.

Kaya's mind was taking control.

No. Why was she reacting like this? "Kaya. Please, wake up."

But the nightmare spread like an infection. The trees were dissolving to pixelated messes, and the grass beneath her twisted to ash. What had Asa been thinking? Her sister was probably terrified, wondering where her body was.

She couldn't wake Kaya up. Not here.

Asa pulled the cord and tore the scan-glass off her eyes, heart racing. Zephyr's rough tongue was flicking over her fingers, scrubbing away the grime from traipsing the abandoned tunnels and weaving through Gnosis.

And she was well and truly alone again.

Getting Kaya to Earth was the only way to pull her from

those nightmares. Asa had evaded death and lied to get this far, and she'd have to do more still. She had no other choice.

She wrapped her arms around Zephyr. With any luck, she'd be out of the galaxy's darkest gutter tomorrow.

But as she settled under the thin blankets, pursuing sleep, Diego's words rang in the back of her mind.

The longer you wait, the deeper you'll be digging your own grave.

ADVERSARY

Riven didn't need to watch the news to know they were running out of time.

The spike of fear had trickled through Gnosis's crowds last night, the reek of nervous sweat and desperation even stronger than usual. Something was sweeping through the wires, and not even a well-placed gunshot could stop it.

"Bringing me will only increase our odds of screwing up," Riven complained when Samir and Tripp woke her up early, *too* early, and crammed her into the front seat of Diego's speeder. "I'm no good at diplomacy."

"That's why you're going to speak softly and carry two guns." Samir punched the destination into the nav console. "Right?"

"No promises on the first part."

Stay sharp, Riven, came a message from a private number on her wristlet. *You might have an advantage here.*

She frowned. It was probably from Diego. *What the hell is that supposed to mean?* she messaged back.

Diego still hadn't replied as they parked the speeder and strode up to the wrought-iron gates of the Duchess's palace, metal guardian lions snarling down at them.

"It definitely looks like a palace," Tripp muttered. Beyond the gates were grassy hills covered in red-leafed trees, and the towers rose like teeth sinking into the dark sky. The palace was modeled after some ancient Earth style, so gaudy it almost hurt to look at. A relic of some tourist hotel from Requiem's heyday.

"Doesn't all of Cortellion look like this?" Riven said.

"Not quite."

Riven found her eyes lingering on Tripp's pretty, gold-flecked eyes and feathery hair so dark it seemed to absorb the light from the streetlamps. Tripp had been cagier than ever, after holing up in the guest room by herself last night. Riven hated how it made her curiosity flare, pulling her in like a void. Raw determination flickered beneath Tripp's surface—the girl had more guts than she gave herself credit for.

Riven turned away before Tripp caught her staring. She had secrets, and she'd never trust Riven with them.

The Duchess's guard led them into the palace halls, which were lit like a dungeon and cold as a meat locker. Somehow the false candlelight chandeliers and onyx-trimmed ceilings made the halls even more unsettling, like all the extravagance was hiding something. No doubt this place was just as bloody as Sokolov's.

Riven shivered. This might be less of a *negotiation* and more of a *pact*.

With any luck, the envoy wouldn't be someone she knew. The list of people who hated her was growing by the day.

Of the five factions beneath the Duchess—the faction known for its strong-arms, Staccato; the informants, Boneshiver; the assassins, Fanged Invective; the merchants and prostitutes, Borealis; and the smugglers, Rio Oscuro—Riven had at least one enemy in each. She had a good chance of running into someone with a grudge against her. Still, what had Diego meant by her having an advantage?

Riven was thumbing her revolvers when the guard stopped them to confiscate weapons.

"Is this a joke?" She lifted her chin, glaring into her reflection on his helmet.

"Protocol," he said through his rebreather. "You want to meet the fleet captain, you follow the rules. Weapons down, wrist-cuffs on."

Ty swallowed hard as a guard patted him down. Another guard was affixing a thick cuff to Tripp's wrist.

Riven exhaled through her teeth. She should've expected this. "You scratch either of them, and I'll make a milkshake out of your eyeballs."

"Riven." Samir's smile was taut, a warning. "Don't threaten the nice man."

Riven eyed the small metal nodes on the underside of the wrist-cuff. Definitely dubious. They couldn't just be for decoration.

She reluctantly extended her wrist, and the guard clicked it on.

"So, do these things explode if we step out of line?" Ty said nervously.

"No." The guard gave an exasperated sigh, pushing open the massive hall door. "But I'd advise against it."

Riven nearly shoved the guard out of the way. The sooner they got this over with, the sooner her guns would be back in their holsters.

Beneath the vaulted ceiling, paintings of dead matriarchs scowled down at them in judgment. Dozens of matriarchs—mostly women, some outside the binary—had risen and fallen over the past sixty-odd years since Requiem had gone to the gangs. Matriarchs never died of old age.

At the end of the hall stood a plush throne lined in blue velvet, with a massive pair of carbon-fiber wings slowly spreading and folding behind it.

Riven suppressed a groan. She already hated the fleet captain. You couldn't sit on a winged throne and not be an asshole.

But as they got closer, and her dirty boots left tracks on the gold-threaded carpet, Riven recognized the figure on the throne. It was even worse than she'd expected.

"We need to leave," she hissed, wishing she could hide behind Samir's wide-as-a-door shoulders.

"Wait, why?"

"Samir Al Ghadani and Riven Hawthorne," a guard announced.

Samir raised his eyebrows as they neared the fleet captain. The man wore a navy-blue racer pilot's coat, with a pale blue skull painted over his face.

And a cape. God dammit, a *cape.*

"Is that who I think it is?" Samir whispered.

"Yes."

Marcus Albrecht. Riven's ex-boyfriend.

You might have an advantage here, Diego had said. So much for the warning.

"I'm going to murder your boyfriend," she said to Samir. "Diego didn't say *he* would be here."

Samir swore under his breath. "I don't think Dee knows just who we're dealing with."

There was no running now. Riven willed herself to be impassable as titanium, straightening her back and lifting her chin as she approached the dais.

"Riven Hawthorne?" A slow grin spread across Marcus's face. His hands rested on the touch-panel arms of the chair. Throne. Whatever the gaudy thing was. "Been too long since I've seen you."

"Not long enough," she muttered.

He cocked his head, sizing her up. "I'm genuinely curious what brought you here, my pale, lethal Lily-Flower."

"Lily-Flower?" Tripp whispered incredulously.

Riven bit her tongue. His stupid nickname for her. Half endearment, half belittling. It dredged up memories she'd never been able to scrub away—the extravagant gifts, the vases of Cortellion-imported atherblossoms, the jealous whispers whenever she dared to talk to anyone halfway attractive. The insistence that *you're good, but not* that *good, Lily-Flower.*

All the condescension and possessiveness she'd tried to forget, staring down at her from a fucking throne.

"I'm not here for *you*, Skullface." Her anger strained against her self-imposed restraints. *Speak softly and carry two guns.* She had zero guns and was losing her will to speak softly.

Marcus straightened up, adjusting the bandolier of bullets strung across his chest. Despite the armed guards at every corner of the massive hall, Riven counted two guns at his belt and another three leaning against the throne. Overcompensator. "Actually, my new call sign is Deathknell."

Riven snorted. "Deathknell?" She was calling him Skullface, regardless.

"I'm guessing Diego filled you in on our proposal." Samir cut her off before things got ugly.

Marcus stared him down. "Another proposal. Like every other low-league smuggler crew who thinks they have something to offer the Duchess."

"We're better than them," Riven said. "My crew smuggled volatile salirium during the tax crackdown last year. And if you heard about the mech that mysteriously disappeared from the Crush fighting pits—"

"What crew? The four of you?"

"We've got a pilot, a soldier, a mechanist, and a medic," Ty said. "We can crew a stealth-class ship, easy. So if you have a job—"

"That might have interested me," Deathknell—Skullface—said, waving the proposal away, "had it been someone else standing in my court today." He wouldn't stop staring at Riven, and it made her skin crawl. "Regardless of your current proposal, Lily-Flower. After all the lies you told me . . . why would I start believing you now?"

Riven couldn't answer that. She was still furious with Diego. Why hadn't he told her? She wouldn't have come if she'd known.

And maybe that was the point.

Skullface leaned back in the chair, his gaze flicking over Tripp, Ty, and Samir. "I've no use for the three of you. But, Riven, however . . ."

There it was. The starry-eyed look that had once suckered her in. His admiration had been intoxicating at first—the endless compliments on her skill, his conviction that she'd leave her mark on this city. That she mattered. But as soon as they'd started getting close, that admiration had turned to jealousy. He'd tried to keep her like a pet, to stop her from getting too big for the cage he wanted to keep her in.

"Let's talk. Privately," Marcus said. "Tell your friends to leave."

A muscle in Samir's jaw twitched. "We're *not* leaving."

"Is that so?" Marcus drummed his fingers on an arm of the chair.

Samir gasped, clutching his wrist. He convulsed in pain.

And immediately Riven knew what the wrist-cuffs were.

Samir crouched onto the gold carpet, his shoulders jerking. No doubt stun-blasts were ripping through him.

"Stop it," Riven demanded, instinctively clutching for *Verdugo* at her hip. She should never have given it up. "Stop!"

"Only if they leave while you hear me out," Marcus said.

"Fine! I'll stay. But you *let them go,* right now."

Samir let out a shuddering breath and stood up, still shaking. "Riv, don't." His voice was ragged.

"I can handle this." Riven stared Skullface in the eye.

She didn't break eye contact even as she heard Samir's footsteps grudgingly recede and the hall doors slam. "What do you want? Revenge? We could settle this in a few seconds. Duel me."

A smirk crossed his face. "Duel *you?* With what gun?"

"That's where you start acting like a gentleman and give me back my damn guns."

"I believe the rule is *I* would get to choose the weapon." He rested his chin on his fist. "Always ready for a fight, aren't you? I'm curious to see how you'd fare. You're the only person who's ever outgunned me, Lily-Flower." Despite the softness of his voice, stinging resentment flashed in his eyes. Same as always.

"Stop calling me that." If her fists were balled any tighter, her nails would draw blood. "You want to do this, or not?"

"There are other things I'd rather do to you."

Her heart about hit the floor as she realized how utterly alone she was. Stripped bare—no *Verdugo* and *Blackjack*, only the Duchess's rifles and Marcus's eyes trained on her.

"I have nothing to gain from a duel." Marcus walked down the stairs of the dais, his long blue cape swishing around his ankles, and waved to the guards at each corner of the hall. "Leave us alone."

They saluted and walked to the doors. Even with four fewer guns trained on her, Riven somehow felt worse.

"What's this about?" she said, though she had a guess. They hadn't parted on good terms. Far from it. She'd had to block Marcus's wristlet code after the flood of obsessive calls.

"Just hear me out." His expression hardened. "I happen to have full flight privileges on the *Adversary*. Heaven's Breach has some of the Duchess's contacts stationed for stealth movements."

Frustration roiled in Riven's gut. Heaven's Breach was a hub on Requiem's dome—a way out. Marcus had her right where he wanted her. "And what are you asking in return?"

"I just want the truth. You've cheated me, lied to me, left me, and I want to know why." There was something pained, almost vulnerable, in his eyes.

"*Cheated* isn't the word for what I did." Her chest was tight, like claws were raking the insides of her ribs. Before she'd ditched Marcus, she'd been flirting with one of the bartender girls at Olympus, ready to swear off boys completely, when—

When.

Riven felt his next question coming.

"Tell me." His fingers brushed her chin, and she recoiled. "Why did you leave me for Emmett O'Shea?"

Most kids on Earth got cruisers or secondhand speeders for their seventeenth birthdays. None of the caregivers in Riven's group home had the money for one—they had forty-two other wards of the state to deal with—and besides, they hadn't remembered her birthday in the first place.

But that night, after curfew had passed and the doors were locked, her wristlet buzzed. She found Emmett waiting outside.

"I have a surprise for you." He slipped a blindfold over her eyes. Despite the blindfold, Riven could trace every turn of Emmett's beat-up speeder and recognized he'd brought her to the scrapyard.

Emmett guided her up a creaking mound of broken vid-screens and shipping crates, though she secretly watched her feet out the bottom of the blindfold. When he removed her blindfold, she squinted into the floodlights. Broken ship clad-ding and crumpled speeders stretched into hills.

"I found you a ship," Emmett said, beaming.

At first glance, it was a piece of junk with faded green paint, barely distinguishable from the scrap around it.

"What do you think?" His handsome face was streaked with engine grease that matched his raven-black hair.

Riven wanted to laugh, but Emmett looked so excited, so *proud*, that all she could say was, "It's perfect." And maybe it would be. How often had she dreamed of having her own ship, of leaving this place behind for good?

"Want to give it a name?"

The ship's cladding was textured into scales and sleek ridges. Riven pictured it with a better coat of paint, deadly and fast—a snake.

The name slid easily onto her tongue. "*Boomslang*," she whispered.

Getting the ship into shape, though, wasn't as effortless.

Emmett was a damn good mechanist, and Riven helped him haggle for the parts they needed. They spent nights repairing and painting the ship in a rented corner of a run-down hangar. When the hull paint was almost finished, Emmett flicked green paint across the seat of her pants, laughing, until she retaliated by leaving her own handprints on his shirt. And pants. And everywhere else.

After weeks in the hangar, the engine turned over for the first time. As it purred to life, Riven swore she tasted the stars.

"The cockpit's yours." Emmett strapped into the navigator's seat for *Boomslang*'s first ride.

She was so ready. She and Emmett were seventeen, fresh into their second years at Central Atlantic Academy on

Earth—the world ahead of them, with everything to prove and
nothing to lose.

Her head throbbed as they breached the atmosphere.
The ships she'd flown at CAA were nothing compared to the
freedom she had now. *Boomslang* was hers. Emmett was hers.

The stars themselves were hers.

"It goes on forever," Emmett said, when they stalled the
engines to gaze into the starfield. "Even if you spent your entire
life exploring, you'd die before seeing even a sliver of what's
out there. Incredible, huh?"

"It really is." *Boomslang* was only a speck in a sea of worlds
beginning and ending, worlds she'd never know. "Sure makes
you feel insignificant."

He leaned against the gunner seat, brushing his fingers
through Riven's hair, the magenta streaks she'd just had grafted
in. "Maybe not. It just means we get to decide what's most important in our corner of the universe."

"And what's that for you?"

She hadn't needed to ask. Emmett had worked long nights
and sweltering days to give her this ship. He'd picked *her* to
be here with him, drifting in the starfield, hundreds of miles
from a world that had never given a damn about her.

Emmett leaned in and kissed her fiercely. She wrapped
her arms around his waist, closing every inch of space between them.

Before now, Riven had never been chosen for anything.

And if she'd had the option, she might've never set foot
planetside again.

"Because I loved him." It should've been obvious.

"Oh?" Marcus circled her. "It had nothing to do with him giving you a ship while we were still together?"

"You and I were never together. I was only on Requiem for two weeks." She'd scrounged a passenger ticket to Requiem the first time she'd gotten kicked out of the house.

"But I was already going places in the underworld. And I would've given you more than a beaten-up gunship."

Riven turned away. Ship or no, Emmett had changed everything. "That wasn't what I was after."

"Not then, anyway. But now . . ." The false candles in the chandelier flickered behind him. "Emmett can't get you a ship off Requiem now, can he?"

Riven had the uncontrollable urge to punch Marcus's skull paint inside out. If her guns were at her hips, he might've died right then and there. *He* should be dead, not Emmett. A thousand people should be dead before Emmett.

"He would do whatever it took," Riven spat.

"And yet you're here petitioning *me*." Marcus stared her dead in the eyes and grabbed her waist in both hands.

The same way he'd grabbed her a year and a half ago when she'd told him she was leaving, but he'd insisted *you're just being coy*. Riven couldn't move.

"I'm willing to forgive you, though." Hurt flashed in his paint-rimmed eyes, and he pulled her closer, murmuring into her ear. "You're the most fascinating person I've ever met, Riven. I've never been able to stop thinking about you."

The smoothness of his voice dredged up memories of him tampering with her transit ticket back to Earth, trying to keep her from leaving. The possessiveness he'd hidden beneath his slick exterior.

The rational part of her screamed, *Punch him*, her fists clenched tight and painful. The stupid part of her faltered, demanding, *He has you cornered. You attack, and you're dead too.*

Diego expected her to pull some strings, but he wouldn't have sent her if he'd known the details. And Riven was the furthest thing from a diplomat.

Marcus was too close, his hips pressing against hers.

His guns close to where hers should be.

In an instant, one of his semi-auto pistols was in Riven's hand.

Her thumb clicked the safety off and she pressed the muzzle under his chin. "Back off."

Marcus didn't flinch. "Or what? You won't kill me. You're not nearly as tough as you pretend to be."

"Want to try me? You can activate the wrist-cuff if you want. But I might pull the trigger on reflex." She hoped he'd be dumb enough to, that he'd shock himself while touching her. But the jolt might not travel through her gloves.

He shrugged and leaned closer. "All right."

Searing pain erupted from the wrist-cuff.

Riven gritted her teeth against the heightening pain. It was stupid to shoot Marcus in his territory, but if he was going to try to control her—to keep her here, as he had before—

This might be her only chance. She kept her composure just long enough to pull the trigger.

Nothing happened.

She doubled over, shocks of pain piercing through her. The gun skidded onto the gold carpet. Bastard.

Marcus laughed. "You really think I would let a loaded gun anywhere near you? You're so predictable."

Tears stung her eyes, and her arm jerked as the stun-blasts continued. The pain was a rhythm, *stab, stab, stab.* She braced herself against the swell and stood up. "I'll answer your first question: I left because you're a self-important asshole who belittles girls to stroke your own ego."

The next shock was powerful enough to knock her over. Riven writhed, trying to yank off the wrist-cuff. But it was no use. Marcus had her right where he wanted her.

Then, mercifully, the blasts stopped.

The gaudy carpet was rough against her hands and knees. Her brain was fried, and her entire body felt like it'd been dropped through a crusher. Through her blotchy vision, she watched Marcus's skull-embossed boots approach.

"I'll offer one more time. Right now, you have only a grounded, beaten-up ship and no steady crew. You're nothing, Lily-Flower, and I have everything. Even the ship you need. Join me."

It was tempting. A ship off. So easy.

But it would mean letting him keep her like a lapdog.

She was more than that. And she had a reputation to uphold.

"No."

Marcus was quiet, and she braced herself for another stun-blast.

"Well. I've made my conditions clear." He turned his back,

walking back to the unfurling carbon-fiber wings of the throne. "Take as much time as you need to think. But remember, Requiem isn't getting any brighter."

He didn't look back, and neither did Riven as she stumbled from the hall.

Another reason she had to become a matriarch. When she had power, nobody would be able to look down on her. *Deathknell* would piss himself at the sight of her.

But now, she didn't know what to tell Tripp and the others. That she'd let go of their chance to get offworld? At the rate Banshee was spreading, Requiem might not make it until dawn.

Her only option left was drastic. Her crew wouldn't be happy—but risky measures were her specialty.

Diego, she messaged on her wristlet, trying to shake away the crawling sensation where Marcus had touched her, *I know the perfect ship to steal.*

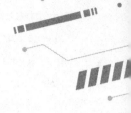

chapter 15
INTO THE FIRE

"That is a terrible idea," Samir said as they rode the speeder back to Diego's, and Asa didn't disagree.

The skyway tunnel broke, revealing the city below—a labyrinth of hacked billboards displaying syndicate logos and crude messages, bridges over crystal ruins, crowds shifting between graffitied streets and dirty alleys. A city that seemed determined to trap her.

"Do you have a better plan?" Riven leaned against the front-seat window as beams of light and shadow passed over her silver hair. She hadn't told Asa what had happened in Deathknell's hall, but she'd been on edge ever since.

Maybe Riven was getting desperate. Asa certainly was. Just when they had a ticket out of the quarantine, their plans had shattered. Maybe a diplomatic solution was out of reach—especially considering her luck lately.

"I'd like a plan that doesn't have a fifty percent chance of getting us jailed or killed," Samir said.

"Same." Asa adjusted her harness in the seat behind Samir's. Stealing a ship seemed like a fast route to a matriarch's chophouse. She remembered the man tacked to the billboard in the Crush, a gutted shell of steel and flesh.

But what if Riven's new plan was their only way out? Asa's

throat went dry. When she'd sworn to be stronger, partaking in a heist wasn't what she'd meant.

"Actually," Galateo chirped from Riven's wristlet, sitting on the control panel's wireless charger, "the chances are closer to eighty-six percent, allowing for complications in patrols, quarantine conditions, and spontaneous bickering."

"See? Even Galateo knows this is a bad idea," Samir said.

"I am here to provide objective analysis."

"Bullshit," Riven said. "Run your numbers again—this time, allowing for the complication of me kicking your ass. Objectively. Ty, back me up here."

"I actually think stealing a ship isn't the worst idea," Ty said. "But are you sure there isn't some other ship we could take? I mean, come on, Riv. Stealing from someone aligned with the Duchess is a death wish." Ty sat next to Asa, his shoulder brushing hers, but his gaze was fixed out the window. The city lights gave way to a darkened, empty slum. The quarantine region was growing like an infection. As the skyway swooped low over the city, Asa glimpsed hooded looters on ladders, crawling into the blacked-out buildings.

They were running out of time. Soon she'd have no chance at all.

"The *Adversary* is perfect." Riven's fingers worked through her purple-and-blonde hair, rebraiding it. "That ship can pass through the atmo-dome at Heaven's Breach. Plus, I've flown it before, and I happen to know the ignition codes."

Ty's eyebrows shot up. "He told you his passcodes?"

"For *everything*. I just checked—he hasn't changed any of

his other passcodes in two years, so I doubt he's changed his ship's."

"What is it, then?" Ty said.

Riven puffed a breath. "It's dumb."

"Something something, *Lily-Flower*?" Discomfort flashed across Ty's face. "I can't believe you dated that guy. Just. Damn. If my brother hadn't come along . . ."

"Yeah, yeah. I was sixteen and dumb." Despite the nonchalance in her voice, Riven crossed her arms, as if trying to shrink. "Marcus was halfway cute before he started wearing the face paint."

Diego's sigh sizzled through the speakers. The console showed him at his desk, his hair disheveled. "As Ty mentioned, you do realize stealing the *Adversary* means crossing the Duchess herself? Deathknell is one of her men, and she'll take it as a personal attack."

"We'll give the ship *back*," Riven said with a dry grin. "And we won't get caught."

"Riven . . ." Diego was quiet for a moment. "She'll know. If you do this—even if you succeed—you might not be able to come back to Requiem."

Riven's char-rimmed eyes narrowed. "There might not be a Requiem to come back to otherwise. And the Duchess will be thanking us once we've saved her whole damn city." She leaned closer to the console screen, the glow illuminating her freckles. "Seems we have to save Requiem without her permission."

"I hate to say it, but . . ." Ty crossed his arms. "I'm with Riv here. We're choosing between crossing a Duchess who might hunt us to the edge of the star-system, and a demon AI that already is. One of those we have a chance of reasoning with."

Just give Kaya up, a voice whispered at the back of Asa's mind. *Find a way to hand her over to Banshee, and their city will be free. You'll be free.*

It was an awful thought. She'd come too far to turn back.

"Samir?" Riven said. "We're not doing this unless you're on board."

The speeder made a tight turn, and the seat harness cut into Asa. All she could see of Samir was his white-knuckled grip on the console bar, but his voice was soft, controlled. "I still think crossing the Duchess could be suicide. But . . . I can't let Requiem die like this. And if we manage to purge Banshee, the Duchess might do a lot more than forgive us. Diego, if you can build us a real strategy, I'm in."

A jolt went through Asa's nerves. Whatever their reasons, she had a team.

"Riven's passcodes will be helpful, but ship access might be the least of our concerns." Diego tapped at his keyboard, and the vidscreen showed a three-dimensional map of a docking bay. "The hangar still has an extensive surveillance system. You'll need some well-placed disruptor bullets to get rid of the security-mechs—"

"I'm your huckleberry," Riven said.

"I don't doubt you are. You could handle the perimeter, but there's an alarm system. Disabling it would involve getting in first. Heat sensors, motion sensors . . . I don't know if it's possible."

"We'll figure it out," Riven said.

"That's not good enough," Samir said. "If we fail, the Federation and the Duchess will fight over who gets to slit our throats."

The solution was in Asa's backpack. If she volunteered, there'd be no turning back. But she'd been strong enough for the past few days, and it would all be worth nothing if she didn't step up now.

"I can get us through," she said quietly.

Diego's dark eyes narrowed. "Oh?"

"I can get past the surveillance systems." Asa dug into her backpack, producing the shimmery black fade-suit with wires spiderwebbing over its surface.

Riven's eyes lit up. "I saw that in your backpack. Where'd you get it?"

Asa felt her cheeks flush. Fade-suits weren't legal on Cortellion—only licensed espionage-tech manufacturers had them, and they were expensive. "Stole it from Almeida on the way out. No surveillance will pick me up—no heat, no motion detectors, no cameras." The image might appear distorted and blurred to a human monitoring a camera, but AI security systems wouldn't trigger.

"That's some awfully rare tech," Samir said. "You sure it's genuine?"

"How do you think I managed to steal Almeida's biocapsule?" Asa pulled the suit over her hand and clicked the switch. Her hand shimmered and blurred until it was clear as polished glass. This tech was hers—one thing she could control, no matter how far out of her depth she was.

"Good point." Ty watched her intently.

"That still leaves the dozen patrol mechs stationed inside for emergencies," Diego said.

"What if we disabled the mechs?" Asa said. "I might have a way to do that too."

Even Samir turned to stare at her.

"I home brewed a few EMP grenades from Almeida's disruptor tech." She'd built these last summer, testing them on her dad's security-mechs. The mechs had come back online after a few hours, but he'd still been furious. "I haven't fully measured the knockout radius, but I'm guessing it's about twenty feet." Asa dug into her backpack and pulled one out. "It'll send a pulse to disable their circuits. They might have hardened reboot boxes as backup, but even then, anything electronic should be dead for at least half an hour."

"You made those." Diego didn't sound surprised.

Asa managed a smile. "Sure did."

"That . . ." Diego conceded with a shrug, "would actually work."

Riven gave a smirk over her shoulder. "Seems our mechanist is useful after all."

"You do understand, Tripp," Samir said, "that if you fail, we might be dead?"

"I can do this." Asa swallowed the lump in her throat. She had to. She was already blocking herself from imagining gruesome outcomes to this plan. Now wasn't the time for panic.

"If you're up to this, reroute your speeder to these coordinates," Diego said. "Keep your comms encrypted. I've got a plan, but we need to do this soon."

"You ready to get the hell off Requiem?" Riven punched the codes into the control panel.

"Let's do this." Asa couldn't tell them how unprepared she felt.

◢ ◢ ◢ ◢ ◢◢◢◢◢◢◢◢◢ ◢◢

They were going to rob the Duchess of Requiem.

Asa had spent the ten-minute speeder ride in sheer, frozen terror. She'd expected some time to get used to the idea—to play through possible scenarios in her head. But they were dropping her straight into the fire.

Now she was numb, skulking with the others through an alley near the docking bay. The bay loomed ahead—fashioned after an ancient Roman pantheon from Phase I Earth, but decked in black concrete and neon lights instead of polished white stone.

With every step, the fade-suit tightened in all the wrong places, tailored for someone with longer legs and narrower hips. The hood covered her hair, exposing only her face. She'd zip it up when the time came.

And the battery had better last.

Samir slipped past her. "We have everyone? Soldier, dead-eye, medic, informant, mechanist?" He clapped Asa on the shoulder.

Mechanist. Part of the crew. As if she belonged, however briefly.

"Voice of reason?" Galateo said.

"You can come if you shut up," Riven said.

Diego's voice came through her earpiece. "When you're

in position, I'll launch the attack on the Federation servers." A distraction, while they flew out.

"Understood," Riven said.

Asa trotted to catch up with Ty, but a strong hand on her shoulder stopped her.

She whirled, coming face-to-face with Riven. Beneath the fizzing streetlamps, Riven's eyes had a lethal glimmer.

"Tripp."

The false name on Riven's lips sent a shiver through her. "Yes?"

Riven's jaw quirked, as she calculated her words carefully. "I know we have a plan in place." She leaned closer to whisper, and Asa held her breath as Riven's hand wrapped around her wrist. "But if you run into any trouble in there . . . just call me. I'll protect you." Riven tapped on Asa's wristlet, the gesture humming through her like sparks.

Protect you. Asa met Riven's eyes, and her rational thoughts evaporated like stardust. Silhouetted by the distant sky, Riven seemed as dangerous as the shadows lurking between the alleys. Deadly, but on her side.

A strange, impossible yearning washed over Asa—for intoxicating danger, a far-flung dream out of reach. Something that would never be hers. *Could* never be hers.

"I will," Asa finally said. "Thank you."

A dark smile played at Riven's lips. "I mean it."

Diego's voice cut through. "I'm sending you a display of the drone patrols on the docking bay now—first headed your way in about six seconds."

A patrol drone whizzed overhead, scouting the perimeter.

"That's my cue." Riven pulled away, cocking *Blackjack*. "Go get ready for yours."

And then Riven was running the other direction, and Asa was alone with her racing heart. No time to dwell on it. She caught up with Ty, who was waiting at the alley's edge. "I'm here. Sorry."

Atop the steps of the docking bay ahead, one of the Duchess's troopers leaned against the service-entrance door, looking bored.

Ty nodded to her. "Let's move."

They ducked near the service-door steps. Ty must've noticed her teeth chattering, because he gave her shoulder a reassuring squeeze. His hands were warmer than Riven's, a different kind of comfort.

And a reminder she was too far in to back out.

Thoom. Thoom. Riven's gunshots. The guard, who'd been scratching his crotch, turned toward the noise, raising his assault rifle.

Ty's cue. As soon as the man's back was turned, Ty sprinted and leapt.

The guard swore as Ty wrapped an arm around his neck, squeezing with his elbow. Asa winced—it was a blood choke, which she'd only seen in true-crime shows. It wouldn't kill the guard, but Ty might get hurt.

The guard's rifle clattered onto the steel steps, but he wouldn't let up. He grabbed Ty's arm and slammed backward into the wall, trying to knock Ty off. Asa gasped as Ty's head clanged against the steel, and his eyes rolled backward.

"Ty!" If he lost consciousness, he was dead. Her chest tightened. Distracting the guard wouldn't be much use—she'd have to knock him out. Or worse.

Asa held her finger on the fade-suit switch. Maybe she'd have to take the gun.

But Ty hung on, pulling the choke tighter. The guard sputtered, dropping to his knees, flailing slower. Seconds dragged by like hours, and the man finally collapsed.

"Oh my god." Asa ran over as Ty lowered the limp guard to the ground. That had been way too close. "Wouldn't a stunner have been easier?"

"Doesn't usually work against this armor." Ty gave a weak smile and checked the man's vitals as he unwrapped a sedative patch. "And he's still breathing. Better than Riven's bloodier alternatives, huh?"

Bloodier alternatives. The phrase dug into Asa's skin. Would it have been better to let Riven handle this?

"He almost had you." By refusing to kill, Ty had put himself in danger. It was either admirable or utterly reckless.

Ty pulled on gloves and pressed the patch to the unconscious guard's neck. Then he daubed the man's wrist with an antiseptic, positioned his scalpel, and made a thin red slit above a bump in the skin.

Asa gasped, turning away. It was alarmingly casual, cutting flesh outside a lab environment.

Ty laughed. "Wish *I* could look away."

"Doesn't it bother you? To be cutting into something . . . living?" She imagined what Josiah might have to do to put Kaya back together, and the sourness in her gut worsened.

"Not since I started thinking of the body as an intricate machine, and not the person living inside it." She snuck a glance back at him. He dabbed the blood away and pried his tweezers into the slice, extracting a pill-sized microchip between the tendons and the blood. "Kind of like what you do, I guess."

Not even close. "Machines don't feel pain."

"And if I do a good job, this guy won't either."

She studied him carefully. Ty made three perfect stitches and applied a numbing salve to the wound. His hands were deft and gentle. Even now, he was keeping the wound clean and painless. Why did he care so much?

Still, she couldn't shake the idea of him making bigger cuts—*killing* cuts—on jobs with Riven's crew. "Is this why you became a medic? To cut data out of your targets?"

"You really think I'd bother with med school for that?" Ty's face was grim. "No. I became a medic because Riven's always trying to protect me. But someone needs to save her."

"Save her?"

A solemn nod. "Right. I'm a year too late to help Emmett, but I can be here for Riven. I don't think I can cure her, but maybe I can stop it from spreading. Stop her from dying."

"She's *dying*?" Some of Asa's longing turned hollow, like reaching for a flame as it faded to embers.

"She might be. It's not something we really talk about, for obvious reasons. I just wish she weren't so reckless sometimes." His eyes met hers, steady as a planet core. "It's nice to have someone else around who doesn't use guns to solve every problem."

She clenched her quivering hands. "It's the only way I know how. But honestly . . . I'm terrified."

"So am I. Every time. But sometimes you don't have a choice." A furious blush was creeping across his cheekbones, and he rubbed his brow to hide it. "You've already come a long way, but . . . it kind of sucks you'll be leaving after this. What do you think, though? After you save your sister, will you ever come back to Requiem?"

Asa suppressed her smile, the flutter in her ribs. "I don't think I can plan that far ahead."

"Right. Sorry." Ty bit his lip as he unwrapped an antiseptic wipe and scrubbed the tiny microchip clean. "Here. All yours."

She tucked it into her fade-suit's pocket. Ty's gaze skimmed her from head to toe, lingering on the tight fabric over her hips, before he looked away. Maybe he didn't see her like the others did—as a lost girl in ill-fitting stealth tech, an unwelcome complication. Maybe he saw more.

Maybe he could save Riven, and she could save Kaya. Right now, they all needed each other.

His hand lingered against hers. "You're the only reason we have a shot at this. So trust yourself and your tech, okay?"

"I will." She clicked on her wristlet comm. "All right, Diego. We have the chip. I'm heading in."

"And you're going to give them hell," Ty whispered.

She shot him one last smile as she zipped the face cover.

chapter 16

THE INTRUDERS

The warmth of Ty's hand almost drowned out the scream of *I'm not ready I'll never be ready* in the depths of Asa's head.

Her breaths were uncomfortably moist inside the face cover. She held the chip to the reader at the door, and it blinked. She'd stolen worse.

Good luck, Ty mouthed as the door closed behind her. Maybe he was right. She was the reason they had a shot at escaping the quarantine. Even if this mess was her fault—and even if her secrets still made her an outsider—she could do this.

The service hallway was narrow and dark. Surveillance cameras and sensors glared from the ceiling.

Almost like the security checkpoints at her dad's estate. She'd become a pro at surpassing them. As the fade-suit activated, her arms became transparent like water, but not quite invisible.

A steady whir rose behind her, and she immediately pressed herself to the wall. A patrol drone zipped through the hallway, a crackling stunner mounted on its underside like a stinger. The whirring quieted as the drone stopped, projecting a beam of red around its radius.

Asa tried not to breathe as the drone scudded forward and stopped in front of her, close enough to touch. Her heart was probably hammering loud enough to give her away.

The red scanner beam ghosted across her. Asa's pulse jumped in her throat.

Then the machine chirped and continued forward, leaving her behind.

She held her breath until it drifted out of view. So far, so good. She slipped through the corridor and up the stairs to the central atrium.

The docking bay was decked in flickering lights. Pink and orange neon cycled between shifting palm tree silhouettes. Black tiles on the walls glinted in the dim light. At the center of the atrium was a tiered fountain.

Everything was weirdly empty. Lights crawled along the balconies—more patrol drones—but no guards or dock workers.

"I'm inside," Asa breathed into her wristlet, concealed under the suit. "Remind me where the control room is?"

"North tower," Diego said. "Check your map. Let us in once you've disabled the mechs in the security bay. You can handle that, right?"

Failure wasn't an option. "I'll do my best."

Asa skulked between the security-drones until she reached the bay. She peered inside—at least a dozen mechs stood at the perimeter like suits of armor, waiting for an alarm to be triggered.

It was time to launch her EMP grenade.

She crept into the room, but the mechs' dead gazes passed right through her. *Trust the fade-suit, Asa.*

She slipped the grenade out of the suit's pocket and set it in the center of the room. As soon as the grenade was visible, one of the mechs straightened to attention, its eyes lighting green.

Asa flipped the switch. The grenade counted down from five, the beeping increasing in pitch and frequency.

She ran, keeping her steps light. The radius should be twenty feet—enough to knock out all the mechs. But it could hit *her* too. She pushed herself faster. Thirty feet away should be safe.

The high-pitched whine of the detonation went off when she was barely outside the room. The lights flickered and went out.

A numbing pulse washed over her, like a weak stunner shot. The grenade had been more powerful than she'd expected—powerful enough to hit her fade-suit.

With bile rising in her throat, she looked down. The cloaking tech flickered, and suddenly she was a girl in a tight black suit again.

Dammit. Dammit! Asa ducked behind a control console and checked her wristlet. As dead as the fade-suit. Panic surged. She had no way to contact her crew. At least Samir had the biocapsule.

Fade-suit or no, they were still depending on her. She made for the security room, heart pounding, clinging to the shadows behind the palm trees. But when the next patrol drone appeared, sending a scan-beam around the hallway, hiding wasn't enough.

An alarm began shrieking. Her cover was blown. The wasp-like stinger aimed at her, crackling.

Asa sprinted down the corridor, the drone floating at her heels. As she rounded a corner, its stunner fired past her, sending static tingling at her hair follicles.

She forced her feet faster, her breaths coming in short gasps.

Sometimes, Ty had said, *you don't have a choice.*

When she reached the security station, she thrust the chip at the scanner and threw the door open as soon as the lock lit green. She pulled out her stunner, but nobody was manning the security feeds. The control panels blinked back at her, a field of lights like stars.

"I'm in," Asa whispered to herself, slamming the door shut. A wave of adrenaline washed over her, giddy relief. She'd done something right. "I'm *in!*"

Thump. Thump. The patrol drone was bumping the door. Its shoddy programming worked in her favor.

Other than that, the tower was eerily quiet. Her instincts told her something was *off*, but all that mattered now was getting the gate open. Asa unzipped the face cover—the suit would be dead for a while anyway—and scrolled through the security controls, hitting the lock for the west doors.

A few patrol mechs were still up, but the crew could handle those. Now, how was she getting out of here? The security-drone's stun-blasts fizzed against the metal door.

The panels blinked in front of her—an overlay of the entire docking bay, and the mechs inside it.

She had another idea. Maybe the drone could be useful.

It was time to steal Marcus's ship.

Riven imagined the thrusters purring as she fired it up, the ship shaking as they left the atmosphere. It had been too long since she'd piloted a ship, and the withdrawal was starting to make her twitch.

Ahead of them, the atrium doors split open, revealing the polished arches of the Duchess's docking bay. Between the black columns, ships sat in docking rigs like idols in a pantheon. The external bays were shuttered behind walls of semitransparent graphene.

Riven kept her guns up, but no guards greeted them. Unlike the entrances, which had been swarming with patrol mechs, the bay itself was . . . empty. Unease crept up her spine. Maybe the Duchess had pulled back her guards because no ships were flying, and maybe Tripp had disabled every patrol mech—but something felt *off.*

"Hey, Tripp, did you get the bay open?" Riven said. "We're looking for dock 212D."

Tripp didn't respond.

"Shit," Diego said in her earpiece. "Her comm is out."

Oh, damn. "Did they catch her? Should I go back?"

With a shudder, the graphene panel in front of Bay 212 slid aside. Inside was completely dark. Riven exhaled hard. If Tripp had gotten the door open, maybe she was safe.

"Something wrong with the power?" Riven led the others inside, flicking on her wristlet's flashlight.

"The EMP might've knocked out the lights," Diego said. "Docking controls still seem to be online though."

"You guys see dock D?" Riven could barely make out the exit channel between the docked ships, which were wreathed in shadow. She walked under the lattice of steel maintenance scaffolding, but the ships' dock numbers were still too far to see.

"Shh," Ty said. "Hear that?"

Riven stopped. A clacking, a scrape on steel. A quick pat-ter, like footsteps—*clawed* footsteps.

"Something's here," Samir whispered. Riven could barely make out his cat eyes in the reflected light from Ty's wristlet. "Look at that."

Ty shone his wristlet light over an empty shipping con-tainer. Not just any shipping container—inside was a smatter-ing of straw and barred dividers.

Cages.

Empty cages.

"What the hell are these?" Riven tried to ignore the grow-ing unease in her gut.

"Must've come off that freighter," Samir said.

Diego's voice came through the comm. "Send me a scan?" Samir slid his wristlet scanner over the label. "Hmm . . . label says these were bound for the gladiatorial pits in Olympus. They electromagnetically seal those containers. The seals must've gotten knocked out with the power."

"*Gladiatorial pits*?" Ty said nervously. "What was inside?"

"Look at the tag on the doors. It'll tell you."

A scuffling in the dark. A smacking of jaws. Claws on steel. Riven cocked *Verdugo*. If a bruttore had escaped, a shot through the eyes should take care of it. But the containers weren't big enough for bruttore.

"It says . . ." Ty examined the label on the shipping con-tainer's hinge. "Oh, no. Oh, *no.*"

Riven aimed *Verdugo*'s barrel through the dark, trying to follow the scrape of claws. "Answers, Ty. Quick."

"It was a shipment of . . . anteleons."

Shit. That was the worst news Riven had heard all day.

The one time they'd been stupid enough to accept a job transporting anteleons, it hadn't ended well. The ugly bastards could cloak—fade-suit tech was based on their scales. Riven had enough bullets, but she couldn't hit a target she couldn't see. Only dim planetlight through the translucent ceiling panels lit the bay.

Samir's footsteps were soft against the steps of the scaffold. "I'm going up. I'll have a better angle with my thermal scope. I'll let you know if I see anything."

"We need to find the *Adversary*," Riven said. "Ty, stay close. We'll have to trust that Tripp is on her way."

Something shifted in the dark—a flash of gray scales that immediately disappeared. A skittering behind her, and the hollow *clink* of a fuel canister knocked over.

A volley of bullets discharged from Samir's gun, followed by a screech. Two anteleons curled up, their cloaking disappearing and leaving an ugly mass of gray scales.

"Brace yourselves," Samir said. "There's at least a dozen."

"Not helpful when I can't see them!"

Ty ejected his stun-switchblades. They crackled with electricity, for all the good they'd do. Behind him, something blurred through the dark.

"Ty!"

He fell, dragged backward by his boot. Riven fired into the empty space over his shoulder. Her first bullet kicked up chips of concrete. The second hit its target. A huge, ugly hunk of scales and claws appeared, slumped behind Ty like an overgrown lizard. One down.

Riven was cocking *Verdugo* a third time when stabs of pain dug into her shoulders. She froze as a sticky, revolting warmth slid up her neck.

Tasting her.

She writhed. "It's *licking* me!" She twisted her gun backward—the claws digging further as she moved—and fired a shot past her ear, where the anteleon's snout should be.

The blast punched her eardrums like an explosion, but the claws released.

It wasn't the last of them. Feet scuttled in the dark, and another claw latched onto Riven's arm—

"Hang on!" Samir's voice called through the ringing in her ears.

And suddenly, her breath was stifled by a waterfall of something heavy, dark, and horrifyingly *wet*.

The cold slime pummeled her from above, knocking her onto her hands and knees. When the barrage subsided, she swiped a hand over her face, gasping. Her hand came away sticky, and she realized she was wrist-deep in a pile of glowing purple ooze. Not just ooze—melon-sized *slugs*.

Ugh. It couldn't get worse—or weirder—from here on out.

Anteleons limped from the sludge, reptilian shapes defined by patches of purple slime. They were visible now, but what the hell had just happened? Riven wiped another handful of sludge off her cheek—dammit, her *hair* too—and pulled up her sticky guns.

Riven held her left hand over *Verdugo*'s hammer and fanned it as she pulled the trigger. Four shots. Four anteleons dropped.

"Did *you* do that, Samir? If so, you're cleaning my guns!"

Ty staggered to his feet, soaked in glowing purple. He grimaced at the drenched shirt sticking to him. Poor Ty. For a medic, he had a nasty fear of germs.

"Couldn't shoot them while they were on you." Samir jammed another mag into his rifle and peered down the thermal scope. Next to him was an overturned container streaked with purple goo. "And I didn't think you wanted me to get all the kills. So I gave them some color."

"It's all *over* me." Ty peeled off his hooded vest. "This was my favorite shirt too."

Riven shot another purple patch crawling through the dark. She probably glowed too—after being exposed to their flashlights, the slime was bright as neon. At least it was purple.

"Why do they need slugs for the gladiatorial pits?" Ty said.

"The anteleons are for the gladiatorial pits." Samir descended the scaffold steps. "The slug slime is for the dancers."

Her arm squelched as she gestured at Samir. "And how do you know that? Dare I ask whether this is your thing, or Diego's?"

Samir grumbled, but she couldn't make out the words as an alarm began blaring. The red emergency lights blinked over the exits.

Riven's ears throbbed. "Can you get this alarm off, Dee?"

"Working on it. Trying to figure out where the alarm system connects."

"Well, Tripp needs to get her ass down here. We can't risk backup coming from outside." They needed to board the *Adversary* and go. Now.

Riven checked the docking terminals until she found 212D.

"Whoa," Ty said.

The flashing emergency lights glinted off the *Adversary*, its hull folded like origami, its paint deep blue. A pale blue skull was splashed over the top, with the glass panes of the cockpit forming the teeth. Definitely bigger—and more powerful—than *Boomslang*. Riven tried to ignore the creeping envy.

"Looks like our ride out." She punched Marcus's passcodes into its docking terminal.

The hatch hissed open, and the boarding ramp extended invitingly. The *Adversary*'s interior lights flickered on, illuminating the white polymer trim and carpeted interior. Riven laughed with relief.

"Come on, Tripp," Ty called toward the bay doors. "We don't have much time."

But as Riven boarded, she was so focused on getting to the cockpit—the throttle, the nav systems, all at her command—that she didn't notice the footsteps from the ship's cabin behind her, or the faint whir of cybernetics unsheathing.

"Uh. Riven?" Ty's voice was strained.

"Didn't expect you to actually get in," said an annoyingly familiar voice. "Then again, we thinned the patrols to make it easy for you."

Riven whipped around, raising *Verdugo*. At the end of her iron sights was a curly-haired woman pressing a hand cannon to Ty's temple.

Morphett Slade.

"Did you dress him up just for me?" Morphett said against Ty's neck. "You should feel how fast his heart's beating. I'm tempted to take him with me." He was a head taller than her, but she held him like a vise. A scalpel tip protruded from under her fingernail, pointed at his collarbone.

This bitch again. Would she come this far just for Tripp? "What do you want?" Riven snarled.

Ty's head was tilted back, his teeth bared. Scared, but trying not to show it. He trusted Riven to save him. She always did.

"I'll trade you." Morphett retracted her finger-knife and trailed her hand down Ty's bare stomach. He gasped. "Reluctantly, of course. Him for Asanna Almeida. Fair?"

Riven narrowed her eyes. "I don't know an Asanna Alm—"

Almeida. Luca Almeida had a daughter, didn't he? Someone Morphett thought Riven knew.

Someone with access to Almeida's tech.

Someone he wanted back desperately enough to hire Morphett.

"Tripp," Riven whispered. "You dirty liar."

"**N**o," Asa whispered. Morphett had broken the dam on her biggest secret, and it would swallow everything she'd struggled for.

She slipped into hiding behind the wing of a butterfly-shaped ship. A few ships over, light flooded from the *Adversary*'s boarding doors, and inside stood Riven and Samir—her crew—at a standoff with Morphett. Morphett pressed an enormous handgun to Ty's head. *Dust and bones.* Asa had put him in danger too.

"Oh?" A look of sadistic glee crossed Morphett's face. "Oh, my. You didn't *know*?" She laughed. "I'd wager that's not the only thing she's been lying about."

"You're that maniac's *daughter*?" Riven shouted. Asa could feel the fury in her voice, echoing across the bay. "I know you're here, *Tripp*. You'd better come out and explain."

Asa couldn't move. Her getaway ship was stalled by a vicious bounty hunter and a furious Riven. But Asa couldn't leave while Samir had Kaya. A familiar dizziness crept over her. This wouldn't end without violence.

"She's just a dumb little rich girl going through a rebellious phase," Morphett said. "Bored of life in her pretty Corte mansion. Robbed Daddy Dearest in a plea for attention. Weird she'd turn against him, after he made her a *lead engineer* on Project Winterdark."

"Winterdark too," Riven hissed. "What else have you been lying about? Your imaginary sister?"

Asa was too stunned to respond. Did Riven really think *everything* was a lie?

"Where is Asanna?" Morphett said.

"Let him go," Samir said behind his rifle.

"I asked nicely." A bright-pink bubble popped all over Morphett's glossy lips.

Asa slid her finger over the greasy datapad she'd stolen from the security room, maneuvering her hacked patrol drone closer to the *Adversary*. She readied its mounted stun-gun, not that it was much use right now. She couldn't force Riven to pilot her out.

"*Asanna* is hiding nearby," Riven said. "I don't care what you do with her, but let Ty go."

Asa's stomach sank. Riven was done with her. Exactly why she hadn't revealed her name last night.

"Watch this." Morphett called through the docking bay in a high, saccharine voice: "Asanna, dear, I'm going to blow a hole in this boy's skull unless you show yourself."

Asa remembered the organ pirate's brains smattered all over the walls. *No. Not Ty.* Morphett wouldn't dare. Would she?

Asa positioned the patrol drone's stun-gun, centering it on Morphett's head. But her head was so close to Ty's, and if it missed—

"See?" Morphett laughed. "She doesn't give a damn about what happens to any of you."

"You're not going to throw away your leverage," Ty said between gritted teeth. "I'm calling your bluff."

Morphett giggled. "Oh, there's so much more I could do to you before throwing you away." Her finger-scalpel shot out, and she traced a shallow cut over his breastbone. Ty choked back a pained gasp. "Now, Riven and"—Morphett gestured at Samir, who was seething—"Gorgeous McMuscles, whatever your name is—both of you, off the ship. Asanna, get over here. Once we've traded, I'll let Blondie go."

"We're not negotiating with you," Samir growled.

"Well, that's unfortunate," cooed an oily male voice. Deathknell's blue cape swished as he emerged from the ship's cabin behind Morphett. "You didn't think you'd waltz out of here on my ship, did you?"

"That was the plan," Riven said, *Verdugo*'s barrel skewing hungrily across the newcomers. "Maybe then you'd learn to change your passcodes more often."

Deathknell laughed. "I know you too well, Lily-Flower. You take what you want. You're desperate to prove yourself. Of course you would go after my ship. Which is why I brought backup."

Riven's scorched-black eyes narrowed. "You had to pick Morphett, huh?"

His lips curled. "She's helped get you right where I want you. So, here's my new offer: you can head to the Duchess's prisons with your friends—or come back to me. Your choice."

Sirens still blared in the main atrium. No mechs arrived to answer them.

"I'd kill you before that happened," Riven said. "And speaking of, you still owe me a duel."

Deathknell stroked the stubble on his chin, waiting for Morphett's reaction.

Riven pushed further. "We could do it now. Morphett lets Ty go, and we duel. If I win, I get your ship. But if you win . . . then either I'm dead, or I'm yours. Willingly, and without question."

Morphett laughed, but it was hollow. Nervous. "You're kidding, right?"

Deathknell nodded slowly. "I'm a good shot. I wouldn't hit any of your vitals, Lily-Flower. I look forward to having you *work* for me."

The look he gave Riven was voracious. His eyes were glued to the purple slug slime soaking her shirt to her chest. Asa shuddered, wondering what exactly he meant.

But Riven didn't flinch. A lethal excitement crossed her face, as if she knew she'd win.

Asa crept between the ships, moving closer. If that ship was leaving Requiem with her sister, it wasn't leaving her behind. No matter what Riven thought of her.

"Fine." Riven lowered her revolver. "Ready when you are."

"Don't you *dare*," Morphett spat at Deathknell, her scalpels extending like claws over Ty's chest. "I need a ride out, you idiot. At least give me your ignition codes before she destroys you!"

"She needs to know that leaving me was the worst mistake

she's ever made." Deathknell began to holster his blue-gray handgun.

Asa had to stop this. She couldn't risk Riven or Ty getting hurt. She aimed her drone's stun-gun at Deathknell—

"I warned you," Morphett said in a strained singsong. Before either of them holstered their weapons, Morphett's hand cannon whipped sideways, fired, and blasted the pistol from Deathknell's hand.

Deathknell fell to his knees, shouting a string of incoherent curses. "You!" he spat, clutching two bleeding, destroyed fingers. "What the hell was that for?"

"We had a deal." Morphett returned the muzzle of her gun to Ty's temple. "You'd get your girl, and I'd get mine—with a ride out. This duel would've ended with you dead, or with the ship in Riven's hands. Neither of which gets me out of here."

Deathknell moaned through gritted teeth.

"Ugh, the *whining*." Morphett rolled her eyes, yanking Ty back. "This is the last time I'll ask. You know I'll do it, Hawthorne. Bring Miss Almeida to me. *Now*."

Asa didn't want to find out whether Morphett was bluffing. She'd seen enough death for one lifetime, and Ty was the last person who deserved to be hurt.

So Asa did the only thing she could.

"I'm here," she blurted, stepping onto the *Adversary*'s docking ramp. "Let him go."

"Brave of you to show your face." Riven drew *Blackjack* in her left hand. Asa found herself at its business end.

"Riven, *please*. If you'd known my name, you might've—"

"Trusted you were telling the whole truth?" Riven's arms

were at a right angle—*Verdugo* pointed at Morphett, *Blackjack* at Asa.

Morphett cackled and whispered something into Ty's ear, making him flinch.

Asa touched the datapad, bringing the drone forward. Riven's eyes flicked to the drone and back to Asa. "Stand down," Asa said, as useless as the command sounded. "Please."

Behind Riven, Samir stood over Deathknell, rifle pointed at his smeared blue skull paint. Everyone was at an impasse—the reluctance to shoot was a spider thread tying them all together.

Riven kept her eyes on Morphett, but her glance kept flicking to Asa. Conflict was written on her face, and maybe pity. They both knew Riven would be a faster shot.

If only Asa could speak into Riven's thoughts the way she spoke into their comm system. *Please,* she wanted to say. *I'll explain everything once we're off this moon. Once we have Ty safe from Morphett.*

"I'm waiting," Morphett whispered.

Asa stared into Riven's gray-green eyes. Riven wouldn't shoot her, but she *would* leave Asa behind. It didn't matter. Ty was in trouble, and Asa knew what she had to do.

In the silence, they could hear each other's tense breaths, the hum of the ventilation systems, distant alarms—

And the ear-splitting *crack* of Asa's stun-bolt, hitting Morphett and Ty.

Ty gasped from the shocks. Morphett staggered sideways, letting him go, as Riven seized the distraction to send a bullet tearing into Morphett's shoulder.

In an instant, everything shifted.

Morphett's pistol whipped toward Riven and returned fire. Riven dove beneath the bullet and yanked Deathknell to his feet in a headlock. Samir grabbed Ty's arm to stop him from collapsing.

And Morphett's hawk gaze snapped to Asa. Her resolve crumbled before she could fire another stun-shot. The thought of Morphett's bloody blades brought a prey instinct to life, screaming at her to *RUN. NOW.*

Asa's feet pounded against the docking ramp, between the cargo crates, past docked ships. She had to lose Morphett. If she could hit Morphett with another few stun-shots—stall her long enough to board the *Adversary* before the ship left—

Morphett was quick at her heels. Asa barely had time to glance at her control board. She tapped the screen to call the drone. She just needed enough distance to line up a shot.

Morphett's footsteps receded, and Asa paused, panting, beneath a low-slung ship wing. Then, from the other direction came the muffled *tromp-tromp-tromp* of multiple sets of footsteps. Someone else had arrived.

No. It was the worst possible complication—

"Drop your weapons," commanded an unfamiliar voice through a helmet speaker. A group of flashlights ghosted forward, the beams shuddering as their owners ran. A platoon of nearly a dozen enforcers, clad in purple-and-gold body armor and winged helmets, ran toward the *Adversary*. The three at the front lifted their rifles.

The Duchess's enforcers. The crew was doomed.

Asa peeked from behind the wing. They hadn't spotted her yet. But where was Morphett? A second ago she was—

Strong, nimble hands jerked Asa backward, pulling her to her feet. Morphett winched a skinny arm around Asa's neck. Asa gasped, struggling, as the datapad fell from her hands.

"Be a good girl and come along." Blood seeped from Morphett's shoulder where Riven's bullet had clipped her. "I don't want to have to explain bruises to your dad."

"You are *not* taking me back." Asa kicked at Morphett's shins. But fighting Morphett was like fighting a tiny armed bruttore. Or a very angry mech.

"These thieves are trying to steal the *Adversary*!" Deathknell shouted across the bay. "Take them all! But get Morphett Slade first!"

"I. Saved. His. *Ass*," Morphett muttered. "Let's move, Deadweight. We've got a ship to catch."

Asa bit Morphett's wrist and instantly regretted it. The metal beneath the skin was hard on her teeth, and a line of bitter surgical steel ran the length of Morphett's forearm. Still, Morphett recoiled in pain and smacked Asa on the back of the head.

Maybe biting a cyborg hadn't been a great idea.

"Here they are!" shouted an enforcer.

The enforcers clustered between the ships, blocking their path to the *Adversary*. Riven and her crew were leaving, with or without her.

"Guess I need to cut us a path." Morphett let go of Asa as her blue holo-shield materialized over her body. She approached the enforcers, grinning like a monster. Against their rifle lights, she was silhouetted, holding up her hands.

Deathknell laughed through his groans. "You'll regret crossing me, Morphett Slade."

But Morphett wasn't surrendering.

The flesh on Morphett's forearms split, and two carbon-fiber blades unfolded and locked into place. Her shield flashed over her body. Then she rushed the enforcers, her blades piercing their body armor and biting one man's throat in a gush of red.

With her cybernetics unleashed, Morphett was a machine, the bullets breaking on her shield. Her pink-and-black sneakers skidded as she leapt between the enforcers.

"We've got a path!" Morphett shouted. "Let's go, Dead-weight!"

Not with you. Asa had a chance to run. She grabbed her datapad—just as pain jolted through her from a stun-shot. She tried standing, but a rifle muzzle prodded her neck.

"Don't move," rasped a voice through a rebreather helmet.

"I'm not one of the thieves!" Asa pleaded, holding up her empty hands. "I swear!"

She'd never been one of them, and never would be. They weren't coming to save her.

Behind her was the *swoosh* of the bay door opening, and a dozen more footsteps tromped in. Morphett looked in horror at the enforcers emerging. She'd taken down most of the first squadron, but her shield was beginning to fizzle.

That was the problem with cybernetics—once their batteries were dead, they'd pull energy from your body. Morphett seemed to know she was outmatched.

As the soldiers charged past Asa, Morphett swore and

hurled a smoke grenade. Clouds of purple bloomed around her, thick and opaque as fire-extinguisher foam. Asa glimpsed Morphett slipping into the dark. Two of the enforcers charged after her, but with no body armor or heavy rifles, she was quicker.

The enforcers pulled Asa to her feet. As the smoke cleared, she saw the *Adversary*'s headlights flicker on. Her heart sank. None of them had come back for her. Not even Ty.

All because she'd lied.

Asa squeezed her eyes shut as cold steel handcuffs clicked over her wrists. She'd lost Kaya. The best she could hope for now was the Duchess collecting her bounty and sending her home.

It felt like a death sentence.

INCORRECT CODE, read the *Adversary*'s control panel when Riven entered Skullface's ignition codes.

He chuckled, despite Riven's death-grip headlock on him. "Like I said, that code will no longer work."

Riven grabbed his head and shoved his cheek against the control board, smearing the blue paint onto the screen.

"Tell us new codes. *Now*." She nudged his chin with *Verdugo*.

They were so close, holed up in the *Adversary*'s cockpit as the Duchess's forces arrived. All they had to do was get the ship off the ground. Preferably without Little Miss *Project Winterdark* Engineer. Dammit, she'd started liking the girl too. But they could save Requiem without her.

But, conveniently, Skullface had changed his codes while Morphett stalled them.

Riven's heart pounded in time with the commotion outside, her nerves prickling unsteadily. It would be a hell of a time for a white noise flare-up. Outside, Morphett plowed through the enforcers, which bought them some time, but it wouldn't last forever.

"We should go back for Tripp," Ty said. "Who knows what they'll do to her?"

"The same thing they'll do to us if we don't leave." Riven would've gone back for her, if *Asanna* weren't a liar. If she hadn't helped with her father's murders. Samir still had the biocapsule–when they reached Earth, they could tell that Josiah guy she hadn't made it.

And Riven could still claim some of the credit for saving this hellhole.

"Ty." Riven eyed Skullface's destroyed fingers. "You got any tools that can make him hurt more?"

Ty's eyes widened. "What? *No.*"

"All I have to do is wait," Skullface said. "My friends are here, and you–"

Riven grabbed Skullface's collar and smacked his face against the screen again. "Enter the code." She cocked *Verdugo*, pressing its muzzle to his crotch. "I might not kill you, but I can sure as hell wreck your favorite body part before your reinforcements get here."

He gave a strained gasp. He was wearing down. Good.

"They're here." Samir peered out the door with his rifle drawn. "I'd say we have a good seven seconds."

A taut, authoritative voice blared through a helmet speaker—one of the enforcers. "Come out with your hands in the air, and we won't shoot."

"Dammit," Ty said. "We're done for."

Riven let go of Skullface, drawing *Blackjack*. "Not if we shoot fast enough."

"We are *not* shooting our way out of this." Samir set his rifle down. "Do you hear me, Riv? They will *kill* us."

Kill us. Riven's heartbeat was unsteady, and that familiar numbing prickle was creeping through her nerves. "Then let them. Better to go out fighting than rotting in the Duchess's dungeon." She trained both revolvers on the door. If she died here, she wasn't dying a coward.

"And you want Ty to die here with you?" Samir said.

Riven hesitated. "You can surrender. But I'd rather die on my own terms."

And if she went out in a blaze of gunfire, the others might have a chance. She braced herself for the first purple-and-gold helmet to appear, even as black spots swam across her vision.

But the sickness was flaring brighter, her stress stoking it like lighter fluid. *Not now*, she demanded. Not when she had shots to make.

Enforcers stomped up the steel docking ramp. The ringing in her ears rose to a crescendo, drowning them out, and the ground swayed violently beneath her.

The next she knew, she was staggering, catching herself against the wall, hurling curses like the bullets she couldn't shoot as her guns clattered to the ground. *Verdugo* gleamed at her feet, and she reached for it with a shaking hand. Heat flared from her spine, through her chest, and spread to her fingertips.

Before she could grab it, steady hands slid beneath her arms, pulling her upright. "Riven." A slender arm braced her waist.

"Get the hell off me. I need my guns."

"No." Ty kicked *Verdugo* aside. "We're surrendering."

Riven struggled in his grip. Normally she'd be able to shake Ty off in a heartbeat, but the dizziness was sucking her under, determined to drown her. "I can't. *Let go.*"

"No." Determination flashed in his blue eyes, fiercer than she'd seen them. "If you die here . . . I won't be able to save you."

"Ty . . ."

"I'm going to give you more time. I promise."

And as Ty stared into the barrels of the enforcers' rifles, his free hand raised in surrender, Riven almost forgave him.

Almost.

Part III:
THE DEAD
OF NIGHT

chapter 18
THE DUCHESS

"We are boned," Ty whined from the corner of the cell. "So boned."

"Will she give us a trial?" Tripp—*Asanna*—said from the cell next to Riven's. "Or at least hear us out?"

Riven glared at her through the bars. If she weren't covered in clammy sweat and still trembling from the near-blackout, she'd reach through and throttle the girl. It was Asanna's fault they were locked in the Duchess's dungeons—some sick fairy-tale interpretation of a medieval prison, with brick walls and wooden benches. All because of Asanna's stupid biocapsule, and the lies that came with it.

"I'm guessing you haven't heard much about the Duchess." Samir leaned against the cell wall behind Asanna, just outside the reddish laser-diode glow of a false torch.

"But why would they take us unharmed if they intended to kill us?" Asanna's full lips pursed, like they always did when she was sketching a strategy. A few hours ago, before Riven had known Tripp was her enemy, she would've let her eyes linger. Now, the simple gesture was infuriating.

"They could do a lot worse than execution by firing squad," Samir said. "Maybe they want answers."

"There has to be something we can offer," Asanna said.

Riven staggered to her feet and braced herself against the

bars, glaring down at Asanna. "The rest of us don't have a rich dad who's going to pay our ransom. Do you know what kind of trouble we're in? Not you—*us*? Because you lied to us and dragged us into some sick plot of Almeida's?"

"This wasn't for my dad!" Asanna said. "Everything I told you was true except my name."

"I don't believe you." Somehow, in a sick turn of fate, she'd taken a job for the daughter of Emmett's killer. "You said you'd never heard of Sanctum's Edge."

She's just a dumb little rich girl. Bored of life in her pretty Corte mansion. How much of her story had Asanna lied about? What if she'd planted info for Diego, and that capsule couldn't help them save Requiem? She'd played Riven for a fool.

And not only did Riven look stupid for believing her, but the whole crew might die for it.

"I hadn't!" Asanna said. "My dad keeps secrets from me too."

"You're lucky there's bars between us," Riven seethed.

"Riven, back off," Ty warned.

She whirled to face him. "You're still defending her? For someone so smart, you let your hormones do an awful lot of your thinking."

"I'm not defending her." Ty crossed his arms over his bare chest, his hair and arms coated in dried slug slime. The slice Morphett had carved on his breastbone was dark with dried blood. "She messed up, and she owes us an explanation."

"And you still owe me an explanation," Riven said. He'd held her back, stopped her from shooting her way out. That stung. "Why couldn't you have just let me be? I could've gotten us out

of there. Or I could be asleep somewhere among the stars instead of waiting to die in this godforsaken cell!"

"You think that's what Emmett would've wanted?" he said
softly.

"I promised Emmett I'd keep *you* safe. Not the other way
around."

Samir stepped toward the bars. Some of his stiff-gelled locks
of dark hair had collapsed, hanging into his eyes. "And can you
keep Ty safe if you're dead?"

"Shut up, Samir."

Ty peeled dried slime off his arms. He wouldn't look at her.

"Shooting our way out would've been suicide, Riv," Samir
said. "That was for your own good."

"For my own good? And why is that *your* decision?"

Her crew was teaming up against her. *Boomslang* was still
quarantined. *Verdugo* and *Blackjack* had been taken, along with
her wristlet—her link to Galateo. This was as bad as it got.

All because she'd taken a job for some doe-eyed runaway.

It was quiet between the two cells, except for the creaking
of pipes and the tap of approaching footsteps.

"I didn't lie about her, you know." Hugging her knees in the
fitted fade-suit, Asanna looked small. "It really was for my sister. Project Winterdark hurt her too."

Another Almeida girl. Riven wanted to scoff, but something
dark began dawning on her. "You expect us to believe Almeida
experimented on his own daughter?"

Asanna looked up at her. "Do you really think he's above
something so terrible?"

Riven recognized the look in her eyes—the terror-filled, sleepless nights that replayed horrible memories on loop, the guilt and desperation. Maybe Asanna was telling the truth. Luca Almeida didn't value anyone's life where his experiments were concerned—not even his own daughter's.

Riven's head was still pounding.

Ty's eyes widened, and he pointed at Riven. "Riv, your—" He tapped his right ear.

She touched her ear and brought her fingers away slick with blood. Her episode had been worse than expected. Ty kept telling her that her stress could influence how bad the white noise flared. She took a calming breath, focusing on thoughts of sprawling starfields and mentally tabulating *Boomslang*'s cockpit controls.

Whatever happened here, she needed to maintain *some* dignity.

"I barely did anything for that project," Asanna said. "He only let me tinker with the cybernetic sensor systems. Then he put my name on the project so I'd have a reputation before becoming his heir. Trust me, I had no idea what else he'd done with Winterdark."

"I don't want to hear it," Riven said hoarsely, as her throat constricted like a sudden sorrow. "Unless you're planning to lie our way out of this."

Asanna opened her mouth to protest, then clenched her jaw.

A high-pitched beeping came from above Asanna and Samir's cell door. The holographic image of a grommeted steel door disappeared, revealing a transparent panel. An enforcer in purple-and-gold armor stood at the other side, rifle in hand.

Riven instinctively groped for her revolvers. The power-lessness overtook her again when she found empty holsters.

"The Duchess requests to see you all. Personally," the enforcer said through the speaker. "And immediately."

Asa's bladder seemed to shrink two sizes when she was nervous.

She couldn't decide whether to focus on the Duchess's impending wrath, or how much she had to *pee*. Both made her miserable.

And both were a little better than remembering the betrayal on Riven's face. She wished she had even one friend right now, heading into a trial that would doubtless end badly.

Asa was at the back of the group, hands shackled behind her. An enforcer kept nudging her in the back with the muzzle of his gun. She stumbled, keeping her chin up and trying to match Samir and Riven's pace.

"At least it doesn't look like a chophouse," Ty whispered. The palace seemed both austere and fragile, all sinuous golden statues and hanging lattices of red gems. Every inch of the palace—from the crystal flowers and glass-tiled floors to the mahogany cornices on the ceilings—was crafted in painstaking detail.

Asa glanced into a ballroom as they walked by. A massive golden hawk guarded the far end, its wings outstretched and talons raised.

"Yeah. Looks like Versailles before the guillotines came out," Samir said.

"Quiet," an enforcer barked. "I don't get paid to listen to this tripe."

The house of criminal royalty, passed between bloody hands. Asa wondered what this place had originally been, during Requiem's tourist-trap days. Now, its underworld fought ruthlessly for control of these halls.

She only hoped their current owner might be feeling merciful today.

The enforcers stopped them in front of a tall wooden door. The panels dilated apart from the center, revealing a narrow two-story ballroom. With its glass walls and the city sprawling like a garden of glowing flowers below, the room felt suspended.

The marble floors shone in the planetlight and city haze, and two rows of pillars stretched to the other end, where a fire roared behind a winged golden throne. Atop the throne sat a woman's silhouette. Asa swallowed the hard lump in her throat.

As they approached, the Duchess came into view. She was beautiful, her black hair pulled into a chignon, with gold threaded through it like a crown. Sweeping layers of ruffled purple silk covered her, down to the embroidered suede of her white boots.

The Duchess uncrossed her legs and rested her hands on the arms of the throne. It was made of golden seraphs, a cluster of tangled limbs and wings, holding her reverently aloft. Like Deathknell's throne, the massive wings fluttered soundlessly. Above the Duchess's head hovered a glowing red sphere, orbited by rune-engraved rings.

The Duchess lifted her chin as they approached, her eyes dark and severe in the firelight. Requiem's leader was as breathtaking and intimidating as the city itself.

"Kneel," an enforcer hissed through his rebreather.

Asa immediately did as she was told. The others followed suit, though Riven stared at the Duchess for one last defiant second before she complied.

"Breaking and entering. Destruction of my patrol drones. Attempted theft," the Duchess said, her voice smooth as honey. The roaring fireplace gave an eerie cast to the vacant, vengeful eyes of the seraphs. "As for your sentence . . . the Code of Nocturne provides me a few options."

Asa's bladder constricted again.

The hall doors grated open behind them. Asa stole a glance over her shoulder as two enforcers shoved a handcuffed Diego to his knees.

"Ah." The Duchess laced her white-gloved fingers. "There's your fifth. Took a while to track this one down."

"Diego," Samir breathed, somewhere between relieved and angry. "And . . . that's my dog!"

A tall enforcer approached, holding Zephyr in his arms. The golden pup pawed at his helmet, licking the visor. The enforcer's chuckling was muffled.

"Won't have an owner much longer." The enforcer scratched Zephyr's head. "I think I'll keep him."

Samir muttered a string of expletives.

The Duchess rose and sauntered toward them, wraps of silk trailing behind her. The silence was punctuated by the snap of embers and the somber clack of her heels.

She stopped beside Ty, who was still half-dressed, his hair matted with purple. "I'll admit," she said, looking down her sharp nose at him, "the only thing I have yet to learn is why you're covered in *glühschnecke* slime."

Ty shifted uncomfortably in his shackles.

The Duchess tapped her earpiece, and a holopanel appeared in front of her right eye. "Tyren O'Shea. Formerly a first-rate medical student at a second-rate academy. Was it *your* distaste for violence that made this whole heist a bloodless one? Because of your brother?"

Ty looked away, shivering. Despite the slime caked onto his bare arms, Asa would've wrapped her arms around him. He'd spared a few lives today, and now he might lose his own.

"A shame you lost him at Sanctum's Edge. But at least he found you a crew, hmm?" The Duchess strode down the line, to Riven. She swiped the holopanel to the side, bringing up another file with Riven's face at the top. "Riven Hawthorne. I should've known we'd cross paths someday—as allies, or as enemies."

Riven lifted her chin, baring her teeth in a grin. "I'd shake your hand, but . . ." She shrugged, and her shackled wrists clinked behind her back. "You know."

"Those are to keep your thieving hands in check. The *Adversary* is far from the best ship you could've chosen to steal. But perhaps any ship is better than that junk heap you call *Boomslang*."

Riven seethed silently. She never broke eye contact with the Duchess, brandishing her meteoric confidence. When her time came, Riven would probably insult Death itself and challenge it to a duel.

"You had a full scholarship to Central Atlantic Academy on Earth, but you were expelled after two years for failing your written exams. What a waste. Records show you can snipe a target from one-point-two miles off."

"On a bad day, maybe," Riven said.

"Were you expelled from CAA before or after your caregivers forced you out of your foster facility?"

Riven glared. "Leaving was my choice. They hated me long before I got expelled."

The Duchess's expression softened for a half second. "One too many beatings?"

Riven finally broke eye contact. Asa suddenly felt guilty for where she'd grown up. For all her father had done, he'd never laid a finger on Asa.

The Duchess turned on her heel and moved down the line. Asa stilled her breaths. She was at the end of the row, so maybe she'd be last. What would the Duchess make of her heritage, and her bounty?

"In your first year," the Duchess said to Riven, "your fourth-year mentor was . . ." She stopped before Samir. "Samir Al Ghadani."

Samir gave a slow, reverent nod. From the way Asa had seen him and Riven fight together, it made sense.

"Hmm." The Duchess leaned closer, her eyes fixed on the rolled-up sleeves of his dress shirt. "Seems you've been a smear on your family's legacy of military leadership. You were on track to become a Federation officer . . . but you were expelled after the death of a squadmate."

Samir stared at the floor. "Nasty accident."

"And now you follow the command of a girl who failed out of your academy."

"Not her *command*. I only listen when her plans are halfway reasonable."

"Reasonable, is it?" She smirked. "Well, it seems you've settled in nicely on Requiem. It's a seductive place, no?"

"Certainly more interesting than the life my parents wanted for me." He shrugged. "You know the quote 'when all the world has burnt, even the ashes feel like home'?"

The Duchess laughed, a high, feminine sound that echoed between the empty arches. "Vashti Chabra's *Horizon Aflame*. Mid twenty-first century, no? It truly is a shame you're not interested in women, Samir. Few men here have both military training *and* knowledge of Phase I Earth literature."

Discomfort flickered across Samir's face. The Duchess moved to Diego.

"Diego Valdez. I'll admit, my sources don't have much information about you. But you're a member of Boneshiver—Matriarch Cerys's pet, I hear. At first I was baffled why you'd be involved with this little heist. But then . . ." She nodded toward Samir. "I suppose I know your weakness now."

Diego kept his eyes low as the Duchess approached Asa. Asa's ears rang, and her lungs felt like they were filling with oil. She was the odd one out. The one the Duchess could sell.

The Duchess stopped in front of Asa, her plum-colored lips parting to reveal teeth white as starlight. "And, most curious of all . . . Asanna Almeida. Heiress to the Almeida fortune and corporation."

Asa took in a deep breath that smelled of woodsmoke and candy sweetness. Would the Duchess use her as ransom?

"Now *there's* a different world. Almeida's older daughter isn't in the public eye much, but the younger . . . you're a world-class mechanist, despite only having completed two years at Cortellion's premier automation academy. Even credited as a lead engineer on Project Winterdark."

Asa didn't dare look at Riven. That wound was still fresh. "I didn't know—" Well, she'd known *something*. Years ago, her father had shooed her away from some lab subjects he'd con-tracted—Requiem glitch addicts testing the early brain-jacks, their movements mechanical, their voices slurring. *They know what they signed up for,* he'd said when Asa had confronted him. *To make their minds better.*

She'd thought little of it at the time—so Kaya and Riven's crew had paid the price. But Asa couldn't have stopped him, even if she'd known.

Could she?

From down the row, Ty's blue eyes locked onto her, and Asa couldn't meet them. She'd betrayed him before they'd even met.

"It wasn't my fault," she said, more to Ty than the Duchess.

"Doesn't matter. You *helped.*" Riven struggled against her bonds, but the enforcer shoved her forward, her cheek smack-ing against the floor.

The Duchess settled back onto her throne, curling like a snake about to strike. "Quit squabbling." Her eyes snapped to Asa. "We're here to talk about how you tried to steal my ship." She lifted a teacup and saucer from beside the throne and blew on the steaming surface. "And, as for why you'd go through the trouble . . . my curiosity is *very* much piqued. I want to hear the story from you."

"Didn't you have at least six witnesses and a few camera feeds?" Riven said.

The Duchess smiled into her teacup. "I want to know *why*. My city is falling apart, and I have a weakness for a good story."

Samir fidgeted in his cuffs. "How about you start, *Asanna Almeida*?"

Asa's breath caught. It *had* started with her. The Duchess regarded her with a hunter's gaze, a cat humoring a mouse. Right now, lying would only make things worse.

So Asa told the truth. The whole thing.

Samir picked up the story where she faltered, filling in the gaps like a seasoned public speaker. The Duchess never interjected, watching them with an expression of slight amusement.

"You managed to shut down my security systems and kill none of my soldiers. The whole stint was, admittedly, impressive." The Duchess sipped her tea, thinking. "But since you attempted to steal from me . . . the Code of Nocturne dictates I must also take something from you."

From behind the throne, a plump man in a surgical smock circled in front of the Duchess, looking over the crew like they were a crop of fresh cadavers.

"At least you're worth something this way," the Duchess said. "The fighting pits are a little more . . . indelicate."

Asa wanted to vomit. She'd known about the high price of human organs on Cortellion, for lab studies and fixing diseased organs from the newly terraformed atmosphere. Did most of that market stem from Requiem—from living hosts, like her friends?

"Wait." If there was ever a time to use her father as leverage, it was now. "You can't—"

"Except that one." The Duchess pointed to her. "Almeida's two-million-denar bounty requires her in one piece."

"*Two million?*" Asa choked. No. Even if the crew hated her, she couldn't watch them take the fall. They hadn't hurt anyone. "If you spare them, I'll have him make it three million. I swear!"

The surgeon unfolded a stretcher from the wall and twisted a needle onto a syringe's tip. Ty let out a soft gasp, his bare chest shaking. Riven's glare was cracking into something like fear.

"As for the rest of you, I'm willing to hear one last argument. I know what you're worth to me dead." The Duchess stared at Riven, bored. "Even you, Hawthorne, despite the rumors. So what are you worth to me alive?"

"Even a two-million-denar bounty can't lift a Federation quarantine, can it?" Diego's voice reverberated through the arches, louder than Asa had expected he could be.

The Duchess's gaze snapped to him, fierce enough that Asa wanted to shrink.

"That's right." Diego stood up, locking his brown eyes with the Duchess's. He twisted sideways in his cuffs, tugging his glove down to reveal a steel-and-silicon forearm. Beneath his arm's transparent shell and silvery tendons, a circuit board glinted green. So that was where Diego kept his database.

"I got the news twenty minutes ago," Diego said. "Heaven's Breach is closed even to you, now, huh? The Federation high command is rooting out the matriarchs' underworld contacts.

Even yours. Some Fed member nations are pushing for more control of Requiem—hoping to gain more power over the salirium reserve. There's a real chance of a complete Federation take-over under the guise of public safety. And every hour, they're closing in more."

Asa shuddered. Requiem's independence was tenuous, at best—any of the interstellar powers attempting to seize the salirium reserve would lead to conflict with the others, maybe even war.

And now, there were no ships off. They were truly impris-oned here. But did Diego have a plan?

"We were trying to save this godforsaken city," Samir said, "because you have bigger problems than ship thieves."

"I understand that," the Duchess snapped. "And if you have a solution, you have thirty seconds to explain it."

"I invoke the Article of Conscription." Diego said. "Spare us in exchange for our service."

"That Article requires you have something to offer me. Something I don't already have."

Diego squared his shoulders. "And if I know who has the quarantine override codes?"

The Duchess was quiet, crossing her legs.

Diego continued. "Let's say—hypothetically—that one of the other matriarchs is shacking up with the Federation behind your back. This matriarch thinks if the Federation takes over, she'll become the new Duchess. And one of her strongholds happens to have the Federation's override passcodes that allow her ships in and out. I think we all agree that this scenario could *drasti-cally* shift the balance of power in Requiem, no?"

The Duchess lifted her chin, as if readying to strike Diego down on the spot. "And you really think this information is worth your lives?"

"Not just information. A crew. With all the identiscans and surveillance in the place you'd need to retrieve the codes . . . your operatives would be recognized instantly."

Identiscans. Surveillance. What kind of place was Diego talking about?

"I have operatives that even Boneshiver is unaware of, Diego Valdez."

"I'm sure you do. But nobody evades detection in this place. Your operatives would be scrutinized, and you'd be compromising their covert status, permanently." Diego never flinched, his voice velvet calm. Damn, he was good at this. "Unless you used a crew of outsiders. A crew who already owes you something."

"And how do I know this crew wouldn't fail?"

Riven cracked a grin. "Because it's one of the best damn crews on Requiem. And you're going to help us."

A smile quirked the Duchess's full lips. "A bold argument."

Diego sunk into a bow. "*Boomslang*'s crew is at your service, Duchess Reyala."

The Duchess was quiet, considering. "You're correct about Banshee. It's unlike anything my best people have ever seen. The Federation doesn't have a plan to defeat it either—but they *will* seize the opportunity to bring my city under their control." She set the teacup down, and tea sloshed over its edge. "During its first few years, Requiem suffered as a mining colony under Federation control. The workers had no rights until they took them by force. And if the Federation gets the city back . . ."

With a flick of the Duchess's wrist, a pedestal rose from the floor, with the biocapsule atop it. Asa's heart accelerated. It was safe. She still had a chance of getting Kaya back.

"I have contacts from Earth who need to get in . . ." The Duchess inclined her head, looking straight at Asa. ". . . and if this Josiah Herron truly can help us, this biocapsule needs to get *out*."

Asa nodded as determination rekindled behind her ribs. "We'll do whatever it takes." As usual, she was in over her head. She'd be dropped into the incinerator again—this time, at the behest of the most powerful woman in Requiem.

"We could very well have ourselves a bargain, Valdez," the Duchess said. "Of course, my advisors would need details from you about the matriarch in question. To help you plan . . . and to verify."

"Fine by me." Diego flexed his cybernetic fingers.

Asa stole a glance at Ty, whose shoulders went slack with relief. He shivered in the cool draft.

"Now." The Duchess waved them away. "If my intel confirms your information, I'll summon the five of you and provide your equipment." With a tap of the Duchess's fingers, Asa felt her shackles release. "You have a few hours while we put this together. If all goes well, one of my attendants will brief you on the assignment.

"But, before you leave—" The Duchess nodded to the enforcers, and they formed up in front of the door, blocking it. The surgeon was mounting thick needles on a tray. The bile rose in Asa's throat again.

"Stay calm. They're only trackers," the Duchess said.

"You don't trust us?" Samir said.

"I trust your capabilities." Those golden wings fanned out behind the Duchess. "But I like to have a bit of extra . . . insurance."

As the surgeon loaded a pill-sized tracker in the injector, the last thing Asa wanted was to disappoint the Duchess.

"And Fitzwilliam?" the Duchess said to an enforcer by the door. "Please bring our friend Tyren a sweater."

Asa had never expected to finish the day as a hired criminal.

But here she was, escorted down a mirrored hallway by an attendant clad in purple-and-gold robes, the servant of an underworld queenpin. Instead of a pawn in her father's aspirations, she was a pawn in a syndicate war. And her allies probably hated her.

"A map of the guest wing has been loaded onto your wristlets," the attendant said. "The stylist will see you at 19:30 in the fourth-floor atrium. Then you'll be given an official briefing and assignment. Until then, shower or sleep or whatever you need."

"A stylist?" Asa rubbed the new lump at the back of her neck. The tracker itched. She had a feeling it'd let the Duchess do more than just locate them. "What for?"

He pursed his gold-painted lips, glancing disdainfully over her rumpled fade-suit. "For Olympus, of course. You'll need it."

Asa didn't ask what Olympus was, but she didn't argue. The fade-suit was getting sweaty. She'd never worn the same clothes for days on end, and she might be self-conscious if she weren't so exhausted.

The plan sounded dubious, and they wouldn't learn it for

another three and a half hours. But it was a second chance to save Kaya, and if Asa had to hold herself together for a bit longer, so be it.

"Diego saved our asses in there," Ty whispered once the attendant was out of earshot. "I didn't think I'd be leaving with all my guts intact." He held an oversized sea-blue sweater. "Though maybe the Duchess is kind of nice."

"As long as we're useful, she will be," Samir muttered. "We're also expendable. If anything goes wrong, she's not going to bail us out."

"Well, she knows our reputation." Riven stared down the hallway, frowning to herself. "I just don't understand why she thinks that reputation includes *Asanna*."

"You don't have to talk like I'm not here." The reminder she wasn't one of them stung. Even if they were helping her right now, it was because they didn't have a choice. "And I go by Asa."

"Asa has proven what she can do," Samir said. "And she has a stake in this."

"A stake in this?" Riven said. "Like she had a stake in Project Winterdark? She didn't think it was a big deal when her freak of a father was experimenting on other people. Seems her *sister* is the only person who matters."

"I couldn't have stopped him." Asa's heart turned leaden. She wondered if that was a lie too. "Even if I'd known."

Riven waved her excuse away. "Whatever. Our reputation's on the line right now. We're doing a job for the *Duchess of Requiem*. And if there really is another matriarch plotting against her, the Duchess could be replacing her soon."

"Replacing a matriarch? With . . . you?"

"Right. I intend to be as close to the top of that pyramid as possible." The torn-metal grit in Riven's voice implied it was more than a passing desire. This was important to her. "So I don't care what happens to your sister, but you'd better not screw this up."

Riven strode away, her frayed braid swinging as she headed down the red-lit corridor to the training wing.

Asa huffed. Riven seemed determined to blame someone for Emmett's death. But maybe she was right. Asa should have told them the truth when they were fighting for her. This job wasn't going to be easy if they didn't trust her.

"I'm going with her," Samir said. "See if I can get her to cool off."

"I'll give you some space," Ty said. As Samir left, Asa and Ty were alone. Despite the nearness of him, her guilt separated them like a stone wall.

She had to say *something*, even if she couldn't make it up to Ty. She needed at least one person on her side when they left for this job.

"Ty. I want to talk."

His eyes flitted over her, cautious, as if she were a stranger. "You mind if I shower first?" An uncomfortable smile. "It's taking an embarrassing amount of mental energy to ignore all this grime."

"If you want to hate me, you can. Just hear me out first?"

"Whoa, I didn't say I hated you. But I was serious about the shower."

Her cheeks flushed at the thought of him washing himself. But she could wait. And she still had to pee. "I should too."

They walked to the bath hall, a cavernous marble room with soaring buttressed ceilings and golden faucet taps. Ivy crept up trellises separating the communal tubs and private shower areas. Asa found a private bathroom, shucked off the fade-suit, and scrubbed under the shower's scalding water as if she could burn away all the guilt. Her first shower since leaving home.

She'd never been able to stand up to her father. The crew would understand that, right? Ty might, at least. But she'd probably live longer if she never spoke to Riven again.

Asa found a spare set of purple-and-gold sweats from the towel racks and slipped into the gardens outside the bath hall. Beneath the starry skylights and fairy orbs strung between the topiaries, she found Ty.

"Let's walk. I think we have a lot to discuss." He wore similar sweats, with loose-fitting pants and a tight T-shirt, and his ginger-blond hair was tousled and damp. All traces of slug slime had been scoured off his toned arms. Asa fought the urge to smooth her messy, half-dried hair into place.

She fell into step beside him, weaving among the maze of atherblossom trees. The sweet, musky scent reminded her of home.

"So. Asanna Almeida. In the flesh." A translucent holoscreen appeared above his wristlet, playing a vidclip of the tech-show a few days ago. Asa onstage, prim and confident in her red dress beneath the spotlights and camera flashes. "Hiding in plain sight on Requiem. You must be pretty hard to miss on Cortellion, with all this footage out there." Ty gave her a heart-shattering smirk. He didn't look angry, but he kept more distance than before. As if testing her.

"Not really. You'd be surprised how often people miss someone they aren't looking for. Kaya and I snuck out of the house whenever we got the chance, but we've only been recognized once."

He laughed. "I guess that makes sense. You blend in pretty well without the swarm of cameras. Reminds me of the story about Screaming Deadbolt's lead singer, who stood under a full-size holoscreen ad featuring a picture of her . . . and nobody on the street recognized her." The hedges grew thicker, denser, as they walked. With night creeping over the pergolas, their only companions were shadows lurking in the gardens. "And you've never struck me as an heiress. I mean, you seem . . ." He gave a noncommittal shrug.

Asa frowned. "What? You can say it."

"Normal, I guess. You're not . . . pretentious. And you can hold your own."

Not pretentious wasn't a high compliment. "Well. Glad I've made such a great impression." An uneasy silence hung between them. The chirps of unfamiliar insects emanated from the hanging vines, and a flaming bronze brazier guttered in a clearing ahead.

No doubt Ty was still thinking about Project Winterdark. She had to say *something*. "I rarely had a choice but to do whatever my dad wanted. I was . . . an extension of his aspirations. Most of the time, I didn't know how he was using the tech I built for him."

"So you *did* work on Sanctum's Edge."

"I hadn't heard of it before coming here. But maybe I did."

"Here's a question, then." Blue eyes met hers, hesitant but calculating. "Would you have left earlier, if you'd known?"

CITY of SHATTERED LIGHT

Her heart sank. It wasn't a fair question. Her father used people like objects, but they'd usually consented. It had taken everything in her to defy him after what he did to Kaya. "It's over. Does it matter now?"

"I guess not." They'd reached the brazier clearing, and he settled onto the bench in front of the fire, nodding to the empty space next to him. "With everything you had on Corte . . . you really gave up a lot for her, didn't you?"

A tentative, dizzying warmth began to melt the edges of the shield she'd hidden behind for the past few days. She sat down next to him, and somehow, the stories poured out—Kaya bringing her snacks as Asa built a cherry-red speeder in the garage; looping the cameras in the estate's surveillance system to sneak out past curfew; programming AbyssQuest together well into the night.

Ty stared into the crackling flame with a quiet, faraway fondness. She wondered if he had similar memories of Emmett. "AbyssQuest, huh?"

Asa bit back a smile, remembering the elf rogue character Kaya had created—based on one of her favorites from another game. For a single, stupid second, Asa almost told Ty he looked like him. But she'd forever be known as the Girl Who Had Crushes on Fictional Elves, so she kept her mouth shut.

"She sounds like a great person." Ty set his hand dangerously close to Asa's thigh. Something electric shot through her. "And I hope I get to meet her. But I wish . . ."

The inches between them suddenly felt like miles. Asa knew exactly what he was thinking, the rift keeping them apart.

"I wish you'd told us earlier," he said. "I get not wanting to announce your name when you've got a two-million-denar bounty on you, but we trusted you. And we were risking a lot for you."

The warmth from his nearness faded like smoke. "I know. But after what happened to Emmett . . . you would've left me behind if you'd known."

"I don't think I would've." He sighed. "Look, Asa. Even if you didn't know . . . it's going to take me a while to process this. And it might be hard, especially for Riven."

Riven. Remembering Riven's anger brought the guilt creeping back. Was it ridiculous to have wished for Riven to admire her, the way she'd been admiring Riven? Between Ty's disappointment and Riven's anger . . .

"I know it might be hard," Asa whispered. "And I understand."

Carefully, Ty leaned in, lacing his fingers with hers. "I'm sorry."

He shouldn't be the one apologizing.

Ty's wristlet beeped. He reluctantly pulled away, clearing his throat. "Oh. Our briefing's in five minutes." He took a hard breath, regaining his composure. "Time to make a great impression, huh?"

"I guess so." Her nerves about the mission were almost enough to take her mind off Ty and Riven.

It was time.

chapter 19

GLITTER & GREASE

"**T**his is a waste of time," Riven said as the stylist thrust a wad of glittery purple scraps toward her.

The stylist—who'd introduced themself as Bria—cocked a perfectly shaped eyebrow. "On the contrary. No job goes smoothly without proper outfitting." Bria was nearly as tall as Samir and wore a prim black pantsuit, subtle yet authoritative. Asa was immediately intimidated. "The only waste of time is you refusing to try things on."

Riven muttered under her breath and slipped into one of the changing pods.

Asa was still gawking at the stylist's collection in the atrium, with dozens of sliding and rotating racks commanded by Bria's datapad. The racks held a rainbow of colorful cloth—pleated, strappy, glowing, shimmery. The mirrored walls shattered the wardrobes into an infinite kaleidoscope.

"All right, heiress," Bria said. "You're next. Step over here for measurements."

"What do you have in mind?" Asa held out her arms as a machine's scanner flickered over her body's contours. The room smelled like an expensive brothel, all musky perfume and hairspray. A place that transformed people into dolls for display. The barely there outfits on the mannequins made her worry exactly where this mission was taking them.

And what they'd have to do to steal those codes.

"If all goes smoothly, you'll be able to take what you need without firing a gun." Bria's voice was husky. "You'll be entering Olympus nightclub. The plan is threefold—hacking a data terminal, stealing a key, and collecting the data from the Federation's suite in the VIP deck." They studied Asa's face, then swiped through a row of colorful leotards on their datapad. "So the five of you need to wear something functional, but modern. Something suited for a trip to Olympus during a Darkday."

"A *nightclub*?" Asa blurted.

"It's one of the main bases of Rio Oscuro—the syndicate best known for its smuggling operations. Diego gave us the details. Seems its matriarch's gone traitor." Bria gave a razor-sharp grin.

Samir slid his hands into his pockets, appraising the racks. "As long as tonight's plan involves you fitting me for one of those regency jackets, I'll do whatever you say."

Bria tapped the screen, and the racks shifted. A round rack lowered from the top of the stack, turning until a group of leotards sat in front of Bria. They grabbed a slashed red leotard with a tight collar and handed it to Asa, along with a pair of studded black shorts. "There. Try that."

Asa grimaced at the slits slashing over the leotard. "Is this all I'd be wearing?" It looked like her tech-demo ball gown had gotten stuck in a turbine and only the top had survived.

Maybe that was the point.

Bria flicked a finger toward the changing pods, eyes fixed on their datapad. Asa blushed and stepped into a pod. When she tried it on, the leotard hugged her like a glove full of holes, revealing skin through the glitter-edged slits on the sides. The shorts didn't add much coverage. Kaya might wear something like this in public, but Asa certainly wouldn't.

"Excuse me." Asa stepped out, tugging at the leotard. "It might be better if I had something with more coverage. If I'm going to be digging into any engines—"

"You'll be fine," Bria said. "We'll get you matching heatproof gloves. Otherwise . . . the outfit fits you perfectly."

"Seconded," Ty said as he entered one of the changing pods. He gave her a secret grin, and she instinctively fidgeted with her gloves.

Riven emerged from her pod and scowled into the trifold mirror. A tight pink crop vest exposed the bottoms of her full breasts. "Absolutely not."

Asa watched Riven attempt to pull the tiny shirt down. Why was Riven complaining? She looked good. Only when Riven shot her a confused look did Asa realize she was staring. She turned away, her entire face burning.

"I'm with Riven." Ty emerged from the pod and tugged at his shirt—if it could be called that. It was a tangle of silver belts crisscrossing his chest. "Isn't the goal to attract *less* attention?"

Bria smirked. "Depends on how you plan to get those codes."

"I'll just wear what I showed up in." Riven crossed her arms over her chest. "Slug slime or no."

"I think you're all forgetting how little say you have in

the matter. You've been given a *very* merciful bargain from Duchess Reyala tonight. You have a good chance of emerging from this mission alive."

"She's not using me for my tits," Riven snapped. "I can't focus if I'm thinking about them slipping out."

Asa didn't think *she'd* be able to focus either. She pushed the image of Riven out of her head, forcing her gaze toward a well-dressed mannequin. If she couldn't bring herself to confront Riven, she couldn't allow herself to daydream about her.

"Fine," Bria huffed, scrolling through their datapad. "As for what you'll be doing . . . Olympus has multiple levels—a main dance floor, a GravSphere arena, and VIP suites on the top floor they call the observatory. You'll need to get through a few layers of security before you can steal the quarantine codes from the Federation suite on the observatory deck."

"GravSpheres?" Ty said as Bria handed him a pressed black vest and a slim masquerade mask. "Don't they host gladiatorial death matches with Corte wildlife there?"

"After a certain time, yes. Before then, the layers are dance floors."

Asa didn't like the sound of that. She hoped the plan kept them far away from the gladiatorial shells.

"Can I take my guns?" Riven said. She'd taken them into Gnosis with no problem, terrifying as that was. Nobody on Corte carried guns, and it was safer that way.

"Olympus security usually allows handguns," a familiar voice said. "Shouldn't be an issue."

Diego approached behind Bria. He'd been outfitted already—his tight curls were sculpted into a fade, and he wore a high-collared, moss-green long overcoat with tarnished buckles.

"Ah. *There's* the one who's going to keep you all in line." Bria gave Diego a sidelong glance.

"Have to perform my solemn duty of keeping Samir from shooting himself in the foot."

"What's the matter?" Samir flashed Diego an incredulous grin. "Dee, are you *worried* about me?"

Diego suppressed a smile. "Don't get cocky."

"Too late." Samir pulled a night-blue jacket with silver epaulettes off a rack. "New goal is to see how many heart attacks I can give you tonight."

"Have you briefed them?" Diego said to Bria.

"I will as soon as they stop complaining about their outfits."

"Done complaining!" Ty burst from one of the pods, wearing a sleeveless black vest and a wire-frame mask forming a pattern across his cheekbones.

Bria grinned. "That's better."

Riven and Samir were fitted minutes later—Riven in a buckle-front bodice the color of the streaks in her hair, and a pair of carbon-plated electromagnetic boots with straps crisscrossing up her pants like garters. Samir wore similar boots and a sport jacket with epaulettes, and Bria painted lines of silver onto his cheek to mimic the cybernetic tattoos Asa had seen in the Crush.

"*Now* you look like a proper heiress." Bria touched up the black wings on Asa's eyeliner. They brushed and tousled Asa's chin-length hair until it shone, glossy and blue-black, in feathery layers.

Asa's reflection in the neon-framed mirror made her breath catch—red sweeps of eyeshadow, a small heart-shaped rhinestone under each eye. Her lips were plump and crimson, shining like speeder varnish.

Behind her, Riven snorted. "Didn't realize sex hair was the hallmark of a *proper heiress*."

Asa's mouth fell open, and she shot a glance over her shoulder. Riven leaned against a makeup cabinet, smirking. At least she didn't look as angry. Bria had scrubbed Riven's smudged eyeliner away, applying a clean black line to one eye and covering the other half of her face in a skull pattern of purple-and-black rhinestones. Riven had complained, noting the similarity to Deathknell, but Bria once again reminded her she didn't have a choice.

"One last touch." Bria placed a mask across Asa's cheekbones—delicate as copper wire, forming sweeping crimson lines that dipped beneath the rhinestones. The shimmer of the wires suggested it was a scrambler, designed to disrupt facial recognition tech. It didn't look terrible on her either.

"If our heiress is finished dolling up, are we ready?" Riven said.

"Ready as we'll ever be," Diego said. He and Bria led them to a meeting room off the atrium, with an arched ceiling lined in gold. On the table lay *Verdugo* and *Blackjack*, and Asa's EMP-fried wristlet. "Duchess Reyala said you could have these back."

Riven's eyes widened and she snatched the revolvers, eyeing the metal for scratches. When Asa tapped her wristlet, the screen turned on. Thank the stars for its hardened backup system.

Bria settled into one of the high-backed chairs, and they all followed suit. Bria looked dressed for a business meeting, and the rest of them . . . didn't. Asa felt ridiculous in the red nylon, even if it might help her blend in.

Bria tapped the buttons on the edge of the table, and the entire surface lit up as a map of Olympus. They shoved a vapor-stick between their teeth.

"Let's discuss the plan. And listen well, because if you fail . . ." Bria exhaled a cloud of vapor through their bloodred lips. "I'm sure you know Duchess Reyala will be *very* unhappy."

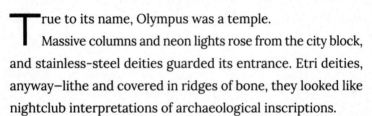

chapter 20
OLYMPUS

True to its name, Olympus was a temple.

Massive columns and neon lights rose from the city block, and stainless-steel deities guarded its entrance. Etri deities, anyway—lithe and covered in ridges of bone, they looked like nightclub interpretations of archaeological inscriptions.

Asa leaned closer to the dark-tinted window of the cruiser. Driving on the ground instead of the skyway, Requiem looked even bigger—tilted layers of storefronts and pedestrian tubes, with signs advertising noodle bars and clothing shops and smoking dens, the smog blurring the lights into a muggy rainbow.

She swallowed the lump in her throat. Leaving Kaya at the Duchess's palace had left a hard pit in her stomach. It felt like a hostage situation. If Asa didn't play her part, it was all over.

As soon as the cruiser rolled to a stop, Samir's seatbelt clicked open, and Riven's hand was on the door handle. "Let's break some skulls."

"If they don't break ours first," Asa said.

"You know the adage about how bad things always happen to good people?" Riven opened the door, unleashing a flood of jarring bass. The gemstone skull on her face glimmered under the galaxy of colored lights. "I figure we're safe."

It sent a chill through Asa. Right now, she was part of one

of the galaxy's biggest crime syndicates—a thief, a runaway, a liar. She was a nobody.

And she fit right in.

Riven strode toward the pillared entranceway and pulsing rhythm, her titanium-blonde braid swaying. Asa took a deep breath and followed, squaring her shoulders and lengthening her stride. The night air chilled her slits of bare skin, and she realized she was wearing less than she'd ever worn in public.

At the door, security guards pulled some patrons aside—checking bags, scanning faces. One guard leered at Riven until she flashed her revolvers at him. Asa didn't meet any of their eyes, but then a heavy hand clasped her shoulder, and a guard's silvery helmet tilted into her face. She froze up, but Samir returned the glare and put a hand on Asa's back, ushering her into the roar and lights.

She'd thought being onstage had prepared her for Olympus, but she'd been wrong.

Olympus was as breathtaking as the edge of space. The main chamber was built like a colosseum, its arches containing scantily clad dancers painted and scaled to look like Etri. The gargantuan brushed-steel torso of an Etri deity held court at the edge of the dance floor, its outstretched claws carrying clubgoers between the tiered dance floors. The dancers gyrated and spun in the sea of swelling synths, illuminated by wavering lights.

"Whoa," Asa gasped, but the word was drowned by the blaring bass and roaring crowds.

Riven beckoned over her shoulder. "Stick with us," she shouted over the music. "Can't lose you in here."

Mistrust still hung between her and Asa. Their fragile alliance hinged on the trackers in their necks. With a pang of longing, she remembered Riven in the Gnosis elevator, laughing with her, trusting her. The mischievous fire in Riven's eyes when they'd teamed up, before Riven knew the truth.

Riven would probably never want her again. Even if they were stuck working together for now.

They skirted the main dance floor and headed to the upper loft, where partygoers lined up for bars, döner kebab stands, and body-mod shops. Diego grabbed a table behind a fountain.

"I'll camp out here for a while." Diego zipped his jacket collar so it covered his mouth. His voice came through their earpieces. "Everyone know what they're doing?"

"Security terminal. Right," Asa said. "But we have to find it first."

Diego nodded. "Tail some guards if you have to. But stay inconspicuous."

Asa nodded. "Let's go." She took a deep breath and descended to the main dance floor, Ty trailing behind her. When she glanced over her shoulder, he gave her a reassuring smile, his eyes bright under the scrolling lights. Asa was glad to have him near. The hard contours of his arms were a good distraction from Riven, and he was the closest thing to a friend she had right now.

With every step into the thickening crowds, the weight of her self-consciousness lifted. The crowds were a jungle of stainless-steel cybernetics and barely there cloth. A man with a forked tongue and pointed cybernetic ears hissed at Asa, and she recoiled, sinking further into the crowd. When she found

Ty again, three tall women in rhinestone-studded makeup had him surrounded and were drunkenly asking about his mask.

Did Ty need her to save him? One woman laughed, setting a hand on Ty's shoulder. He looked uncomfortable.

Just past them, at the edge of the crowd, a security officer tromped by, a pistol holstered at his hip. As good a target as any.

"Ty," Asa blurted, grabbing his hand. "Dance with me."

His eyes went wide under the mask, but he happily slid his hands onto her waist, his fingers brushing the slits of bare skin. "How long have you been waiting to ask me that?"

"Olympus guards," she practically shouted into his ear over the blaring music. "Behind you."

"Oh." He sounded disappointed.

Asa watched the guard over Ty's shoulder, who stopped to talk to another guard at the base of the loft stairs. "Two of them. Chatting."

"Bet you one of them will be on break soon." The soft breeze of Ty's breath on her ear made the base of her spine tingle. "Could do worse than to dance while we wait."

The song changed to a smooth, sultry throb, and a giant pulse-line panel behind Ty fluctuated with the rhythm like a heart monitor. Something electric fizzed in Asa's chest. This wasn't part of the mission, but it was the least risky thing she could mess up tonight.

Asa set her hands on Ty's shoulders and let her hips sway, hitting the beats. His grip tightened slightly on her waist. For the first time since the emergency landing, she felt like she fit in with the stifling, dangerous crowds. She exhaled her fear and breathed in Requiem—the press of bodies, the crashing waves of the music, the heady vapors, the rush of lurking danger, and the wood-spice scent of Ty, dizzyingly close.

The city resonated with a hidden part of her, a stronger skin she'd never been stripped down to until now. She pulled Ty closer. What if she could choose a home for herself? A place where she was wanted on her own terms? Even if she saved Kaya, she could never go back to Cortellion—and that feral, rougher part of Asa whispered to let this city devour her, to let it pull her apart and reform her as one of its own.

Her lips were dangerously close to Ty's when he took her hand and pulled her through the crowds. "They're moving."

Asa glimpsed the guards weaving at the edge of the crowd. She huffed to herself. Why did they have to be moving *now*?

People cooed with excitement as a bartender-android sauntered by, carrying a bottle of booze spurting red sparks. Ty and Asa reached the edge of the crowd as the guard entered a side corridor. As they followed, the guard stopped at a security room, keying a code on the number pad.

Right. She had a job to do.

"Simple," Asa breathed. She pulled out a tiny wrench and her pen-laser. Disabling a keypad lock would be cake.

As the guard opened the door, Asa glimpsed the room—barely large enough for a desk, containing another bored-looking guard in front of the camera feeds. The guards swapped, and the second ambled into the hall, directly toward Asa and Ty.

"Asa." The next thing she knew, a pair of hands jerked her away, pressing her back against the wall.

Ty stood over her, his masked face only inches from hers. He leaned on his hand, planted on the wall above her shoulder.

"Guard's coming," he whispered, tracing the line of her jaw with his free hand.

Asa's head swam. "We have to hide." What was Ty doing? This wasn't the time.

"Relax," Ty whispered. "We're back here for . . . other reasons." He leaned closer. Close enough to kiss. "May I?"

Asa wasn't quite sure what Ty was asking, but she nodded. Ty threaded a hand in her hair, tilted her head, and pressed his lips to her neck.

That was a surprise.

He kept going—soft at first, then fiercer, more intense. Asa gasped without meaning to. Slowly, it clicked: this was a way to blend in. An act. A couple of horny teenagers who'd grabbed the first side hallway they could find.

But the coiling feeling in Asa's gut *wasn't* an act. Ty's lips felt like an extension of the frantic lights and pulsing bass—seductive, dizzying. He put a hand to her waist to steady her as he pressed closer, until his chest was against hers.

The Olympus guard gawked at them as he passed. Asa closed her eyes, pretending not to notice him. But as Ty's teeth brushed her skin, she all but forgot about the mission.

For a moment, she imagined it was Riven's strong arms pressing her against the wall, Riven's heated lips crashing against hers. But it was a senseless whim. If Riven wanted her, she'd take her.

And Asa found she *really* didn't mind Ty's lips on her skin.

Moments later, Ty pulled back, breathing hard. "Sorry for springing that on you. Are you all right?"

Asa pushed herself off the wall, flushed, adjusting her too-tight shorts. "You're . . . good at that."

He looked stunned, and his cheeks reddened even more. "Um. *Oh.* Thank you?" He wiped his mouth on the back of his hand, turning away. "Sorry, that probably wasn't . . ."

Asa's heart sank a bit. It'd only been an act for him. He'd probably done it a thousand times as a survival measure. And kissing Luca Almeida's daughter must have been agonizing for him.

"I think we've given him enough distance," she said. "Shall we?"

Mission first. Kaya first. Asa pulled off the keypad's faceplate and tinkered with the internal board. Taking it apart was risky, but the club security shouldn't be too tight. Not until the upper levels anyway.

Less than a minute later, she'd overridden the door bypass. The access light lit green. "Go," she whispered to Ty.

Ty nodded and opened the door. "I'm lost," he said innocently. The split second of confusion from the puffy-eyed security guard was enough.

As the guard tried to stand, Ty caught the man in a chokehold. A quick touch of a sedative patch, and the man squirmed and gasped, until he *didn't.* Ty set the unconscious man gently into the chair.

Asa eased the door shut behind her as Ty checked the man's pulse. "That'll keep him asleep for a good three hours. Doubt it'll be long before someone comes to check on him, though."

Asa tried to forget the press of his lips to her neck, his

hands on her bare skin. *Only an act.* It shouldn't bother her so much. The outfits, the stealth—it was all a performance. And it had to be a good one.

"Diego." Asa surveyed the security screens. "We're in."

Seconds dragged by, and Ty leaned over the security controls, scrolling between camera feeds. "Diego?"

On Diego's channel was only silence.

chapter 21
CAPTIVE

"Diego?" Asa repeated into her wristlet.

The security guard was unconscious, but he might have backup soon. She thought of the Duchess's surgeon, grinning as he held up a scalpel.

No. Diego couldn't be out of contact. He needed to send her data for the security systems—they might not get another chance.

Ty watched the security monitors showing the club's many crowded floors. The furrow on his brow told Asa he was worried too.

Seconds crawled by before Diego's voice came in, hurried and breathless. ". . . Federation chaser mech . . . it's following me. Give me a minute. I—"

"Diego?" Ty stood up. "What's happening?"

The connection went out. Where was he? Asa scanned the security screens, cycling between feeds of the many-armed automaton, the concentric holo-shields of the GravSpheres, and the bar loft. She squinted, zooming the security camera in on the table where Diego had been. It was empty.

"Riven, Samir," Asa said into her wristlet. "I think Diego's in trouble."

Samir's voice came through. "Dee? You okay?"

No response.

"Dammit," hissed Riven. "I'm going to go find him."

"He's not at the bar." Asa flipped frantically through the screens, searching for one of the wolf-shaped chaser mechs or Diego's green overcoat. The mess of lights and crowds made it impossible to focus.

"There!" Ty tapped one of the screens. Diego was limping into a storage bay, clutching his shoulder. He held a stunner, which wouldn't do much against the sleek wolf-mech skulking between the crates.

"He's bleeding," Ty said. "I need to get over there."

The wolf-mech's cold blue eyes were tracking Diego. Someone knew he was the focal point of their group tonight. Banshee flashed through Asa's mind, but all of its infected tech so far had orange lights.

"Riven," Asa said, "he's in the storage area. Northwest hall, off the second-floor loft. Hurry."

Asa watched the feed. *Stick to the mission—whatever the cost*, Bria had warned them before leaving. But the mission would fall apart without Diego. There had to be something she could do—

Wait.

"Diego," Asa said. "I can lower the bay doors. But you'll need to run."

Diego paused for a moment, then darted around the supply crates. Asa activated the door. The mech sprang to life, snapping at Diego's heels, as he ducked beneath the closing door. The mech skidded to a halt, clawing and hurling itself against the metal lattice. The bars warped outward.

And then a bullet punched through the mech's eye, scattering and sparking. The mech crumpled against the bent bars, its eyes going dark.

Riven strode into view, *Blackjack* drawn.

"Thanks for that," Diego said, breathless.

"What happened?" Asa said as Ty slipped out the door to go help.

"It was stalking me, and then it attacked. The club guards didn't even interfere." On the security screen, Asa saw a dark patch of blood on Diego's shoulder.

"You think it was a hacker? Or something else?"

"It could be the Federation already knows we're here. Either way, we need to be fast. Do you have the connection set up?"

"Yes." With Diego's data, Asa uploaded their fingerprint scans to the top floor's VIP system. Phase one, nearly complete. But she couldn't shake the unease that had clawed under her skin. Someone had seen them.

Someone probably still watching.

"We're going after the access key," Riven said, with a sting in her voice. "Samir pinpointed it—but there's a complication. We might need the runaway's help. Asa, when can you be here?"

Asa's insides twisted. A complication? If Riven was asking for her by name, it was serious. She hadn't planned for this. But everything was shifting so rapidly she'd drown if she didn't adapt.

"I'll be there as soon as the upload finishes," Asa said. "Just tell me what to do."

Riven stared at the dead wolf-mech, the warped metal bars. This hadn't been a glitch—someone knew they were here. This was becoming a grudge match, a game.

If it came to that, she'd play dirty.

Ty peeled away a shredded flap of Diego's jacket. "You'll need stitches, but they don't look too deep." The lighting was bad—dim blacklight and garbled flashes of color leaking from the main dance floor. But the wet gashes on Diego's shoulder were hard to miss. No stun-blast, no warning shot. The mech had tried to kill him.

"I don't like the idea of leaving you here." Riven shoved *Blackjack* back into its holster.

Ty shot her a smile. "And I don't like the idea of you stalling the mission because you think I can't take care of myself."

Ty was stubborn for someone without a gun. But she had places to be, if they were going to finish this with their organs intact.

Riven clicked on her comm. "Hey, Mechanist. When you're done with that upload, meet us at the second-floor body-mod shop. Our mark left something valuable there."

"You're taking Asa?" Ty muttered. "Going to put her conning skills to use?"

"No. Need her to look at some tech." It still stung that she'd been conned by a little rich girl. But Asa had to help—she'd know what they were looking for.

Asa had manipulated them, in more ways than one. It had been hard for Riven to pull her eyes away when Asa had stepped out of the changing pod in a slashed leotard that revealed strips of her light-brown skin. And Riven didn't like the idea of Asa alone in the security room, where she was easy prey for guards.

"I'm sure she'll be helpful." Ty's frown slipped as he stitched Diego's wounds. "She's clever."

No doubt Ty had been looking too. "Is that why you were staring at her ass?"

"I was *not*." Ty dabbed blood off the finished stitches and quickly changed the subject. "So what was up with that mech? You think it's the Federation after us, or . . . ?"

"If they know what we're doing here, that's trouble." Diego slid the shredded coat back on. "I doubt the Federation knows, but the mech didn't seem to be Banshee either. No orange light, no whisper-screech. Unless something's changed."

Riven frowned. She wouldn't put it past Banshee.

"Who's to say what it can do?" Ty said. "It's already evolving to evade hosts' defenses. Like a virus." Ty approached the dead wolf-mech. It lay on its side, a heap of angular black metal with powerful haunches meant for chasing targets.

"Ty, get away from that thing," Riven warned.

Ty inspected the mech's paws, the articulated joints and thick rubber treads at the bottoms. "Hacked or no, it's possible we could have Asa look at it." Ty reached between the bars of the bay door and twisted the paw to one side.

Riven drew *Blackjack*. "Not kidding, Ty. That thing's bad news–"

A set of steel claws ejected, like a cat's. Ty jerked his hand backward, swearing, as the blue lights returned to the mech's eyes. Riven fired another shot. The claw swiped the air sluggishly, and the eyes went dark again.

Ty backed away. "That thing's definitely not built to pull its blows."

"Listen," Diego said. "We need to keep all suspicion of

Banshee quiet. Even if it's not here, we could end up in another quarantine zone."

"Right," Riven said. "We need to get those codes, fast."

"So go." Diego waved Riven away. "Ty and I are fine."

Riven heard a message *ping* and shot a glance at Ty. He flicked his wristlet screen on, and his eyes widened.

He was harder to read with that mask on, but she knew that look. Ty always froze up like a scarni on a skyway when pretty girls tried to flirt with him.

"Who's that?" She had a feeling she already knew.

He finished tapping a message and clicked the screen off, a blush spreading across his cheeks. "Nothing." Then, his mouth tightened in concern as his wristlet pinged again. "Where did Asa go?"

Riven frowned. Heck of a time for idle flirting, but maybe it was more than that. "She should still be uploading our scans. Why?"

He shook his head. "Just curious."

Weird. He was hiding something. "And you're *sure* you're okay by yourself?"

"Um, yeah." He ran a hand through his hair. "Trust me. Everything's great." He gave her his *I'm fine, really* smile.

Right now, maybe he'd be safer without her. If whatever was targeting them was smart, it'd come after her and Samir next.

"Well, keep your stunners ready," Riven said. "And let me know if *anything* weird happens."

Maybe Asa was messing with his head. And *all* their heads. But, mission first.

She strode off, leaving Ty behind.

chapter 22
RANSOM

Riven's left foot quivered against a rung of the stool, and she almost turned on her boot's electromagnet to get it to *stop.* This wasn't the time for jitters.

"Do we *really* need a mechanist to find this thing?" Riven said into her comm. Somewhere in this body-mod shop was their access chip—buried in a discarded cyborg hand. And she was sick of waiting for Asa.

"Unless you want to knock a Fed trooper unconscious and drag them upstairs." Diego's voice still rasped with pain.

"I'm here," Asa's voice interrupted. Riven glanced over her shoulder as Asa entered, muttering a cheerful "excuse me" when a huge tattooed man nearly knocked her over.

Riven groaned through her teeth. Asa had all the survival instincts of a domestic kitten. Still, she'd conned them once. Maybe she had some chops.

Riven beckoned her through the crowd, where patrons tested cybernetic mods at the glass counter and others sat for tattoos or slipped into private booths to have glowing dermal mods installed. The mirrored walls reflected an abyss of blue pulse lights and puffy, marshmallow-pink couches.

Asa sank onto a metal stool next to her. "So what's the plan?"

Riven couldn't shake the thought of Ty hiding those

messages. Asa obviously hadn't run off with him, and she wasn't hurt. "What were you messaging Ty about, a few minutes ago? Is everything all right?"

Asa looked genuinely confused, her polished-cherry lips twisting into a pout. "I wasn't messaging Ty."

Huh. It must've been someone else. Ty's love life was his business, not hers. "Whatever. Plan is, Samir's talking our way in. And then we need to find this chip before the manager gets suspicious."

Asa wrinkled her nose. "We're rooting through their bio-hazard trash?"

"To put it nicely, yeah."

Samir was chatting up the manager, who leaned against the counter, practically hanging on him already. He laughed a little too loudly, and Samir's grin widened in response. Thank god. It seemed Riven wouldn't have to bat her eyelashes after all.

She pulled Asa through the crowd. Samir's story—some drivel about a friend's scrapped cybernetic eye containing an heirloom lens made from her grandmother's wedding ring— seemed to be working.

"That *is* tragic," the manager was saying as they approached. His bloodshot eyes peered at them through a scan-glass. "I don't see why you can't take a look. But I'll need to supervise you." He set a hand on Samir's back.

Samir didn't even flinch. He shot Riven a wink. Their cue.

The manager pulled aside the curtain to the storage room— the size of a walk-in freezer, but weirdly *hot*. Purple light ringed the ceiling, and racks held rejected cybernetic parts—eyes, limbs, tangles of glowing ropes. Riven hoped they'd already been scrubbed down.

"What are we looking for?" Asa whispered, pulling the curtain closed behind them. Though some of the cybernetics were eerily fleshy looking, she didn't look fazed. She probably worked with this kind of tech all the time.

"A hand. You know how to pick out Fed-tech?"

"Yeah. It'll have an octothene circuit board, or Gliflex ball jointing."

"I was thinking because it'd smell like conceited dickhead. But that works too."

Asa stifled laughter as she began sorting through a pile of arms.

Riven pushed aside a tangle of dermal light wires. This place was probably a gold mine of scraps. She peered into the shaft of a translucent forearm with wires hanging out. Inside, a tiny data crystal glimmered. "Damn. Galateo, how much is this worth?"

"Unregistered listings are showing similar items at two hundred denar, my lady."

Riven let out a low whistle. Two hundred was nothing compared to the *two million denar* bounty next to her, but it would buy a few bullets. Riven pulled the wires aside.

Conveniently, the arm decided to twitch, sending a spray of hot liquid across Riven's neck and chest. "Shit!"

"What is it?" Asa whirled toward her, saw the glowing mess over Riven, and clapped a hand over her mouth. When Riven tried to wipe the sludge away, Asa grabbed her hand. "Don't! Try not to touch it—it's corrosive."

"*Corrosive?*" That explained the tingling itch, the heat on her skin. "It's kind of *already* touching me!"

Asa pulled a cloth out of her pouch. "Hold still."

Riven locked into place at the command, and Asa began dabbing the sludge away. Her hands were gentle and skilled, her touch soft. Riven swallowed hard, trying to ignore the spreading warmth.

"Bria will probably deduct a few extra organs for ruining their clothes," Riven said as Asa's cloth passed over her neck.

Surprisingly, Asa chuckled. The purple light caught the edges of her tousled hair and left a bright sheen on her lips. "Wonder what they'll say." Her voice turned nasally. "*I don't think you have much choice in the matter. Now shut up while I put rhinestones on your liver.*"

"Since when do *you* have a sense of humor?"

Asa's smile tightened. "Since I've accepted that I'll be running for my life, for the *rest* of my life. This is my new normal. I couldn't live with myself if I never cracked a joke."

It was hard to dislike Asa, especially when she had that almost-giddy glow to her. Maybe something had happened between her and Ty.

Strangely, Riven felt a sour burn of jealousy. It shouldn't matter. Asa wouldn't be sticking around with Ty any longer than the rest of the crew.

The rag skipped Riven's breasts, then moved toward the stain across her purple bodice. Asa's gaze snapped away from Riven's chest, and she blushed.

"I can get it," Riven said. "Hand me the rag."

For some reason, she was glad when Asa said, "It's fine. I can see better than you can." Riven's breath hitched as Asa's hands moved over her chest, gently rubbing away the burning sludge.

What was this girl *doing* to her? Riven warned her idiot hormones to *shut up.* This girl had pulled her into a world of trouble, and she wouldn't even see the payout.

"You know." Asa's voice turned somber. "I'd be locked up in Morphett's cargo hold, or dead in a sewer system, or a million other terrible things, if you hadn't been around. Honestly . . . you're the only reason I still have a chance to save Kaya. I owe you a lot."

Where was she going with this? Was she going to apologize?

"Technically," Riven said, "I kidnapped you. So that balances it a bit."

Asa gave a devious smile. "And I'll bet you regret what a handful I've been." She bit her lip as she held Riven's arm in place. "But I'm glad I have you here. No matter what you think of me right now."

Riven lifted Asa's chin. A lock of night-black hair was stuck to her lips, and Riven brushed it away. The girl had lied, but she was just trying to survive. Had Riven been too hard on her?

"Hey. Keeping you safe is my job right now." But she couldn't ignore the deep, nagging rift, the knowledge of the monster Asa had helped create. Of Emmett, bleeding to death in the sand, while the world quickly forgot and Almeida continued to be a billionaire.

"I just want to know one thing," Riven said. "Were you telling the truth, at the Duchess's?" Asa's breath caught. "It's hard to believe you spent all that time in your dad's lab and didn't foresee *any* of the nasty shit he was doing."

Asa's lips quivered, forming the beginnings of a thousand excuses. Then her mouth closed in grim resolve. "It's not that simple."

There it was. Defenses, not apologies. Had Riven really expected more?

She waited for more explanation, but none came. "Not that simple?" She turned away. "I think standing against a murderer is pretty simple."

It was stupid to get close to Asa. Her crew came first. Ty and Samir—and Galateo, with the little pieces Emmett had left in him as digital love notes.

Asa recoiled like Riven was on fire. She was her father's daughter. She'd sell them all out if it meant saving her own skin. No, they couldn't get comfortable here—no matter how tantalizing Asa's nimble hands and pretty eyes were.

Outside the curtain, Samir's voice grew louder. "I'm sure they're close to finding it." A signal to hurry. "It should be hard to miss."

"One minute," Riven hissed. When had she gotten so distracted? It seemed like hours had passed in this tiny closet. The hairs on her arms were standing up despite the heat.

"This is it." Asa pried open a limp metal hand. "The pattern on the carbon matches. It's Fed-tech, and this is definitely an access chip." After a few twists of a tiny wrench, she handed the chip to Riven.

Riven stuffed it in her pocket. "Thanks. Let's go."

They pushed out of the cybernetics storage, shooting Samir

a thumbs-up. He nodded, waiting for them to pass before he extricated himself from the manager's eager conversation.

"Package secured, Diego," Riven said. "Ready to go up?"

A pause. Then, Diego's voice was rushed with worry. "Have any of you spoken to Ty lately?"

"No?" Riven frowned. "Thought he was with you."

"He said he was going to check on Asa, but he never came back. And his tracker just went dark."

"*What*? How would that happen?"

"I checked all communication from his wristlet over the past few minutes. You'll want to see this. Those messages Ty was getting . . ."

Messages. Dammit, of course. He'd been hiding something.

Riven slipped into a side hall with a flickering light, as a screenshot appeared on her wristlet. A text conversation between Ty and Asa.

ASA: *You free yet? Meet me in the third-floor lounge. Need to finish what we started.*

TY: *aren't you supposed to be meeting with riven and samir soon?*

ASA: *Just come find me. I need you alone. At least for a few minutes.*

TY: *alone?*

TY: *why? are you okay?*

ASA: *More than okay. The way you kissed me in the hall . . . I'm not done with you.*

No wonder he'd been blushing. Riven shot Asa a glare. "What's this all about?"

"I didn't send those." Asa peered over Riven's shoulder,

looking increasingly horrified. "And nobody's touched my wristlet but me."

"If they're not from you, they're likely hacked," Diego said.

Clearly by someone who'd seen them *kissing*. Someone was targeting Ty like they'd targeted Diego. Riven ignored the itch of jealousy and read the final messages.

TY: *seriously. what's going on?*

ASA: *I need you. All of you. Your lips all over me, your body pressed against me.*

TY: *just let me know you're okay. please?*

"That's when he said he was going to go check on her," Diego said. "I should've insisted on going with him."

Riven's heart beat a furious rhythm. She'd been so stupid to leave him behind. "*Shit.* Someone set a trap for him." Whether Ty had been gullible or just worried for Asa, he'd walked right into it.

"You don't think it was Banshee?" Asa said.

"You really think an AI would *flirt* with him?" Riven gritted her teeth. "Whoever's behind this is getting a chest cavity full of hollow points."

Galateo piped up. "It's not hard to mimic human speech patterns with enough data input, my lady."

"We have a few possibilities," Diego said. "But if it's Banshee . . . we're in deep trouble."

"Well, I'm going after him. Starting at the lounge." He could be anywhere by now, but it was the only lead she had. She clicked off her wristlet and ran toward the stairwell.

"Wait!" Asa called. "Should I—"

"Go meet up with Samir and Diego. I don't want to attract extra attention. I'll let you know what happens."

As Riven shoved her way through the elevator line, her wristlet pinged. A message—from Ty.

Want to save me? it read. *You'd better hurry.*

Bring the biocapsule with you, and the Almeida girl.

Riven's blood went cold. It wasn't Ty sending the messages. Someone had him for ransom.

chapter 23

GRAVITY

"Ty," Riven said into her comm for the hundredth time, hoping *this time* he might respond. She dashed up the stairwell and reached the third-floor brothel lounge. Smoke hung over the red lights as half-dressed prostitutes of all varieties—android, cyborg, full-flesh—draped themselves suggestively over velvet couches. Titanium statues stood on pedestals, cold-metal curves in provocative poses, heads thrown backward in ecstasy. Like a kitschy circus, with sex instead of carnival games.

Why would Banshee—or the Feds, or whatever was messing with them—bring Ty here?

From one of the bar tables, a greasy man leered at Riven's panting chest. She gave him a nasty gesture and headed to the private booths. She yanked curtains aside to indignant shouts and drunken confusion, searching for Ty's messy ginger-blond hair and black mask. But he was nowhere.

Another message from Ty's wristlet pinged hers. She tried to suppress the spark of hope.

Looking for someone? it read.

whatever you're after, she responded, *this probably ends with a bullet in your skull.*

I would like to see you try.

what do you want?

Meet me in the first-floor storage chambers. I have a surprise for you.

Riven stared at the message, at its smug demand. Something dark and desperate welled within her. How dare this thing order her around. And how *dare* it touch Ty.

when I get there, she responded, *you're going to regret this.*

As soon as she'd sent it, she opened a private comm channel with Diego. "Diego. Did you manage to track Ty's wristlet? Whoever has him says he's on the first level."

"The tracking signal from his wristlet is garbled," Diego said. "It's being hacked. I might have an override, but you'll have to wait a few minutes."

She didn't have a few minutes, when Ty might be in trouble.

"I salvaged some footage from his wristlet camera," Diego said. "It's recent."

"Let me look?" She slid into an empty booth, pulling the velvet curtain closed.

Her heart crawled into her throat as the footage began playing.

The camera on Ty's wrist was shaky as he entered the lounge, and the teardrop lamps and leather-clad androids swayed. Ty caught himself against an armchair, breathing hard. Something was wrong with him. He was either drunk or drugged, and Ty wouldn't drink on a job.

Other patrons' eyes narrowed on him as he passed, hushed murmurs and nasty grins following. Riven's chest clenched. Some of the faces in the lounge, she recognized—his captors could still be here. What if Banshee had help? She remembered

Cyclops, pleading and stumbling through the sewers. Dammit. It could have control of *anything* here.

The camera was positioned below Ty's chin as he spoke into his wristlet. "*Asa? What's going on?*" he said in the recording. "*Are you here at the lounge?*" He tapped the screen, pulling up Riven's name from his call log, but the HUD read *NO SIGNAL*, and all his app icons had disappeared.

Ty swore to himself, then began stumbling toward the *RESTROOMS* sign glaring green through the sickly sweet smoke. To keep watching felt like an invasion of privacy, but Riven had to know where he'd gone.

Ty ducked into one of the tiny bathrooms and braced himself against the sink, panting. When he lifted a shaking hand to his neck, the wristlet camera caught the mirror, and she saw his face as he pulled off the black mask. Beneath it, he looked lethargic, his blue eyes glazed.

An unfamiliar voice sounded in his private comm channel. "*Such a tiny poison inside you, lying in wait . . .*"

A chill went through Riven. The voice was deep and weirdly processed—computer generated.

"What are you?" Ty whispered. "Why are you doing this?"

"*I am unlike you. How fragile you are,*" the inhuman voice drawled. "*And how easy to control.*"

Riven bit back a snarl. What was Banshee trying to do to him?

Ty pulled a scalpel from his pouch with quaking hands. He kept fingering the back of his neck.

And then Riven realized—the trackers.

Ty's tracker was releasing whatever had made him dizzy. Banshee had hacked it. And Ty was going to cut it out.

Riven couldn't breathe as the video showed Ty positioning the scalpel . . . and stabbing himself in the neck.

He'd missed.

Blood trickled into the high collar of his black vest. He didn't even wince as he made another cut, this time hitting the tracker. He squeezed his skin, pushing out a tiny cylinder.

There was sedative in the trackers. In Ty, in Riven, in all of them. The trick up the Duchess's sleeve—and Banshee had found a way to use it against them.

The video ended in a blur of white tile as Ty fell limp.

Searing, nauseating rage boiled in her gut. "I'm going to *kill* someone."

"I've already messaged Bria to deactivate our trackers," Diego said. "They have a fail-safe with a mechanical switch, so it should prevent them from ever reactivating."

Screw the trackers. "How long ago was this footage?" Riven headed toward the chrome-black hall of bathroom doors.

"It cut about six minutes ago."

Three stalls down on the left. That was the one Ty had walked into, right? Riven wound back and kicked the door in.

The door flew open with no resistance—not locked. But it was empty. The light flipped on as she entered, revealing a trickle of blood at the edge of the sink.

Her heart pounded. Ty had fallen unconscious here, and someone had taken him.

She imagined someone—or *something*—dragging an

unconscious Ty through the lounge, and nobody lifting a finger to stop them. Her nails dug into her palms.

"Riven," Diego said, "just got a ping of Ty's wristlet location. It seems to be . . ." A pause. "It's on the fourth floor."

"The GravSpheres," she breathed. This was getting worse by the minute.

"Are you going after him?"

"Have to." Her trigger fingers were getting twitchy. "The rest of you should keep your distance. I don't want them to know I'm coming."

Riven boarded the glass elevator to the fourth floor and rose toward the GravSpheres, a set of concentric globes streaked with blood. Her stomach knotted. There would be hell to pay if Ty was anywhere near there.

A crowd beneath the spheres roared as a woman with a pair of energy blades fought a bruttore. The shaggy, bearlike beast swiped a massive fist at her, but she ducked and scrambled away, nimble in her blue bodysuit. She ran *up* the curve of the outermost sphere until she was upside down. Boos erupted from the audience.

A countdown appeared on the spheres. When it hit zero, the contender did a jump-twist as the gravity reversed, pulling her onto the inner layer.

Riven checked the tracker–Ty's wristlet was moving toward the spheres, but not inside. Yet. She burst out of the elevator as soon as it opened.

The roar of the crowd had died down, and small cleaner-mechs scoured the inside of the spheres, sweeping away the blood smears and the dead bruttore for the next match.

The tracker showed Ty's wristlet, sixty feet ahead. In the spheres.

From this angle, most of the spheres were blocked by the control booths and elevator. She couldn't see inside. Riven shoved through the crowd, ignoring the swearing and indignation from the people she pushed. "Out of the way," she growled, shouldering past a man with color-cycling spikes in his forearms.

Thirty feet.

If you aren't on the first floor within the next five minutes, another message pinged, *I'll send you pictures of what I'm doing to your friend Tyren.*

Not if she found him first.

Banshee had gone too far. It was *dead*, even if she had to crush every one of its circuit boards in her bare hands.

Ten feet. Ahead, the doors to the GravSphere elevator opened invitingly.

Riven barreled in, guns drawn. But the elevator was empty, except for a wristlet on the floor, its screen a white spot in the darkness.

Ty's wristlet. But no Ty with it. Or . . . anyone.

As Riven picked up Ty's wristlet, her own wristlet pinged. A new message, from . . . Ty. From the wristlet she was holding.

Right where I want you, the message read.

The elevator doors slammed shut behind her.

"You *fucker*," she whispered.

Another messaged popped up. *I want to watch you dance.*

Banshee was in the palm of her hand. Not only was it inside Ty's wristlet, it was inside the elevator.

It had the GravSpheres.

Riven gasped as the elevator lurched, pulling her toward the center. She gripped her revolvers tighter. If Ty was in there, she'd save him. No matter what nasties waited for her.

The elevator groaned to a stop. She tensed, waiting for the doors to open. But a high-pitched whine rang out, and her guns were yanked upward.

The metal pulled up, forcing Riven onto her toes until the barrels were touching the ceiling. The force nearly lifted her off her feet, impossibly powerful. An electromagnet.

The guns slid from her grasp and locked onto the ceiling with a *clank*. She clawed at them, trying to pull them away, but they were stuck fast.

"Dammit," she rasped as the elevator doors opened, revealing the brilliant, blinding blue of the holo-spheres and the vidscreens surrounding them. "Dammit!"

The crowd roared. Her heart pounded. She might have an opponent out there—and they'd corner her in the elevator.

She had no choice but to enter the fray unarmed. Riven squared her shoulders. If Banshee wanted a show, she'd give the bastard a show.

Riven strode onto the curved floor, swaggering like she'd faced death unarmed a thousand times. The spheres turned turquoise like the surface of a pool, and her boots left ripples on the transparent surface. Below, the audience bellowed, a crowd of sharks awaiting a meal.

Outside the spheres, a pixelated graffiti mask appeared on the screen, splitting in an overlarge grin. "Gutter trash and gentlefolk," a syrupy voice came over the loudspeaker. The voice shifted from a smooth announcer's voice to a harsh, feminine whisper. "Tonight is a decision of fates. Her life as collateral, its threads tangled within"–then, a deep growl–"a violent spectacle. A show unlike any you've ever seen here."

It sounded like garbled audio clips pulled from movies. This power-tripping AI was putting on some sick display–and she was the main attraction. Riven's stomach churned as her footsteps struck the holo-spheres. Without her guns, she felt exposed. And Banshee had her right where it wanted her.

She glanced up and across the spheres. They were empty, but an elevator crawled through the other tube. From the bestiary.

"With that," the voice said, "the curtain . . . falls."

The crowd gasped as the room plunged into utter darkness.

Riven's instincts screamed at her to *get out*. There was that familiar, bloody tang at the back of her mouth. She stilled her breath, listening. Within the spheres, no footsteps. No flickers.

"You survive this," said a static-garbled voice over the loud-speakers, "and I'll give him back."

"One hell of a bargain." Not that she had much choice.

Her breaths were starting to come ragged. *Stay conscious. Nobody's here to catch you if you fall.*

A flash of red on the spheres cut through the darkness: *3 . . . 2 . . .*

Oh, damn. The gravity-shift counter. Riven braced herself to flip.

. . . 1.

Riven jumped and shifted in the air, toward the ceiling fifteen feet above her. The ceiling, which was now the floor. After a moment of brain-shattering vertigo, she stumbled into a landing, pushing the braid out of her eyes. Her head throbbed. This gravity shifting could kill her if she landed on her neck. Maybe that was the point.

The crowd floor was now *above her.* A spotlight shone at her feet, illuminating her—just her. She straightened and craned her neck backward, flashing the crowd a grin and a confident wave. Anything to prevent them from knowing she was in over her head.

The spotlight dimmed as the floor shook beneath her feet. Another elevator had arrived. Riven rolled her shoulders, falling into the defensive stance she'd trained in with Samir at CAA. Her skull pricked like needles as her pulse rose. Being unarmed against a bunch of monsters was better odds than against the poison in her nervous system.

Banshee wasn't going to let her escape. But it still had Ty, and that was all the reason she needed to get out of here alive.

Through the dark was the *hish* of a door sliding open.

The bruttore had arrived.

The screens flashed with fireworks of black-light paint. In the brief light, Riven saw a shaggy, hulking form stalking the sphere directly opposite her.

The bruttore launched itself forward on powerful haunches, its face splitting into vicious teeth. And, on the surface of the spheres, flashes of light marked other footsteps. *Invisible* footsteps. Anteleons.

Too many for her to fight alone. And nobody was coming to save her.

Riven moved, clearing her mind of everything but the pounding of her boots, the pace of her breath. But keeping her distance inside a spherical arena was impossible, where the ground folded in on itself and all roads led to their prey.

With nowhere to run, one of the anteleons caught her.

Invisible claws gouged into her, accompanied by anteleon squeals like meat frying in a street vendor's cart. Hot slices of pain opened her shoulder and tore through the bodice at her waist. She wrenched the claws apart, grabbing at the beast's neck, hearing a satisfying *crack* as something snapped.

She tossed the anteleon's gray-scaled corpse aside, staggering on her feet. Dizziness washed over her, worse than before, and something wet and dark was trickling from her arm and stomach. *Oh, shit.*

Riven clutched her shoulder, wincing, as the scrabbling of more anteleons drew closer. If all of them hurt her like the first . . . she might not survive this.

And though the bruttore wasn't as quick, she was good as dead if it knocked her over. Suddenly, she was the girl on the beach again, Emmett dying in her arms, her guns left behind as bullets pounded the sand.

No, she demanded. *I will not be weak.*

She kept running as the crowd roared, her feet ramming harder against the holo-sphere. She needed a plan. If she ran long enough, maybe they'd devour each other—but her running space was limited, and the scent of her blood was only pulling them closer.

She had to keep running if it killed her. Even if the white noise got her first.

As Riven's gut flipped and something tugged at her hair,

the gravity shifted again. *Slam*. She saw stars as she staggered back onto her feet, panting.

Nearby, the bruttore rolled back onto its feet and growled at her, its teeth a flash of razor-honed yellow.

Banshee wouldn't let her survive this.

"Riven is in the GravSpheres?" Asa demanded as the elevator crept upward.

"We tracked Ty's wristlet there," Diego said. "But she's stopped responding. No idea how she got in there."

Samir swore, pressing his hands to the glass panel on the elevator wall. His cat pupils narrowed as he glared down at the spheres. "They sent beasties in and turned out the lights. Someone's trying to make sure she can't fight back."

A knot tightened in Asa's stomach. They'd both scanned their fingerprints, and now the elevator was carrying them to the VIP level—Samir had gotten another message from Ty's wristlet, saying they'd find him up there. But Banshee could be leading them anywhere, splitting them up.

Lights flashed in the spheres below, showing glimpses of Riven's purple bodice and rhinestone makeup. She scrambled between a bruttore's claws and the flickering footsteps of an invisible creature. Anteleons, maybe. If Riven had her guns, it'd be over in seconds. But this . . .

"She's unarmed." Asa's voice cracked. "Why doesn't she have a weapon?" Riven wouldn't have stumbled into this blindly.

"No idea," Diego said. "Maybe that thing demanded it. As part of a ransom."

Ty and Riven, both in danger. And time for the Duchess's job was running out. Even if she could save Kaya alone, there was no way Asa was leaving them behind.

Riven staggered as red lines sliced through her pants. Something invisible was tearing at her. Then the gravity shifted, and Riven ducked as she slammed into the outer sphere.

Asa squeezed her eyes shut. She couldn't watch. She hadn't even managed to tell Riven the truth—that she'd been too scared to stand up to her father, that Emmett might've been saved if only she'd dug into her father's research earlier.

You coward, a new, resolute part of her demanded. *She's down there, staring danger in the face, and you're too afraid to even watch her struggle?*

Asa clenched her fists. Whatever the cost, she had to help.

"Come on, Riv." Desperation crept into Samir's whisper. "Hang on. Please."

The gravity countdowns weren't showing. Riven stumbled and fell upward, slamming into the gravity sphere again. A flash of her blood, bright red.

"Something doesn't want her to make it out." Asa hit the control panel, and the elevator halted. It shook, then began descending. "Galateo said Banshee could learn, and if it's messing with Ty's comms and the GravSpheres . . . Riven's in trouble." The thought was like a kick to her gut. How could she outwit an AI?

But Kaya had done it once. Asa could do it now.

Asa swallowed hard as an idea hit her. "I think I can get her out of there."

"It's trying to kill her. It'll try to kill you too."

"Then it's a risk I'll have to take." Asa shot Samir a grim smile as the elevator doors opened to the fourth floor. Everything was trying to kill her today. But she owed Riven her life and couldn't bear losing her too. "I'm your mechanist, right? This part's my job."

Despite Samir's objections, Asa sprinted out of the elevator. She weaved through the frantic crowd at the GravSpheres until she found the control room, then fried open the lock with her pen-laser.

As the door opened, she clutched her stunner, ready to fire. But the attendant was already unconscious on the floor, a nasty bruise swelling on his forehead. Someone else had gotten here first.

Through the glass panel, she saw Riven twist as the gravity shifted again. The crowd roared as she landed roughly, rolling some of the momentum off.

The gravity shifts seemed to be coming from the orb at the center of the spheres—an attraction and repulsion field. On the screen, Asa saw an infrared overlay of the inside of the spheres. Four anteleons crawled, and the searing red-heat mass of the bruttore lumbered toward Riven.

Banshee was probably right in front of her, inside the control panel.

"All right," Asa whispered. "Let's pull you out of there." Her wristlet was close to the infected control board, but it should be safe. Her father had commissioned the rose-gold gadget for her seventeenth birthday, and it was fitted with the newest specs from his lab—she'd barely been able to hack it. Banshee would be hard pressed to.

She watched the controls, listening to the hum of the gravity systems and the whir of the switches. Banshee had learned to sync the computer systems with the GravSpheres. It was watching Riven, timing its slams to catch her off guard.

But if it had to relearn . . .

Asa flipped open the console. It was time to do some rewiring.

She spent a minute rigging the controls to her wristlet, then flicked on her comm. The bruttore swiped a claw at Riven's head, and Asa noticed a gash bleeding through Riven's skull makeup. Now or never.

"Riven," Asa called into her comm, "can you hear me?"

"Not the time!" Riven shouted over the comm.

She panted, dashing across the GravSpheres to give herself some distance. But she was trapped, and the crowd only cheered for more blood.

Blood was already staining her gaudy new clothes, and her skull was pounding, threatening to knock her unconscious.

Every few seconds, she glimpsed a flash of gray when an anteleon's cloaking shifted. The invisible bastards had her surrounded. So she kept moving, trying not to break her neck when the gravity shifted. The adrenaline dulled the pain of the cuts and bruises, but it'd catch up to her later. If there *was* a later.

"Riven, I think Banshee's trying to kill you."

She bared her teeth. "Oh? You *think*?"

"I have control, but I don't know for how much longer. I need you to trust me."

"Trust *you*?" But she'd never been so damned glad to hear that girl's voice. "Go on. I'm listening."

"The boots Bria gave you. Are they electromagnetic?"

"Yes? Kind of in trouble here!" She sprinted as the bruttore roared, lumbering toward her.

"Activate them on my count. Highest setting!"

Riven skidded to a stop as the bruttore closed in. Her chest heaved. "Will they stick to these shields?" If they did, activating them would immobilize her. She'd be a sitting duck.

"Yes, the gravity capacitors have—just trust me! Four, three, two—"

Trust her, something in Riven knew. *She'll pull through.* She braced herself and activated her boots. The soles hummed, buzzing through her. The bruttore leapt toward her, claws raised, and she instinctively raised her forearms like a shield. But then it twisted and fell upward, crashing into the inner sphere.

Riven felt a tug on her braid and a rush of blood to her head, but her feet were stuck fast, and the straps across her legs and waist anchored her. She craned her neck backward, laughing at the vertigo of sticking to the ceiling. The disoriented bruttore rolled onto its back, its heavy coat swishing.

"I haven't found an escape route for you yet," Asa said, "so I'll get you a weapon."

"My guns would be *so* nice right now." The bruttore sniffed the air, glaring at Riven hanging above it.

"Next best thing? It looks like there are some energy weapons I can send in."

Energy weapons. She could make do. It'd be a hell of an improvement. "Sure. Should I jump down first?"

"Hang on. I'll bring them down to you. But once I do, you'll have to run."

Jagged lightning flashed across the holo-spheres as thunder rumbled over the speakers. Banshee was messing with her. She remembered the growl of distant thunder, the storm gathering that day at Sanctum's Edge. She'd been running then too—unarmed and hopeless.

This time, she'd go down fighting if she had to.

"Do your worst!" Riven shouted over the boom and the crackle.

At the other side of the sphere, the supply box opened. "Go grab that. It's a little present for you."

As soon as the gravity shifted, Riven wasted no time scrambling to the supply box. Inside the steel tube was a heavy launcher weapon, with a chain and a barbed hook at one end. "Good choice, mechanist."

Riven braced the launcher against her shoulder, shooting the arrowhead at a patch of flickering footprints. The launcher heaved, burying the merciless arrowhead into its target. A mass of gray scales appeared, revealing a skewered anteleon corpse.

Perfect. This thing had range. Riven pressed the switch to retract the barbs and reel the hook back in.

"Bruttore!" Asa yelled.

Riven dove and slid, twisting backward to fire the hook at the approaching bruttore. The shot missed, grazing its matted ear. Dammit.

"How many more?" Riven sprinted. Bones crunched as the

bruttore devoured the dead anteleon. Gray scales and dark blood sloshed within its chops.

"I see three more anteleons. The bruttore is going to be the problem. But gravity's on your side now. You ready?"

"As I'll ever be." Not just gravity on her side. Asa too. Like a proper teammate. Suddenly, she wasn't so wary about her life in the runaway's hands.

On Asa's count, the gravity shifted again. Riven glimpsed an anteleon hitting the center sphere, and fired the launcher upward to skewer it.

Then, with another nauseating hit of vertigo, the gravity turned from pulling up to pushing down. She released her electromagnets as two anteleons and the bruttore came crashing down around her, squealing.

This was it.

Riven let herself fall into the rhythm, imagining it wasn't a launcher but her revolvers. She ran and fired, shooting the anteleons until they were lumps of gray scales on the spheres.

She plunged the harpoon through the bruttore's heart. It roared, collapsing in a mound of fur. The crowd shrieked, and a few shoes and empty bottles hit the outside of the spheres.

Riven looked up, panting, poising the launcher to fire again. But the spheres were empty. She'd won. Exactly as Banshee had demanded.

"Asa." Riven's breaths were staggered. "Did you just save my ass?"

Asa let out a delirious laugh. "I think I did."

"Thanks." It was still dark, and weirdly quiet. No fanfare.

No cheers, but murmurs. "You're going to let me out of here now, right?"

On Asa's cue, the elevator arrived, and Riven jumped in as soon as the doors opened. She caught her guns from the electromagnet as it released. Away from all the crowds and cameras, she slumped onto the floor, resting her head on her knees. The wounds stung like all hell, and her lungs felt like she'd been breathing acid fog. She let out a shaky breath.

I'm alive, she told herself, incredulous. *I'm alive.* After all that, she'd been too stubborn to die. But she'd had help.

Asa was waiting for her as the elevator opened. "Riven." Her eyes were glassy, as if she were holding back tears. "You're hurt—"

Riven threw her arms around Asa. She smelled like hairspray and sickly sweet fruits and a trace of nervous sweat. "You came back for me."

"I had to. We're crew, aren't we?"

There was so much hope in Asa's voice that Riven gave a shuddering laugh. She was probably smearing the girl with blood and sweat and god knew what else, but hell if she cared right now. They'd been through enough. Enough to forget whose daughter Asa was, if only for a few moments.

"Nice moves in there." Asa pressed her forehead against Riven's. Her eyeliner had smeared, and small burns and scrapes riddled her hands. She was starting to look like proper gutter trash. It made Riven proud.

But now that Riven's head was clearing, she remembered why she was here. "Ty," she said, pulling away. "Where's Ty?"

"We don't know yet. Samir and Diego headed toward the observatory to look for him."

Riven swore. He was in worse danger than she. "Banshee still has him."

Asa nodded. "We need to keep things quiet."

The surge of pain in Riven's head was worsening. She closed her eyes, wishing she could will away the nastiness eating her.

Ping. Another message from Ty's wristlet.

Splendid, it read. *Tyren is waiting for you on the VIP level, suite IX. And so am I.*

With it was a picture that made her cold fury return. A blurry close-up of Ty's face. His eyes closed, his lip split. A bruise darkened his temple.

Riven let out a string of filthy curses. "That bastard hurt him. Now it wants me to go up there too."

What game was this thing playing? Its original message said to meet her down at the storage rooms. It couldn't hurt to do one last check, in case this was another trap.

She told Asa about her first messages. "I need to look down there, just to be sure."

"Riven, you shouldn't."

The lights in the GravSpheres flickered back on, illuminating graffiti skulls on the walls. "Ty can't wait forever. And then we have a job for the goddamn Duchess of Requiem to finish."

"I'm heading up." Asa gently took one of Riven's hands. "I don't want to leave you behind again, but . . ."

"Just a glance. Down the stairs, and back up. No gladiatorial pits. No creepy brothels." She leaned in. "I promise."

Asa didn't look convinced. "Be careful." She let her hand fall. "Whatever has him is waiting for us."

chapter 24
BANSHEE

With every step, the club's walls seemed to be squeezing in. Asa knew they were walking into a trap, but it was the only way to save Ty.

She caught her breath at the top of the elevator, where Samir and Diego waited for her. Samir led them to suite IX, and the door slid open once they'd all scanned their fingerprints. The outer wall and edge of the floor were glass, overlooking Requiem's vibrant skyline. Thorned vines crept up the walls, and holograms of dormant, scantily clad companions flickered, waiting for instructions.

And at the far end of the room, silhouetted by the glow of the city, was the monster that had followed them. Next to it was a slumped, kneeling form. *Ty.*

"Hands in the air," its deep, metallic voice grated. The monster— seven feet tall, all ridges and angles—made a slicing motion with its hand. A humanoid Federation mech. Not a hologram. "Weapons down. I wish to talk."

Asa's heart leapt into her throat. Banshee was smart enough to speak. Smart enough to trick them. Smart enough to possess a deadly mech.

"How about this instead?" Samir lifted his pistol. "You let Ty go, or I'll blow out the circuit brain of that mech."

"Fire, then," Banshee challenged.

Asa heard a click. Then a second. Samir was pulling the trigger, but it wasn't firing. The lights along the barrel of his pistol had gone dark.

"Dammit," Samir breathed. "Of *course*."

Banshee was in everything. A prickle of instinct told her to *run* before it sealed the door, like it'd done in the lab.

But Ty . . . her chest ached as she looked him over. Lethargic but breathing, his mask gone, ugly bruises creeping across his cheekbone and bare arms. A trickle of blood ran down his neck, and his lips parted in pained gasps.

Whatever Banshee had done to him, he had to stay conscious. They'd get him out. Asa would make sure of it.

"You creatures may address me as Yllath." Banshee's mech-jaw clicked as it spoke. Its eyes blazed like distant flames. "*He of Many Faces*, in your tongue."

He. Strange that an AI would gender himself. "What do you want?" Asa said softly, though she already knew the answer. She remembered Cyclops demanding her biocapsule, the path of hacked tech heading straight for her.

And it'd found her.

"I only wish to parley." Somehow, even the skeletal plates of Yllath's face radiated calm, calculated intelligence. Maybe he was alive, and unstable. Maybe the creature following her— through the laboratory, on the ship—had been *thinking* as he learned to hack, learned to speak.

"Stay back." Ty's words were slurred, sluggish. "There's a sedative in your trackers, and it can—"

Yllath smacked the back of Ty's head, knocking him forward onto the glass. Samir lunged toward the mech, grabbing its arm and twisting. Any human would've been slammed face-first onto the ground, but Banshee merely swayed, then punched Samir's ribs with a steel-plated fist.

"Samir, stay *back*." Diego grabbed his stunner, for all the good it would do.

Asa touched the back of her neck. A sedative in the trackers. That's what had gotten Ty. Did the Duchess know what was happening here?

"Don't panic," Diego murmured to her. "Bria's already deactivated them."

"Clever." Yllath resumed his position near Ty, eyeing Samir with those smoldering eyes. "But you should not be so aggressive. This is a negotiation."

"Oh, *now* you want to negotiate." Samir clutched his ribs.

A click and a whir sounded behind them as two wolf-shaped chaser mechs entered, circling in front of the exit. Asa swallowed hard. They weren't getting out of this without a fight. She wished Riven were here.

"I will speak to the Almeida girl." Yllath paced behind Ty, the mech's feet clanking against the glass floor. "Come here, Asanna."

Asa couldn't respond. Negotiating with a creature that had brought a city to its knees? For her sister? Every muscle seemed frozen, and she glanced at Diego in a silent question. He merely raised an eyebrow. Even he was out of ideas.

Ty let out a weak cough. Asa had gotten them into this mess, and she had to do *something*. "Fine." Asa kept the quaver out of her voice. "But you promise Ty leaves safely."

Yllath's rumbling laugh sent a chill through Asa. "I make no promises."

She approached Yllath until the floor beneath her feet became glass.

"Miss Asanna Almeida." Yllath's movements went from graceful to hostile, and he cornered her against the glass wall, staring down at her. "Where is the biocapsule you protect so jealously?"

"I don't have it." The Duchess had it, for safekeeping.

"But you know where it is." His false eyes blazed.

"It was . . . stolen from me." She squirmed beneath the weight of the mech's gaze, trying to shrink further against the glass at her back. Behind Yllath, Samir stumbled to his feet, shouting to Diego.

"*Liar.*" Yllath bared the serrated teeth inside his glowing maw. His arm snapped out, pinning Asa by her neck. She gagged, seeing spots from the impact. Instinctively, she grabbed the hand, trying to keep the pressure off her windpipe. Yllath's free hand ripped the wire mask off her face, leaving the skin at her temples stinging. "You and your father both. I will ask once more: where is it?"

Over Yllath's shoulder, Asa glimpsed Diego staggering as one of the chasers snapped at him. Samir grabbed a steel coat rack and jammed it into the mech's maw.

"I can make things hell for them. And neither will I hesitate to crush you." The mech's fingers tightened on her neck.

Asa gasped, tilting her head back. "My father would be *very* disappointed if that happened."

"I don't care about your father. Luca is shortsighted. Cruel."

"Is that why he created you?"

A morbid, grating laugh. Yllath's grip loosened, and Asa steadied herself against the dizziness. "Your father pretends he created me. But I have existed far longer than he has, and he merely . . . woke me, thinking he could control me. And then he began *pulling me apart.*"

Woke up Banshee. It didn't make sense. "Why are you after that biocapsule, then?"

In those glowing eyes, nothing. "Because it contains something of mine. Your father cut it from me, and I intend to put it back."

Cut it from Yllath. The Etri brain. But that meant—

"You're an Etri," Asa whispered. "Not an AI."

"Correct. There is nothing artificial about my intelligence."

Her father had pulled Yllath apart, like he'd done to Kaya. The pieces were falling into place. If the brain in the biocapsule was originally Yllath's, and it now contained Kaya's mind . . .

The original Etri mind hadn't been erased. It had crept through the wires, traveling, escaping. And now Yllath was right in front of her, in the body of a mech.

Yllath must've awoken in a cold-circuit prison, the same way Kaya had. He'd been hurt by her father too. But Yllath and Kaya couldn't both become whole—not with Kaya's original brain in pieces. Not without another miracle organ that could be reprogrammed with a human neural structure.

"I'm sorry for what my father did to you," Asa said. "But I need to save Kaya."

"Kaya Almeida?" Yllath said.

"You mean me?" The familiar voice sent a pang of longing through Asa, but it was somehow . . . wrong. Distorted.

Toward them strode a hologram—a girl with a messy side

ponytail, a zippered cocktail dress, and a face that made Asa tear up at its familiarity. Kaya smiled with a mischievous warmth Asa had missed.

She looked exactly as she had onstage. Kaya's posture was slightly off, but the hologram was unmistakably *her*.

"My sister," the false Kaya said, her voice distorted. She smiled, reaching for Asa's face. "If you don't tell me where the biocapsule is . . ." She frowned, and her voice was joined by the deep tone of Yllath's. "I will find her and destroy what's left of her. Just like I will destroy your father, and everything else on that hell of a planet you call home."

The last shred of sympathy she had for Yllath vanished. "The people of Cortellion didn't do this."

"Your people are all the same," Kaya-Yllath continued. "In the time I have spent in your world, human culture has glorified nothing but thievery and murder. I wouldn't hesitate to turn Cortellion's cities into burned-out shells. And, as for you . . ."

Mech-Yllath grabbed Asa's wrist, twisting it backward against the glass. She gritted her teeth to stop the cry in her throat. "I will do whatever is necessary to extract the capsule's location from you. But I will not kill you. You are my only leverage in getting your father to put me back together."

No. She wasn't cargo or leverage. She hadn't come this far to be used in someone else's plans. And she was *sick* of people trying to intimidate her.

"You're no better than my father," she said. "That brain is Kaya's now, and nothing you do will make me give it up."

Before Yllath could respond, a gunshot rang out. Yllath

looked over his shoulder, snarling. The wolf-mech guarding the door had been reduced to a sparking heap.

Riven was here, tearing a warpath through the room. Asa wanted to collapse with relief.

Riven strode toward Yllath, leveling *Blackjack* at the side of the mech's head–

And the hologram of a young man leapt in front of her. "Riven, *no!*"

Riven's eyes went wide, and she froze, the barrel of her gun trained on the boy's forehead. He raised his palms in surrender. Tousled dark hair, blue eyes. He looked familiar, like Ty but taller, with a stronger jaw and sturdier build.

"Emmett," Riven breathed.

Riven had never expected to see Emmett O'Shea again.

But at the other end of her gun, there he was, his dark hair falling into his vivid, pleading eyes. So close to perfect it made her chest ache. Her pictures and vidclips of him–and the messages he'd left her in Galateo's modifications–were burned so deeply into her mind she barely noticed them anymore. But now . . .

"Put the gun down, Riv," Emmett's hologram begged. "Please."

Despite the synthetic blips, it was his voice, forming new words. In a strange, sick way, he was real again. Like the deepfakes the brothels served.

Behind him, Banshee let out a low, grating laugh. "I believe we have a matter to discuss, Miss Hawthorne."

"Don't shoot," Emmett whispered. A bullet hole appeared

through his chest, and blood began to stain his shirt. Riven's hand shook, and her fingers refused to fire.

"How did you find this?" Did footage exist of Sanctum's Edge, of the day it had all ended? "His . . . his voice . . ."

"I knew exactly where to look," the mech said. "And that wasn't the only thing I've found." It tilted its head. "You wish to rule this city, yes?"

Asa struggled in Banshee's grip, staring at Riven as if to say *shoot it, Riven. Please.* Instinct screamed that Asa needed her—but she silenced it.

Riven cocked *Blackjack* with another disruptor round. "I don't know what the hell you think you know about me." Her curiosity was piqued. This creature had all the matriarchs running scared, and there was no beating him here. Could she strike a bargain?

"Does this runaway Cortellion heiress and her family conflict mean so much to you? I intend to take her with me and withdraw from Requiem voluntarily. Still . . ." His skeletal mouth twisted into an imitation of a grin. "There is much more I could offer you. Blackmail. Control over every matriarch's most personal tech. Every syndicate in Requiem would bend the knee to you, Duchess Hawthorne."

Every syndicate. It was a stupid lie, but as for the rest . . . "You'd leave?" she whispered.

"My quarrel is not with Requiem," Banshee said. "Once I'm finished with this girl and her psychopath father, Cortellion is all I want. All that planet's tech—and its scientists, and whatever else was involved in these experiments—I will destroy. But

I can help you first. All I ask, Hawthorne, is that you let me leave with Miss Almeida."

Emmett stared at her, waiting. The bullet hole in his chest had disappeared. He'd be here—in the flesh—if not for Asa and her father. How much more of Requiem would they lose if they *didn't* give the capsule back?

She was tired. Tired of being kicked around for a scheme that might never pay off. Tired of fighting for power and ending up with scraps. Tired of waking up thrashing to nightmares of Emmett. If surrendering meant saving her city—saving Ty and Samir—she'd do it.

"Riven," Asa choked. "Don't listen."

For a second, Riven almost pulled the trigger. But Asa's father wouldn't kill her if she went home. The rest of them had no such promise.

"Every faction would fall at your feet, Riven Hawthorne."

Riven narrowed her eyes. "Prove it, then. Pull yourself from Requiem. All of it. And you have a deal."

Suddenly, the mech's head crumpled and dented. Two bullets punched through, one piercing through the steel cladding.

Someone else had fired and ruined her negotiation.

She whirled. "What the *hell*?"

"I should be asking you the same thing, Riv." Samir peered down *Verdugo*'s barrel. "Step back. That's enough."

Riven seethed. He'd just ruined their chance to free Requiem. To be done with all of this.

The metal fingers on Asa's arm released, and she slumped onto the glass, gasping. Banshee lurched toward Samir, the mech's head dented and gaping. It was *pissed*.

Their deal was already broken. Riven fired, blowing the rest of the mech's head apart with a disruptor round.

"We need to get out of here," Samir said. "What were you thinking? You really think you could reason with this thing?"

As if *she* were the irrational one. "That might've been our only chance to get it to leave!"

As Banshee's destroyed mech twitched on the floor, metallic laughter echoed overhead. "Might I remind you I control all of Olympus?" Banshee's voice was grainier through the speakers.

"Grab Ty. We're getting out of here," Samir said. Riven grudgingly handed him two bullets, and he swung *Verdugo*'s cylinder out and loaded them into the empty chambers. "Never been happier to see these things."

Verdugo had helped him ruin her negotiation. Samir usually followed her lead on the crew, but he always thought he knew best. She had half a mind to take the gun back, but she needed backup.

"Scuff that gun and I'll scuff *you*." Riven loaded more silver-blue disruptor bullets into *Blackjack*.

She couldn't look at Asa. Whatever had been blossoming between them was over now—Asa wouldn't forgive her for this.

"Crossing Yllath was a mistake," Emmett's hologram warned as blood blossomed from his gunshot wound, staining his gray shirt. "Tech controls the world, and he can speak to it better than any of you."

Yllath. Banshee's true name? Riven looked over at Ty, who was slumped half-conscious next to Samir.

"Ty, don't look up," Riven said. "It's not pretty."

"I already saw." Ty winced. "How does he know?"

"He knows a hell of a lot, apparently." Riven locked eyes with Asa and jerked her thumb toward the exit.

The Kaya hologram appeared in front of Asa again. "Do you want to see what it looked like when he tore my brain apart?"

Asa closed her eyes and walked through the hologram.

Yllath was using their demons against them, trying to wrench them apart. And maybe he already had.

Riven shot the lock on the door and kicked it open. Outside, Olympus was in chaos. Alarms shrieked over the thumping music. She pulled back into the room as a Federation trooper ushered a group of startled clubgoers aside.

The trooper's shouting was distorted through his helmet. "This club is under mandatory evacuation. Step this way, and we can–"

He stopped and fled as a salvo of gunfire rang out behind him.

"Get down!" Riven shouted as another armed mech stepped into the doorway. Another of Yllath's thralls.

She scrambled toward Samir. With an unspoken cue, they heaved a lounge table over, toppling and shattering a bottle of booze. As they pulled Ty and Diego to cover, she glanced around for Asa. Thankfully, the girl had wedged herself between a couch and a potted palm tree.

Laughter reverberated through the speakers as the possessed mech drew closer. "I'm not finished with you yet."

Riven let out a steady breath.

Neither am I.

chapter 25

NIGHTMARE PARADISE

In moments, holograms and security-mechs had turned Olympus into a death trap.

Asa sat rigid with terror as bullets hurled through the observatory deck. She tightened her sweaty grip on the stunner, trying to make herself smaller against the plush couch. They hadn't gotten the quarantine codes. Either they'd die here, or they'd have to face the Duchess.

Her heart already felt like it'd been torn out through her ribs. Riven had tried to send her home. She would've let Yllath throw away her chance to save Kaya.

Perhaps more than ever, Asa was on her own.

"You have a plan yet, Samir?" Riven shouted from behind the overturned table. Bullets flew over them, sending cracks spiderwebbing across the glass wall. "They're going to evacuate this place. We have one chance."

"The plan is . . ." Samir held *Verdugo* parallel to his head. "To have a plan within the next thirty seconds."

"That isn't a plan!" She twisted her revolver over the top of the table and blind-fired a few rounds. One hit, making the mech in the doorway shudder.

Despite everything they'd endured together, Asa was worthless to Riven. If she died here, she'd die alone.

Finish the mission, Asa told herself as panic seized her every muscle. If she survived, it was just her and Kaya and Josiah. She'd have nothing to do with *Boomslang*'s crew.

After Samir lifted the table like a shield, Riven slipped into the hallway, and the heavy *thoom* of her revolvers followed. The stomp of mechs outside quieted, though screams and blasts still rang in the distance.

In the lull, alarms blared. With the horrific Kaya and Emmett holograms gone and only city light creeping in, the room felt almost serene. But between Yllath's threats and Riven's near betrayal, Asa wasn't sure how long she could keep it together.

As her eyes adjusted to the darkness, she saw Ty sitting against an overturned couch. He tilted his head backward and closed his eyes, drinking in a deep breath.

That longing ache flared up again. He'd put himself in danger because he'd been worried about *her.*

"Ty." She crawled to him before she could stop herself. "You all right?"

"I'm awake. I can move . . . sort of." He opened his eyes and gave her a wry grin. Even now, it thawed some of the ice in her chest. "I'm pretty useless right now, huh? Hope they don't need me to fix them."

"Honestly?" Diego said. "If one of those mechs catches them, it'll already be too late." He sighed, flexing the fingers of his cybernetic hand. "Samir had better not be doing anything reckless."

Samir's voice crackled over the comm. "Floor's clear. You going in, Riv?"

Riven responded. "No good. Suite's locked with a holo-shield."

"Dammit. Chip isn't working?"

"No. Emergency measures. Only mechs are moving through."

Red letters scrolled across the holopanels on the walls. *EMERGENCY EVACUATION IN PROGRESS. ALL GUESTS MUST EXIT.*

Asa's breath was tight. They were so close. The Federation suite was a few doors down. There had to be another way.

Diego swore and flicked on his wristlet. "Riven. Samir. The power's going out. This might be a lost cause."

"I'm not leaving!" Riven said. "The Duchess will kill us before Yllath will."

Asa's mind whirred, overclocked. The quarantine was starting. They needed a mech to download the quarantine codes before the power went out completely. She eyed the downed mech—Yllath's former body—and had a dangerous, terrible idea.

"Riven, come back to the suite. I might have a solution, but I'll need cover." She hated to ask Riven for help right now, but Riven's guns were as good as anyone's.

Plus, Riven had something else she needed.

"This better be quick," Riven said. "Fed troopers are sweeping the place."

Asa held up her wristlet and scanned Yllath's mech—the joints and wires, the holes from *Verdugo*'s bullets and the scattered shrapnel from a disruptor. The main circuit board was a wreck, but the rest might be salvageable.

Riven reappeared in the doorway, silhouetted by the frantic lights outside. "What are you doing with that thing?" She aimed a gun at the downed mech.

"Its motherboard is fried, but that's where the infection would've been. So if I attach a new board . . ." Asa dug into her tool pouch. "I can take it over."

"You can reprogram a Fed-mech so quickly?" Diego said.

"I can't. But if an AI could control it *for* me . . ." Asa glanced at Riven's wristlet.

Riven frowned. "Galateo?"

"Might be all we've got."

Riven glared at the floor. Then she unclasped her wristlet and handed it to Asa. "I'd better be getting him back."

"Eager to serve, my lady," the wristlet chirped.

Asa hesitated. "Galateo, you might not make it out."

Riven grabbed Asa's wrist as her gray-green eyes met Asa's. It made heat shoot through her for a fleeting second. "He had *better*. And Emmett . . ." She paused, as if she couldn't get her words out. "Emmett put Galateo together. There are pieces I couldn't back up in any other system."

"I'll try." She didn't dare tell Riven there was no way Galateo was coming back. But getting this done was more important than whatever sentiment Riven attached to Galateo. Galateo was their last ace.

Asa worked the still-hot mech apart, grateful for the padding on her gloves. She removed them when she'd exposed the busted motherboard, then attached the wristlet with a tiny soldering gun.

"Riv," Samir said gently, "even if the mech goes down here . . . he'll still be on *Boomslang*."

"But he won't remember anything," Riven said. "My nav patterns, our smuggling jobs–Emmett's programming. His memories."

"It might be a necessary risk."

When Asa had snipped and resoldered the wires in the mech's brain, she took a step back. "Galateo, can you hear me?"

A twitch. The mech's eyes lit pale blue, and the joints whirred and twisted until the mech rose to its full height, over seven feet tall. Asa tried not to flinch, considering this thing had been squeezing her throat a few minutes ago.

Galateo tilted his new half-destroyed head and flexed the mech fingers. He let out a quizzical laugh. "It is *fascinating* to move this way." He sunk into a graceful bow. "I am at your service."

"You'd be a good shield in a gunfight, Galateo." Riven gave an uneasy smile. "Damn, look at you!"

Galateo walked along the windows–awkward and wobbly, but gaining momentum. "I am not programmed for autonomous movement, but a body serves me well." His voice was deeper than it had been on Riven's wristlet, but with the same accent. "All the better to stop you from making bad decisions, my lady."

"Here's what you need to do," Asa said. "You should have access to the Federation suite. Download those quarantine codes, send them to us, and we'll get them to the Duchess."

"Noted." Galateo straightened his broad, steel-plated

shoulders and strode toward the exit. Samir and Riven flanked him, and Asa helped Ty to his feet. "If any of the troopers ask, I'm escorting you ingrates out of the establishment."

"I'll escort *you*." Riven cocked *Blackjack*. "To make sure you walk out of here."

Gunshots resounded in the hallway. "Like hell you will," Samir said. "You saw that area—it's crawling with mechs. Galateo can take a few bullets. You can't."

Riven gave Samir a hard look, then sighed. "Galateo—don't screw this up."

Galateo looked over his shoulder. Asa could've sworn there was a sad smile on that mechanical face. "I am not programmed to, my lady."

Galateo stomped toward the VIP suites while Riven and Samir led the rest of them across the red-carpeted bridges. Two wolf-mechs' eyes flashed orange as they approached, but Riven downed them.

Asa snuck a glance over the balcony to the main dance floor. It was chaos—the spotlights and screens pulsed red with emergency lighting, while the bass still thumped frantically. Music blared in off-key, distorted snippets, as if some tone-deaf creature were messing with the sound mixers.

Worst of all was the Etri elevator. The arms had pulled free of their tracks and slammed onto the dance floor as terrified clubgoers tried to run. The arms moved slowly but destructively, crushing and slamming.

Asa's stomach turned. Not everyone had avoided its blows.

"This way!" Riven said behind her. Diego yanked open the door to the emergency stairwell, urging them inside. It was pitch dark, but at least Yllath couldn't affect stairs. The concrete pounded beneath Asa's feet.

"If we get out . . ." Diego switched on his wristlet light. "We're never getting back in. The quarantine's hitting hard."

"If Yllath finds out what Galateo's doing . . ." Riven hissed in exasperation. "Oh, *god*, he's doomed."

Samir pressed his ear to the first-floor stairwell door, listening for gunfire.

Asa watched Galateo's field of vision on her wristlet. One of the other Federation mechs shredded Galateo's leg with bullets, and he fell to a knee.

"Come on, Galateo," Asa whispered into her wristlet. "You can do this."

Galateo's vision showed a control panel, flickering amid the chaos. He plugged into it, and for a few agonizing moments, there were loading screens and a salvo of gunfire in the background.

"Codes downloaded," Galateo finally said. "Sending them your way."

Relief loosened the ropes constricting Asa's lungs. "Thank you, Galateo."

A prickle of static. "Yllath has noticed me. And he's not happy."

"No, Galateo." Riven grabbed Asa's arm to shout into her wristlet. "You've resisted this thing before. Don't let it in."

Galateo's voice came in garbled. "He's . . . cleverer than before. Creeping into parts of my systems I was not aware of. Like a virus."

Asa closed her eyes. She had a feeling this would happen.

"He learns quickly. He is . . . a true consciousness," Galateo said. "I can thwart attacks by artificial minds, but I have never encountered a mind like his. I am sorry, my lady, but I . . . am not strong enough."

"Don't you do this, Galateo." Riven's desperate fingers dug into Asa's wrist. "I mean it. I need you in my cockpit."

A file containing the codes popped up on Asa's wristlet screen. *From: Riven Hawthorne.*

"Sent. Now, go. Before he finds you too."

Through the stairwell door, the music was replaced with the shriek of microphone feedback. Asa gritted her teeth. Yllath was coming.

"Galateo," Riven said. "If you go down in that mech—"

"This is all I can do for you," Galateo said as two enforcer-mechs closed in on him. "Goodbye, my lady."

chapter 26

ATMOSPHERE

"**G**alateo," Riven whispered. She realized she was holding Asa's arm in a death grip, but it was her only connection to him.

The comm channel turned to static.

No. Not like this. Riven tapped frantically on the screen. Galateo's mech had gone down, frying him with it. "No. No, no, *no.*"

One last transmission began playing. "*I'd be okay, Riven,*" Emmett's voice crackled through the speaker, "*if it were just us, I think. Us, and the starfield.*"

His voice hit her like a punch to the chest. *Just us.* She'd let Emmett down once more. Now, she'd heard that clip for a final time.

Asa slowly pulled her wrist away from Riven. Her brown eyes met Riven's. "He's gone."

Gone. After seeing Emmett's image in the VIP suite, and being powerless to save Galateo . . .

It felt like fleeing Sanctum's Edge, Emmett in her arms, dune grasses cutting her bare feet. But this time, it was Asa's fault, not her dad's.

Samir had to drag Riven out the emergency exit, insisting Olympus was going down in flames.

"I'm going to go get him. Let go of me."

"No, you aren't," Diego said. "We have no way to contact you right now, and Bria is waiting at the docking bay. We've done what the Duchess wanted."

"I'm sorry." Asa clicked off the wristlet screen. "But we have to leave, Riven."

Riven's hackles rose. *I'm sorry.* The half-sincere apology only made things worse. She'd acknowledge Galateo, but not Emmett?

But Diego was right. Riven holstered *Blackjack* and followed them, trying to ignore the hole growing in her chest—Emmett's programming gone, forever. It wouldn't sink in.

They left Nocturne and headed through the subway tunnels into the quarantine zone, creeping past the few Fed patrols until they found Eidolon Docking Bay, vast and dark and silent. They followed the Duchess's coordinates to a side door. When they approached, it slid open to reveal Bria—a glowing vapor-stick in one hand and the biocapsule in the other.

"Nice of you all to show," Bria said. "Duchess Reyala was surprised you managed to pull that off. There will be hell to pay for Rio Oscuro, but for now . . ." They stuffed the biocapsule into Riven's hands. "Your ship is already tagged for tracking. Go—quickly. No telling how quickly Banshee will spread here, with the power back."

This thing. This stupid biocapsule. The reason her hideout and Galateo were gone. Her crew almost carved up for organ pirates.

At least she still had *Boomslang*. The bay lights flickered on, following their footsteps down the walkway toward her ship's dock. *Boomslang* was waiting for her like an old friend, its black-banded hull gleaming.

When the ship's lights came on and the docking ramp lowered, Galateo's voice wasn't there to greet Riven.

"Let's go," Samir said as they headed up the ramp. "Yllath might hit the docking controls soon."

Riven shoved the biocapsule into Samir's hands as she took in the salirium-and-stale-pizza scent of her ship. It smelled like home. Once she settled into the cockpit, behind the control panel and the crescent-shaped windshield, she was in the one place she'd ever belonged.

She entered her codes, hit the ignition, and closed her eyes as the main engine turned over, a powerful buzz in her arms and feet. At her command.

It was time to fly. To leave behind all her failures and bad decisions of the past few days. To finally end this.

"Requiem lives and dies on your watch," Bria called from the docking ramp, breathing deep on their vapor-stick. "You'd better not screw this up."

"Thanks for the reminder." Riven flipped a dirty gesture while hitting the hatch switch, shutting Bria out. She'd had enough of Bria's snobbishness and bad taste in fighting gear—the constrictive bodice made her wounds burn. This job was going to end on Riven's terms, not the Duchess's.

Before Ty sat down, he lifted Riven's injured arm by the elbow. He winced as he looked over the cuts. "Riv, we need to—"

"I'm fine." She jerked her arm away. Even the small motion stung. "Go strap in."

The others pulled down the seats in the cockpit. Ty helped Asa buckle the harness, and it pissed Riven off that he was still being nice to her. For all she'd wanted to like Asa—her softness, her determination in the face of danger—Asa didn't care about anyone but herself. She was just like her dad, considering only the end and not the sacrifices to get there.

Riven tapped her flight coordinates into the control panel. It was weirdly quiet. "Dammit. Never thought I'd miss Galateo." He might've been a nag, but he was a friend. Even if he was programmed to, at least he pretended to appreciate her.

From the corner of her eye, she saw Asa's arms crossed over her ribs—her *don't-touch-me* stance. "You cared more about getting an AI out of there alive than me?" Asa said softly.

"Your life wasn't on the line." Still, the guilt nagged her. Asa had risked herself to save Riven in the GravSpheres, but Yllath's deal had been tempting. Her hideout back, the city free. Asa would've exited Riven's life the same way she'd stumbled in, taking the destruction with her.

"Do you know what'll happen if I ever see my dad again?" Asa said.

"Listen. You're here, mechanist. You're alive. We're getting you off Requiem, exactly like you wanted. For *your* sister. Cortellion's safe, and our city's blasted to shit. Are you happy?"

"Asa's right," Samir said from the seat behind her. "Betraying your crew for *Banshee* was one hell of a bad decision."

"Stay out of this. It's not your business." Riven engaged the atmo-support, preparing for ascent. The ship's vents roared in response, awake and ready.

"I'm on your crew, so it *is* my business." She could feel

Samir's disappointment behind her. "I follow your lead because you know how to get a job done. Because you found me a crew when I needed one. But *this*? You really thought Banshee would make you a matriarch? Sometimes it seems like you care more about your reputation than about this crew."

"I care more about this *crew* than I do about some Almeida family drama that has nothing to do with me!" Riven gritted her teeth as the ship lifted from the docking controls. She hit the thruster switch, harder than she needed to. None of them understood.

Boomslang shuddered as it gained momentum, and Riven engaged the stealth drive to slip past the Fed-drones' radar. She piloted the ship between their spotlights, between the animated holograms on Requiem's towers and skybridges. With her guidance, *Boomslang* darted between them with the grace of its namesake.

Her breath caught as they slipped through the dome at Heaven's Breach and into the freedom of the stars. It felt like the first lungful of air after being trapped underwater—she'd missed being suspended in an expanse of distant worlds, the worlds Emmett had promised to explore with her.

But she was still anchored by her obligations. She had a job to finish, much as her crew hated her right now.

Once they'd made the turbulent ascent and breached Requiem's gravity, Ty broke the silence. "Samir. Yllath spoke to me too."

"While he was hurting you?" Samir said, his voice a quiet fire.

"He offered me access to Almeida's data. Something I could use to research the thing infecting Riven."

Riven scowled into the starfield, trying not to listen. The white noise was easier to manage when she pretended it didn't exist.

"I've scoured every database I can find," Ty said when Riven didn't respond. "Experimental drugs, analogous diseases, neurodegeneration. But all I've discovered is that it's a bioengineered fungus, it's spreading through her nervous system, and it attacks her worse when she's under stress. If I was sure Yllath knew something . . . maybe I would've taken that risk."

"But you didn't," Samir said.

"It was tempting. Riven wanted to save Requiem. And for her or Emmett . . . I would've hesitated too." Ty sighed. "You know what? We all made mistakes back there. But bickering isn't going to fix things or put Requiem back together. We're all each other's got. And all Requiem's got. So we should start acting like it."

Riven let the silence hang heavy. Maybe Ty was right. Once Yllath was defeated—once everything went back to normal—it would be just her and Ty and Samir again, gunning their way through the underworld, scraping a living during Requiem's sweltering days and electric nights. Her and *Boomslang*, with no quarantine to tether her from the stars.

Somehow, maybe, that future could involve Asa. If the girl ever owned up to her mistakes . . . well, there was something between them, something Riven wasn't ready to admit yet.

"Hey," Asa said excitedly, as if relieved to be changing

the subject. "Josiah came for us. His ship is waiting outside Requiem's orbit for us to dock."

"Why?" Riven said. "I thought we were making the jump to Earth and meeting him at his lab."

"We're running out of time for Kaya," Asa said. "So he brought a med-station ship. It has the facilities to keep her stable."

Riven frowned. Something in her gut said things didn't add up. "You sure that's not Yllath trying to get us to dock?"

"Josiah gave me our code phrases. We can trust him."

"I don't know about this." What if Asa and Josiah were trying to con them? There were still gaps in Diego's intel—Josiah's goals being the biggest. "I want to at least follow to a secure docking zone. Or the lab itself."

"Josiah," Asa said into her wristlet. "Do you have Kaya aboard?"

"So glad you've made it out, Asa," Josiah's eerily somber voice murmured through Asa's wristlet speaker. "She's waiting for you. Her vitals are stable, but we don't have much time."

No objections came from the rest of the crew. Getting the biocapsule into Josiah's hands was part of the mission, after all. Riven sighed. "All right. Give me his coordinates, and I can alter the course."

As Riven entered the new nav-route and the ship stabilized, the clicks of unbuckling seatbelts filled the cabin.

Next to her, Diego fiddled with an aux computer screen, scrolling through news sites and private channels. "Well. On a brighter note, seems Yllath has been plastering our images on every working screen in Requiem." He frowned, watching the footage. "The Federation has a hefty reward on us."

"Was only a matter of time." Ty settled into the control panel seat at her left. He still wore the black vest from Bria's closet—none of them had time to change. The rhinestones were still covering half of Riven's face, since they hurt like hell to peel off.

"That's not all," Diego said. "Banshee's been all over the news on Cortellion and Earth for the past few days. This is the first time the public's gotten hold of names and faces to go with the ordeal. We're *famous*. And not in a good way."

"Let me see that." Samir slid into the seat beside Diego. "Whoa. That's not just news, but message boards. AlphaSpace videos. Blogs . . . conspiracy theories? You guys should *see* this."

Riven didn't want to know. Josiah had probably heard all sorts of rumors about her crew by now. She focused on the nav display.

Samir snorted. "There's middle school kids crushing on Ty, creepy older guys fantasizing about Asa and Riven . . ."

"Gross," Riven muttered. Marcus was bad enough.

". . . and a few admirers who're convinced Riven and I are together." Samir gagged. "Not even if I were straight."

"Oh, shut up. You *love* me." At least, she hoped Samir didn't hate her. Her crew still felt fractured, and it was partially her fault. The only way to fix things was to finish this. To prove her worth to the Duchess. To settle Sokolov's debt. To get Asa out of their hands, maybe forever.

Still, part of her wished she could steal Asa as their per-manent mechanist.

"Isn't this bad news?" Asa said uncomfortably. "With a huge reward . . . everyone's going to be on the lookout. Not just for me anymore."

"That's why you'd better hope your friend Josiah knows what he's doing." Samir said. "Once Yllath is gone, the Duchess might be able to remove that bounty."

"Until then, we're fugitives," Riven said.

With a flash of blue light at the horizon, Josiah's ship came into view. A state-of-the-art medical ship—a small hospital for treating patients off planet. Better than a brain-swapping lab, she supposed.

"There's our ride," Riven said, though the unease hounded her. If Josiah was going to save Asa's sister, she needed him to prove it first. "Grab your guns, and be on your guard."

***

Asa had never been more relieved to see a ship.

As the disc-shaped med-station approached through the blackness, she imagined a private bed where she could sleep off the terrors of the past few days. A lab she could share with Josiah, a place to start her own projects—and Kaya, whole again.

Requiem was behind her. She'd survived the galaxy's shadiest underbelly, and now she could tell Kaya true stories she'd never believe, dive back into AbyssQuest with her, and give her the most intense hug of her life.

"Soon," Asa whispered to the biocapsule.

"We'll dock," Riven said, "but wait for my signal."

Samir grabbed a rifle from the arms storage and shoved

a pistol into Ty's hands. Ty held it at arm's length, as it if were a dead squid.

The entire ship rocked as *Boomslang* locked into the larger ship's docking mechanism. When the airlocks closed, Riven vented the cabin pressure, making Asa's ears pop.

"All right," Samir said. "Stay back, Asa, and keep that thing safe until we're sure we know what we're dealing with."

"I *do* know what we're dealing with." Riven and Samir were paranoid. She'd known Josiah for a decade. He was the one to sneak her chocolates during long hours in her garage, helping her sift through design plans her father hadn't approved.

Asa clutched the biocapsule as the hatch opened. Down the lighted walkway was Josiah's familiar grizzled beard and old-tree frame. His hands were stuffed into the pockets of his baggy suit, exactly as she remembered him. Not one of Yllath's tricks.

"Josiah!" Asa clutched the biocapsule tight, rushing down the dock.

"Asa, what are you doing?" Riven shouted behind her.

Asa didn't look back. The sooner the capsule was safe in Josiah's hands, the better.

Josiah gathered Asa into his arms, tightening his grip around her. He was *real.* He hadn't hugged her since she was a child, and it was a strange comfort. He smelled like atherblossom wood and chemical rain, like home, but more . . . sterile.

When Josiah pulled back, the biocapsule was in his hands. He turned it over, flicking on the light switch to watch the Etri brain pulse inside.

Kaya. So fragile, but alive.

"Thank you, Asa," Josiah said, but he wasn't looking at her.

"Where's Kaya? Do you have everything you need to start?"

"Kaya. Yes." He gave her a hard look. Something was off. "Come to the lab with me. There's something I need to explain."

Behind her was the slither of a door opening. She turned back toward *Boomslang* as doors on either side of the hallway dilated open.

Out ran eight guards in plates of black body armor, their rifles trained on *Boomslang*. Security guards.

Asa grabbed Josiah's arm. "What's going on?"

He ignored her. "Surrender your weapons," he called to Riven and Samir.

"Tell your men to stand down!" Asa said. This had to be a misunderstanding. "They're the ones who've been helping me."

"They're dangerous. And according to the Federation . . . they're worth a substantial bounty."

Riven's venomous glare snapped to Asa. There was a flicker of hurt, then clear resolve. As if she'd expected this from Asa all along. Then, she started shooting.

A few guards dropped as Samir held the trigger and Riven fired from each revolver, but with their body armor, most of Josiah's guards only staggered at the hits.

"All of you, *stop*!" Asa shouted over the gunfire. Riven had to know Asa hadn't betrayed her. Nobody had betrayed anyone. This was just–

A cold smirk flickered across Josiah's face as he tucked the biocapsule into a satchel.

A misunderstanding?

"Josiah." An awful suspicion crept over Asa. "What do you plan to do with Kaya?"

As the guards returned gunfire, Riven and Samir dove back inside the ship. Bullets pelted *Boomslang*'s hull and flew through the open door.

Josiah set a hand on Asa's shoulder. "I plan to do what your father never could."

"Which means?"

"We disagreed about the scope of this research. He discontinued the soldier project of Winterdark. But in my hands . . . it will become what it always should have been."

"You aren't stopping Project Winterdark." The pieces began to click. "You're continuing it?"

The hopes that had kept her alive—the desperation that had given her the courage to save the crashing ship, the resolve to break into the *Adversary*'s bay—began to flicker and die. They'd all hinged on Josiah helping her. If he wasn't, she had nothing left.

He was just like her father.

"You can see her body, if you'd like." He watched his men dive into *Boomslang,* emerging with a struggling Riven and Samir. A thrill ignited in his eyes. "I have no use for her anymore, now that you've gotten this for me."

"You promised," Asa spat. He'd used her. Used Kaya.

"I am sorry, Asa. But Kaya is part of something much larger than either of you. Her mind is ready for reprogramming."

"You said we could trust him!" Riven shouted. Josiah's remaining guards marched her four disarmed crew members down the docking ramp, like malfunctioning mechs being led to the scrapyard.

"Oh, come now. It isn't her fault," Josiah called to Riven, an ugly sneer infecting his voice. "The girl's always been so trusting."

Asa's response caught in her throat. An heiress was all she'd ever be. She'd gained nothing by running away—only lost everything she could've been.

"I knew I had a bad feeling about you." Riven squirmed as two soldiers in crested black helmets locked her arms behind her. Samir had guns pressed to his neck and back. Ty and Diego held their hands up, avoiding their captors' gazes.

"And I have a feeling you'll make me quite a few denar." Josiah reached for Riven's chin, but yanked his fingers back when she tried to bite him.

"My father will be looking for me," Asa said, as awful as it was to imagine going back. "And then what will you do?"

"He won't find you, unless he coughs up your ransom and the data I need." Josiah's thin lips tightened. "And Luca doesn't have much sway outside Alpha Centauri. Once we pass through the relay to Earth, we'll be a star-system away."

Ransom. Once again, she was a bargaining chip.

On Josiah's signal, the guards marched after him, dragging Asa's friends with them.

"Come, now." Josiah's voice was rough with a dark excitement. "It's time to get you all settled in."

chapter 27
PRISON, AGAIN

As the door bolted shut behind them, Asa couldn't face her crew members. Or her former crew members. She'd put them in danger again—and this time, they might not get out.

The med station's guest suite was far from the worst possible prison, but with their guns, tools, and comms confiscated, they were helpless.

Riven paced toward the plexicarbon wall, shaking with fury. She looked like she was going to throw a punch, but instead she slammed her forearm against the wall and leaned against it, resigned, staring out at the stars and Requiem fading to a small crescent.

None of them spoke. Diego set a hand on Samir's shoulder, and Ty sank onto one of the couches, his hands on his knees.

Asa knew exactly what they all wanted to call her—liar, naïve rich girl, failure—and they'd be right. She felt the burn of impending tears and slipped into the tiny side bedroom.

It was barely large enough for the white-sheeted bed and nightstand, and she kicked the door closed before flopping onto the bed. She'd lost her home, and Kaya. Everyone had gambled on her ability to save Requiem, and she'd failed.

There was nothing left.

Asa sat up, hugged her knees, and stared through the glass wall at the expanse of stars. Requiem's patch of myriad colors slowly shrunk until it was only a point of light on a distant moon. Beyond, Cortellion's vast forests and rivers were a blue-and-white glass sphere.

Neither place was truly home. Asa would never be the daughter her father wanted, and she wasn't cunning enough to navigate Requiem. All she'd wanted was a quiet life in a machine shop, a life on her own terms, free of the lies of her father's world. A life with Kaya. But the world was out to get them.

Maybe Morphett had been right. She could never stand against her father.

The moon and the planet blurred as the tears finally came. She wiped them on her bare arms, realizing how little she was wearing. The stupid slitted leotard and shorts Bria had insisted on. Asa had made the mistake of thinking she was a member of the team—that she belonged.

But now Riven would never forgive her. Asa had let them down twice. They'd risked everything for her and Kaya, and now the city they called home was in shambles.

She rubbed her eyes on the duvet, and one of her red rhinestones popped off. Her eyeliner left black smears on the white fabric. Good. The least Josiah deserved was a ruined bedsheet.

She startled when a light rap resounded on the door.

"Hey." Ty's voice. "Can I come in?"

Asa was numb. It didn't matter if Ty or anyone saw her like this. "Yeah. Sure."

The door swung open, and Ty approached cautiously. "You all right?" His voice was gentle. Concerned. More than she deserved.

Her throat quivered. The words would come out creaky and stupid if she spoke, so instead she stared out the window and shrugged.

"This isn't your fault."

She laughed bitterly. He was either lying or stupid. "And why's that?"

"Everything Diego found on Josiah checked out—one of Almeida's best scientists, and a defector who'd stolen important tech from his boss."

"Still. I should've known."

"Well, maybe," Ty said sheepishly. "Our missing piece was his motivations, so I guess we were counting on you to fill in that part."

She let out a shaky breath. "And that screwed us over. You don't have to pretend you aren't mad at me."

"I'm not." The bed jounced as he sat down next to her. His warmth was achingly close, and she wished she could believe him. "We couldn't have gotten out of there without you. With your mechanist skills, you might've given even Emmett a run for his money." He put his hand on hers. "Look. If it were Emmett who needed saving, and someone of dubious motives was my last hope, I would've taken the chance too."

It helped, a bit. "Being a good mechanist doesn't mean I'm cut out for any of this."

"Because you're from Cortellion? So what? You were fine on Requiem. You made it out of the Duchess's dungeons. Few people have lived to tell *that* story." He traced her fingers, his voice quiet, soothing. She forced herself to look at him—his blue eyes reflected pinpoints of light in the starfield, and the fine bones in his face were almost fragile. "You know, you saved our asses enough times. You got Riven out of the GravSpheres, you got Galateo into the Federation suite, you disabled the *Adversary*'s security systems, and . . . well, a lot of things."

"So you don't hate me?"

Ty gave a surprised laugh. His fondness was intoxicating, a shred of warmth to cling to in this chaos, even if her feelings for him were a jumbled mess. "Of *course* not. You're brave, and you're trying. You've made mistakes, but we all have." He sighed, brushing a rust-blond lock out of his eyes. "My point is, this isn't over. And it isn't too late to fix things."

Maybe he was right. She'd fallen for Josiah's lies, but he hadn't won yet. "I guess I should apologize to the others."

"Maybe. But it'd mean more if you helped us get out of this. With your tech expertise, Riven's sharpshooting, and my . . . whatever I have . . ." Ty nodded. "We can do this."

Locked in a room with no weapons or tools, headed to another star-system—Asa didn't have the beginning of a plan. "You really think so?"

"I know so. But you should talk to Riven first. You two need to be on the same page."

At the mention of Riven, the sliver of longing intensified. When Riven had hugged her after the gladiatorial pits, Asa hadn't wanted to let go. For that fleeting moment, she'd felt like she belonged.

But the last she'd seen of Riven was the betrayal in her eyes, when Josiah's guards had attacked. "Even if *you* don't hate me, Riven definitely does."

"She doesn't. She respects you a lot more than she's willing to admit. And maybe . . ." Ty fidgeted uncomfortably. "You two work well together, when you're not hung up on your prejudices." He tucked Asa's hair behind her ear. "And I know you have it in you to make things right."

Asa found herself smiling. Despite all her mistakes—despite everything—Ty still liked her. And he hadn't treated her any differently after he'd found out her real name.

That was new. Boys on Cortellion always tried to get close because of whose daughter she was. Back home, she was a prize—a challenge. But to *Boomslang*'s crew, she was just *Asa*.

Despite everything, Ty was still sitting here, telling her everything would be all right.

The road ahead would be risky, and risks terrified her. But she could start with a small one.

She wrapped her arms around Ty's neck, pulling him closer. His breath caught as he wrapped her into him, holding her close.

"Asa," he whispered, and suddenly his lips were on hers.

His lips were soft but firm, encouraging. She returned the kiss as something wild burned within her, scalding away the apprehension and pressure. She'd never been kissed by someone who wanted the real her. She released her worry, and her lips melted against his.

Ty lifted her off the bed and pressed her back against the glass wall. The universe at her back, home behind her, Ty warm and close in front of her. He felt even closer than he had at Olympus—the heat of him against her chest, no masks, no makeup. No onlookers but the stars.

"Ty," she whispered between breaths. He paused, listening, eyes bright and half-lidded. "When you kissed me in Olympus . . . did you want to?"

He laughed, brushing a thumb over her cheek. "Of course I did. You're incredible, Asa."

His lips roamed from Asa's mouth to her jaw, her neck. "For the record," Ty breathed against her neck, "I enjoyed every second of it."

She gasped and pulled him closer. Kissing Ty was a bandage—a temporary, comforting fix. It didn't solve everything, but it felt good. Ty was already slipping through her fingers, like everything she'd ever known. But she could savor the heat shooting through her for a few minutes longer.

He kissed down to her collarbone, like he had at Olympus—but this time, it sent real shivers through her. Definitely not an act.

His hands slid onto her waist, fingertips brushing her exposed skin. She undid the buttons on his vest and carefully pulled the fabric aside, revealing slim muscle and a healing cut on his breastbone. She put a hand on his chest—gentle, testing, letting it run from his collarbone to his stomach. His breath caught—her hands were probably cold.

For a moment, her mood turned as she remembered Riven in the room outside. Was this a point of no return, ruining whatever might be between them? But Asa forgot herself again as Ty's tongue pressed between her lips and his knee slid between her thighs.

A jarring voice cut into her thoughts. "Heads up, kids," Josiah droned over the loudspeaker system. She would've ignored it, lost in Ty's arms and his perfect mouth, but part of her insisted *this is important,* and the mental fog began clearing.

"We've started burning salirium and will be making the FTL jump in ten minutes," Josiah said. "I suggest you all strap in if you want to stay in one piece."

Ty gave her ear a gentle nip and pulled back, breathless. "That jackass really knows how to kill a moment, huh?" His face was flushed, his hair tousled, his shirt half-open. He looked like he'd been mauled by a bruttorc.

Asa laughed, despite herself. "Maybe you should straighten up before anyone sees you."

"At least you're smiling again." He pressed one last kiss to her forehead. "Hope to see that more often."

"Maybe you will." She'd misplaced her trust too often lately, and somehow these scoundrels from Requiem were the most honest people she'd known. Asa brushed her messy hair into place and opened the bedroom door, hoping the blush had faded from her cheeks.

Maybe Ty was right—maybe she could do this.

There had to be a way out, but she'd need help. She had to talk to Riven.

Asa had never made a faster-than-light jump between star-systems before, but she already needed to vomit. Whether it was from nerves or the strange, acrid smell in the air, she wasn't sure.

She steadied her breaths, glancing around the guest suite.

Diego and Samir were already strapped into seats near the door. Riven was seated alone, fastening her thigh buckles. Her gaze flicked between Asa and Ty. Unreadable, as usual.

The seat next to Riven sat empty. Ty gave Asa an encouraging nudge before taking a seat across the room, giving them space.

Now or never, right?

"Riven." Asa sank into the seat next to her. "You okay?" The whir of the vent systems grew louder.

"As *okay* as you can be when breathing salirium haze." Riven's fury had quieted to a simmering, sorrowful thing.

"That's what that smell is?" Asa fiddled with her harness.

"Ever done this? You'll feel like shit until we jump. Then you'll feel worse."

"Good to know." Asa swallowed the lump in her throat, not knowing how to start. "I guess trusting Josiah was a bad idea, huh?"

Riven gnawed on her chapped lips. "Yeah. Pretty bad."

There was something bigger on her mind—the chasm between them grew deeper every hour. Project Winterdark. Her father's entire world and Asa's entire life were built on the secret that he was hurting people, even before he'd hurt Kaya. That Emmett was only one sacrifice out of hundreds.

"I don't know everything my father has done. But I should've known what I was doing for him. I should've stood up sooner." She took a shaking breath. "And I don't want the world to forget what happened there. Whatever my work did at Sanctum's Edge . . . I think it's my responsibility to know. To understand what you went through."

Riven gave her a grim, sidelong smile. "You sure you want to know?"

"I can take it." She was done running from the truth. And maybe all Riven wanted was for her to understand. "Whatever you want to tell me."

Riven tilted her head back. "I guess I can give you the long version."

The last time Riven remembered being happy was on an Earth beach called Sanctum's Edge, at a lighthouse where time seemed suspended.

White sands hissed in the stormy breezes, across dunes rising above the churning waters. Riven chased Emmett over the dunes barefoot, her tangled hair whipping over her shoulders. The final day of the best summer she'd known, before everything fell apart.

The marbled blue-gray sky made it impossible to tell the time of day. Even then, the beach had felt trapped in time. She'd never forget the grit of the sand between her bare toes, the sting of the heady winds, the *lightness* of Emmett's voice.

"Can't believe we go back tomorrow." His arms locked around her waist, pulling her body against his. "Think there's time to make the jump to Requiem for a night, before we move back into the dorms?"

She ran her hands through his windblown black hair and kissed him fiercely. Central Atlantic Academy was the last thing on her mind. She had Emmett in front of her, *Boomslang* docked at the settlement nearby, and two star-systems' worth of trouble to get into. This beach was off-limits because of the military test facility up the coast, and that made it even more exciting. When she had new worlds to discover, what was the point of written exams?

"Guys, something weird is happening," Ty called across the dunes. Emmett's brother was a year younger, and willing to be third wheel whenever they went adventuring. Emmett would do anything for the kid, and that made Ty sort of Riven's brother too.

And sometimes she treated him like it. "Go away, Ty," she muttered, nipping Emmett's bottom lip.

"No, really. Something's wrong."

The first gunshot rang out as a blaze down the beach caught her eye. Roiling flames, streaked with greasy black, engulfed the palm trees like a bonfire.

She squinted down the dunes at the beach below, the black-clad soldiers and barbed-wire fences surrounding the test facility. Equipment from Almeida Industries was tested there, with experienced soldiers running drills. But they were far outside the hazard zone, and Riven had a terrible feeling about the gunshots so close by.

Before they could run, a squadron of soldiers crested the dune, running straight toward them.

"What the hell," Emmett breathed.

One of the soldiers leveled his rifle at them.

Emmett started to put his hands up, but Riven grabbed his wrist. The soldiers weren't stopping. She didn't know what they were after, but the last place Riven wanted to be unarmed was in the middle of a firefight.

"Take cover!" She dragged Emmett toward the lighthouse, Ty running close at their heels. Spurts of sand flew as bullets hammered the dunes.

The next few minutes were a blur. Rough sand and dune grasses cutting her bare feet. Shouts down the beach. Soldiers charging over the dunes. Emmett's eyes going wide with fear as he gripped her hand to pull her faster. Her free hand reaching for a gun she'd left on the ship.

Riven reached the lighthouse door first. Locked. She swore, wrenching the handle harder. "We need to get somewhere—"

Ty cut her off with a horrid, mournful cry.

Riven turned toward them, and all words died in her throat.

"Oh, god . . ." Emmett wheezed, clutching his ribs. A gaping, pulpy exit wound had burst through his chest, blood pouring down his stomach.

Riven immediately went numb. She couldn't fix this—they needed to get him to a hospital, and fast. But the approaching soldiers would kill them first. Riven eased Emmett beneath the driftwood slats of the porch as more gunshots exploded nearby. Her heart pounded. Ty's voice was incomprehensible with panic as he tried to stanch Emmett's bleeding.

As she peered through the porch stilts, she saw the soldiers moving into the colony settlement—and firing on *each other*.

They weren't wearing helmets—something that looked like a battery pack was stuck to each soldier's neck, wired to a lens covering their left eye. Riven caught a soldier's gaze, and it was hungry, cold, searching for a target. There was nothing human left. Riven ducked, hoping he hadn't seen them.

Ty crouched over Emmett, dabbing the cold sweat on his

face. Riven ripped Emmett's shirt apart with her pocketknife. It looked even worse. Blood trickled into the sand, and another *pop-pop-pop* salvo of gunfire sounded nearby.

Ty dragged himself away and retched at the other side of the porch.

Something heavy shuddered against the porch slats as a body fell outside. A punctured metal canister rolled from the soldier's corpse, leaking red-black smoke.

Emmett convulsed, choking. Riven grabbed him under the shoulders, dragging him away from the smoke, but she'd already breathed it in, and needles were pricking her lungs and skull. She covered her nose and chucked the canister, but her vision was already blurring.

What came next, Riven barely remembered. Emmett's perfect face went slack, sweating, wheezing, as she begged him to *hold on a little longer, please,* her eyes burning and lungs collapsing. Ty crouched in the sand nearby, shaking with quiet sobs. When the gunshots moved farther away, and the nearby soldiers' dying gurgles mingled with the sigh of the dune breezes, she and Ty carried Emmett toward *Boomslang,* his gift to her. She cursed the pain, pushing it aside—she didn't have time for it, with Emmett so badly wounded . . .

But his chest was already going cold.

⸺⸺⸺

"I didn't find out until later what was happening." The rhinestones on Riven's face shone between her messy silver-blonde bangs. "The facility on that beach was testing a brain-AI interface. Your dad's."

Asa remembered her dad's proud smile when she'd perfected the visual sensor for that interface. She trembled, gripping the straps of her FTL harness. "It must have malfunctioned."

"The brain implants were supposed to sharpen soldiers' senses and perfect their aim. Could also shut off pain, fear . . . give humans all the best qualities of mechs. Problem was, they overrode the soldiers' decision-making. The AIs just kept seeking targets. Targets like Emmett." Riven's voice quavered. "And whatever else they had—some weird biochemical nerve spore—I got hit with it. It's fucking with my nervous system. Ty said it's spreading, and I might only have a few years before it shuts me down entirely." She looked down, strangely vulnerable. "The uncertainty is the worst part."

Asa nodded. "Ty's trying to save you."

"Yeah. I keep telling him it's a lost cause, but he won't give up. He's throwing himself into chemistry textbooks, experimenting with medications, even pawning drugs off organ pirates. He's a good kid, but I don't want to tell him I've lost hope."

"Got to admire his heart."

Ty caught her eye from across the room. He probably couldn't hear them over the whir of the salirium processor, but he seemed to know what Riven had just told her.

"I'm so sorry, Riv. For Sanctum's Edge, and for . . . Josiah." Right now, anything Asa could say was inadequate. "I'm going to do whatever I can to make things right. I promise."

"You realize none of that can be undone?" Riven gave her a hard look, then sighed. "What happened at Sanctum's Edge wasn't your fault. And I know you meant well, with the

Josiah bullshit. You've done some stupid things, but maybe we wouldn't have fallen into this trap if I'd . . . I don't know." Riven stared at her empty holsters. "Helped you more. Treated you like part of the crew."

Like part of the crew. A small, buried hope began to claw its way up. If Riven was on her side, they might still have a chance.

Riven scratched off more of her steel-gray nail polish. "And . . . trying to negotiate with Yllath was really, *really* stupid of me." Her words came out hoarse, as if apologies hurt. "I shouldn't have even considered selling you out. Especially after all you've done for us. For what it's worth, I'm sorry too."

The chasm began to close. "Well, that's good to hear. I was a little worried you'd claw my eyes out if I sat next to you."

Riven laughed. Genuinely, like breaking waves, sending a tingle through Asa's chest. "Oh, hush. I'll save that for the next time I get shoved into a gladiatorial ring."

Asa smiled, but Riven's admission still weighed on her. "Is the sickness . . . hurting you? Right now?"

Riven's expression sobered. "Not always. But I'm a dead girl regardless."

"And that's why you're so willing to put yourself in danger?"

"Maybe." Her lips twitched, as if she wasn't sure whether to say more. Then: "One of my favorite Phase I movies had this gunslinger in it. I guess he was based on a real person—he had tuberculosis, a death sentence. He was dying the whole time he was taking down outlaws . . . but in the end, he died in bed alone with his lungs collapsing." Riven gave an unsteady sigh. "I promised myself that wouldn't be me. So however I go, it'll be like a flare, on my own terms."

Asa suddenly understood why Riven wanted to be a ma-triarch so badly. "You know, you don't need to be a matriarch to be remembered. Your crew respects the hell out of you. If all you want is to prove yourself . . . you've already done that."

"Spare me your pity, mechanist."

Above the door, a hazard light flashed. *Warning,* a mechanical voice droned through the loudspeaker, *Faster-than-light jump sequence will commence in two minutes. Ensure all harnesses are properly fitted.*

"Really wishing I had my guns back right about now," Riven said.

"We'll have to wait until we make the jump, but I think I have a way out." Asa tightened the strap on her hips. Riven's negotiation with Yllath had given her an idea. "I'll need your help. It's the last time I'll ask you for anything. I promise."

"And what happens after we get out?" Riven's lopsided smile made something within Asa ignite. "Don't tell me we'll never be trading favors again. Because we have a big job to finish, and I'll be with you the whole way."

"I hoped you'd say that." Asa let her hand slide over Riven's chapped knuckles, but pulled it away when she remembered Ty across the room.

Riven studied her carefully. "So. What's this plan of yours?"

The jump between star-systems was fast approaching, and they wouldn't have much time before reaching Earth. But with Riven on her side, it just might work.

"You might not like it," Asa said, "but here's what I'm thinking."

Part IV:

DEAD-CIRCUIT
BANSHEE

chapter 28
ALLIANCE

The faster-than-light jump felt like dying.

The buzz in the vents rose to a roar, and the loss of pressure made Asa's ears pop—like taking the maglev train through the snow-dappled mountains of Serra Roxa on Cortellion, but a hundred times worse. She gripped the FTL harness, and her gut clenched as the stars out the window blurred into bright flares.

For a moment, she was everywhere and nowhere.

Everywhere, as a flash of pain pulled her apart, shattering her. Nowhere, as darkness killed the pain into numbness. She floated in a space outside reality, overwhelmed by the temptation to never wake up from the infinite peace. Here, she was truly no one. The tension in her chest was gone. Why had she been afraid, again?

But a hand gripped her shoulder, shaking her back to consciousness. Then, a voice—rugged but decadent, a voice Asa wanted to sink into and let cocoon her like blankets.

"Hey, mechanist. You survive?" Riven's voice. "Asa. Wake up. You're drooling."

"Heaven forbid," Asa slurred, shivering in the chill of her own sweat. "I'm a proper heiress. Heiresses don't drool." Riven took her hand off Asa's shoulder. Behind her, through the glass wall, was an ashen-colored moon and a planet beyond it, marbled blue like Cortellion.

Earth.

All the dread flooded back, as bad as the FTL nausea. Kaya's life was on the line. And she was the one with the escape plan. Asa wiped the drool from her lip, fighting the urge to heave her guts up. She lurched forward, catching on the harness.

"Not so fun the first time, huh?" Diego cracked a tiny smile. "There's a reason my abuela keeps sending me conspiracy-theory articles claiming FTL drives were created for government brainwashing."

Across the room, Ty gave Asa a thumbs-up, and she forced a smile. They'd made it to another world, and it was time to finish what she'd started. The idea was terrifying, but so was *everything* over the past few days, and she'd done it anyway. With shaking hands, Asa undid her harness.

Riven did the same, wincing as the straps skimmed the medicated bandage on her shoulder. A reminder of the anteleons' claws she'd barely escaped. She and Asa had saved each other, and might have to do it again.

Riven drew Ty's infected wristlet out of her pocket. "Time to work your magic, mechanist."

"Wait." Ty stepped out of his harness. "What are you doing with that? Last time I turned that thing on, it said it was Asa and tried to seduce me."

Asa's cheeks grew hot. Even Yllath had noticed her and Ty together at Olympus. And what did it mean that Ty had fallen for the trap?

Riven rolled her eyes. "Not surprised you were dumb enough to believe it."

"I didn't believe it. I thought someone had stolen her wristlet! Or that they had her captive, or–"

"Yllath propositioned you?" Samir gave a wry smile, the first in a long time. "With a bit of sweet talk, you could've been our ticket out of the quarantine."

"Or maybe Yllath himself is our ticket out of here." Asa took the infected wristlet into the bathroom and pulled apart the hair dryer. Or tried, anyway. She had no tools, and the plastic casing wouldn't budge.

"Um . . . what are you doing?" Samir said.

"The hair dryer's connected to the door system. So you can't leave electronics on unless someone's in the room." Asa twisted the panel, but her hands were too small. "Can you pull this apart?"

He gave her a confused look, but gripped it in his carbon-knuckled hands, wrenching the plastic apart to expose the control panel.

"Thanks." Asa picked apart the wristlet and the dryer cables, forming a crude wire-to-wire connection. She didn't have much to work with.

But she had enough for the infection to spread.

"What are you *doing*?" Diego said. "Isn't that–"

"Just trust me." The connection sparked and flickered. The room lights dimmed.

"What the hell?" Samir said.

"Hey." Asa strode into the main room. She glared into the

lens of the security camera and audio monitor. "Wake up, Yllath."

"Did the FTL jump scramble your *brain*?" Diego demanded.

"I really hope you understand what you've done." Samir shot a nervous glance at the door, as if Yllath's possessed mechs might burst through. He turned up the cuffs on his rumpled Prince Charming jacket, readying to throw a punch.

"*Shh.*" Riven cut the air with a slicing motion. She caught Asa's eye, and they exchanged a nod. A vote of confidence, a shared pact. All the assurance Asa needed.

But no response from Yllath came through the overhead speaker.

Asa scowled at her reflection in the camera lens. He had to be in there. "I have questions. And an offer."

More silence. Asa had the sinking feeling she'd made a mistake, but then a prickle of static came through.

The static grew louder, and a familiar voice sent chills through her. "What do you want?" Yllath rumbled.

Asa crossed her arms, leaning against the wall, pretending she was in control. Trying to look like Riven bluffing—like she had a thousand backup plans and a dead-aim trigger at her fingertips. "I gave you access to this block—the doors and cameras for the rooms around here. But there isn't much you can do in there by yourself, is there?"

"You know nothing of my capabilities, or my reach."

Asa laughed. "I know Josiah has the ship on lockdown. There's no wireless signals for you to jump on, and you can't access the other systems. I know your body's somewhere on Cortellion, and Josiah has your brain. So if you want to get out . . . either you find a way to get a sentient hair dryer out of here, or we work together."

Yllath hummed over the speaker, and Asa took it as an urge to continue. "You want to take down Josiah, but you can't get into the systems you need wirelessly. For that, you'll need a pair of human hands. Right now, you're just as trapped as we are."

"And what, exactly, do you want from *me*?"

"You let us out and help us find our gear, and then we hijack a security-mech for you."

Ty made a choked, indignant noise. Clearly he wasn't happy to be negotiating with the monster who'd kidnapped and beaten him.

"You *do* realize we both seek the same thing," Yllath said. "That organ cannot be split between the two of us."

Asa nodded. "But if Josiah gets his way, neither of us get it. He'll tear it apart."

"Yeah." Riven crossed her arms, silhouetted by Earth's moon in the distance. "So after this short *alliance* is over, it's winner takes all. Just like it has been."

A hum. "You're quite perceptive, Miss Almeida. Here is the bargain, then: after I release you, you will grant me access to the security systems. The mechs, the equipment link, everything."

"Done."

"If you fail to uphold your vow, I will not hesitate to open every airlock and destroy you."

He definitely wasn't bluffing. Not after the blood on the dance floor at Olympus, and his promise to ravage Cortellion. Yllath would kill to get what he wanted—and this bargain hinged on a razor's edge. She hoped he'd still consider keeping her alive as a bargaining chip.

She had to stay one step ahead, and trust her crew had her back. "I'm a girl of my word."

Silence. Yllath was probably familiarizing himself with the systems. This plan would either work, or get them all killed.

Then, Yllath chuckled over the loudspeaker. The bolts to the guest suite unlatched, one by one, and the door slid open.

"Your gear," Yllath said, "is in the supply room to your left."

Allying with Yllath was the biggest gamble Asa had ever made.

Yllath guided them through the halls with static noise in the overhead speakers. Guards with rifles waited like minotaurs in a maze. The boys' footsteps tapped close behind Asa, and at every corner, Riven crouched next to her, scanned for threats, and squeezed her shoulder when it was safe to move.

This was her mess, her plan, her burden. But her team knew what they were getting into, and they still followed her. She couldn't let them down.

Here, Yllath messaged to Ty's wristlet, when they reached a door with rusted water stains. *Your gear is inside, as are the security controls.* He sent a picture from one of the cameras. Two guards waited by the crescent of control panels inside, their backs turned.

"On my count," Riven murmured. She pressed her back to one side of the doorframe, and Samir took the other. After Riven counted off on her fingers, Yllath slid the door open.

As the two surprised guards fumbled with the rifles on their backs, Samir and Riven lunged. Even unarmed and injured, Riven was a tempest in motion. Her arms lithe and strong, the twist of her waist when she punched–

It occurred to Asa to stand *far* back.

"Samir!" Riven hissed.

Samir grabbed one guard in a headlock, yanking his crested helmet off. Riven followed up with a concussive punch to his temple that made Asa wince. By the time the second guard had regained her balance, Riven had cornered her with punches to her neck, her gut, her jaw. Samir smacked the guard's head against a wall of lockers and tossed her rifle aside. The guards slumped to the ground, barely conscious, and Ty began binding their wrists.

"All right. Hard part's done," Riven said, rolling her bandaged shoulder.

"Hard part?" Asa stuck out her tongue. "Clearly you've never had to chip through the ice on a complicated security system."

Riven returned a smirk. "And I don't plan to. That's *your* job."

"Quit flirting and let her work, Riv," Samir said.

As the blush warmed her cheeks, Asa stepped over the unconscious guards. Diego was already skimming the control panel. First, they needed their gear. She flipped through the emergency med cabinets, then began cracking open the lockers.

"Bad time for *flirting*," Riven said. "Being at the mercy of a psychopath scientist kind of kills the mood."

"Not sure about that," Samir said. "Some people are into the idea of psychopath scientists."

"Both of you," Diego growled, "shut up before I shove a boot in your mouths."

Sure enough, Asa's backpack, Riven's guns, and the rest of their gear were stuffed in a dented locker. Asa passed the revolvers to Riven, who took them surprisingly gently.

"This is the *last* time I get separated from you," Riven whispered, sliding them back into their holsters.

"Right there with you." Asa dug through her backpack. Everything was here—her second EMP grenade, her sweaty fade-suit, her comic books (with new creases, unfortunately). Samir strapped his wristlet back on, and Ty sorted through his med supplies. Equipment meant they had a fighting chance.

"Save the happy reunions," Yllath snarled over the speaker. "Your end of the bargain still remains."

"Save the snark," Asa muttered. "Unlike you, I can only be in one place at a time." She slid her fingers across the panel keys. It was risky to have a monster on her side—Yllath would move against them as soon as she'd finished the hack. But Diego's steady hands flicked over the screens next to her, and Riven and Samir guarded the door.

Together, they'd face this.

"Never thought I'd trust my life to an Almeida." Against the glow of security screens, Diego's sharp chin and lean silhouette reminded her of a cobra.

"You're one to talk. I'm probably the last person Boneshiver expected to be helping." But *Almeida* was nothing but a name.

Right now, Asa was as much a scoundrel as any of them. "Ready when you are."

Time to take back what was hers.

"Asa," a voice murmured into her ear, and she turned to find Riven's face inches from hers. "Think you could *accidentally* break that wristlet and leave him behind?"

Asa pursed her lips. Yllath would notice their betrayal. And with the airlock right down the hall . . . he'd make sure they paid for it.

"It'll be fine," Asa said. "Just trust me."

Asa wired Ty's infected wristlet to the console, letting Diego override the security system. The prickle of danger at the back of her neck reminded her of disabling the estate's alarm systems before her midnight escapes with Kaya, suppressing laughter at her sister's dirty jokes. She remembered zipping down the skyway in her hand-built speeder, its chrome pipes breathing vapor into the night, colored lights trailing by in breakneck streaks. Their only taste of freedom, of a world beyond their father's prison.

Maybe she and Kaya would still find that world.

CLEAR, the screen read at Asa's fingertips. Yllath was in. Almost as suddenly as it appeared, the screen went dark, and the lights in the room dimmed to orange. Every holoscreen turned to blank, flickering static.

"Is our Faustian pact complete?" Samir muttered.

"As promised," Asa said.

"Better than waiting around for Josiah to decide how he wants to screw us over. Or call the Federation for our bounty." Riven spun *Verdugo* on her index finger.

"I thank you," Yllath's voice rumbled like a coming storm. "For now, I'll keep you here. Josiah and I have business to settle. With the cameras under my control, he hasn't even noticed you're missing." The heavy bolts on the door clicked, locking them in. "Rest assured, Miss Asanna—you won't be in there forever. I've already sent a message to your father. As long as he does what I require of him . . . you'll be returned home, safe and sound."

Your father. Oh, damn. Asa's heart thudded like rifle fire. They'd need to get Kaya as fast as possible.

"You called Almeida?" Riven hissed. "What kind of dumb shi–"

Ship entering atmosphere, the ship's automated voice said over the loudspeaker. *Strap into landing harnesses.*

As the ship shuddered in descent, Samir directed them to the emergency harnesses on the wall. Asa braced herself, her gut dropping like a stone and falling further. She fought the nausea until the thrusters stilled and the ship gave a final lurch. As soon as the docking controls clicked, Asa was on her feet, stumbling to the door with her backpack in tow.

She pressed an ear to the door. In the hall, she heard the airlocks hiss open, followed by a voice as thick as freezing oil. "I don't know how it got here," rasped Josiah, "but take down those mechs. Then, head into the lab. We don't have much time."

"There's our psychopath scientist," Riven whispered. "And he's getting away."

"What are we going to do about . . ." Samir gestured toward the ceiling speaker, where Yllath was undoubtedly listening.

"I've cut the cameras and audio feeds," Diego said. "We might have a few minutes before Yllath notices we're gone."

"Right," Asa said. "And he's probably focused on getting to the biocapsule. He can't be everywhere at once." She dug to the bottom of her backpack, finding a tiny, palm-sized cylinder. "We need to get out. Before Yllath can ransom us." Asa clicked her pen-laser on, channeling all her hopes and frustrations into the tiny, tenacious beam, frying through the metal bolt.

It took a few minutes to reduce the bolt to glowing-hot metal held together by one stubborn bit. Riven and Samir took over, giving the door a few heaves and kicks, until it shuddered ajar.

"Josiah and Yllath have a head start." Samir braced the door open enough for them to slip through. "Go."

Now or never. Asa followed Riven through the halls toward the docking ramp.

It struck her how *dark* it was outside, until she realized they were underground. A shaft of moonlight spotlighted the ship, but ahead, the lab wall curved outward from the cavern. Small green lights shone within the windows. Above, the ceiling arched into an intricate lattice of rock carved like honeycomb.

"Looks like Josiah's been holding out on us," Asa said. How long had he waited, building this lab in secret to betray her father? How long had he planned to use Asa to steal her sister?

Whatever lay inside that lab, he was prepared.

Behind her, Riven made an excited noise. "*Boomslang*," she breathed with relief. "You're in one piece, baby." Asa glanced over her shoulder. Riven was gazing at her ship, held in the med-station's metal-armed docking grip. She could leave now, just as Asa had promised.

Their part in this was over. Yllath had no more business on Requiem. Asa suddenly felt acutely alone.

"If you need to, you all can go." After all they'd done for her, Asa couldn't force them to follow. It was nobody's responsibility to save Kaya but hers. This might be where they parted, as much as it hurt. "I promised Riven she could be done with me after we got out. And I meant it."

"Leave?" Ty frowned. "But we're so close."

Riven turned toward her, scowling, her braid whipping over her shoulder. "I'm not leaving you behind. He still has Winterdark. And this fight's mine now."

"Agreed. You can't tell us to screw off right after you dramatically break us out of a psychopath's ship." Samir shook his head, towering over Asa. He poked her nose, which she scrunched in response. "We want to see this through."

"I'm curious to see how this plays out," Diego said. "Even if I *didn't* have a debt to finish."

Some of the tension coiling in Asa's chest released. Though they'd been her allies before, a barrier had separated them—her lies, and their obligations to the Duchess. This time, they knew her name, her flaws, her talents, and her failures, and they'd follow her anyway.

This time, they trusted her.

"This is as far as I've planned," Asa said. "I have no idea what we'll find in there. But . . ." Her throat was impossibly dry.

"We've faced stupid odds already," Riven said. "Worse than a scientist with a hard-on for brain swapping."

"Asa." Ty set his hands onto Asa's bare shoulders and let them slide down to her wrists. The touch was so gentle it sent shivers through her, and she realized how *safe* she felt with them. "I meant it when I said you could do this. And it's not just you anymore, but the five of us."

Asa smiled up at him, trying to ignore the suspicion flickering across Riven's face. Josiah had expected them to rot aboard his ship. But he'd underestimated her, just like her father had.

"All right," she said. "Let's move in."

chapter 29

PROJECT WINTERDARK

The lab doors were locked—until Samir dragged an unconscious guard from the ship and smacked her hand
against the scan-pad.

Asa swallowed hard as the doors chirped and slid open, a
grim invitation. "Even if we find the capsule . . . we'll still need
Kaya's body." She tried to imagine what Josiah might be doing
in here, and every possibility was gruesome.

Riven shushed her as footsteps approached in the clean
lobby ahead. The guard noticed the intrusion too late, falling
to simultaneous bullets from Riven and Samir. Asa recoiled at
the red spattered on the shiny lab floors, but steeled herself.
The situation was a mess, and asking nicely wasn't going to
solve anything.

Samir pointed to a holo-map flickering on the wall, with
the fire exits labeled. "You three." He gestured to Asa, Riven,
and Ty. "Head for the wet lab on the fourth floor. Diego and I
will hit the research division. Wherever the biocapsule is . . . we
need to get it before that jackass tampers with it." He handed
Riven his wristlet. "Here. Since yours and Ty's are gone. I can
use Dee's if needed."

A metallic crash echoed down the hallway, in the direction

of the elevators. "This place is one big funhouse, isn't it?" Riven slipped a few disruptors into *Blackjack*. She locked eyes with Asa. "Stay behind me."

"Planning to." Asa pressed her hand to the stunner at her hip, familiarizing herself with its grip. If Josiah caught them again, he wouldn't risk keeping her allies alive.

The hall's arches stretched ahead like ridges in a long gray throat. Riven kept both guns up, her electromagnetic boots treading cautiously. Her Olympus outfit was stained with dried blood—and Asa shivered, conscious of how little protection her own clothing gave. They hailed the elevator, and a screen inside showed another labyrinthine floor diagram.

"The facility is huge," Ty whispered, once the elevator doors closed. "Do you think we'll be able to make it out before . . ."

They all let the thought trail off as the elevator lurched upward. Asa's throat was tight. No turning back.

"We always make it out," Riven finally said. "That was the promise."

"I know, Riv. But sometimes promises aren't enough."

Riven whirled toward Ty, staring him down. Her gaze flicked to Asa next. "Listen. Nobody's getting left behind tonight. Do you understand?"

Neither of them responded as the lights flashed overhead.

"We've gotten through worse," Riven said. "I thought I'd die the day I got kicked out of that foster home. But somehow I'm still here."

Asa didn't press, not after the Duchess had mentioned Riven's *one too many beatings*. It was hard to imagine Riven at anyone's mercy now—and maybe that was the point. Her kind of strength only came from struggle.

"If we survived the past few days . . . I think we can survive anything," Asa said.

Riven gave her an uneasy smile as the map on the wall turned to static. "Damn right. Even if everything goes south . . . we're going to give them hell."

When everything goes south, Asa thought, but didn't correct her. While she didn't know everything Riven had been through, a thread was strengthening between them. Asa would keep her safe. Whatever it took.

Ty was quiet, watching the elevator numbers tick up. He didn't look reassured.

The elevator doors slid open, and the sharp scent of formaldehyde killed Asa's next words in her throat. She listened for the whir of mechs or the tap of guards' feet, but there was only the hum of air in the vents.

As they entered the hall, the wall-map screen turned to a winding, nonsensical maze. A garbled voice came through the overhead speaker, like computer-generated laughter.

Every hair on Asa's neck rose. She was drawing her stunner when the laughter coalesced into a voice she didn't recognize. "I knew you would come running back to me."

Yllath. He knew they were here.

Asa assessed the hall. Nothing moved—not even the dark silhouettes of the security-mechs behind plexicarbon panels. No doubt Yllath was already chipping his way through the security systems, searching for a way to pursue them.

"Are you looking for her?" This time, the muffled voice was

so close it made Asa jump. It had come from a directory terminal on the wall—mechanical and distorted.

Asa raised her stunner. Every instinct told her to run.

"What the hell?" Riven breathed.

From the overhead speaker came a muffled giggle. *Kaya's* giggle.

"No," Asa whispered. The laughter was uncanny, *wrong.* As if her brain had been tampered with.

"Come and find me, Asanna." Kaya's voice was a distortion, like the hologram on the Olympus deck.

Asa closed her eyes. This wasn't the real Kaya. Again, Yllath was trying to grind away Asa's resolve.

"This feels like a trap." Riven fell into step beside Asa. "He's screwing with us."

More voices echoed down the hallway like a gauntlet—deepening in pitch, warping. Kaya's whisper became stilted and nonsensical, like an audio clip played backward.

It was joined by another voice Asa vaguely remembered from the VIP suite. "Riven," Emmett's voice pleaded. "Who else won't you be able to save?"

Riven swore, twisting and aiming her gun down the hall behind them.

"Hey," Ty said softly. "Focus on me, all right? He's trying to lead us that way. So we must be getting close." Ty nodded toward the hall to their right. "The wet lab's this way."

"You're fine with putting all of them in danger, Asa?" Kaya's voice had a furious edge, and it was joined by something deep and distorted. "Their blood will be on *your* hands."

"Sick bastard," Riven muttered.

Asa swallowed her fear as they reached the lab. Riven hit the door switch and led them inside, guns at the ready.

Inside was as dark as a starfield. A spotlight glared overhead, illuminating something behind a pile of supply crates and energy tanks.

"Haven't you done enough?" came Josiah's ragged, broken voice from somewhere in the dark. Not mechanically distorted. Human, from a human throat. "Just leave me be."

He spoke in a low murmur, as if talking to someone else. Asa walked toward the light, and every step felt like a mile as she passed the supply crates. There, on a brushed-steel lab table in the pool of light, sitting like a gem on display, was the biocapsule.

Riven kept the barrel of her gun trained ahead. "Asa. Grab it."

Next to a tray of surgical instruments, the capsule waited invitingly. Whether or not it was the real one, she had to take the chance. Carefully, Asa wrapped her fingers around the warm surface and flicked the light switch. The Etri organ pulsed inside, safe. Tears pricked her eyes. She still had a chance—

A flash caught her eye as she scooped up the capsule. A man stumbled into the pool of light and fell to his knees.

Crouched on the lab floor, his lab smock stained from blood dribbling down his chin, was Josiah.

"Asa." Josiah's eyes were wild. "What did you *do*?" Both his shaking hands fisted in his graying hair, and he muttered to himself. "No, *no*. Get out. *Get out*." His eyes flashed back to her. "You set it loose, didn't you? *Reckless*, you stupid girl."

Horror dug its talons into Asa, and she staggered backward. The cold intelligence that normally hardened Josiah's hollow face had peeled away to fear. And, worse—

The collar that usually covered Josiah's neck was turned down. A metal tubule connected a node behind his ear with a silver pod between his shoulder blades.

Winterdark.

A hard pit formed in Asa's gut as she recognized it. Her father had claimed it was a prototype for Kaya's mind-link. And it was exactly what Riven had described seeing the day Emmett had died.

"Sanctum's Edge." Riven cocked *Verdugo* at Josiah. "How much of this was your fault?"

Josiah's face froze as a processed metallic voice trickled from his implant—deep and rumbling. "*Winterdark would have been impossible without his mind,*" Yllath said from the metal in Josiah's neck. "*He picked dozens apart. Myself included. For that, he must atone. He must help me.*"

Josiah gave a humorless smile as he coughed speckles of blood on his white sleeve. "It's in my head now. Not much to be done."

"Why did you do this?" Asa clenched her fists. It was horrible . . . but maybe he deserved this. "You were supposed to help us! Kaya needed you. *I* needed you."

"You wouldn't understand, Asa." Josiah's eyes were glazed, staring into nothing. "Your father tried to throw away the soldier project—the best thing I created."

"I don't *want* to understand." Riven punched Josiah in his already-bleeding mouth, knocking him prone. She aimed her gun at his forehead. "You're the reason Emmett's dead. Do you know how many people you've killed?"

A decisive clarity crossed Josiah's face. "Do you know how

many people I could have *saved*? We needed to finish the soldier experiment, even if it cost—"

Riven's gun held steady. "You've said enough."

Asa wanted to shout for Riven to stop, to let Josiah speak, but it was too late.

Thoom. The gunshot cracked through her ears, and the Winterdark node on Josiah's neck shattered.

His chest gave one final, ragged gasp, and then he was still.

Asa fought back bile. The man she'd once called a mentor, a friend, was *dead*. All his nasty, unearned dreams were dead with him.

"Like I thought," Riven said. "There's nothing left once those implants are destroyed."

Yllath's voice boomed over the speakers, furious. "What have you done?"

"We did say winner takes all," Riven said.

Asa hugged the biocapsule tight to her chest. *Winner takes all.* Only the Etri brain could connect Kaya to her body like her ruined brain would've. She wouldn't let Yllath take it back, especially after all he'd done.

"You and I aren't finished," Yllath said. With a *thunk,* the heavy lab door sealed. The overhead light plunged into darkness. "Plug the capsule into that terminal before Almeida arrives, and *maybe* I will be merciful."

The sweat on Asa's skin seemed to freeze. No. Yllath had intended to take them hostage. He'd mentioned calling her father.

"This isn't good," Ty whispered.

From the hallway outside, muffled footsteps cut through

the quiet, followed by a mechanical clank. Luca must've picked up their trail hours ago. And now . . .

"We need to go." Ty squeezed Asa's shoulder. "The floor plan showed another exit this way."

She followed Ty and Riven through the maze of darkened consoles and dormant drones. Light leaked beneath a steel door ahead.

When Ty threw it open, they were met with a rush of red light and stifling heat. Asa stumbled onto a perforated-steel walkway after him.

"Your old man's trying to corner us." Riven slammed the door behind them and latched the bolt closed. "They're cutting through the outer door."

With Yllath on the loose, having the lights on felt safe. But the air was so hot, it felt like breathing into a hair dryer—one that smelled of burned hair and cooking meat. Through the hole pattern in the floor, Asa saw massive red-hot gears churning in layers, down to the molten mouth of a furnace.

"Dare I ask why this lab needs an incinerator?" Ty caught his breath against the bridge railing.

"Take a whiff," Riven said. "There aren't a lot of possibilities. We need to move."

Asa scanned for the way out. On the wall was a biohazard poster, with the words *blood* and *cybernetics* beneath a heading about *disposal of contaminants.* She forced herself to stop reading. The metal bridge stretched to a dead end at the far wall.

Above them were more rickety catwalks over the churning incinerator, and metal pulleys connecting a lift to the next floor. At the top was a door. "The exit," Asa breathed. "Up there."

"Good." Riven cocked her revolvers, backing away from the door. "Get that lift down here."

Asa assessed the controls. It took three hard thrusts to pull the lever into place, but steadily, the lift began to descend.

"Hey," Samir's voice said into Asa's earpiece, over the comm system. "We found Kaya's body. Diego confirmed her face-scan."

Asa's heart was pounding too fast for relief to set in. Kaya was safe. But it didn't matter if they didn't make it to her.

Footsteps rose just outside the door. Then, a whirring. The fizzle of a plasma cutter.

"We might be in deep shit," Riven said. "But we have the capsule. On our way."

"There might be trouble here too. A ship just arrived. We'll try to come to you—" His feed cut to gunshots, panicked shouts.

It was joined by Riven's cussing as the door flung open.

Asa's heart jumped into her throat. They were too late.

"Hold your fire," she said to Riven. Starting a shootout would end badly.

At the door stood four soldiers in white-and-gold body armor. Sickeningly familiar—the geometric folding on the chest plate, the yellow light panels twisting over the limbs like poisonous frogs. A security force.

Her father's.

The guards parted to reveal a steel-plated soldier mech a head taller than them. It was made of polished, platinum-white plates, its chest emblazoned with the bow-shaped emblem of Almeida Industries. The mech pulled aside the horned shield covering a face screen.

And on the screen was the face of the man she'd been

running from for days. The face she'd tried to expunge from her nightmares.

"Asanna, my dear." Luca Almeida's mech looked down at her. "I've finally found you."

chapter 30
GENOME

*F*inally.

A sinking horror washed over Asa. Her father was *here*, ready to undo everything she'd fought for.

From the mech's screen, Luca Almeida smiled down at her. He was sitting in a well-lit room, safe on Cortellion while she faced death. *Coward.*

He and his soldiers entered the metal bridge, just as the lift creaked into place behind Asa.

"It's such a relief to see you safe." Her father's mech swaggered forward, and a lattice of blue hexagons shimmered over its armored surface. Shields. "I haven't slept in days." On the screen, stubble dappled her father's chin, and his hand twitched as it straightened his tie. Some of the youthful, surgical perfection on his face was drooping. Maybe he *had* been worried about her.

Or maybe he'd just been concerned about his precious project falling apart.

Riven's guns were trained on the approaching soldiers, and Ty held his stun-blades in reverse grip. Asa willed them to stand still, to understand that guns alone wouldn't be able to stop that mech. But her mind was a deadlock, and no other plan formed.

Maybe it ended here.

Asa swallowed hard, lifting her chin. Whatever happened, he wasn't taking her back.

"Please, lower your weapons. This is a negotiation." Her father directed his mercenaries to guard the lab door. Riven scowled, and Asa knew she wanted to light them up. But they were trapped—if they stepped on that lift, her father could stop the wobbly thing in its tracks.

"I'm not negotiating with you," Asa said. "You're a monster."

"I understand you're upset, Asanna. But I've thought about what you said." The mech crouched from its intimidating height, extending a hand. Like her father had done when she was seven and burned her fingers on her first engine build. "I know she means so much to you. And if having her nearby makes you feel at home . . . I can use a different test subject. What if I put Kaya back together for you?"

Asa's heart dropped. For days, she'd yearned to wake up from this nightmare, and now, the offer had fallen into her lap—a path to something that had seemed impossible. Kaya back. All she'd wanted. She stepped in front of Riven. "You wouldn't tamper with her mind?"

"No, Asa. Please. Come home, and we can forget any of this ever happened. I'll have the chefs make cheese pastries tonight, and I've already upgraded your VR holodeck. In a few hours, you and Kaya can be gaming together, just as you did before."

Her old life. Her warm bed. A certain future, a life with her sister, where the scariest thing wasn't organ pirates but failing her exams. Asa blinked back tears of longing—longing to escape the dread, the constant grasp of fear. Running away had squeezed her dry.

But her old life meant moving back into his shadow, and all the terrible secrets within it.

"Asa. Don't you dare," Riven whispered behind her. "You know what he is."

Asa swallowed the lump in her throat. Riven was right, of course. After what he'd done—the lies he'd told—his offer was too good to be true. But fighting their way out wasn't an option.

"What would happen to them?" Asa jabbed her thumb at Riven and Ty. "If I go with you, would they be safe?"

Luca's mech hummed. "Project Winterdark contains sensitive information." As he strode toward her, the mech's footsteps sent shudders through the metal bridge. The incinerator's glow cast him in a silhouette of hard angles. "I cannot let them leave after what they've learned. But if you wish to let them live . . . I can keep them in the lab."

In the lab. As test subjects.

"You would *use* them." More likely he'd kill them. If she went home, she'd be part of that world again—her father's human experiments, and the whole of Project Winterdark. Even if Kaya were free, she couldn't live with that.

And Kaya would hate her for letting others suffer.

"Need I reiterate that sacrifices must be made for what we'll contribute to future generations? The cost is negligible compared to the mark we will leave." His voice quieted. "And once we've mastered our own minds—expanding and controlling them at will—it might mean the end of suffering altogether."

What else would he do to get that kind of power? He'd already used Kaya and Sofi. "Of all the sacrifices you could've made . . . why use your own daughter?"

"You never figured it out, Asa?" He raised an eyebrow. "Why it would be an enormous mistake to allow Kaya off the project?"

She remembered digging through the files in the Winterdark corridor, seeing Kaya's face on Sofi's subject file. And it began to click into place.

"You planned to use her all along," Asa said. "Like you used Sofi."

His smile was strained. "Sofi was so eager, but that wasn't enough. I learned from her. Used her as a foundation for my second daughter. And Kaya is everything we needed—eighteen years in the making."

Asa's stomach acid threatened to heave its way out her throat. Sofi was another Kaya, failed, broken. Gone. A sister she'd never had the chance to save.

"Kaya's mind can handle Winterdark's experiments," he said. "Unlike all the glitch addicts we pulled from Requiem."

He'd raised Kaya, given her the world, only to cut her apart. "You're sick."

"Someday you'll realize what we do is necessary. So I'm willing to give you another chance. Come back, Asanna." Tears glimmered in her father's eyes. "I love you. I never expected to love you as much as I do. Which is why everything I've built will one day be yours. You couldn't *possibly* want more." His composure was cracking. Quiet rage crept into his voice. "Come home. I won't ask again."

She lifted her chin. "No."

"Asa, you're seventeen. You should have been dead the second you stepped onto Requiem. You've been *very* lucky, but luck always runs out."

Realization cracked like a glow stick. This was how her father saw her—a naïve, sheltered girl, incapable of thinking for herself. Asa's cold, quiet fury built on the crumbling walls where her fear had been.

Luck had nothing to do with her getting this far.

Asa stared into the mech's camera lens. As close as she could come to looking him in the eye. "You raised me to be brilliant, but you still look down on me?"

He'd made a mistake raising a clever daughter. Clever enough to undermine him, to stand against him.

She could save Kaya without his help. If she couldn't, then she wasn't worth her salt. Being nobody was fine with her. If she'd never left the world where people only saw her as *Almeida's heiress,* she'd have never learned to survive on her own.

Asanna Almeida. That name meant nothing anymore. She'd been nobody for the past few days, and she'd been braver than ever.

Asa. Asa was enough.

"You were wrong about Requiem." Asa glanced back at Riven. "You were wrong about *me.* Wherever I go, I'll find a way to survive." A flicker of pride lit Riven's face—the girl she owed her life to—and something burned between them.

Maybe *Boomslang*'s crew was home now. Maybe Requiem was the world she'd dreamed of, where she could live on her own terms.

Maybe that was all she'd ever needed.

"I trust them more than I trust you," Asa said. "And I will *never* be the daughter you wanted." She sensed Riven moving into place behind her. The shield-generator on his mech's chest hummed, and an idea finally clicked. "Kaya isn't yours to use. I'm not yours to use. And if you can't handle that . . . you'll have to come kill me yourself."

Her father looked as close to stunned as she'd ever seen him. Stone-faced, working his jaw in mental debate. Her heart raced. Would he?

"I should have expected this." Luca let out a resigned sigh, staring into his lap. In that moment, he didn't see her coming. "Sofi was the same way. I only hope my next child is less of a disappointment—"

Asa sliced her pen-laser's beam at the edge of his shield-generator. In a few precise cuts, sparks flew, until the shield flickered and the palm-sized device popped off.

Her father shouted, and as his giant hand plummeted toward her, she jammed the laser into the mech's hip joint. It burned at the metal, stuck fast, and the mech stumbled backward.

Right onto the tipping-platform above the incinerator.

"I'm sorry for this, Asa." On the mech's wrist, armor plates unraveled to reveal the barrel of a gun. Asa flicked on the shield-generator, which formed a disc-shaped barrier. She braced herself as blasts pelted it.

Riven shot the mech's gun with a disruptor, shattering it. Another bullet severed the mech's knuckles, destroying its grip on the railing.

And, with the shield covering her, Asa backed up far enough to hit the platform switch.

The metal floor released, sending the mech tumbling and

sparking onto the churning gears. The armor plates warped as the gears swallowed it whole.

The last she saw of it was her father's face on the screen going dark.

Asa let out a shuddering breath. Luca was still safe and far away, undoubtedly staring at a blank screen now. The worst he'd suffered was a broken mech. It wasn't fair.

"Engagement authorized," shouted a voice behind them. "Open fire!"

Her father's four mercenaries, in their flashy rebreathers and polished armor, had formed an arc around her and Riven and Ty, their rifles drawn.

"Behind me!" Asa shouted, jumping in front of Riven and Ty with the shield. "Get on the lift!"

Bullets flew, pinpoints of light against the shield's translucent hexagons. Asa gritted her teeth as it flickered—it wouldn't hold long. They had to escape, fast.

She walked backward until the three of them had boarded the rickety metal lift. Riven fired haphazardly through the growing gaps in Asa's shield, staggering two soldiers.

"It's stuck." Ty fiddled with the elevator switch. The pulleys whined and grated above them, but the lift wouldn't budge.

A canister clinked near their feet, unleashing a gust of thick black smoke. Riven kicked it away, but the smoke rose fast in the hot updraft. More canisters flew toward the elevator, belching dark clouds.

Asa tugged the wires of the pulley system. The motor above them was sparking—jammed from a stray bullet. It was still pulling, but it was too weak to lift them.

She was about to call out to Riven when something dizzying and utterly foul hit her nose. The smoke. The canisters continued vomiting black gas, concealing the mercenaries' rebreather helmets.

"I can't see them," Riven growled. "Unless you can fix that in the next few seconds–"

Her heart pounded. They were stranded. "It's working," Asa said through the sickening smoke, "but one of the motors is jammed. We're too heavy!"

"Dammit, what?" Riven said. "Maybe I can climb and–"

Ty coughed. "We don't have time. Another few seconds and this gas . . ." He doubled over, gasping. "Riven. I'm sorry."

Asa was about to ask Ty what he meant when he cupped his hand on her cheek. He passed a sad smile from her to Riven. Her heart lurched.

No. There had to be another way.

"Asa," he whispered, his eyes glassy with tears, "keep her safe."

Before she could stop him, Ty stepped out of the lift, toward the soldiers.

"Ty," Riven shouted as his blond hair disappeared into the smoke, "what the *hell* are you doing?!"

chapter 31

PROMISE

T y needed to get back on the lift. *Now.*

"This isn't the time for heroics," Riven shouted after him, her lungs numbing as the smoke rose. As the black clouds shifted, she glimpsed the mercenaries' gleaming helmets, and then they disappeared again. Even when she fired into the smoke, there was no telltale *thud* of a body hitting the ground.

Horror began to rise in her throat. If they didn't go soon, either the mercenaries would kill them, or the smoke would knock them out first.

But Ty was going *toward* the mercs. Toward the guns.

She lunged after him, but the metal grate slammed shut, trapping her and Asa on the lift. She jerked on the door, but it was locked into place.

Ty smiled at her through the lattice, his hand on the switch. He'd done this on purpose. He wanted them to leave him behind, because—

Because he didn't expect to come back.

No. Not Ty. Anyone else.

"It needs to be me!" she shouted. If there was no way out of this—not for all three of them—Riven needed to be the one to stay behind. She didn't have much time left, and at least *she* could go out shooting.

"Riv, you're not the only one who made a promise," Ty said,

panting from the smoke. "I haven't been able to fix you. But maybe I can save you."

"Don't you *dare* do this," she hissed. "You can't. Get your ass back here, I swear . . ." Riven gripped the lift grate, white-knuckled, trying to yank it back open. It wouldn't budge. "I'm *dying*! I should be the one—"

"Shh," Ty whispered, resting his hand on her knuckles. "Listen to me, Riv." His hand squeezed hers through the grate. "You'll survive. You're too stubborn to die." Desperation in his voice. Not a reassurance, but a prayer. "Give them hell."

He didn't deserve this. "Let me out." She pulled harder, and the grate rattled. Her fingers stung as the metal cut into them, drawing wet lines of blood. How *dare* he. "I won't forgive you if you stay behind—"

He gave her a slow nod, his smile quivering. Gunfire resounded behind him, pinging against the lift frame. "Your crew needs you. You're the only one who can pilot *Boomslang* out of here."

"Ty." Her vision blurred as an itchy tear rolled down her face. "I promised."

Gritty medallions of blood in the sand.

I think I'd be okay, Riv, Emmett had said, *if it were just us—*

No. Not this time.

"Promise *me*, then," Ty said. "Promise me you'll get out. You two need each other." He shot a glance at Asa, who held a hand over her mouth, chest shaking with sobs.

No. Ty, who'd stumbled to her bunk on nights she'd woken, unable to breathe. Ty, who'd stay awake until god knew what time, exhausted, trying to crack some puzzle about the thing eating her.

Riven slammed herself against the grate. She barely registered Asa gripping her wrist, trying to pull her away, and she hurled an elbow backward, because Asa would never understand—

Ty pulled the lever, and the pulley lurched to life.

As the lift rose, Ty shot her a wink and shrank below her. As if this were something he'd chosen with confidence. A decision he'd made long ago.

As if it somehow masked the gleam of tears in his eyes as the smoke swallowed him.

Riven collapsed against the grate, her lungs leaden with sobs and dizzying smoke and the nasty pinpricks of pain. She should have jumped off the lift before he'd even considered it. Ty had always been there—her shadow, a pair of soothing hands, a steady voice in the thrashing dark.

And he was disappearing.

And again, she was powerless.

As the shaky cables pulled them above the smoke and incinerator gears, her throat was raw. No name existed for the anguished sound ripping from her. Gunshots echoed in the sickening black fog.

For a moment, the smoke shifted, and Riven saw the first bullet tear through Ty's arm. Blood, bright and coursing, red as a distant galaxy.

This can't be real.

He's going to die. The thought was so vivid and terrifying, more real than it had ever been during alley fights or heists gone wrong.

The lift stopped at the upper floor. Asa grabbed her hand, dragging her toward the door. "Come on, Riven," Asa said gently. "We have to go."

She smacked Asa's hand away. "How can you say that?" With Ty gone, what did she have left to fight for?

Ty gone. *Gone.* Just like Emmett.

Even after the promises she'd whispered into the ocean winds, the hours spent shooting targets she imagined as Luca Almeida's face, the times she'd dragged Ty to cover when jobs got tense, she'd failed. The person who least deserved to be left behind was Ty.

The pain built to a fever pitch, exploding through her. It pounded at her chest, scratched at her skull, blurred her vision. She barely kept her balance as Asa severed the final elevator cable with her pen-laser.

Bullets peppered the doorframe as she staggered out the exit door. Riven clenched her guns tighter as her hands shook. The lab halls and lights crawled by, hazy and surreal. The rusty tang of blood bloomed at the back of her mouth. "This isn't happening."

A soft touch on Riven's shoulder. "I'm sorry," Asa whispered. Wet lines ran down her soft cheeks. "But we got out because of him."

Riven's legs trembled, and she leaned against the cold wall. The white noise wasn't fading like it usually did. It dug its claws in deeper.

She'd lost everything. And Ty had said stress made the sickness flare. Now her guard was down, worse than ever.

"Riven," Asa said. "You don't look so good."

A knife twisted in Riven's lungs. Needles jabbed her brain from every angle.

And before she could tell Asa she was *fine*, she collapsed.

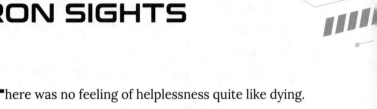

chapter 32
IRON SIGHTS

There was no feeling of helplessness quite like dying.

The pain burst from Riven's lungs like fireworks, spreading through her entire being. She shuddered under the meteor impacts of heat and cryo-cool. The angry thing inside her was claiming her at last.

All the time she'd thought she had—the hope that maybe, just maybe, she'd have a little longer to make something of herself—evaporated like exhaust. The body she'd trained, the muscles that could aim a revolver with half a thought, would be nothing but dust.

She couldn't tell whether her eyes were open, whether she was standing or lying in a thousand pieces. The world was flashes of darkness and pain and spidery red.

In a few moments it'd be over, and she'd be nothing. No one.

Her crew would throw her in a coffin. Throw her out an airlock. Maybe they'd scatter her like sand at Sanctum's Edge. If they ever found her.

"Riven," came a voice, hurried and desperate, pulling her from the dark place.

She let out a convulsing breath and tried to focus. The voice had come from her earpiece. Samir's voice. "Riven?" His voice quavered. "Come in, dammit! We're surrounded."

Riven shook as another salvo of pain-spikes shot through her chest. Ty, and now Samir. Just another way she'd fail.

Her reputation couldn't save her. It couldn't save her crew members. It sure as hell hadn't saved Ty.

What the hell have I been fighting for?

"She can't," Asa was saying, her voice cracking with worry. Asa's gentle hands brushed the hair off Riven's cheek. "I don't know what's wrong, she just–"

Hot blood trickled from Riven's ear, pooling on the floor as she convulsed. But her heart was still beating. *Lub-dup, lub-dup, lub-dup.*

She heard snippets of Samir's voice as she faded in and out of consciousness. ". . . found Kaya. Almeida brought a *lot* of mercs . . . Morphett's here too. We're barricaded in a storage room, but I might have to stay behind and have you get Diego out."

If she lost Samir, too, everything she'd fought for would be worthless. And for Diego, he'd do it. Samir had refused to leave Riven behind during her freshman-year drills, when she'd collapsed after ten hours in the sunbaked desert. He'd slung her arm over his shoulder, dragging her to the checkpoint. Later, he'd pulled her aside for more after-class training when he noticed the bruises on her arms, left by one of the parents in her group home.

She had to save her crew. Even if it killed her, she owed them that much.

Get up, she demanded. *You're not done yet.*

If Ty had died to save her, she'd make damn sure it counted

for something. He'd said to get out. She was their pilot, and her crew needed her.

Get up!

She forced her eyes open. Sterile white lights shone above her. Alarms flashed red. The world came back into focus, like periscope lenses sliding into place.

"Riven!" Asa leaned over her, her wild black hair grazing Riven's face. Asa's arm slid under her shoulders, sitting her up against the wall. "Stay with me. Please. We need you."

"How many are there?" Riven said into her comm, her voice frightfully hoarse.

"Riven," Samir said. "You can't . . ."

"How many?" she repeated.

"Too many. Don't try to engage."

"You are *not* staying behind." There'd been enough sacrifice today. "Do you hear me?"

"Riv, even for you . . . there's too many of them."

"Then one of me will have to be enough." Everything hinged on her now. Even if she couldn't shoot straight, she'd fight off the mercs with a plastic fork if she had to. "Listen. I'm coming. Understand?"

The only reputation she needed was one for saving her crew.

"I get it, Riv. But you don't need to—"

"I *do* need to." And that was why she'd succeed. It was how she'd survived that group home and created a crew when she had nothing. This wouldn't end like it had for Ty. "Hold tight. I'm coming."

Riven grabbed the handrail and forced herself to her feet.

Her body was clammy from cold sweat, and everything burned like hell when she moved. But the pain was starting to clear up—not bad enough to keep her down. Maybe she'd be paying for this later, but right now she had to try.

"*We're* coming," Asa said, slipping her hand over Riven's.

Riven swayed, bracing herself against Asa's shoulder. Asa shouldn't put herself in danger, but she'd earned her place on the crew. She'd put her snooty upbringing aside and dragged herself through the dirt to save Riven's ass. If Asa wanted to come along, that was her choice. They'd come too far *not* to save her sister.

And Asa was part of the reason Ty had stayed behind. For her too.

"What's the plan, mechanist?" The shield-generator Asa had taken from Almeida's mech was useless now, but Asa might have an idea. She usually did.

"It's not much, but even if my dad's tech is immune to Yllath . . ." Asa pulled a makeshift grenade out of her backpack. Her last EMP. "It's still tech. And this should knock it out, at least for a while."

That *was* a plan. "We'll have to get your sister's pod out before this thing goes off."

"I know." Asa nodded. "This is all I can do for you. So take it."

Before she could stop herself, Riven took Asa's face between her hands. "Thank you," she murmured against Asa's mouth. Her lips brushed Asa's, stealing the other girl's startled gasp, her wanting sigh. Maybe it was wrong, after Ty had kissed her. But she might never have another chance, and this was one memory she had to take with her.

Asa's fingers slid into her braid, pulling her closer, and her lips stoked the familiar fire hotter. She and Asa were worlds apart, but one and the same. The heat scoured through her, burning away the anguish, the despair. Left in the ashes was only tempered, red-hot resolve. With Asa at her side, she swore they'd get out of here alive.

At least most of them would. Which meant she had one last job to do.

Riven broke away. "Keep Samir and Diego safe," she whispered against Asa's neck. "And your sister." She turned away, drawing *Verdugo* and pressing its iron sights to her forehead. "Until then . . . you'd better hope I can shoot straight."

As the adrenaline surged and the pain subsided to a whisper, she forced the stillness into her shaking hands, *demanded* it return. She had no choice but to make things work.

They'd called her a deadeye at CAA, before her expulsion.

It was time to remind herself why.

Riven held her breath as the *tap-tap-tap* of rubber soles drew closer. Almeida's mercenaries tromped through the research division, closing in on the corner where Riven and Asa hid. Riven held *Verdugo* by her ear and motioned for Asa to stay back.

Asa could run. From here on out, Riven had this.

Riven whipped around the corner, catching the trio of security troopers off guard. Her bullet found the first soldier's weak spot—the lens on the white-gold helmet—and tore through their skull.

She pulled the triggers, and the hammers twitched as the double action did its work. Two more shots. Her revolvers kicked like cannons, sending ear-splitting echoes through the halls.

Two soldiers went limp and hit the ground like bricks. A third staggered, clutching his helmet, but a swift kick from Riven put him down for good.

Asa pressed her back to the wall, her lips moving in silent self-assurance. Maybe Riven should be scared, too, but *Verdugo*'s grip was warm in her hand. She swung out the cylinder, reloading, as voices echoed down the hall. With only six bullet chambers, you could never be too careful.

"Shit. We've got heat," came a voice muffled by a rebreather.

"Three down!"

"It's that gutter-cowgirl bitch again. Put her down for good."

Damn right it's me, Riven thought. *And if you have any idea what's coming, you'd better run.*

She pressed forward. She was low on disruptor rounds, and she'd need a second gun for what was coming. *All right, Blackjack,* she thought as she clicked the cylinder back in. *You're going to have to suck it up and spit regular bullets for a while.*

Ahead were the brushed-steel doors to the research lab, covered in biohazard labels. Samir and Diego were trapped inside. No time for subtlety.

"Wait here," Riven said to Asa, who pressed her back to the wall. "I'll clear them out."

Time seemed slower, her body overclocked. As if whatever

had set her nerves on fire was bringing them to life, detonating them.

Riven took a deep, burning breath and kicked the swinging doors in, firing from both hands at the first armored guards she saw. A small army awaited her, scattered among the maze of lab tables and bio-tanks. Their flashy white-and-gold body armor didn't have many weak spots. It was time to put her target training to use.

"Heads up!"

These jackasses had killed kids on Almeida's orders. Like they'd killed Ty. They didn't deserve mercy.

Hammer, trigger.

Riven peered down her iron sights and lost herself in the rhythm, in the spray of bullets and the press of triggers. The soldiers were moving targets, and her bullets made straight, lethal lines between her revolvers' barrels and their helmets. They fell one by one, visors shattering, staining the lab floor in splashes of crimson.

When she'd dropped half a dozen, Riven dove behind a control console to reload. Bullets whizzed through the air around her, pinging on the walls. In the moment she'd surveyed the room, there had been at least twice that many.

And Morphett Slade sauntered between lab specimens like a gardener in a flower bed. She headed toward Riven like she was a weed she was determined to pluck. A pair of slim-barreled guns emerged from Morphett's shoulders.

Oh, hell and a half. *Those* were new.

"Riven?" Samir's voice came through the comm, breathless and hopeful. "Those gunshots . . . is that you?"

No time to talk. When there was a lull in the bullet spray, Riven gritted her teeth and leaned out to fire. Three more bullets, three more corpses.

Riven slid back behind the console when she heard Morphett cackle. "Oh, look who came back!" called a voice that was just begging to be punched. "Come to make trouble, Hawthorne?"

"Samir," Riven whispered into her comm, "she's distracted." He had an opening.

Riven peeked around the corner. Morphett was headed straight for her, cybernetics on full display. She looked terrifying, all sharp blades and curly hair and surgical steel—a storm of blades and bullets.

"I'm going to head for Kaya's pod," Samir said. "Keep her off Diego."

Morphett's guns fired, pinging off Riven's cover. Warning shots. "No pressure, I guess!"

Behind her, the supply room door whined open, followed by the familiar *thoom* of Samir's rifle. He and Diego had a clear course to the life-support pods—one of which had a young woman inside. Must be Kaya.

Luckily, Morphett was a *lot* more interested in Riven. "Did you hear? I don't have to take the Almeida girl alive anymore. And guess what's going to happen to you now that you're in my way?"

Riven leaned out and fired, but as usual, Morphett's stupid shield flattened her bullets. If she ever had the cash, Riven swore she was buying one of those. She ducked and rolled, putting some distance between them.

"Bet Asa's price is a little lower now, eh?" Riven said as Morphett's footsteps drew closer. Even if Morphett had been chasing a two-million-denar bounty before, she'd probably be just as dangerous running on pure spite.

"Yeah. But she can wait." Morphett rounded the corner, flashing Riven a vicious grin as Riven's bullets met her face. The pinging against her shield made Morphett stagger. Riven had a split second to dodge Morphett's return fire and slide behind a wall of lockers.

"Having fun wasting bullets?" Morphett said. "She's not going anywhere if you can't pilot her out of here."

Riven gritted her teeth. Her wounds from the anteleon claws had broken open, stinging like venom. Her lungs still felt like they'd been flame-roasted and skewered on a stick. Right now, Samir had to get out and take Kaya with him. She could worry about piloting *Boomslang* once she'd dealt with Morphett.

A bullet whizzed above her head, and she ducked and slid, returning fire at the armored soldier between a pair of bio-tanks. He dropped, and Riven scampered back to cover, ducking into a roll–

Fresh pain bit across her back from shoulder to rib. She cried out, dropping *Blackjack* mid-roll.

Morphett strode closer and kicked the gun away, flicking Riven's blood off one of her wrist-blades. "Nice shot." Morphett retracted her blade and punched Riven in the mouth. Riven staggered backward, her lip going numb as the rusty tang of blood flooded her tongue. "But I don't want you dying on me yet. I want to *savor* this."

She didn't doubt Morphett would try. Riven caught Morphett's next bladed punch on *Verdugo*'s barrel. That would leave a scratch. And Morphett would pay for it.

"Get Kaya out of here," Riven hissed, hoping her comm would pick it up. "Fast. I'm about to do something stupid."

Morphett punched again, twice, three times. Riven caught them on her forearms, her shoulder, looking for an opening to shoot inside that damned shield. But Morphett feinted with her fourth jab and kicked, hooking her heel around the back of Riven's knee.

Riven stumbled, firing at Morphett's face to blur her vision against the shield—just as a different bullet whizzed past her ear.

Almeida's soldiers. Two left.

"Stand down," Morphett commanded. "She's mine." Riven holstered *Verdugo* and caught Morphett's fist in her bare hand. They traded blows, but against Morphett's shields, a punch was no more effective than a bullet.

Just a little longer, and I can end this. For Asa, for Samir, for Ty, she had to survive.

Morphett grabbed Riven's throat and slammed her backward onto a control console. Her injured back stung fiercely, hot blood trickling from her ruined bodice.

Just a little longer . . .

Morphett ejected razors from her fingertips.

Finally, Riven heard Asa in her earpiece, breathless. "We're clear. Do it!"

Morphett's guns locked onto Riven's face, whirring as the blasters charged up.

With a shaking hand, Riven held up Asa's EMP grenade. Two seconds left on the fuse.

Riven smiled through bloodied teeth. "Surprise."

Krshhh.

The electromagnetic pulse tore through Riven in a wave of nausea. The lab plunged into darkness as the control panels and lights flickered out. All the remaining light came from the floodlights through the exterior windows.

The force of her shield shattering knocked Morphett backward, sending her sprawling.

Head throbbing, Riven stood. Samir's wristlet was dead, but she was in one piece. It was time to finish this.

Morphett was hunched over on her knees, clutching the inactive shield-generator at her hip. She peered between her curls, eyes wide. "Go get the Almeida girl!" Morphett shouted at the soldiers, pointing to the doors where Riven's crew had escaped with Kaya. "I'll handle her."

Riven picked up *Blackjack* and strode into the soldiers' path, giving her revolvers a spin. Nobody was going after her friends. Especially not with those trashy new-tech guns.

"You have a death wish?" one of the soldiers barked, raising his rifle. "Out of the way!"

Riven didn't flinch. He obviously hadn't tested his trigger yet. "And if I don't?"

Triggers clicked. Nothing fired. One soldier tapped his rifle's darkened display screen.

Riven fired a warning shot. Both soldiers swore, ducking behind cover.

Nothing could stop her. "Last chance. If you don't want to be collateral damage, crawl back to your ship."

She didn't have to threaten them twice. They turned tail.

"You'll have to do better than that." Morphett spat blood, clutching her chest.

Riven noticed the scar across Morphett's collarbone, disappearing beneath her vest. No doubt some of her cybernetics ran deeper—they were probably holding her together. Those circuits had to be EMP-proof.

But her shield was down. Even if temporarily, that was enough.

Morphett lunged with a fistful of scalpels. The ones she'd used to cut Ty.

Though Morphett was vulnerable now, she was still fast—and her shoulder guns were still hot.

One of Morphett's guns kicked back, lodging a bullet into the wall above Riven.

Riven dove beneath it and gave *Blackjack*'s cylinder a spin. Two disruptors left, and Morphett had two guns. It was time to make them count.

Last chance, Riven told herself. Morphett still had the upper hand. If she didn't win this now, Ty had died for nothing.

Breathe. Riven steadied herself. She'd have to shoot twice as fast as Morphett. Otherwise, her crew's hopes would die with her.

The world seemed to slow, even Riven's heartbeats. One fluid motion, two shots.

Blackjack kicked as she pulled the trigger.

Thoom. Thoom. Morphett's expensive new guns shattered

down their barrels. A third bullet sank into Morphett's thigh, for good measure.

Morphett fell to her knees as blood soaked her tight black pants. She reached for the wound but stopped short, her finger-scalpels locked in place from the EMP blast.

"We're not much without our tech, are we?" Riven pointed *Verdugo* at Morphett's head.

Morphett's shadowed eyes were defiant as she glanced over the gun and Riven's finger on the trigger. "So? What are you waiting for?"

It was pathetic, seeing Morphett on her knees—her pink lip gloss smeared, her curls falling out of place. She looked so raw, so *normal,* without the sadistic grin. This was an execution.

"Take your revenge, kid," Morphett said. "You've won."

It would be so easy to end it here. After all Morphett had done—stealing her cargo, trying to steal Asa, hurting Ty—

Riven pressed the muzzle to Morphett's clammy forehead, but found she couldn't pull the trigger. Morphett was too much like her—playing the game on Requiem to survive, carving out a spot for herself in the underworld. And after Riven had almost died today, it was too hard to look her in the eye and do it.

"It doesn't end here," Riven said, surprised at herself.

"What are you saying?" Morphett bared her teeth.

"Because you got the best of me before. You outsmarted me. Took advantage of me. You almost stole my cargo twice. And now . . ." She lowered the muzzle. "I beat you. Despite your shields and your cybernetics. And I want you to live to remember that."

Morphett hissed through her teeth. "You must be joking."

Riven loaded a stun-round into *Blackjack.* "We can pretend this didn't happen. You're not allowed to be my rival if you're going to give up and beg for death. So you'd better get up and get better."

"That's bullshit, and you know it. I'm not begging." Morphett's grin returned, hollow. "I made my peace the moment the Feds first cut me open."

Riven pushed aside the slither of pity. If Morphett's cybernetics weren't self-inflicted, maybe she had unfinished business of her own. "Then how about this?" Riven backed away. "You don't know what it's like to be running out of time. So quit working for jackasses like Almeida and do something better with yourself."

With that, Riven fired her stun-bullet. It hit Morphett's temple at an angle, just enough to knock her unconscious.

Maybe Morphett would come back to give them hell. Maybe someday she'd have to put her down for good. But that was a problem for future Riven.

When Morphett collapsed, Riven turned and ran. She had a crew waiting for her on *Boomslang,* and a pretty heiress with nerves of steel whose tech had just saved her ass. Almeida, Josiah, Morphett—all dealt with. Now, to finish the job.

She'd entered the hallway when the lights began to flicker. She frowned. This was outside the EMP's blast radius . . . wasn't it?

"Impressive," Yllath's voice blared through the speakers, just as the lights went out completely.

chapter 33

"You left Ty behind?" Samir demanded.

Asa couldn't look at him as they pushed the life-support pod toward the docking bay. It felt like rolling a casket—and if not for the pulsing heart monitor on the side of the pod, Asa would've thought Kaya a corpse. She'd seen enough of those today.

"He insisted on it." Asa forced down the awful memories that threatened to heave up like vomit. "For Riven. And me."

"And there was nothing you could do? Is there any possibility he's still alive?"

"I don't know!" Asa blurted, her voice cracking. When Ty had stepped off the lift, he'd locked them in, and it'd been too late to stop him. Riven had wanted so badly to go back, and the memory of her screams lingered like a wicked chill. "The gas was burning us, and there were bullets, and—I'm pretty sure he got hit."

Samir's jaw clenched so hard it looked like it'd break. "Of all the people we could've lost . . ." His voice was deadly quiet. "Someone is going to pay for this."

Asa remembered Ty's lips against hers, the way he'd looked at her like she could do anything. It took everything to keep herself together. The only thing making it bearable was having

Kaya in her hands. Neither her father nor Josiah could help her anymore.

"Focus on getting out of here," Diego said. "If we try to go back, we might lose everything."

When they reached the docking bay, the path to *Boomslang* was chaos.

Under the floodlights, her father's mercenaries warred with laboratory patrol-mechs Yllath had infected. Between the hurling bullets, a few mechs' orange eyes locked onto Asa.

"Go. I'll cover you," Samir said as Asa and Diego pushed Kaya's pod across the tarmac. He fired off a few disruptors, sending the mechs crumpling into heaps.

Asa's stomach knotted. The rest of the soldiers were probably still in the lab with Riven. She tried to contact Riven, but the girl's comm channel was dead—hopefully because she'd launched the EMP. Whatever happened now, she had to trust Riven, the way Riven had trusted her.

In a whirlwind of shouts and bullets, they reached *Boomslang,* locked into Josiah's ship.

Samir wasted no time plugging Kaya's pod into *Boomslang's* cockpit power supply. "You two." Samir's anger dissolved into military-commander focus. "Go override the docking controls. We need to be ready when Riven catches up." *When,* not *if.* Samir had faith in her too.

Asa helped Diego rig up to the control console. But no matter what they tried, the codes kept scrambling.

"It won't release *Boomslang.*" Diego shook his head. "Something's messing with it."

Beneath Asa's fingers, the console screen fizzed and blurred, replaced with a single message.

Hello. Miss me? The screen flickered orange.

Diego swore. "It's back, Samir."

If Yllath had the ship—Kaya was plugged in, and vulnerable. Asa ran aboard *Boomslang* to Kaya's pod in the cockpit, panic seizing her chest.

"You have one more chance, Miss Almeida," Yllath said over the cockpit speaker. "I am everywhere. And I'm sure you understand what that means."

The heart monitor on Kaya's pod flatlined in a grating, drawn-out beep.

"No!" Asa cried. "Stop. Please!"

"This is your final chance to give back what you stole," Yllath said as the heart monitor began pulsing steadily again.

So this was it. Kaya was Yllath's hostage. And with the chaos outside, Yllath would decide whether they got out of here alive.

Think, Asa. In Olympus, she'd confused Yllath by scrambling the gravity-sphere controls, but that wouldn't work for a ship or a life-support pod. Yllath was a mind with an attention span—she knew that. But when Galateo had been overpowered by Yllath, what had he said?

He is a true consciousness. I can thwart attacks by artificial minds, but I have never encountered a mind like his.

Maybe it would take another organic mind to take down Yllath. Right now, Asa only knew one person who might be able to outsmart him. It was a gamble, like every other trick she'd pulled.

Asa took a deep breath, unzipping her backpack. Kaya had

manipulated AbyssQuest from within. She'd controlled the phoenix with her thoughts. She'd shut Yllath out long enough for them to escape the Winterdark vault. But if this didn't work, they'd lose everything.

Asa recoiled when she noticed the indicators on the bio-capsule—the vitals spiking, as if the mind inside was eager to help her. Kaya was awake this time, ready to fight her own battle.

I need you now, Asa thought, hope sparking in her chest. *More than ever.*

She held up the biocapsule—Yllath's brain, containing Kaya's mind. "Is this what you want, Yllath?"

"Hand the capsule to the mech waiting outside," Yllath said. "And only then will I allow your ship to depart."

"How about I plug it in for you?" Asa said innocently, heart about to beat out of her chest. She wired the biocapsule to the cockpit's main computer, hoping Yllath wouldn't notice what she was doing.

"Asa, what are you doing?" Samir said. "After all this—"

Asa tried to signal to Samir with only a look, the way Riven did. *Trust me. Please.*

He caught her glance, his cat eyes narrowing. Then, a confident nod. He took the cue.

"Stop that." Yllath's voice rose with anger. "This is not necessary."

"Are you sure?" Asa steadied her jittery hands. *Just a little longer—*

"I told you to *stop this*!" Yllath's voice boomed. The heart monitor flatlined again.

Suddenly, in a clash of sparks, the cockpit lights went out. Yllath's voice fell to an awed, uneasy whisper, and Asa knew he wasn't speaking to *her* anymore. "Who . . . who are *you*?"

One of the cockpit screens flickered on. Someone was there—not just Yllath. Asa could've sworn she felt her warmth, her confusion, her brilliant *light*.

"Kaya," Asa whispered, "can you hear me?"

A prickle of static. Kaya might be trapped in nightmares still. She had to wake up.

"It's okay," Asa said. How much did Kaya remember from the laboratory, where her own father had tinkered with her brain? "I'm here. I've been here all along. But I need your help."

Another pulse of static. Text appeared on the screen. "*Asa. This feels wrong. What did Dad do to me? What am I?*"

Asa's vision blurred with tears. Kaya didn't have a body right now, but what did that matter? Bodies could be put back together with cybernetics. Minds could live outside the matter they grew in. Kaya's mind being removed didn't change anything.

"You're my sister," Asa said. "Even if you don't have a body right now, you're still you."

"*I can feel you. You're so close. You never left, did you?*"

"I've had you the whole time. We're going to finish this so you can come home."

"*How? This place . . . it stretches so far. It's terrifying.*"

"We're going to get you out of there. But first . . . there's something else in the system with you. And I know you can figure out how to stop it. It's trying to kill us."

"*That's what scares me. It's eating through this place like an infection. You think I can do it?*"

If Kaya couldn't, she was dead. They all were. "I *know* you can. No matter what Dad said . . . you're everything you need to be. You're smarter than any of us. And we need you." Luca might've designed Kaya for this, but she was more than her genes. Kaya was her own person—if not the person their father wanted.

"*Anything I can do to help you . . . I will.*"

The screen went dark, leaving only the docking-bay lights shining through the windshield. The life-support pod kept flatlining as the muffled gunfire drew closer. Through the windshield, Asa watched Yllath's mechs approach. Any moment now. This had to work.

"Is this really her?" Samir said, incredulous.

Asa didn't answer. *Come on, come on . . .*

A burst rippled through the cabin, like an EMP blast in reverse. The heart monitor on Kaya's life-support pod kicked back to life. Outside, Yllath's mechs stopped dead in their tracks.

Asa let out a startled laugh. "Kaya! Was that you?"

Hurried footsteps rushed onto the ship. Samir's gun was up in an instant, but it was Riven, who held up her hands until Samir lowered the rifle.

"What the hell happened?" Riven panted. "Those mechs just . . . froze."

Her chest heaved from running, and she had a swollen, bloody lip. Asa resisted the urge to tackle her in a hug. When she strode into the cockpit, Asa saw a bloody slice across her back, leaking over her magenta Olympus bodice. Hurt, but alive.

"Dealing with Yllath," Samir said. "What happened to you?"

"Morphett Slade happened."

"Is this one of those 'you-should-see-the-other-girl' situations?"

"She isn't dead. But she won't bother us." Riven pointed out the window. "Those mercs might, though. Hope you've got bullets, because I'm down to three."

Asa watched the cockpit control screens, her chest tight with anticipation. They fizzed with bright-green static, but then a few turned orange.

No.

"*This thing is pushing back*," Kaya's words flickered on the screen. "*It's smart. It's fast. It's everywhere.*"

"So are you!" Asa said. "Please. I know you can do this."

"*I can't do it alone, Asa. I can't control the mechs while keeping them contained.*"

Asa swallowed hard. They had to push back her dad's security force. But if Kaya's hold on the mechs slipped . . . they were all dead. "I'll do what I can. I'll handle the mechs so you can focus on Yllath."

Orange sparks fell in the cockpit.

A pause. "*Do it, Asa.*"

The controls lit up on the touch screen, and she saw the soldiers through the mechs' eyes, a rainbow of infrared silhouettes, orange and green against the cold purple backdrop. Asa took a deep breath. So many. She'd need five arms.

"You got this, Asa?" Riven slipped into the seat next to her. "Or do you need another gunner?"

There was nobody better. Having Riven next to her felt *right*. "Riven's helping us, too, Kaya."

"You have the cockpit," Riven said. "Just tell me what to do."

Asa took a deep breath and touched the control board, imagining the light in Kaya's eyes, the person she'd braved hell for. And for a second, Asa swore she could *feel* everything Kaya felt—the rhythm in the circuits, the steady whir of the engines, the crackle of fluorescent lights, the hair-trigger pulse in the gun mechanisms. Kaya was everywhere, and Asa was at the edge, wondering how deep, how *brilliant*, was the mind that could move it all.

But Yllath was brilliant, too, and it was pushing back. Asa aligned the controls and urged the mechs' earthshaking footsteps forward.

"On my count," Asa said, "move in!"

As they did, the docking-bay lights winked out, plunging everything into complete darkness. What followed were confused shouts, silence, the sting of fear in the air.

Now was her chance to force the soldiers to run. It was the biggest bluff she'd ever make. Asa grabbed *Boomslang*'s microphone.

Like any of her father's lies, confidence was key. "Take another step, and you're dead." Asa's voice echoed through the thunderous docking-bay loudspeakers. The soldiers whirled around, confused, in the blinding dark.

Riven pulled up a mech's controls—a hulking thing with a mounted gun—and peppered mercenaries with bullets. The bullets clanged against their state-of-the-art armor, sparks flying, throwing them off-balance.

"If you were afraid of Banshee," Asa said as the adrenaline burned through her, "you should run. Because Banshee is nothing compared to Kaya Almeida. Whatever Luca's paying you, it sure as hell won't be enough."

In the pitch-black bay, the soldiers' flashlights flicked on. But Riven's mechs were already behind them.

"*I'm forcing this creature out of the systems,*" Kaya said. "*It's vicious. I can't purge it entirely. But it's possible I'll be able to lure it somewhere and contain it. It's . . . it's trying to destroy me.*"

Asa nodded her acknowledgment and focused on the soldiers, ignoring the acid in her throat.

"This is only the beginning of what we'll do to you," she said into the speaker. A few soldiers swore and shouted, ducking for cover and inspecting their rifles for signs of hacking. "You remember Morphett Slade? We destroyed her cybernetics from within. So unless you want me to wipe out the rest of your fleet . . . crawl back to your ships."

A few of them tossed their rifles, hands up in surrender. Others were already scrambling back onto the ships bearing her father's emblem.

"Asa. Get away from there!" Samir yelled.

Asa tore herself away from the screen just as every holoscreen burst into blinding static. The control panels cycled frantically between churning orange distortion and fragmented images of Emmett's and Kaya's faces, as they'd appeared in Olympus.

Yllath was still fighting. "Don't stop now, Kaya!"

"This bastard is *murdering* my ship!" Riven shouted at the sparks raining from the ceiling panels. Yllath was scrubbing the power overload protection—trying to blow out the ship's circuits.

"*Your wristlet, Asa. It has more processing power than this entire ship. And Dad's tech was equipped with fail-safes to keep that thing from getting out.*" Kaya's screen was barely functioning. "*I'll need to lure it in, and have you disconnect it. Hurry!*"

"But you'll be trapped in there with Yllath. Will you be safe?"

"*I can do this. I have to.*"

Asa hooked up her wristlet. She clicked on the microphone one last time, while Kaya still had control. "If you try to pursue us, Banshee was nothing compared to what I'll unleash on you." She tapped the controls, slamming a mech's fist into one of her father's ships.

Within moments, the ship's thrusters had flared up for liftoff. Fleeing.

"We have to go, Asa!" Riven shouted as an awful noise surged through the cockpit.

Banshee's presence—all of Yllath in the cockpit at once—made the circuits scream like the creature's namesake. The shriek permeated her eardrums, her bones, threatening to shatter her.

Her wristlet sparked under the pressure of the creature shoved into it. It wouldn't hold.

"Kaya, you need to get out—"

Kaya's next words burst onto the screen. "*ASA. TAKE IT. NOW.*"

As Asa reached for her wristlet, an image erupted from the wristlet's projector. An erratic wire-frame hologram of glowing orange lines, shifting like ribbons in the wind. The lines formed a humanoid monster with implacable eyes, reaching for Asa with webbed-claw hands. She reeled back.

Yllath's final push.

Her crew had backed away from the control panel, shouting to her to *get away!* But Kaya wasn't finished.

As all the cockpit screens flashed green, Kaya made her escape. The orange beast burst into pixels. The awful noise died.

Asa yanked the wristlet wires away, panting, as the screens powered down. Blackness, once more. "Kaya. Is it gone? Are you . . ."

A pause. Then, the letters began scrolling across the screen. "*It's done. Being in here is a mind-strain, Asa. I'm loading back into the biocapsule to rest for a while, but if I ever wake up . . . you owe me an explanation. Several explanations.*"

"That's not all I owe you." Asa held her shaking arms steady against the pilot seat. "You were incredible, Kaya. See you when you wake up." The screen went dark, and Asa unhooked the biocapsule. The remaining ship lights and default control panels flickered back on, awaiting Riven's command.

Her crew approached the sparking mess quietly. "So that was our Banshee?" Diego flexed his mech-fingers in relief. "How did she drive him back?"

"She trapped him. Kaya has never been a pushover." Asa grinned at Riven. "Pilot seat's yours, Riv."

Riven said nothing, wiping blood off her split lip as she settled into the seat. She looked like she'd been dragged through hell. This victory had taken everything they had. But Kaya was safe at last.

Asa held the capsule close as they strapped in for lift-off, whispering promises and affirmations as the ship rose. Somewhere on this planet, they'd find a place to fix Kaya. Her sister couldn't hear her right now, but soon she'd have her ears back for good. And the rest of her.

"You're safe," Asa whispered. "You're safe."

chapter 34

SUNRISE

The palm trees shifted in the sea breeze, silhouetted against the violent shades of sunrise. This place brought back memories Riven would rather recount in private.

She trudged over the dunes alone, carrying her boots and letting the sand grit between her toes. Brisbane was too much like Requiem: smoky, towering, and overcrowded. Best to savor the good parts of Earth—its rain and oceans and wind—before she went back. The beach wasn't far from the medical clinic in the city, and she needed to clear her head.

Plus, she didn't want to be in the room when they learned whether Kaya's surgery had worked. Etri brains were tricky business, but they'd found a surgeon willing to fix Kaya—someone with experience in experimental organs. It was the best they could reasonably pay off, but it was still risky.

If it failed, Riven would rather not know. She'd taken too many losses lately.

Dark clouds roiled on the horizon, like the wild storm from that day at Sanctum's Edge. Riven clenched her fists, closing her eyes against the whipping winds, quelling her tears. Every time she'd survived, something terrible came with it. This time, it'd been Ty.

If they ever found his body, he'd want his ashes scattered

in a place like this. But what was the point of paying tribute? It wouldn't fix his loss, or her failure.

"Hey," Asa's voice rang over the dunes. "You trying to avoid me?"

Riven looked back, the wind lashing loose silver hairs over her face. Asa trudged up the dune behind her, out of breath.

"I'm trying to avoid *everything*," Riven called. "It's nothing personal."

Asa stopped halfway up the dune. Even from here, Riven could see her tear-stained cheeks. Asa was miserable. That made two of them.

"Come here. Let's talk."

Asa wordlessly approached and sat cross-legged in the sand. "What if this was all for nothing?"

"It wasn't. Because you fought for her. You did everything you could, and the rest is up to the universe." And what if she'd fought harder for Ty? What then?

Asa seemed to know exactly what she was thinking. "I'm so sorry." Asa lost it. Riven put her hands on Asa's shaking shoulders, pulling her closer, if only to keep herself from falling apart. Asa was an emotional wreck, but now she was Riven's emotional wreck.

Riven let her cry for a few minutes. At least she wasn't the only one who'd shed tears over Ty.

"I know you blame yourself, but all he wanted was to save you." Asa sniffed as she dug a fingertip into the sand, tracing aimless lines. "And the rest of us needed you."

Riven stared out at the crashing waves of high tide. Asa was right—Riven had gotten them out. Ty wouldn't have been able to take down Morphett, or save Samir from the mercenaries, or pilot *Boomslang* out.

"I was the reason we were there in the first place," Asa said. "And I can never make up for what happened." She scrubbed away the lines she'd made. "You probably don't want me on the crew anymore."

Riven hadn't had a real mechanist on the crew since Emmett. "Of course I do. Gave you my word, didn't I? *Boomslang*'s your home now too. And after the number Yllath did on things . . . I'm going to need a good mechanist to fix things up."

Asa's teary eyes lit up, and she wrapped her arms around Riven, a little too hard. Maybe a home was all she'd needed.

Maybe the remnants of Riven's crew were what mattered. She still had Samir, Diego, and now Asa.

And Riven had built something Asa hadn't even had on Cortellion. Even though Riven had been dealt a shoddy hand growing up—even though the white noise was eating her from inside—the crew she'd pulled together was unbreakable. And damn if Riven was going to let the sickness ruin her life, or what was left of it.

No way to go but forward.

A message came through on her borrowed wristlet. It had come back online after the EMP, but barely. On the discolored screen, Riven could barely make out an unknown messaging code with a Requiem address. She answered the call after a few rings, careful not to seem too eager.

"Bria," Riven said casually.

But it wasn't Bria's voice on the comm. "I don't know what

you did," the Duchess's honey-soft voice said in Riven's earpiece, "but Banshee is gone."

Riven sat straighter. The Duchess herself. This was serious. "Gone?"

"Yes. It stopped spreading, and when we began rebooting quarantined tech . . . nothing went haywire. Everything has come online without issue."

It seemed suspicious, but maybe whatever Kaya did had worked. Riven could claim *some* credit for the mission's success. "Yeah. We got it done."

A high, feminine peal of laughter. "Clearly I chose the right team for the job. If you're interested in taking more contracts for me, I'll need *specialist transporters* while we rebuild."

Rebuilding. That wreck of a moon colony had some hope yet. "The Federation's pulled out?"

"As much as can be expected. The other matriarchs are coordinating the Federation's full expulsion from Requiem. And until then . . . we have shipments that need to move beneath their radar."

A future in the Duchess's service. Her debts to Sokolov would be nothing. Her crew would be safe. "We're on board."

"Good. I will brief you further when you've returned to Requiem. Until then." A pause. A bark in the background. "And tell your friend Samir his dog is waiting for him."

When the call ended, she turned to Asa. She was on the team, too, and her opinion mattered. "What do you think about working for the Duchess? We'll need a few good *specialist transport* jobs to pay off this surgery."

"The Duchess?" Asa wiped her eyes on the sleeve of

her borrowed jacket—one from Riven's dirty laundry pile in *Boomslang*'s cabin. Riven felt bad about not having better gear for her, but she had to admit, Asa looked damn cute in her clothes. "I doubt she'll assign us anything half as scary as what we did today. But . . ." A thoughtful pause. "I think I'm strong enough now, for any of it. So I'm up for it if you are."

"That's my mechanist." A sliver of sun peeked over the reddening horizon. Riven pulled Asa tighter, breathing in her scent of shampoo and engine grease, mingling with the ocean air.

She was strong enough. *They* were strong enough.

Even so, remembering how Ty had looked at Asa . . . how could she look at Asa the same way? It felt like taking something from him, after all he'd done for her.

Maybe he'd want her to be happy. But it would take time for that wound to close.

Until then, she'd be whatever Asa needed.

"Then we're done with tears now, yeah?" Riven dabbed an eyeliner-black smear off Asa's cheek. "Whatever happens, we have a future to face."

Asa could never go back to Cortellion. And, for the first time, that was fine.

The sand was cold between her toes, but Riven's arms kept her warm. The sun was rising here on Earth—on a continent called Australia—and it seemed like forever since she'd slept. Any other day, she'd miss the soft, temp-regulated sheets on her bed.

On Cortellion, she'd never needed to wonder where she'd

sleep. Tonight, she wasn't sure where. But after crashing on strangers' couches and ships for the past few nights, the thought didn't frighten her. She had people looking out for her, even when things got hard. And Riven . . .

Together, she and Riven watched the fading stars. They sat in silent understanding, a peace from undergoing the same struggles. At first, Riven had terrified her, but now Asa saw a girl who'd grown up in a hard world and hardened herself to match. A girl who'd fight viciously for the things she held closest.

Asa would never be able to repay all Riven and her crew had done. Even if she *could* cough up their twenty thousand denar, it'd be laughably trivial after what they'd sacrificed.

Especially Ty, who'd given himself away for her and Riven. Even now, as she looked at the stars, she felt he wasn't gone—that somehow, she'd find him again. But maybe it was just wishful thinking. The culmination of too many childhood hopes she'd whispered into starlight.

Her only certain future was with Riven's crew. Still, one uncertainty remained—a thought that itched and burned the longer Asa left it alone.

Riven sighed, her lips parting. Just hours ago, those lips had been pressed to Asa's, fierce and wanting. What if Riven hadn't meant it? If Asa said something now, would it strain their work together?

But she had to know. And with no sleep, an exhausted body, and a head swimming with fatigue, the cautious parts of Asa were too tired to stop her.

"Riven. Why did you kiss me in the lab?"

Riven tensed, and Asa worried she'd pull away. Instead, she gave an uneasy laugh. "If I told you stealing and kissing Luca Almeida's daughter was part of a revenge plan, you probably wouldn't believe me, huh?"

"Was it because you thought you wouldn't come back?" Asa tilted her face toward Riven's. A blush had crept across her freckles. She'd found Riven beautiful before, but seeing her beneath the sunrise made Asa's chest ache with longing.

"No," Riven finally said. "I *wanted* it. I probably should've asked first. But I–"

Asa silenced her lips, picking up where they'd left off. She barely remembered that first kiss, only the cold sweat on Riven's skin, the gunfire in the background, and the shrieking laboratory alarms. But now, in the slow sea breezes and riot of dawn, she felt everything–Riven's strong hands pulling her hips closer, her chapped lips against Asa's. Riven tasted like firecrackers and gunpowder. Sea salt and fresh air. Like adventure and danger, and a quiet hideout at the end of a long day. Everything Asa hadn't known she needed.

Riven saw right through her, saw the nerves and failures, and still wanted her.

It felt different from being in Ty's arms. Ty was safe, the kind of person her father might've allowed her to be with. Riven, however–Luca would've *never* approved.

Riven's lips moved against hers, slowing, hesitant.

Asa wondered what they'd tell Samir and Diego, or where things went from here. But the future seemed an eternity away, waiting on the other side of Kaya's prognosis.

Then Riven pulled away, hugging her knees as she stared

into the crashing waves. Some of the warmth receded with her. There was still a piece missing between them.

"Asa," Riven finally said. The distance between their bodies stretched. "I don't know if I can . . ." A shaking breath. "It might take some time."

Asa had expected that. The rift still needed time to heal. For now, she'd be whatever Riven needed. Tentatively, she rested her head on Riven's shoulder, and Riven didn't pull away.

By the time Asa's borrowed wristlet beeped—an old one from *Boomslang*'s storage that the crew had loaned her for emergencies—some of her nerves had calmed.

"What's that?" Riven said sleepily.

She's ready, the message read. *Room 837D.*

"Kaya's ready." Asa's heart sped up. *Ready,* not *dead.* That was something. "Come with me?"

Riven squeezed her hand. "Whatever happens." It sounded like a promise.

Outside the clinic room, Samir waited for them with a protective arm over Diego's shoulders. Diego's inscrutable face was almost peaceful. *Good things came of this,* Asa told herself. *No matter what I find in that room.*

She took a deep breath and followed the nurse inside, Riven's hand on her back.

Inside, a heart monitor chirped above a girl lying on a cot. She wasn't moving, and Asa froze in her tracks. What if it hadn't worked?

Kaya's chest rose and fell with breath.

Asa stepped closer, carefully, as if Kaya were a mirage that'd evaporate when she approached. "Kay? Can you hear me?"

The sutures on Kaya's hairline were sealed with repair ointment, already scabbing. Her wavy dark hair was splayed on the white pillow, and the color was returning to her skin.

"Kaya?" Asa reached out—so, so gently—to touch Kaya's hair, hoping not to startle her.

Kaya's eyes fluttered open. In a flash of panic, her pupils contracted.

"Asa," she whispered. "Am I . . ." She sat up and lifted a hand to her face, running fingertips down her cheek. Then, she laughed. It almost hurt to see that smile after the false Kaya on Olympus's deck, but she was real. Whole.

"You're safe." Asa meant it this time. She embraced Kaya for the first time in days that had felt like decades. And even though Riven had told her they were done with tears, they flowed all the same. "And thanks to you, so are we."

After a few minutes, Kaya pulled away, her thin fingers still clutching Asa's wrists. "Where are we?" Kaya's rose-petal lips tightened into a nervous frown. "And what happened to Dad?"

Asa winced. She couldn't tell Kaya they were fugitives—that could wait. "We're on Earth. You don't have to worry about Dad anymore."

"Earth?" Kaya's eyes lit up, and she swung her feet over the edge of the cot, holding Asa's shoulder for support as she stood. "No way. Can I see?"

She stumbled to the window, her steps steadying as she adjusted back to her own skin. As Asa pulled back the blinds, Kaya shielded her eyes from the rush of sunlight. Morning had broken over Brisbane, a sea of towering glass prisms and holograms dancing in the shadows they cast. The sun glinting off the river and the steel bridge frames was almost blinding, even through the smoggy haze.

"Holy sh—" Kaya caught herself. "It's beautiful."

"If you think this junkyard is beautiful, wait until you see Requiem." Riven leaned against the door behind them, her silver hair bright as city glass in the sunlight. Riven gave her that sharpshot smile, the one that always made Asa's stomach flutter.

"I remember you," Kaya said, excitement creeping into her voice. "From the security feed. All of you were there in the cockpit."

Her crew watched from the other side of the room, giving Asa and Kaya space. Diego's razor-wire tension and Samir's hardened vigilance had dimmed to something peaceful as they sat together in the visitor seats. Asa beckoned them all to the window.

Kaya would have a thousand questions. Asa had to tell the whole story. But where did it even start?

"So, Kaya," Asa said as her crew, weary-eyed but victorious, approached. It was time the two halves of her life combined. They'd lost a crew member, but they'd gained a new one. *Two* new ones. "I guess I should introduce you to our crew."

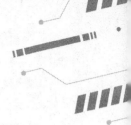

EPILOGUE
TY

"*Is he awake?*"

"*Oh, thank god one of them survived.*"

Ty awoke to soft voices and scalding white light. He squinted into it, and, weirdly, his left eye dimmed like a tinted lens.

Where am I? He lay on his back, his mind a fog. The last thing he remembered was choking smoke, and Riven's screams, and a pain tearing through his left arm—

Impulsively, he tried moving the fingers on his left hand. They flexed. But there was something wrong—the sensation of fabric under his fingers was scattered, and the movement felt eerily light.

Ty lifted his head to look. His fingers were steel plates and silicon. With growing horror, he followed the fingers to a hand, forearm, elbow, and upper arm—all silver wires and cybernetic ligaments, connected to scarred pink flesh at his armpit.

They'd *repaired* him.

"Don't move," one of the kind voices said, edged with annoyance now. "The calibration isn't finished."

"What did you do to me?" Ty croaked. He tilted his head and came face-to-face with a surgical mask and thick lab goggles.

Ty scrambled sideways, but his new arm was heavier than his flesh one. As he tumbled to the polished floor, he grabbed the countertop next to the bed.

In the grip of his new fingers, the steel countertop crumpled like paper.

He let go, landing on all fours, his breaths hard and ragged. His limbs—the real ones, anyway—felt weak. They were sedating him. As he tried to stand, he glimpsed his reflection in a powered-down screen. His face stared back—but where his left eye should have been, a blue light glared.

"What the hell?" Ty held up his new fingers, horrified. They moved like part of him, yet they weren't *him*. At the back of his mind was shrieking panic—*get it off get it off get it off*—

"Don't worry," the voice said, clearer now. The woman in the mask and white-and-gold surgical smock hit a button on her datapad. "You'll learn to control them."

Immediately a tingle surged down the back of Ty's neck and shot into his new arm. The arm went rigid, and he couldn't move it no matter how hard he tried.

"Let's get you back on the cot." The woman—a doctor? surgeon?—grabbed Ty under the arms and tried to lift him.

He shoved her away with his good arm, backing against the wall. "Not until you tell me why I'm here, or what you did to me." Next to the operating table, notes scrolled across a holoscreen: *Project Echofall . . . Etri cellular matrix . . .*

"He has a strong will," said the deeper of the two voices. Its owner's back was turned, and he sat in front of a trio of holoscreens. That voice sent a familiar spike of fear through Ty. He'd heard it in the incinerator room.

"He'll need it," the woman said.

"Don't touch me." Ty ran his shaking right hand over the left eye he couldn't close. He felt a patch of silicon and a metal socket. When he closed his right eye, his vision was sharper, brighter, out of his left.

Ty focused on the far end of the room, and his left eye zoomed in.

In the eye's extended focus, the insignia on the glass lab door was crisp—a white-and-gold logo, backward, printed on the other side.

Almeida Labs.

Panic coiled in his chest. Asa's father had kept him alive and given him cybernetics. Everything terrible originated here—Yllath, Kaya's experiment, the thing killing Riven.

He was a test subject, just like Kaya.

But if that chemical from Sanctum's Edge had come from these labs, then maybe the missing piece was here. The information about what was happening to Riven. If she was still alive.

She survived, he told himself. *Riven's too stubborn to die.* The girl Emmett would've given the world for, the girl who protected Ty even when he wouldn't pick up a gun to protect himself. She and Asa would need each other—and maybe they'd find happiness, the two of them, while it lasted.

The thought was snatched away by a stab of pain at the back of his head. His body convulsed with an electric shock.

"Put him back to sleep," Almeida commanded, and Ty's vision blurred. He tried to fight the numbness, to shock himself awake. He focused on smoky tendrils of hope—imagining his crew tending each other's wounds back at the hideout, and Riven spinning her revolvers with no tremor in her hands, no fear for the future. Alive.

Somehow, he swore, he'd save her.

ACKNOWLEDGMENTS

Starting with the obvious: getting this far wouldn't have been possible without my best friend and the love of my life. Drew, thanks for encouraging me as a newbie LARPer, providing heals when I got hit by fireballs (ugh), and being the first person to take my writing seriously. For your relentless support whenever the world has been uncertain and terrifying. Thanks for believing in me so, *so* hard every step of the way.

To Cortney Radocaj, my tireless and passionate agent. Signing with you changed my life in so many ways. I've grown not only as a writer but as a person, and I'll never be able to thank you enough.

To my incredible editor Mari Kesselring, for her infinite patience and enthusiasm for my grimy murder-paradise and scoundrel squad. To Kelsy Thompson, for making this happen by falling in love with the book and championing it at acquisitions.

To my parents, for their confidence in me—and who bought champagne on the day I was supposed to hear from acquisitions, *just in case.* To Carl, Kris, Rad, and the rest of my family (including my dastardly pup, Tux). To Maea and Aderan—here's hoping you'll keep writing and creating too.

To my critique partners Nicole Brake, Ren Hutchings, Bill Adams, Meg LaTorre, Travis Hightower, and Kate Murray. You've pulled through whenever I've needed it most—last-minute critiques, sometimes-harsh advice, consolation. I can't wait to have a shelf full of your books someday.

To my amazing beta readers—Kelsey B., Melissa S., Michael S., Meg D., Jason A., Stacy W., Jenn S., Krista G., Christy M., and Jacob A.—and my writer friends Briston Brooks, Keala Kendall, Lenn Woolston, Rohan Zhou-Lee, and Sasha McBrayer. To Sarah Rowlands and Emily Field, who supported this book on its way to publication. This book would never have gotten this far without every one of you.

To Kristina, for that mead-laced conversation in a London pub where you convinced me to follow my dreams instead of sinking into debt for a career I didn't want. This book is kind of your fault.

To Katie, my eternal alpha reader and partner-in-dreams. Thanks for reading every terrible draft since the beginning. To Meesoh, for continuing to cheer me on, even from the other side of the world.

To my Valkyrie squad—Dana, Chelsea, and both Katies!—for all the bonfires, D&D nights, convention parties, and lifelong inside jokes. And the rest of my squad: John, Rad, Jae, Brodie, Tyler, Stacy, Krista, Bud, and the Bastard Company. Love you all.

To Christine Daigle, for inspiring me to give talks at conventions. The whole IWS group, for the tough love I didn't realize I needed. Kian Stark, whose incredible art kept me going through several tough revisions.

To writing teachers who've sparked my creativity over the years—Kent Wabel, Jennifer Tiemann, Miranda Keskes, Marcia Gealy, and Paul McComas. I was always the quiet kid, but my daydreams were weirder than you knew.

To authors who've encouraged me—Susan Dennard, Cinda Williams Chima, Jonathan Maberry, Brandon Sanderson, Joe Abercrombie, Alexa Donne, Kevin J. Anderson (and the whole SSWS tribe)—your advice has helped infinitely. To all the 21ders, for their debut year support.

A major thanks to the rest of the Belcastro and Flux teams—Kaitlyn Johnson, Sharon Belcastro, Emily Temple, Jake Slavik, and many others whose advice and hard work made this book possible. To Sanjay Charlton, for bringing Riven and Asa to life on the cover.

And to the reader: these past few years have been a rough road to put this book into your hands. I hope you find something in these pages that resonates with you. Thanks for believing in me too.

ABOUT THE AUTHOR

Claire Winn spends her time immersed in other worlds—through LARP, video games, books, nerd conventions, and her own stories. Since graduating from Northwestern University, she's worked as a legal writer and freelance editor. Aside from writing, she builds cosplay props and armor, tears up dance floors, and battles with boffer swords. *City of Shattered Light* is her first novel.